SPEAK EZ

ELLE E. IRE

Bywater
BOOKS

2024

To my spouse—my first reader always
and the holder of my heart forever.
When they talk about soulmates,
they're talking about us.

Author's Note

One of the greatest pitfalls an author can fall into is starting a million writing projects but finishing none of them. That "shiny new idea" calls writers like a siren to sailors so they'll crash their ships on the rocks. Such was the inception of this book. I was more than halfway through a different project (now three-quarters of the way through) when the concept of *Speak EZ* came to me. I couldn't help myself. I wrote a few chapters, shared them with my spouse, and when they gave me their feedback, it was essentially, "This is awesome. You need to write *this*. You need to write this *now*." I was hesitant, but it kept drawing me back, and eventually, I gave in to that call, hoping it wouldn't be another false start with no conclusion. Three more chapters, and I knew I'd finish this project because I was in love with these characters.

I'm not exactly sure what sparked it. I've always been fascinated by speakeasies, especially authentic ones from the 1920s, and even more so if they are reputed to be haunted. I love to visit them, have a drink, absorb the "feel" of the place. In this book, Ciara describes the sensation of being inside an old building as having "weight" and "substance." In this way, I am like Ciara. When I step inside a 100-year-plus-old building, I sense a heaviness to the air, as if all the years have mass and are layered one atop the other on my shoulders. It's not scary. It's . . . exhilarating. And like Ciara, I appreciate those who preserve their authenticity so others can experience what life might have been like in those places, in those times.

Lastly, I must dedicate a few sentences here to the dog and his demise. I hate it when animals die in books. It's so upsetting to me that I cannot watch a film or read a book where a pet dies. My spouse checks the "Does the Dog Die" website at https://www.doesthedogdie.com/ to determine if there is any animal death in any film we plan to see before we watch it. When I critique work for writer friends, I ask them to leave such scenes to someone else. I swore I would never do this in a book of my own or, at least, I would never make the death permanent. (How fortunate that I write speculative fiction where animals who pass on *can* come back!) If you've read my other work, then you know I did this with a different animal in *Harsh Reality*, and I do it again here. I have tried to keep EZ's death quick and without explicit details for those who would be as bothered as I am. He comes back, and very quickly.

I promise you.

Elle E. Ire
Author & dog lover

SPEAK
EZ

Chapter 1

2:28 a.m., January 1, 1924

MICKEY SURVEYED THE almost empty bar with a sense of comfort and pride that warmed her from the inside out. This was her home, her space, and those she allowed within its walls . . . her family. Here, she could be anyone she wanted to, even if she only aspired to being herself.

Or maybe a happier version of herself. One with someone to care for and care for her beyond her clientele.

She gave a forced smile and a half-hearted wave goodbye to her last straggling customer as he slipped past the door and closed it with a soft click behind him. Good old Jimmy, always hanging around until closing time so she wouldn't be alone. Mickey'd promised him she'd lock up and head out right after he left, but right then, with half a gin fizz in the short glass on the bar in front of her and Bessie Smith's "Down Hearted Blues" playing on the RCA Radiola Grand she'd spent an arm and a leg on, she had no desire to go anywhere.

No one worth going home to anyway, unless she counted her brother, Paul, and she didn't. Since their parents' deaths when she was sixteen, he'd thrown himself into two things—his work as a city beat cop, and replacement parenting Mickey.

She was twenty-nine years old for Christ's sake.

1

Sighing, Mickey took a long swig of her drink, savoring the lemon and frothy sweetness, and reached out to take down the 1923 "Goddesses" calendar from the wall beside the bar, almost falling off her stool in the process. *Show a little decorum, Mick. The customers get drunk, not the owner.* But she'd gotten caught up in the spirit (or spirits as it were) of the evening and this last shot was one too many.

She used the edge of the bar to pull her body square on the padded leather seat, balled up the old calendar between her hands, and tossed it into a small wastebasket, then stretched across the bar's surface and felt under the counter for the new one she'd stored on the first shelf. Drawing it into her lap, she flipped over the cover page and hung it on the wall. January's pinup girl, a buxom brunette wearing a low-cut black evening gown and holding a red feather fan, smiled down at her, and Mickey grinned back before catching herself and frowning. She might be able to charm even a classy dame like that into sharing a drink or a dance. It was an era of taking chances for a lot of folks, in spite of, or maybe *because* of, Prohibition. And Mickey knew her reputation as a real charmer. Prided herself on it, in fact.

But taking a chance wasn't the same as staying. None of them ever stayed. Especially a well-to-do broad like the one in the picture who would have had everything to lose by taking up with someone like Mickey.

Though tonight Mickey hadn't looked too shabby if she did say so herself. In fact, she felt downright handsome. Using the mirror over the bar, Mickey cocked her black fedora rakishly over one eye. Her fingers brushed through the ends of her short brown hair coming just to the top of her collar. Paul was sure to give her a hard time if she cut it again, but she told him long hair got in the way of her day job running the spotlights for the theater company.

"What guy's gonna wanna marry you, with you looking like that?"

That was kind of the point, though she couldn't say so. She'd also overheard the words he'd mumbled afterward.

"Oughta be finding a wife of my own. Instead, I'm a permanent nursemaid."

Mickey forced the painful comments from her mind and stroked the smooth fabric of the gray suit jacket she'd "borrowed" from the give-to-charity corner of his closet along with the matching pants and a pair of slightly too large for her black and white leather men's shoes. Tonight had called for something special even if she did hate holidays.

New Year's Eve . . . well, now actually New Year's Day. The celebratory evening had found her surrounded by her closest friends, everyone cheering at the fresh start the change of date seemed to carry with it.

What would she start this year? Who did she even know to start something with?

Bill had Jeremy. Patrice had Maria. Hell, she suspected her dog EZ had a fluffy little poodle he liked to sneak off to. Everybody she knew had somebody.

Somebody to come here with, dance with, or go home to after leaving the bar behind. She wanted that, all of that, and thought she'd found it. She should have known better.

Mickey's girlfriend, Annie, had broken up with her over a year ago on the Thanksgiving before last. Her longest relationship to date, its conclusion had driven home the idea that maybe she wasn't "forever" material, not worth taking that ultimate chance for.

Mickey took a deep breath, exhaling to let the memory go. Thirteen-plus months and it ached like the breakup had happened yesterday.

She inhaled again the bar's signature scent mix of cigarette smoke, cologne, and sweat, along with a touch of grease paint that came with the territory of their theater basement location. What better place to hide a bar during Prohibition than in a secret gay and lesbian gathering place that had already been there two years before the anti-alcohol laws even got passed? Adding the "speakeasy" moniker was just a formality.

"Mickey's Speak EZ." She couldn't advertise publicly, of course, but she'd had the name framed by a friend of hers and mounted above the shelves of bottles and glassware. It had a nice ring to it, a ring that got whispered backstage and in the dressing rooms and on street corners between friends of friends and word-of-mouth by trustworthy and like-minded individuals. The stage attracted a hefty percentage of men who liked other men and women who preferred women. After every evening performance, Mickey's clientele was already on-site. The idea had been inspired. And tonight, the place had been packed. She provided a space where people could enjoy themselves without judgment.

Even her. But only here.

Mickey downed the last of her drink, walked behind the bar, and set the glass in the sink she'd had installed there. Resting her hands on her narrow hips, she took one last glance around the joint and nodded with satisfaction. Nothing too out of place. Nothing that needed dealing with before she arrived tomorrow night. A few glasses left to wash, the handful of tables to wipe down. Some of the wood paneling and the bar itself could use a polish along with the mirror.

She double-checked that the cash register was locked. No need to count the till when you were owner, bartender, and cleanup staff rolled into one, though if business kept growing the way it had been, she might need to hire someone soon. But that was a thought for a more sober moment. She switched off the radio.

Time to lock up—something she should have done immediately after Jimmy left just to be safe, but Mickey knew the theater was empty, so she hadn't bothered. The actors not invited to her New Year's Eve party would have hurried off to find their own revelries right after the final curtain call. The backstage workers like her would have lingered longer to reset things for tomorrow night's performance, but that didn't take too long, and even if some were around, they all knew about her bar. The cleaning staff had finished hours ago. Nothing to worry about. She was the only one in the building. Yet an uneasy feeling had her shoulders tensed and her hands fidgeting.

A floorboard over her head creaked once, twice.

Her contact with the local booze smugglers had mentioned maybe coming by tonight but then called to say they were all busy celebrating. They wanted their own version of that fresh start—new contracts for her to sign, even higher prices on every bit of illegal liquor she sold. Mickey barely got by as it was. They'd told her to pass the increase in cost along to her customers, but most of her customers made less than she did.

She'd told them to screw off until February. Were they here to push her?

Settling. Buildings settled. Especially heated buildings after the heat was turned off for the night, which was why her customers wore long-sleeved dresses with wraps, or suits with the jackets on the whole time they drank in her establishment. Management also knew about her hideaway. Eli and Richard were frequent guests and wholeheartedly approved. In exchange for her use of the space, she paid them a small percentage of the take each month. But that didn't mean they'd spend money on extra hours of heat for her. She was sure that was all it wa—

More creaks from the ceiling—even, measured creaks that might have been . . . footsteps.

Shit.

Patting the pocket of her suit jacket for her keys, she frowned. No jangling, no bulges. No keys.

She couldn't lock the speakeasy door without the key.

When she'd put this place together, she'd had the locks

on what had then been the largest of the theater's unused set storage rooms replaced so that she could secure the door from either side. This meant during business hours she could wait for a secret knock before opening up to an outsider and also keep potential intruders out when she was upstairs working lights. Lately, though, she'd gotten careless. They hadn't had a new member in over a month, and her customers always gave her a heads-up when they were bringing someone in. She'd stopped locking the door all the time.

Besides, who would think to look for a secret gay and lesbian bar in one of five storerooms in the subbasement of a theater?

Well, somebody's thought of it, because if the footsteps are right over your head, that means they're already in the upper basement, which means they're looking for something.

Her booze suppliers already knew where she was. Someone else was upstairs.

No. No no no no no. She could *not* get raided. She'd lose everything, all the inheritance money she'd poured into outfitting this place. She'd be arrested.

And if she were arrested, her brother Paul, no, her brother *Officer McFadden*, would absolutely find out.

She needed to find her damn keys.

Mickey did a quick run-through of her night. Had she had her coat on the entire time? No, at one point she'd left it hanging off the corner of the bar. She searched around the edges of the dark wood, all across the black tile flooring.

There! At the foot of the storage cabinets under the bar. Her key ring.

Except . . . She picked it up: house key, theater key, locker key, cash register key . . .

The key to the bar was missing.

She had no memory of taking the ring out of her pocket or dropping it. But if her jacket had hung on the corner, that would have placed its pockets right around head height for—"EZ!" she

6

called, not too loud in case someone was in the subbasement already.

A soft yip answered her call, followed by the clicking of tiny toenails on the tile. The terrier/beagle mix came sliding around the corner of the back room. EZ stood on his hind legs, placing his front paws on Mickey's knee with his tongue hanging out like he was laughing at her.

"This isn't funny," she admonished him, giving him a few strokes on the head despite her urgency. It might be nothing after all—someone forgetting something and coming to pick it up, or a diva who needed just the right prop or costume accessory for tomorrow's show.

Except it was New Year's Eve and freezing outside. Anyone sane would wait until morning.

"Where's the other key, EZ? Seriously. Where did you hide it?" He had a habit of this, picking up little trinkets and stashing them in some hidey hole only he knew about. "Please, EZ. It's time to go home."

At the word "home," EZ's pointed ears perked straight up. He barked once and darted off, for all the world looking like he was going to fetch what she'd asked for. Mickey let out a sigh of relief.

The door to the speakeasy swung open.

Mickey didn't even have time to turn around. She caught a glimpse of something metal reflected in the mirror over the bar and was raising her hands in the air when two loud pops echoed through the hidden space.

Pain seared through her lower back and abdomen. Two holes appeared in the side of the rounded end of the bar. She stared in disbelief as two deep red stains spread across the bottom half of her starched white button-down shirt.

Mickey slumped over the polished wood surface, then slid to land in a heap face down on the tile. Why? Why shoot her? If this was a raid, why not just arrest her, charge her a fine, lock her up? If it was something else, well, she couldn't imagine anyone angry enough with her to do this. It didn't make any sense.

Somewhere past her left ear, something metal clinked on the tile. The missing key, she presumed. A cold, wet nose nudged her cheek.

Too late, my friend, Mickey thought, wishing she could stroke his soft fur one last time, but her arms and hands wouldn't move.

EZ barked over and over again. There was a third pop. The dog whined and went silent.

And so did she.

Chapter 2

Sunday, October 23, 2022

THE BIG CITY Little Theater Company had dominated the corner of Gin and Jazz for over a hundred years. The streets hadn't always borne those names, but they were the ones Ciara recognized staring up at the signs while waiting to cross with the light.

The theater rose into the sunlight, its rooftop touched with metal accents to catch the rays and reflect them back at its patrons as if to shout its own "star power." How many ticket holders had stood in this same spot while a Model T, or a Duesenberg, or a Bentley passed by? In its heyday, back in the 1920s, this was the center of culture for the city's wealthy elite, and Ciara pictured them striding up the marble steps—men in tuxedos and top hats with women in long evening gowns.

She let out a wistful sigh, then shook her head. If she'd been among them, she would have preferred a feminine escort of her own, ensuring she'd never have gotten past the front door. No, Ciara was much better off in her own decade, even if she often felt like she belonged in a much earlier time.

The traffic light dinged, and the walking man figure lit up across from her. Ciara glanced both ways to be safe, then double-checked for turning vehicles before making her way to the other side and her theatrical place of employment. Three full aboveground stories and a couple of levels below of pure history. It gave her a shiver every time she came to work.

She'd almost reached the far curb when a flash of brown and white caught her peripheral vision. Ciara turned toward the motion as a little dog with a stubby tail and pointy ears darted out of the alleyway between the theater and the café next door, the café's owner chasing after it with an upraised broom.

Ciara recognized the stray as one who'd been hanging around the backstage door over the past week or so. It had even managed to sneak in from time to time. Performers and stage crew reported glimpsing the animal in the lobby, the labyrinthine corridors that ran throughout the ancient theater, and even in the basement stairwell, and it was usually carrying some small object: a handkerchief or glove from costuming, a flower from the prop department. He was a regular canine kleptomaniac. Ciara had seen him, too, though she'd never gotten close enough to check for a collar before he ran off. She'd taken to leaving bowls of kibble and water at the rear entrance in an attempt to keep him outside, but he never seemed to touch any of her offerings.

She'd always wanted a dog. Her military father had them moving all the time and felt it was unfair to an animal and, besides, her mother was too fastidious to allow any sort of pet, but now that she'd settled into her job and nearby apartment, if she could gain the stray's trust, she might keep him.

Having a permanent residence all to herself was lovely. But it would be nice to have someone to come home to, for both of them.

"No more digging in my garbage!" Antoine shouted in his heavy French accent, brandishing his makeshift broom weapon. Then, "Oh! Oh, no, don't go that way!"

Ciara's breath caught in her throat when the panicked animal bolted straight for the intersection and an oncoming delivery truck. She didn't think. She reacted. Waving both arms frantically in the air, Ciara took three steps to her left bringing herself into the edge of the truck's path.

The driver laid on the horn and swerved, his infuriated grimace visible through the windshield before he missed both her and the dog, which ran off between a bookstore and a barber shop. Brakes screeched as the truck slammed to a halt half a block farther down Gin Street. Leaning out the window of his vehicle, the red-faced heavyset deliveryman shouted, "What the hell, lady? You wanna kill us both?"

"You almost ran over that dog!" she shouted back in between sucking in ragged lungfuls of air.

The driver sobered for a moment, neck craning to scan up and down the street. He scowled. "I didn't see no dog. Stay out of the fucking road." He tossed off a lewd hand gesture and continued on his way.

Ciara pressed a hand to her chest in an attempt to quell her panic and lower her adrenaline level. She staggered the rest of the way to the curb, reached out, and grabbed the light post, letting it support her trembling body. Antoine joined her a moment later, as out of breath as she was, and grabbed the pole right above her own hand, leaning on the broom with the other. He wore his usual attire of black slacks and a black button-down with a white apron stretched over his rotund belly and tied in the back. His graying hair stuck out in all directions from his run.

"Oh, I'm so very sorry," he panted. "I never intended for the little dog to be hurt. It's only that he leaves such a very big mess for such a small animal." His accent made him a little difficult to understand, but after working next door to the café for six months and going there at least once a week on her lunch break, Ciara could make out the words. Antoine frowned down at her, his expression reminding Ciara of her father when he worried. "I am glad you saved him, but that was a dangerous risk to take."

Ciara opened her mouth to respond, then held up one finger and took a few more deep breaths. When she had enough air to speak, she said, "I know. But I felt responsible. I've been leaving food for him at the stage door, so it's partially my fault he's still hanging around. I was hoping to adopt him." She ran a shaky hand through her long dark hair, a few strands from her neon blue highlights catching between her fingers.

Antoine's face softened. "Ah, I see. You would like a pet for company."

She raised her eyebrows.

He shrugged. "You always dine alone at my café. A lovely woman should have a companion sometimes, even if that companion is canine."

Ciara laughed and pushed away from the light pole. She adjusted her backpack that had fallen off one shoulder in her mad dash. "I have work friends. I'll bring some by next time I come for lunch. But yeah, it would be nice to have a friend to come home to if I could catch—" Something moved just below her normal sight line. Ciara jumped, then laughed again. She looked down toward her sneakers and right into the eyes of the little dog. The moment their gazes met, it dropped into a perfect sit. If she didn't know better, Ciara would have sworn the dog seemed . . . contrite.

Antoine agreed, saying, "Now there's an apology if I've ever seen one." He waggled a finger at the dog. "You do know I deserve an apology as well, Monsieur."

As if it understood his words, the dog reached out a paw toward Antoine who took and shook it with an odd expression on his face. "Oh!" Then he blinked and the oddness had vanished. Antoine grinned. "Very well. Apology accepted. Now stay out of the garbage, eh?" With that, the café owner picked up his broom and strolled back to his restaurant, whistling some little French tune Ciara vaguely recognized.

That left the two of them alone on the street corner. This early in the morning there wasn't a lot of traffic, vehicle or pedestrian, with the exception of delivery trucks and shop owners preparing their businesses for the day ahead. The sun had crested the top of the theater, but October meant frosty mornings, and Ciara was glad she'd chosen the sky-blue winter jacket to wear over her thinner navy pullover sweater. She looked at the dog. The dog looked at her.

"I don't suppose you'd like to live with me," she said and grinned. "I don't make that offer to just anyone." *Make that no one.* She couldn't remember the last time she'd even had a friend over. Certainly not since she'd moved out of her parents' house. After so many new bases, new schools, new homes, it had stopped seeming worthwhile to make friends she'd leave again within a few months.

She'd done better in college, making a point of going to other people's dorms and apartments and forging some bonds. Yet even there she'd known it would all crumble to dust at the end of four years, and then after two more in graduate school at another university where she'd had to once again start over. A couple of temporary jobs into her career and she'd become almost as transient as she'd been as a child.

But you don't live like that anymore, Ciara reminded herself. Her current position felt permanent—her bosses much pleased with her, and the rest of the staff friendly and easy to work with. She loved her job. She loved the theater. She loved this city. And still, even her best friend at work, Kate, who headed up the backstage crew, hadn't gotten an invite to her place. Definitely time for a change.

"You want to share my home?" Ciara rephrased her offer to the dog who was still focused on her with intense interest.

At the word "home" the dog's ears perked up and it gave a single happy-sounding bark then turned around and around in a circle, making Ciara laugh.

"Well, you certainly like that word." She began to crouch

13

down, then noticed the thin collar and dangling tag hanging around the dog's neck. Her smile faded. "Oh. Looks like you have a home already." She sighed. "Guess I'd better figure out who you belong to." Ciara reached for the tag.

The dog skittered away.

"Hey! I just want to help you find your owner. I'm sure they must be worried about you." This dog had hung around the theater for over a week. His owner had to be missing him. "Come here little guy."

And on that note, the dog barked three more times, turned, and ran off in the direction of the backstage alley. A moment later he was lost in the shadows between buildings, gone.

Ciara shook her head and went on to work. If he followed habit, he'd turn up again sooner or later.

Stepping inside the theater was like stepping back in time. The small foyer contained a pair of ticket booths beyond which stood ornately gilded quadruple glass doors that opened into a wide lobby where audience members could wait until the house opened. To the left, a bar ran the length of the wall, a newer addition if newer meant within the past seventy years. Ciara paused to straighten the "Show Times" placard in the corner of the closer booth's window and to grab an empty wineglass from the ticket counter that the cleaning crew had missed, then headed to the bar to return the glass for washing.

Even with the horrific cost of retaining their liquor license, the current management continued to allow the selling of alcoholic beverages before performances and between acts, and a rattling of bottles beneath the bar's counter surface told Ciara that Carlos, their bartender, was already on duty. "What're you doing here so early?" Ciara called to the unseen figure. She maneuvered her way between plush velvet couches and chairs arranged in little clusters so elderly patrons would have a place to sit while they drank.

Ciara set down her retrieved wineglass and leaned her arms on the bar, then stood on tiptoe to look over it. Carlos was crouched, his head and torso out of view as he searched inside one of the cabinets.

"Hello, my lovely work wife!" he replied, voice muffled a bit by the furniture.

Ciara laughed. Carlos had been the first employee she'd met when she'd come in for an interview. They'd hit it off, though as a bartender, he got along with almost everyone. Quick with a joke or an amusing anecdote, Carlos had a way of lifting her spirits no matter her mood. When she'd emerged from the owner's office on that anxiety-filled day, he'd been right there with a glass of wine asking her how her meeting went. Since then, she'd been his "work wife," despite neither of them preferring the opposite sex.

He withdrew and grinned up at her while reaching to smooth down his short dark hair. Straightening brought him to his full six-foot-two height that towered over both Ciara and the bar. Pressed beige slacks and a white polo set off his tanned skin. Men weren't her thing, but Ciara considered him very attractive.

"I thought I'd come in and take care of the ordering," he said, "maybe straighten things up a bit, but two of my bar towels are missing, the red one and the green one. I can't find them anywhere."

"You store them down there?" Ciara said, pointing at the lower cabinets.

"Sure, why?"

"Oh, nothing. I'll keep an eye out for them." She had a pretty good idea which small, furry culprit had snatched the towels. Something really did need to be done about the dog sneaking inside, but outside clearly wasn't safe for him, and until she could get a look at that collar and call the owner—

A hand waved in front of her face. "Earth to Ciara. I said, what are *you* doing here? You don't usually work on Sundays."

She shrugged. "Same as you. I've got a pile of paperwork on my desk. Invoices for equipment and materials, requests for season tickets. Things backed up when the pandemic shut you down. I need to catch up on everything the last bookkeeper let go. And the owners don't care which hours I work as long as I put in forty of them." In reality she put in a lot more than forty. She'd spent her first three months figuring out where everything was and deconstructing the filing system before transferring most of the previous year's documents to her computer. Then they'd reopened for performances, and more got put on hold. She had a lot to accomplish, and she hated feeling behind even if no one else seemed to think she was.

Other sounds of life from behind the house doors told her they weren't the only ones putting in hours. She raised her eyebrows at Carlos.

"Yeah, Kate and Jeremy are here, too. Something about the lightboard glitching during last night's show. They're trying to track down the problem."

Ciara had heard about that—lights flickering then going off completely, only for a different set to turn on without warning. "Good. I hope they figure it out. Well, off to the office," she said and waved goodbye. "I'll catch you later."

"Later!" He disappeared back beneath the bar.

She made her way across the lobby, sliding her palm along the backs of the deep blue crushed-velvet couches, the material a decadent indulgence of an earlier time and expensively reupholstered every three to five years according to the previous bookkeeper's records. Someone else in her profession might recommend a cheaper, more durable alternative or perhaps suggest the removal of the furnishings altogether and let audience members stand to wait to be let into the house, but the couches matched the area rugs—deep blue plush with silver threads running through them and making every inch of floor they covered glitter under the crystal chandeliers. The décor suited the theater's origins, and Ciara would cut corners elsewhere to make sure those origins remained as intact as possible. Fortunately for her, the owners shared her nostalgic views.

As she reached the "Staff Only" doors on the lobby's far side, Ciara considered what Antoine had said to her. Maybe she should invite some of her coworkers to join her for lunch once in a while, especially Carlos and Kate.

You've forgotten how to make friends, or at least how to treat and keep them.

She pushed through the right-hand door into her very favorite area of the theater. Most would have chosen the house itself with its red velvet curtains, deeply cushioned seats, and luxurious balconies. Others might have selected the labyrinth of storerooms in the basements—a veritable treasure trove of long-lost period costumes, props, and sets—some of which hadn't been explored in decades.

But Ciara loved this hallway.

Lined with black-and-white photographs on both sides, the hall leading to the theater offices was a tunnel into the past. Beginning with colorful digital prints of the exterior after its recent renovations, each image took her further and further back to the building's origins. There were framed programs, some of them signed by actors who'd gone on to be stars of Broadway and Hollywood. Others displayed professional headshots of the performers from a wide variety of plays and musicals.

She studied the black-and-whites from the sixties, fifties, forties, showing candid shots of curtain calls, makeup sessions, costume fittings. And oh, the costumes, styles from a dozen time periods in all their glam and glory.

But it was the collection of the earliest photographs, the ones from the nineteen-twenties and early teens when the theater first opened, that always stopped her. Not many had survived, but the ones that had, had been carefully and meticulously preserved by the current owners. Ciara stared at the faces of the cast of the first play ever produced there, *A Midsummer Night's Dream*, in 1915. Another showed all the ushers in their pressed black tuxedos and bow ties, along with the ticket takers and office staff in matching long black skirts and frilled white blouses.

Ciara appreciated the lack of a strict dress code now, but thinking of the military she'd grown up around, there was something to be said for the pride and camaraderie a uniform could invoke. Still, even without one, she felt that surge of importance at being a part of this history though she hadn't yet been immortalized on the hallway walls.

She continued on to the final image, and her favorite, depicting one of the first backstage crews, those unseen but vital individuals who operated the curtains and the spotlights, set the scenes and lowered the backdrops.

Ciara trailed her fingers across the glass separating her from the rough-and-tumble bunch posed on and around a stepladder, circa 1921. They wore overalls and loose-fitting shirts, both men and a couple of women. That had come as a surprise until she'd done some research and discovered the 1920s had been a time when women in the workforce were on the rise in all sorts of factories and such, especially in cities. Judging from the determined expressions on the women's faces in the photograph, they'd held their own.

She certainly admired their grit.

Well, she thought, reaching her office door at the end of the hall, her name and the word "Bookkeeper" emblazoned on its frosted glass upper half, *time to show a little grit of my own.*

She pressed a palm to the door to push through and conquer the mounds of neatly stacked paperwork and the full email inbox that awaited her, but a faint scraping sound stopped her. Glancing back, she spotted that backstage crew photo now hanging askew, having come partially loose from the hooks behind it on the wall.

Ciara returned to it, lifted it all the way off, and examined the holders. She tugged on each one. Neither wiggled. They were firmly attached. She supposed the wire on the rear of the frame must not have been placed fully over one of the two hooks. Shrugging, she set it to rights, made a minor adjustment to be certain it hung evenly, and went on into her office.

Chapter 3

Sunday, October 23, 2022

CIARA CLICKED *SEND* on the last of the orders for the maintenance department and leaned back in her swivel chair. Inbox: zero. New achievement level unlocked. She shut down the email program before anything new could come in and ruin her miraculous accomplishment. The clock in the corner of her screen read 4:55. Five minutes before the matinee crowd let out, which meant wall-to-wall people followed by bumper-to-bumper traffic as the families attending *Peter Pan* attempted to leave the back parking lot and make their way home.

So, she was stuck. Maybe she could catch up on her social media, such as it was—

"Hey!" Carlos rapped on the open door to her office. "Want to go on a scavenger hunt?"

She drew her brows together. "Excuse me?"

He held out the clipboard in his left hand, a second one tucked under his right arm. "Props needs all hands on deck. They're trying to complete some semblance of inventory and thought it would be more fun if they made a game out of it. Management approved the overtime and even threw in a free pair of primo box seat tickets to the next Broadway touring show and a bottle of champagne to the winner. I thought we could team up and split the prize."

Frowning, Ciara took the clipboard and studied the multi-page list divided into categories: set pieces, props, costumes, accessories, and "random shit." She pointed at the last header. "Kate came up with that one, didn't she?"

Carlos rolled his eyes. "She is a tad predictable. But I'm not knocking it, you know? Her 'random shit,'" he reminded her, air quotes and all, "can bring in some serious cash, especially if it's old. Remember last year when she found that carbon arc lamp in a box marked 'dishware'? Sold that thing on eBay for close to five hundred dollars and bought costumes for the youth drama program. Who knows what we might find if we help out? Our future kids are gonna need clothes and toys and ... and ..."

"Random shit?" Ciara suggested.

Carlos pointed a finger at her. "Exactly, my lovely work wife!"

She laughed. Could be fun. And she wasn't going anywhere until the roads cleared anyway. Besides, while she received a hefty discount on tickets, the box seats were still out of her price range. And the next touring show was *Hamilton*.

"Okay, I'm in. How does the contest part work?"

Carlos reached over the desk to point at the margin of the page she was looking at. "See these specific items scribbled in?"

She peered at the messy handwriting. Definitely Kate's. She could barely decipher Kate's invoices without asking for a translation. Using her letter sense, she read aloud, "Rubber chicken? Latex gloves, stuffed cat, brown bowler hat, washboard ... what is this?" There were ten random items in all.

"Those are your items for the scavenger hunt. While you're inventorying everything in the storerooms you're assigned to, if you happen to come across those ten things, you check them off and put them in a pile. The person who finds the most wins. I've got different ones." He held out his list, which included a calendar, a radio, and a wine bottle among others. "I figure if

21

we work together on both lists, we have a better chance. And I made sure we were assigned to adjacent rooms."

Sure enough, her printout read Subbasement Storeroom One while his said Subbasement Storeroom Two. She flipped to the very back page which appeared to be a photocopy of an old blueprint plan of the theater with her assignment circled in yellow highlighter. The date in the corner said "1915." "Wow, where'd she get this? And are you sure you want to pair with me and not Renaldo from makeup?" Carlos had been drooling over Renaldo for days.

"Like I said, Kate loves antique shit," he called, already heading out the door. "So do you. I've seen you staring at those old photos. Besides, Renaldo doesn't like to get himself dirty unless it involves powder and rouge. Come on! The others have already started. And as soon as the ushers finish clearing the house, they'll be in on it too. Let's get a jump start!" And he was gone.

Glad she'd opted for jeans and sneakers today since she hadn't planned on leaving the office, Ciara followed. She bypassed the elevator in favor of the stairs. Now that the show had ended, the single-car lift had a huge crowd of mothers with strollers and elderly wheelchair users waiting on the upper levels to get down to the lobby, and it didn't go all the way to the subbasement anyway. Judging from the clomp of footsteps on the stairs ahead of her, Carlos had opted to do the same.

"Wait up!" she called, her voice bouncing off the concrete walls. "Oh, great acoustics in here." She tried a wolf howl, laughing when it echoed and reverberated around her.

"Quit it," Carlos shouted back, out of sight somewhere below. "This place is creepy enough without your help."

She continued to descend, marveling at how the more recently painted walls began to show their age the lower she went. Plaster-covered cinderblocks were cracked and chipping. Tiles had missing corners or entire squares. The moldy, musty smell made her sneeze.

She passed the propped-open main basement entry door where she could hear laughter and conversation and the occasional shout of discovery. It sounded like most of the staff was in there. A head popped around the doorway, and she leapt back against the interior stairwell wall and pressed a hand over her heart. "Don't do that!"

Jeremy laughed and swept his hand through his spikey blond hair. He had dust covering his stage crew black pants and shirt. "Sorry. Didn't see you. You heading down to Creepytown?"

"Um, why do you call it that?" This game didn't sound so fun anymore. She peered down the stairs. Were they talking cobwebs and spiders or . . . something less tangible? Ciara loved the *idea* of spirits lingering around old buildings and cemeteries. That a love for a particular place might transcend death brought out the romantic in her. However, she didn't think she'd want to actually *meet* one. Classic films like *The Ghost and Mrs. Muir* were totally her jam. *Poltergeist*, not so much.

"You've never been to the subbasement?" came a female voice. Kate joined Jeremy in the doorway and wrapped an arm around his waist. They'd been a couple since just after Ciara got hired. "Don't let him scare you. It's just old. And really cool. Almost no one ever goes down there since all the modern stuff gets stored up here. I've made a dent in storeroom three, but I don't get time to really dig in. I think some of those crates and boxes have been in the subbasement since the theater opened. It's a lot. We'll join you two in a few minutes once we get everyone assigned up here."

"And watch out for ghosts!" Jeremy called. Kate smacked him on the shoulder, and they disappeared back into the main basement.

History Ciara loved. Ghosts, not so much.

Most old theaters had ghost stories. Theirs was no exception. Anytime the lights flickered or the sound system made strange noises, some staff member claimed it was a ghost. And the Big City Little Theater Company had suffered its fair share of deaths over its one hundred-plus years of operation. She'd heard all the tales almost immediately after her hiring.

During its construction in 1915, a worker had been crushed by a concrete slab. A pair of actors had shot each other over a starring role in 1918. The early twenties marked a diva's suicide after reading a scathing review in the local paper. Nineteen thirty-five saw a lighting operator fall from the catwalk, and in the sixties two ushers had been found backstage after having overdosed on heroin. The most recent death had occurred only five years ago. The soundboard had shorted out when the operator spilled his water bottle on it, and it had electrocuted him. They'd replaced the equipment, and food and beverages were no longer allowed in crew areas.

Because of all that, lots of staff claimed to have seen and heard things—a flicker at the corner of an eye, a shadow that shouldn't be there, a woman's voice whispering behind the curtain when no one was on stage. Ciara didn't believe any of it, but that didn't mean she wanted to seek it out.

She reached the bottom of the stairs without ghostly incident and entered the subbasement. Carlos stood next to the second door on the right-hand wall. Two more doors were in the left wall, and the farthest wall across from the stairs was blank, which seemed odd for some reason, but she shook it off. There were a few scattered boxes and crates stacked in this entry area, but they looked empty. "Okay, I'm here. Where do we start?"

He knocked on the door beside him. "This is my room. Next one over is yours. Take a look at my hunt list. If you find anything on it, rap on the wall between our rooms and I'll do the same for you."

She took the clipboard from him and quickly scribbled down his ten random items on the back of her first inventory page, then returned it. "Okay. Let's leave the doors to our storerooms open in case . . . well, just in case. I mean, something might fall on us, or there could be mice or rats down here."

"Riiight. Sure. No problem." Carlos gave her a grin, opened his assigned door, and stepped inside. "Damn, this is a lot of shit."

She opened her own door. A small walking path led from the entry to the rear wall with floor-to-ceiling crates and boxes on either side and almost none of them labeled, not that she'd trust the labels anyway.

Two and a half hours and a lot of profanity later, she'd almost finished cataloging her assigned boxes—most of which contained household props from decades long past, two that held gloves and hats, and another with nothing but scarves. Outside the storeroom she'd piled a harmonica, a framed painting of a woman, and a fireplace poker from her scavenger hunt list along with boxing gloves and a top hat from Carlos's.

She stepped out and jumped when something squeaked beneath her sneaker—the rubber chicken Carlos had found for her. With only four checkmarks, she doubted there would be *Hamilton* tickets coming her way.

Carlos joined her, followed by Kate and Jeremy coming out of room three. By the looks of Kate's smeared makeup and their rumpled clothing and messy hair, they had *not* been doing inventory.

Ciara smirked at them. "Find anything useful?"

"Oh yeah," Kate said, squeezing Jeremy's ass and laughing. "Lots of things."

Carlos stood by the stairwell door and listened. "Sounds like everyone upstairs left. We ready to call it quits?"

"Yeah. We've gone through three out of four. Really good progress." Jeremy collected the clipboards.

"Sure, if you consider good progress being half of what Ciara and I did," Carlos muttered, but he grinned to take the sting out of it.

"Five," Ciara said.

"What was that?" Kate turned away to rebutton her misaligned top.

"Three out of five. There are five storerooms down . . ." She trailed off, studying the four doors. "Oh! But on the blueprints . . ." Ciara snatched her clipboard back and flipped to the last page, then tapped the photocopy. "See, I was right. There should be five storage rooms here. In fact, that fifth one would have been the largest, as big as one and two or three and four combined. It even has a second smaller room behind it, according to these plans. But—"

"Yeah, but." Kate waved her arm to the blank far-most wall. "No fifth room. I noticed it too. I'm guessing it was either a mistake on the architect's part, or maybe a change was made after they started construction, and they filed the wrong blueprints." She shrugged. "For whatever reason, they never put that fifth room in."

"Weird," Ciara said, walking over to the blank wall. She turned around and faced the rest of the open space. "And it's asymmetrical." She pointed at each wall in sequence, to her left, straight across, to her right, and over her shoulder. "Two doors, stairwell, two doors, nothing. It looks so odd."

"It could have been anything. Maybe they would have hit a water main or a gas line. Does it matter?" Jeremy said.

"No, I guess not." Ciara leaned back against the blank wall to push herself off toward the stairs. The cell phone in her rear jeans pocket *clonked* as it connected with the bare cinderblock. In fact, it didn't sound much like cinderblock at all.

Kate froze with one booted foot on the bottommost step, the guys stumbling into each other behind her. Slowly Kate turned and looked over her shoulder, eyes wide. "Did that sound . . . hollow . . . to anyone else?"

Chapter 4

????

WHERE WAS SHE? Mickey pushed herself up from the bar, her fingers still wrapped around her gin fizz glass. Had she . . . had she *passed out?*

Impossible. She'd had a few drinks, sure. It was New Year's Eve after all. But she was no lightweight.

Straightening on the barstool, she looked around the empty space. The clock, a showpiece her parents had brought all the way from Ireland, which Paul hated so of course she loved it, read 2:41. The calendar displayed the correct date. And yet . . . and yet. She remembered Jimmy leaving. She remembered cleaning up a little, then getting all maudlin about still being alone after more than a year.

The thought sent her spiraling all over again.

Her chest ached as she replayed the conversation she'd had with Annie on that Thanksgiving night over a year before—a conversation that had come without warning. They'd enjoyed a quiet dinner in the bar after it closed, or at least Mickey had enjoyed it. Annie had been especially thoughtful, almost silent throughout the meal. And then she'd set down her fork, looked up, and dropped her bomb.

"I'm tired of celebrating holidays in hiding. I want someone I can take into the daylight. There's no future for us, Mick." Annie reached across the table and cupped Mickey's cheek in her palm, her expression full of regret.

A wave of panic seized Mickey. They'd been together almost six months, the longest relationship she'd ever had. Annie could take someone into the light. She was attracted to both women and men, a trait Mickey didn't share.

"No!" she said out loud, dispelling the images from her mind, forcing herself to focus on the here and now—EZ, the bar, the odd sense that she'd forgotten something important.

She'd been about to lock the door and head home. That was it.

Mickey patted the pockets of her suit jacket. Her keys were missing.

An odd sense of panic tightened her chest and sent the gin fizz sloshing around in her stomach. Her breath came short and fast. What the hell was wrong with her? They had to be around somewhere. EZ must have taken them. He was always pilfering little things.

"EZ! Here boy!"

On command, EZ scampered into view, skidding on the tiles as he ran from the back office. Something shiny and metal hung from his mouth—her key ring. EZ dropped into a perfect sit at her feet and laid the keys down carefully in front of her borrowed black-and-white men's dress shoes. She bent to retrieve them and froze.

This isn't right. This isn't how it happened. It isn't.

She didn't care.

"Good boy. Ready to go home?"

The dog yipped and jumped up to turn in a circle three times, then ran back and forth between Mickey and the door leading out of the speakeasy. Mickey shut off the radio and all the lights except for the bulb just inside the entry, which she left on so she could find the door easily and see when she returned. Buried deep in the theater's subbasement, it would be pitch dark without that light, and while she loved her private gathering place, she didn't love the dark so much.

Except . . . the dark had never really bothered her before.

Before . . . what?

Mickey reached to retrieve the keys, almost losing her balance in the process. Yep, definitely too much to drink. Good thing home was only a brisk walk away. EZ stood by the door, his stubby tail blurring with excited wags. Her fingers brushed the cold metal ring.

The shock of a static electricity charge so strong as to be visible sparked off the keys and into Mickey's fingers. She jumped back with a yelp, shaking the pain out of her hand, then stilled.

"This . . . isn't right. It's all wrong somehow. This isn't the way—" She stared at the floor beside the edge of the bar, then down at her shirt front, and back to the bar. EZ gave a soft whine.

There'd been three pops. There'd been . . . there'd been . . .

She'd died. They'd both died.

Hadn't they?

"EZ?" Mickey said in a whisper, her eyes wide. Before the dog could respond in any way, someone pounded on something outside the door. Her heart leapt into her throat. Her muscles stiffened. She stood there, paralyzed, listening and trying to breathe as shallowly as possible. They couldn't hear her, whoever they were. That didn't matter. She wanted to hide.

More knocking. Definitely not on the door. It sounded farther away.

"This isn't how it happened," she murmured, more to herself than her dog. "Someone came in. Someone had a gun." The knocking faded away, growing fainter and fainter until she could no longer hear it.

Mickey breathed a sigh of relief. "We have to get out of here. We have to get home."

EZ barked his agreement.

She reached for the doorknob. Her hand trembled. *Open it. Open it now or you never will.*

Mickey threw open the door and staggered backward.

A swirling miasma of cold gray fog greeted her on the other side. She stared into its whirlpool-like depths, like one of her grasshopper cocktails without the green of the crème de menthe. Mickey shivered at the shadows that writhed and moved amid the tendrils of gray. Terrifying.

She couldn't let it touch her.

Mickey slammed the door shut, then threw herself against it. She slid, panting, down to the black tile.

In here it was safe. In here she would stay. Was this heaven? Was this her personal version of an afterlife? If that was the case, was it a privilege or a punishment to be in her favorite place but trapped?

Mickey had no idea. She wondered how long it would take to figure it out.

Chapter 5

Sunday, October 23, 2022

KATE STARED AT the blank wall that apparently wasn't a wall at all. She'd taken her hammer off her ubiquitous toolbelt and was tapping it lightly against her open palm. "What the actual fuck?" she muttered.

Jeremy stood beside her, Ciara and Carlos behind them. Jeremy knocked on the center of the unadorned wall. It resonated. "Not exactly hollow, per se, but not concrete, that's for sure." He exchanged a look and a nod with Kate. As if they could read each other's thoughts, they both began a series of knocks, starting at the wall's center and working outward, Kate going left and tapping tentatively with her hammer, Jeremy stepping to the right using his knuckles, and alternating. When they reached their respective ends, they faced each other, then turned toward their companions. "What do you guys think?" Jeremy asked.

Carlos cocked his head to one side and then the other. "It sounded pretty much the same all the way across. Maybe a little deeper, louder in the center?"

Ciara nodded. "I agree. And according to the blueprints," she said, consulting them for the twentieth time since her odd

31

discovery, "that's about where the missing door should be."

"Hmm." Kate held her free hand over her mouth, her brows drawn together in thought.

Meanwhile, Jeremy went back to the corner and ran his fingers down the seam between the two walls. "Oh wow. Holy shit. You guys aren't going to believe this."

"There's actually quite a lot not to believe here, Jer," Kate said with a roll of her eyes. "Share, please?"

He turned to them, a look of absolute awe on his face, his palm pressed reverently against the blank wall. "This isn't a wall at all. It's a backdrop."

"What?"

"You're kidding."

"Are you serious?" Kate studied it again. "How do you know?"

Jeremy pointed to the corner. "The edges don't quite match up. I can get a fingernail in between where this wall meets the next and it's probably the same at the other end. But you'd have to know to try that. You'd have to be looking for it. Otherwise, it's perfect as long as you don't go knocking." He took a step back and admired the pale white wall as if it were a museum masterpiece. "Color's matched. And painted to look like concrete blocks." He ran a hand across the surface, then stretched and did the same with the adjoining wall. "Even the texture feels right. I'm not certain how they anchored it in place, but then I can't get enough leverage around the edge to try and pry it loose, which may be what they counted on, whoever 'they' were. If you didn't see the blueprints and you didn't bang on it, you'd never know it was a cut set piece."

"But . . . why?" Ciara asked, voicing everyone's thoughts.

Kate shook her head. "No idea. Maybe some accidental damage? Hide things from the owners or the insurance company? Hey guys, we had five storerooms, but we flooded one so now we have four? Management never comes down here. At least ours doesn't. It could have worked."

"Maybe . . ." Ciara said, but it didn't sound right. Something else was going on.

"It would be a great way to hide a body."

The three of them turned slowly to stare at Carlos.

"What?" he said, throwing both hands in the air. "I watch a lot of crime dramas and cold case investigation shows." He gestured at the wall with an outstretched arm. "This would be the ideal setup for murder."

"That's ridiculous," Jeremy said. "If it ever got discovered, the stage crew would be the first people the police would go after. You'd have to know set design and construction to pull something like this off."

"But it never did get discovered," Kate said, "until now. Whatever it's here for, it's meant to hide something. I say let's find out what it is." She stood at the dead center of the wall and raised the hammer to shoulder height.

"Whoa, wait! Shouldn't we tell management?" Ciara didn't know exactly why that seemed like a good idea. It wasn't the actual wall they'd be damaging, just a set backdrop that no one used for the company's productions. But she was the bookkeeper, and this felt like something there should be a record of.

Kate threw a quick and mischievous grin over her shoulder. "Nope." And she brought the hammer down.

It took three bangs against plaster-covered wood to break through, every pounding sending deafening reverberations through the subbasement and forcing the others to cover their ears. So when Kate had a hole about eight inches in diameter and said something, Ciara didn't catch it.

"What was that?" She lowered her hands. Her ears still rang.

"I said someone give me their phone to use as a flashlight. I left mine in my locker backstage."

Ciara pulled the cell from her back pocket, shook it twice to activate the built-in light, and handed it over. Kate aimed it at the hole she'd made, shining it up, down, and sideways. Then she stood on tiptoe and pressed her face to the opening for a better view. When she turned around at last, she crossed her arms over her chest.

"Well?" Carlos asked, bouncing on his toes.

Kate nodded once. "We found our missing door."

Over an hour later they'd smashed their way through enough of the backdrop's center to have a clear view of said door, which, disappointingly, looked exactly like the other four doors in the subbasement except for . . .

"The knob's different," Ciara said. "And the keyhole." She gestured at the rest of the doors. "Those have plain metal hardware. This one almost looks like brass."

Jeremy reached out and gave the knob a twist, then frowned. "Locked. Of course. If you're hiding something, you're gonna take every precaution." He glanced at Kate. "You got a key for this?"

Kate stared at the lock, a thoughtful expression on her face. "Maybe." She dropped her hammer back into its holder on her toolbelt, then rummaged in a belt pouch and removed a large key ring jangling with maybe thirty different keys. "When I got promoted to crew chief, the boss handed me this mess. Said he didn't know what half of them opened, but I'd figure it out." She rolled her eyes. "I still haven't, and I've had to replace a lot of locks over the years just to get in places where I needed to be to do my job. But I've managed to label some of the originals." Kate held up the ring.

Ciara could see tiny white stickers with small print written on them attached to several of the keys. She thought one said "Stage Door," and another said "Dressing Rooms." A third might have read "Storerooms" but deciphering Kate's chicken scratch could be a bear. Kate took hold of that one and attempted to insert it in the lock. It fit, but it wouldn't turn.

"Figures it couldn't be that easy," she muttered.

"So try them all," Carlos said.

Kate tried one key after another. Many wouldn't fit in the keyhole at all. The ones that did wouldn't turn. Ciara found herself holding her breath as Kate came to the last three keys on the ring.

"That one," Ciara said when Kate held them out in her palm separated from the others. Ciara reached a tentative finger to touch the rightmost key, then jerked back when a jolt of static electricity arced through her fingertip. She shook out her hand and laughed. "Wool, metal, and colder weather don't mix well." She pointed to her heavier fall sweater. "But seriously, that one. It's brass like the lock, and it looks ancient."

Indeed, it did, the brass metal tarnished over almost its entire surface, and the end of it covered in scratch marks.

"That . . . would be one helluva coincidence," Kate said, picking up the key and raising it toward the light.

"Why's that?" Carlos asked.

"Because I just found this key today."

"What? How?" Ciara looked from Kate's face to the key in her hand and back again.

Kate grinned. "You know that stray dog that's been hanging around?"

"He's not a stray," Ciara said. "He has a collar. As soon as I can catch him, I'll call his owners. I know he's a bit of a nuisance."

Jeremy laughed. "Hey, don't worry about it. We know you've been leaving food for him, and we all think he's cute."

"Yes, adorable," Kate said with less enthusiasm. "But he steals things—tools, set pieces."

"Bar towels," Carlos put in. "Oh, I got those back, by the way. Turned up in the middle of the lobby. With four holes in them."

"Sorry," Ciara muttered.

"Anyway," Kate continued a little louder, a note of annoyance in her tone, "when I saw him backstage this morning with something in his mouth, I yelled at him to drop it. I heard metal hit the floorboards and he took off." She gestured at the key in her palm. "This is what he dropped. I figured it belonged to one of the actors or was a prop, so I put it on my ring for safekeeping." Without further ado, she inserted it into the lock. It slid in easily. She took a deep breath.

She turned the key.

"No way."

The lock clicked open. The four of them gaped at the doorknob.

"Like I said, one helluva coincidence."

Chapter 6

Sunday, October 23, 2022

"WE HAVE NO idea what's in there," Jeremy said. "So go slow."

Kate eased the door open a couple of inches, then stopped. "It's thicker than the other doors," she commented, holding her thumb and forefinger apart to measure the width. "Better for protecting whatever's inside. Someone call Geraldo Rivera. We've found the real Al Capone vault."

"Or maybe it's to block sound from coming in or getting out?" Jeremy suggested.

"Yeah, like a murder victim's screams."

Ciara reached over and smacked Carlos on the arm. "Quit it with the murder stuff. Please."

"Right, then." Kate wrapped her grip around the doorknob and hesitated before pulling it all the way open, glancing back over her shoulder. She let go of the knob. "You found it, Ciara. Do you want the honors?"

Ciara studied the two-inch gap they'd already made. Nothing but darkness. No light. No sound. Not that a storeroom would have either if no one was inside. Oh god, why had she thought *that*? What if someone *was* inside?

Once, when she'd been a teenager, she and her parents had returned to their home on base at Fort Carson after a rare weekend getaway. It was late and dark. They'd driven for hours. They'd been tired but laughing at some dad joke from her father when he swung open the front door and a large, shadowy figure barreled out of it, knocking her flat on the grass of their perfectly manicured front lawn. Her father subdued the man—a soldier recently returned from deployment who'd broken in through the back window during a rough episode of PTSD—but it scared the bejeezus out of her.

"Nope, I'm good." Ciara hoped she hid the slight tremor she had in her voice. Kate's smirk told her she hadn't.

"Here goes nothing!" Kate reached for the knob once more.

Before she could touch it, the door flew outward, slamming her in the forehead and sending her staggering into Jeremy. A blur of motion at about shin height hurtled out of the darkness of the fifth room causing Ciara, Carlos, and even Jeremy to shriek at the tops of their lungs while Kate groaned.

The trio continued to scream until Kate shouted, "Seriously? Look, people. Look!" She pointed across the subbasement's main area to the base of the stairwell, her other hand rubbing above her left eyebrow. Ciara noted with some satisfaction that Kate's hand trembled. She wasn't as calm as she wanted to pretend. "It's that damn dog!"

Sure enough, the brown and white terrier mix stood on the bottommost step, his stubby tail a blur of motion like he'd just performed the greatest trick of his entire doggy life and was waiting for treats and pets. The dog barked twice, then turned and ran up the stairs to vanish from sight.

"Oh for fuck's sake," Jeremy said, clutching his chest and panting more heavily than the dog. "You okay, Kate?" He gently lifted the bangs off her forehead to study the bump. "That bruise will be a beaut."

She shook him off, but her smile said she appreciated the

gesture. "Been hurt a lot worse working crew. It's nothing."

"But . . . how?" Ciara asked. "The door was locked. And blocked."

Kate shrugged. "Must be another access point somewhere. Hole in the wall between the rooms, heating or A/C ductwork. Lots of renovations done over the years, and we don't actually know how long this room has been sealed off. I've been here longer than any of you, and that's only seven years. Hell, for all we know, there's a connecting corridor back in there that lines up with another part of the theater. The whole building's a minotaur's wet dream. You said the blueprints showed a smaller room behind this one. Could be more."

"I thought you said the dog wasn't a stray," Carlos commented, still staring at the stairs. "I didn't see the collar you mentioned."

Ciara narrowed her eyes. "You had the wherewithal to look for that? While screaming?"

He ran a hand through his short, glossy black hair. "I'm a man of many skills. But yeah, while it was barking and pretty much laughing at us, I looked."

Ciara shrugged. "He must have lost it."

"Are we going in or not?" Jeremy interrupted. "It's almost nine. I've gotta be at my other job at the coffee shop by six tomorrow morning."

"Right. You need your beauty sleep." Kate stood in the dark doorway. She didn't cross the threshold, and no one moved to join her. "Okay, first things first. Lights. In the other storerooms, the switch is right over—" she reached around the edge of the doorframe, moving her hand up and down until, "—here."

Six scattered overhead incandescent light fixtures came on, brightening gradually over several long seconds and bathing portions of the room beyond in warm orange-yellow glows. The one above the entry crackled then burst, showering Kate in a handful of tiny glass particles and eliciting yet another

39

scream, this time from the entire group. Two more, illuminating what appeared to be about a half dozen round wooden tables with seating for two or four, flickered erratically like mistimed nightclub strobes. The final three held steady—one over the end of a dust-covered wooden counter, one positioned just above a faded wall calendar, and the last over a set of shelves where a huge and ancient-looking monstrosity of a radio sat, its dials staring at the new arrivals like a pair of eyes.

"It's . . . it's a . . . bar?" Jeremy stammered, regaining his composure for the second time within a handful of minutes.

Kate shook her long, blond ponytail, bits of glass falling from it like glitter. "Good. After this experience, I could use a drink."

"Seriously, though," Ciara said, moving farther into the converted storage space. "What's it doing here?" She took a few steps to the left between a pair of tables and ran one finger through over an inch of accumulated dust on the back of a generic wooden chair. It flew up in a small cloud, making her cough. Waving it away, she drew in a deeper breath of musty air heavy with the weight of years of abandonment.

"I'll tell you what it's doing here. It's helping me win the scavenger hunt!" Carlos ducked out the door and returned a moment later with the clipboard he'd discarded while they broke through the facade. He pointed at the wall. "Calendar. Check." His finger moved to indicate the counter behind the bar below shelves of foggy bottles encased in cobwebs. "Radio. Check. I think I've got you all beat."

"I think we need to figure this out. Is this . . . for real? Or is it an elaborate set of some kind?" Ciara went to stand beneath the calendar. A woman in a form-fitting black evening gown smiled down at her. "This thing says 'January 1924.'"

Jeremy let out a low whistle. "Damn, that's old. 1920s. Prohibition Era, right? Maybe this was one of those . . . what did they call them? Speakeasies."

40

Kate laughed. "Look at you being all intellectual and shit."

Jeremy grinned and gave her the finger.

"Of course," Carlos said, slapping his forehead.

"Holy crap, you're right!" Ciara imagined the bar full of men in suits and women in flapper dresses sipping drinks made from gin. "I've been to a couple of modern speakeasies."

"The calendar could still be a prop," Kate pointed out. "I remember the owners telling me some of the theater's history when I got hired. They filmed parts of a couple of movies upstairs, and several commercials, back in the late nineties, I think. Maybe the film company stored their stuff down here and locked it separately so it wouldn't get used by the theater and then forgot about it." She shrugged. "Still old, but not noteworthy old."

"I don't think so," Carlos said, crossing a small dance floor to the right of the bar. His shoes left tracks through the dust and grime covering the wooden addition. The rest of the flooring was black tile, also covered in footprints from their entry and wandering. "Why the elaborate backdrop to hide it? Doesn't make sense. And neither does the speakeasy theory, really. It would need to be hidden, sure, but that backdrop? That would keep people out entirely. Look how long it took us to get through it. Someone must have added it later."

"But the dog got in," Jeremy reminded everyone. "So, there's another entrance somewhere. Hide the main door and have a secret one somewhere else? That would fall in with the speakeasy theory." He shrugged. "Won't know until we search everything."

Carlos moved behind the bar. Starting at the farthest corner he brushed off bottles and read the labels out loud. "Gin, whiskey, rum. Can't pronounce the names of the distilleries. Most of them are foreign."

"They'd have to be. Almost everything at that time was either made with a home still or imported illegally from overseas," Kate said. "If those are authentic and unopened, they could be worth a small fortune."

Carlos came to a stop by the radio. "This looks like the real deal. I mean, maybe a film budget would cover using an antique like this, but . . ." He trailed off, his fingers reaching for the dials.

"Don't!" Kate yelled, the sound very loud in the eerily quiet room. The others jumped. Again. She smiled sheepishly. "Sorry. But don't turn it on. That goes for the standing lamps, too." There were a handful of those, one in each of the corners of the room and maybe more in the deeper shadows, all spindly things with gaudy lampshades trimmed with tassels. She waved toward the overhead lights, so much older than the fluorescent tubes in the other storerooms or even the bare bulbs in the larger open space outside the door. "We already blew one bulb, and the wiring in here clearly hasn't been used in decades at the very least. If that radio is an antique, I don't want to damage it, or worse, start a fire in the walls. We're gonna have to be very careful while we figure this place out. And it's not going to all come together tonight. Let's give it a quick once-over, write down anything especially interesting on our clipboards, and come back on Tuesday with some portable lights."

Right. Ciara knew the theater was closed on Mondays, and they ran a skeleton crew Tuesday through Thursday to build sets, check equipment, and let rehearsing casts in and out. Eventually, they'd work back up to a six-days-per-week performance schedule, but that was several months away.

They could still come in on a Monday if they wanted to. Most of them had a key to the backstage door. But Jeremy and Carlos had part-time jobs to go to on the first day of the work week.

Jeremy held his phone up with the screen facing out. "No signal in here, phone or internet. If we want to look up something, we'll need to be in the outer area. I know the rest of the subbasement is within the wireless zone." He flipped the phone around and turned on its flashlight.

Ciara and Carlos did the same with their cells while Kate turned off the built-in lights for more safety. "Do we tell anyone? Like the owners?" Jeremy asked.

Ciara thought yes, but Kate shook her head. "Let's figure out what we've got first. If it's just an old commercial set, it's not worth bothering them. We'll find the production company and let them know we've got their crap. If it's legit . . . well, I for one want to know who set this up, and why they so thoroughly hid it. Don't all of you?"

Three heads bobbed up and down.

"Okay, we're agreed." Kate clapped her hands together once. "Let's stop for now. I can't see anything by our phones. Tuesday we'll meet down here after Jeremy's barista shift, say five thirty. I'll bring a few portable battery-operated spotlights with me. Jer, yes, I know that will be tight for you with traffic, but I want to maximize our hours and match them to the cast rehearsal that day, so people don't wonder what we're doing down here."

"I'll sneak out a few minutes early. This is too awesome to pass up." His grin was infectious.

They returned to the doorway. As soon as they stepped outside the fifth room, Carlos's phone chirped an incoming text. His face lit up when he read the screen. "Ooh, that's Renaldo! He wants to meet me tomorrow morning for coffee. We'll come by your place, Jer."

"Sounds great." He hid a yawn behind his hand. "I'm outta here. You girls good to lock it up?"

"We've got it. Go." Kate waved them along. When they were up the stairs and out of earshot, she turned back to Ciara. "Here," she said, pressing the key into Ciara's palm. "You found the room. You should hold onto the key. It'll just get mixed up with all of mine, and with the climbing around I do, I'm more likely to lose the thing. Oh, take this one, too!" She passed over a second key. "It locks the door to the subbasement. I'll tell the rest of the crew we're 'organizing stuff' and this area is

43

'temporarily off limits.'"

"Sure," Ciara said, slipping both into her pocket. "You go on. If you'll double-check the front and back exits, I'll lock this and the subbasement."

"Got it. See ya!" Kate jogged up the steps two at a time and was gone.

Ciara stood alone in the subbasement, that Creepytown feeling washing over her now that her friends had left, but which was quickly dispelled by curiosity and excitement. Quite the adventure they'd gotten themselves into. And what an incredible discovery they'd made. Her research on the theater after getting hired had instilled in her a love of the era in which it was most popular—flappers, jazz, the Charleston, and with Prohibition the movement among the younger generation of that time to break the rules. Women's fashion, their drive to hold jobs, and more openness about sexual activity strained against the alcohol restrictions like a horse champed at the bit. And here she was, potentially immersed in a piece of that history.

If it was real.

Ciara leaned through the fifth door one more time to see if they'd left anything behind, because that seemed . . . wrong . . . somehow, to leave modern things in that possibly ancient space, but without more light she could see only a few feet inside. Yet, something metal glinted on the black tile, just beyond the threshold and to the right of the entry.

Bending down, she lifted the abandoned red fabric dog collar with its round hanging brass tag and stepped back to examine it under the main room's overhead lights.

Maybe their canine thief was a stray after all if the collar was anything to judge by. The red material was almost worn through in multiple places with strings hanging off and darker red stains on one side, or perhaps that was the collar's original color and it had faded badly. The metal clasp was completely tarnished and the "tongue" or little metal piece that would have been fitted through the holes in the fabric for adjusting the collar had broken away, which explained why it had fallen off.

The round brass tag was also tarnished and dented, but not so much that Ciara couldn't make out "EZ" on one side and "MArket 9847" right above "MArket 9568" on the other.

Ez?

Odd name for a dog, but who was she to judge? And the rest? Had to be an address or maybe two addresses like a split household due to divorce maybe, though in a weird order and with unusual capitalization as if a child had made it for their pet.

Ciara wasn't familiar with a Market Street anywhere in the area, but she hadn't lived in the city all that long and didn't know all the different neighborhoods. She'd do a quick internet search in the morning and see if she couldn't figure out where Ez had wandered away from. He couldn't have come that far with his short legs and tiny paws—

Ciara froze, her fingers closing around the collar in a vise-like grip. A sudden chill raised all the hairs on the back of her neck. She turned slowly and peered through the doorway into the empty bar once more. Her gaze fell on the dusty black tile floor where the imprints of her sneakers and the boots and shoes of her friends led farther inside and faded into the darkness beyond.

There were no paw prints among them.

Chapter 7

????

"EZ! COME ON, boy. Give me that key."

Mickey stumbled over the edge where the dance floor met the tile, almost falling across the expensive polished wood surface, scuffed a bit now from all the New Year's Eve dancing. It was late, after 2:30 in the morning. She wanted, no, *needed*, to lock up and head home, and EZ had decided it was time to play Catch Me If You Can.

But hadn't she just *been doing this? Taking these exact actions?* She shook off the odd sense of déjà vu but it wouldn't leave her. She'd been thinking about Annie stunning her with the revelation that she was ending their relationship. Mickey had tried to convince her to stay . . .

Grasping at hope, her chest tightening, she'd said, "It's getting better. You've seen it. Songs, plays, they're starting to accept us."

She couldn't lose Annie. She couldn't. She needed someone to love. She needed someone to love her.

She needed someone to tell her she was worthy of it.

Annie let go of Mickey's hand. "Are you talking about the so-called 'Pansy Craze'? That's all it is, Mick, a 'craze,' a curiosity, a fascination. They listen to the songs and tittle behind their fans at what they view as risqué. It's daring and exciting to attend those plays where they laugh at us. As soon as they stop being fascinated, we'll be right back where we were, kissing in basements." She gestured around the bar. "Where we are. We've never left. Because it's one thing to see characters in a performance where people can pretend we're playing a part, and quite another to see two men holding hands on the street or two women kissing on the doorstep." She stood and lifted her coat from the back of her chair and put it on, covering an attractive but simple dress of green velvet that reached halfway between her knees and her ankles and flared at the hemline. No flapper style for Annie. She didn't believe in that craze, either.

And oh god, she was leaving.

"Is that all I was to you? A curiosity? You were curious?" Mickey bit out, standing as well. Her face heated. Her hands clenched and unclenched at her sides.

"No," Annie said, staring down at the table's surface, her voice soft and defeated. "No. You were never that. But if that's what you have to tell yourself to replace heartbreak with anger, do it." She turned and crossed to the door but hesitated with her hand on the knob.

It was unlocked. Mickey always left it unlocked when it was just the two of them in the bar. Annie claimed the locked door made her feel trapped.

Maybe there had been a warning after all.

"Tell yourself whatever you need to," Annie said as she opened the door. "But it will never be true. My only betrayal is I can't love in the dark."

And she was gone.

And then Mickey had been too caught up in that ancient memory and had too much to drink, and the dog had somehow gotten the key to the bar off her key ring.

And now here he was, running around with it, darting just out of reach. In her half-drunken state, Mickey wasn't getting it back unless EZ chose to give it to her.

47

Gotta get out of here. Gotta get out of here now.

Mickey didn't understand the urgency wrenching at her insides. Sure, it was late. And she needed to beat her brother home from his night shift and return the clothes she'd "borrowed" from him to his closet. But she still had several hours for that. No work for her to worry about getting to. The theater would be closed on New Year's Day.

So why . . . ?

Because you're about to die.

Where the hell had that thought come from?

Regardless, it sent her into a panic. Her heart pounded. A sheen of sweat formed on her forehead. "Please, EZ. Give me the key."

EZ hopped back and forth in front of the door to the bar, ears pricked forward, tail wagging, having the best time of his little doggy life.

Desperation seized Mickey. She tightened her muscles in preparation to spring and grab him up.

The door to the bar opened outward a crack.

Gray mist seeped around the edge, roiling and undulating, curling in thin tendrils that thickened as they flowed into the room. EZ batted at one with his paw. It wrapped around his foreleg, and for a moment that part of him appeared more . . . solid?

Hadn't he been *solid* before?

"What the hell is happening here?" Mickey whispered. She stared down at herself, only now noticing how the colors of her clothing, her skin, seemed almost . . . washed out. Yes, that was the right description. Here but not *here*.

EZ looked from Mickey to the door and back again, and she had only a moment to realize what he intended. She lunged forward to stop him, but she was too late. EZ threw himself at the opening, flinging the door wide open, and disappeared into the gray fog. Something metal *dink*ed on the tile, and she prayed it was the key, but no. His collar and the bronze tag attached to it had fallen off.

"No! EZ! Come back!" She took a step, but the snake-like fingers of smoke withdrew, forming into a wall of mist. She reached out a tentative hand and touched it with a fingertip.

Solid.

How could fog be solid?

She pressed harder, then laid both palms against it and pushed, but it might as well have been made of brick or concrete. She backed away to study it.

One tendril reached around the edge of the door.

The bar lights sprang on. *Hadn't one already been on?*

Four shapes formed in the doorway and resolved into two women and two men. Their clothing was odd, but they didn't feel threatening. Still, Mickey knew they shouldn't be here.

"I'm sorry. We're closed," she heard herself say, like there was fog in the theater basement and people appeared out of it every day.

It didn't matter. They didn't hear her. They didn't see her.

A heaviness fell over Mickey. The farther in they came, the slower she moved, while all around her, everything *aged*.

It was like that scene in that book she'd recently read—H.G. Wells's *The Time Machine*, when the Traveler raced forward in time and the lab around his machine became covered in dust and cobwebs within seconds for him, while the years flew past his protective bubble.

Desperate to escape her own bubble, Mickey stumbled toward the bar, but each step became more and more difficult. She'd barely gotten behind it—her favorite place in the world to be—when she became frozen in place.

And in time.

Chapter 8

Monday, October 24, 2022

EVEN THOUGH SHE'D gotten to bed at nearly midnight, Ciara woke early, tingles of anticipation and excitement coursing through her. With the theater closed Mondays, she had the entire day to herself for the research she had planned.

And first on her list was to track down the address on Ez's collar.

Ez, the ghost dog.

She let out a little nervous laugh as she pulled a lavender jacket over her black long-sleeved T-shirt and jeans, then added thick wool socks and her sherpa-lined boots.

Ridiculous. There were no such things as ghosts, even dog-sized ones. Besides, Antoine from the café had shaken hands—er, paws—with the dog. You couldn't touch a ghost, right? And hadn't she felt Ez brush past her leg as he ran out of the hidden bar? She'd been so startled, she wasn't sure.

And the bar had no other discernible entryways.

No. Just . . . no. There had to be some explanation for both Ez being in there and the missing paw prints in the dust. She and her friends must have erased the dog's prints walking around in there. That had to be it.

Except the human shoeprints had been sharp and clear.

A shiver worked its way up from the base of Ciara's spine to her neck despite her being in a jacket and a heated apartment. She shook out her arms, then stretched them over her head to work out the sudden tension in her shoulders. It didn't help.

Okay then. Only one way to dispel her insane theory—find Ez's owners.

Who hopefully weren't ghosts.

She settled into her much too expensive desk chair and opened her laptop, then did a quick internet search. Nope, no Market Street. At this rate, her excursion was going to be very short.

Remembering that a lot of street names in the area had been changed during some revitalization efforts, she dug deeper. Her first result indicated those changes had occurred more than twenty years ago. If Ez lived on a Market Street whose name had been switched to something else, the dog (or the collar at least) would have to be over twenty years old.

Very few dogs lived that long, and Ez looked and acted anything but decrepit.

Ciara clicked through a few more pages until she found what she needed. She studied the twenty-five-year-old city map, then did a control-F for Market Street, holding her breath. There had been one, but it didn't extend far enough to have a 9568 or 9847 address on it. Her breath *whooshed* out of her, lifting half of her neon blue tinted bangs off her forehead. Now what?

Leaning back in her chair, she tried to think like a researcher. She supposed the Market Street she needed might be in a different city or smaller town, but when she had first caught sight of Ez, he'd looked healthy and not like he'd been worn down by days or weeks of travel and trying to survive on his own before arriving at the theater.

Another possibility was that he'd been lost by someone visiting the area, a tourist to the city or someone just passing through who'd gotten careless with their dog while letting him out. If that was the case, she'd probably never find Ez's owner.

Which meant she could adopt him. Oh, she'd take out an ad in the local paper and put up some photos on social media. She'd do her due diligence, but Ez was so cute and obviously very, very smart. She'd love to have a dog like him.

Unless he was a ghost.

Back to that again. Ciara mentally kicked herself, but she took the next step anyway. She performed a search for a map of the city dating back to the early 1920s.

This time she wasn't as successful. The downtown library website claimed they had such a map, but only a physical copy, and while they were in the extensive and tedious process (for which they would gratefully appreciate donations) of moving their archive of documents online, they hadn't gotten through the 1920s as of yet.

A library visit was in order.

Twenty minutes and five freezing blocks of walking later, Ciara arrived at her destination. She jogged up the stone steps and passed through the automatic doors. Heat blasted her wind-chilled body as the doors closed behind her, and she shrugged out of her jacket and tied the sleeves around her waist.

A quick chat with the librarian at the assistance desk led her to the topmost floor of the eight-story building. Ciara stepped off the elevator, immediately sensing the weight of time within the archive room, much the same as what she'd felt within the hidden bar. In fact, she always felt this way in old homes and other structures that had existed for many years. Time had *substance*. And that substance commanded reverence and respect.

It wasn't a large space—about four rows with shelved books and binders on either side, a number of filing cabinets lining one wall, and a collection of four rectangular tables forming a study area where only one person was currently working, her head bent over some research materials.

Past those stood another smaller desk and a single librarian, much older than the one downstairs, her gray hair pinned up in a neat bun, round black glasses perched low on her nose, and a smile disrupting the wrinkles in her weathered face. She raised her hand in a quick wave of greeting when Ciara approached. "How may I help you today?" The eagerness told Ciara not a lot of people came up here. The librarian was probably thrilled for the distraction.

"Hi! I'm looking for a map of this area, dating back to the 1920s. The internet said you had one on file?"

The librarian, Ms. Waters according to her metal nametag, raised her eyebrows. "Well, has one of the college classes assigned a special research project? You're the second person to ask me for 1920s materials today." She pointed to the study tables.

Ciara looked harder at the other visitor bowed over a set of blueprints. "Kate?" she said, not that surprised.

Kate looked up from her intense study, the bruise she'd gotten on her forehead the night before now a deep purplish blue. She gave Ciara a sheepish smile. "I couldn't wait for tomorrow," she said by way of explanation.

"Shh," Ms. Waters said, holding a finger over her lips, but there was a friendly smile behind it. "Why don't you go join your friend and I'll bring over the map you requested?"

"Perfect, thank you, Ms. Waters," Ciara responded in a whisper and seated herself next to Kate at the table.

"Call me Claudia, please," the librarian said and headed into the rows of shelves.

"This is our theater," Kate said, pointing at the blueprints with rooms outlined in white and names and numbers in the center of each. Her index finger rested just beneath the words "Storeroom Five."

"Is this the same one you photocopied for the scavenger hunt?"

"It's the same blueprint, but this is the original. The one I have at the theater is a copy and a lot more creased and faded. I thought maybe seeing this one in person might make things clearer." Kate traced her finger around the box that encapsulated the hidden bar.

"You're looking for how Ez got in."

"Ez?"

"Oh! Right. I found this after you guys left." She pulled the broken collar from her pocket and laid it on the blueprint next to storeroom five with the name side facing up.

"EZ," Kate said, reading each letter individually. "Like speakeasy?" She ran her thumb down the length of the collar.

"Hah. I hadn't thought of that. Has to be a coincidence. Different spelling and all. Maybe it's short for Ezra or something." But she doubted it. And she liked it the other way. She'd start saying it like speakeasy from now on.

"Lot of coincidences here," Kate muttered, tone thoughtful. "And to answer your question, yes, and there aren't any."

Ciara had lost her train of thought. "Aren't any what?"

"Other ways into that bar. Look."

Ciara followed Kate's finger all the way around the solid white lines delineating the four walls of the secret bar. Yes, there was a second, smaller room off the back wall of the space, but it, too, had four solid walls. And while the boiler room near the rear of the theater and beneath the stage appeared to be on the same level as the subbasement storage, it was accessed via a completely separate set of stairs, and the two areas did not connect in any way. At least not in any way that appeared on the blueprints.

"Could something have been left off?" Ciara asked.

"That's what I'm assuming. We'll know more when we search the room tomorrow with some good lighting in place. Or there could be a hole somewhere." She shook her head. "I love a good mystery, but it will probably have an easy answer."

"An E-Z answer?" Ciara said, stressing each letter.

Kate rolled her eyes.

Ms. Waters . . . Claudia . . . arrived at that moment with a sealed cardboard tube in her hands. She pried open one end and shook out the map within it, then unrolled it across the table for them. "Are you looking for some location in particular? I don't date back to the 1920s, mind you, but I've lived here all my life."

Ciara wasn't sure what she should say. She hadn't planned on having an audience while she indulged her ghost dog fantasy. Kate and Claudia would think she was crazy if she told them about that. Thinking quickly, she flipped the tag on the dog collar over to show the address. "I'm trying to find the owner of this stray dog hanging around the Big City Little Theater Company. He was wearing this collar before it fell off yesterday. I know the dog isn't a hundred years old," she hurriedly added with a nervous laugh, "but if the collar was passed from pet to pet, like a memory keepsake of dogs who'd passed on or something, then maybe the owner's family has lived at this address for generations. Except there's no Market Street here today, and the one on this map looks too short to have a number 9568 or 9847. I see there's a whole Market *District*," she said, pointing at the words that seemed to jump out at her from the map.

Interesting. The Market District in the 1920s included the theater as well as the surrounding area of historical structures that still stood today even though it was no longer called that.

"Well," the librarian began, her tone dropping into what Ciara would refer to as "instructor mode," "you probably know about the 'revitalization wave' from City Hall that upgraded the entire historical arts district about twenty years back." She paused to meet Ciara's eyes and Ciara nodded for her to go on. "Excellent. You've done your homework."

Ciara couldn't help the small spread of warmth in her chest at the compliment. She guessed a lot of people came to Claudia

Waters asking for things they could have researched on their own, and the librarian appreciated not having her time wasted, even if there weren't a lot of visitors to the archives.

"A partnership between the local government and the historical society raised money and won grants to renovate all the buildings in the Market District," Claudia went on. "Streets had their names changed to 'match the theming' of the 1920s era they'd chosen as their focus since that was the area's most popular time period. Most of the shops and structures received placement on the National Historic Registry ensuring their continued preservation and survival."

"But still no Market Street long enough, and a district wouldn't have numerical addresses, so . . ."

Claudia pushed her glasses back up to the bridge of her nose and leaned in. At first Ciara thought she was studying the map, but then she reached for the collar. "May I?" she asked, glancing at Ciara.

"Oh, yes, of course, go ahead."

The librarian lifted the collar to eye level in a hand that shook slightly with age. "Well, here's your problem," she announced, a satisfied smile on her face. "These aren't addresses. They're phone numbers."

"What?" Ciara said, blinking in confusion. They didn't look like any phone numbers she'd ever seen.

"Oh yeah, she's right!" Kate exclaimed, then lowered her voice at the librarian's frown and repeated, "She's right," in a stage whisper that probably carried just as far. "Didn't you see our production of *Sorry, Wrong Number* last year? Oh, wait, you wouldn't have. You weren't working there yet. God, that one ran so long I think I have every line stuck in my brain. But yeah, it's set in the 1940s and was a radio play before it went to stage and film. The phone number the main character keeps trying to dial is Murray Hill 4-0098, and she has to go through an operator to do that." Kate nudged Ciara's shoulder. "It was also a murder mystery."

"God, don't tell Carlos." She'd heard enough about murders and hiding bodies last night. "So the Murray Hill part and the numbers don't correspond to an address?"

Claudia shook her head. "No. Well, not a home address, anyway. It's like the song 'Pennsylvania 6-5000' also from the '40s. The title refers to a New York City phone number. The word at the beginning stands for the phone company's region of service that the owner of the phone would have lived in. So, in the case of your stray, the Market part very likely does refer to the Market District on this map since the phone company's Market region probably served that area."

"But there are only four numbers for each, not five. And why are the first two letters capitalized like that?" Ciara pointed to the capital MA at the beginning of each MArket on the tag.

"Well, that would make this even older," the librarian said, carefully placing the collar back on the table. "1920s was a rather accurate guess on your part." She raised an eyebrow at Ciara like she thought she was hiding something. Which of course she was.

When Ciara wasn't more forthcoming, Claudia *hmph*ed and went on. "In that decade, very few people had home phones, so they didn't need as many unique phone numbers. Two capitalized letters, representing the first two letters of the region of service, plus four digits was sufficient. The operator would make the connection based on the two letters like you see under the numbers on your phone keypad for the region and then the four numbers for the specific phone in that region."

The three of them stared at the innocent-looking collar, all of them doing the math in their heads, but it was Claudia who brought it into the open.

"Good lord," she said in the hushed tones all librarians seemed to master, "that collar must be about a hundred years old. And I can guarantee if you try to call either of those numbers, the only ones likely to answer are ghosts."

Chapter 9

Tuesday, October 25, 2022

AS PLANNED, THEY all met up outside the fifth storeroom at approximately five thirty on Tuesday. Ciara came early. She checked the food and water bowls outside the backstage door. Still full. But then, ghost dogs wouldn't need to eat. Or he was getting plenty from Antoine's café garbage. Gourmet scraps had to beat kibble any day of the week. No sign of EZ, though.

If she *did* adopt him, if he *wasn't* a ghost, she'd need to pick up a few things: a leash and new collar, a sweater for the colder weather, one of those cute little doggy beds that—

Ciara stopped. No. EZ could sleep with her. It would be nice to have someone to cuddle with instead of sleeping alone.

Jeremy called to say he was running a little late, so she paced back and forth in front of storeroom five for fifteen minutes before anyone else arrived and by the time the barista pounded down the stairs, still wearing his coffee shop uniform that smelled like a latte, Ciara was ready to burst with anticipation.

She had spent the rest of the previous day and all this morning thinking about speakeasies and hundred-year-old dogs and disconnected phone numbers. It frustrated her that she was no closer to finding EZ's owners.

Except maybe by searching the nearest graveyard.

"Finally!" Kate said, throwing her arms around her boyfriend. "Also, you smell delicious. Now I want a caramel macchiato, dammit."

Jeremy laughed. "Damn good thing my girlfriend happens to have a massive caffeine addiction. I never seem to be able to get the scent completely off me. Sorry."

"No worries," Carlos assured him. "I think 95 percent of my blood supply is type C for coffee."

"Same," Ciara put in. "Now, can we go inside?"

Kate and Carlos lifted the four portable battery-operated spotlights they'd brought from upstairs. "Ready when you are, boss," Kate said.

Oh, right. Ciara had the key. She pulled her keychain from her pocket. After fitting the correct key in the lock and turning it, she swung open the door. Everyone held their collective breaths.

When nothing startling ran out, they released them in a massive whoosh that made all of them chuckle.

"No dogs today," Jeremy commented, relief in his tone.

"Or anything else," Carlos added.

Kate took the lead as usual, but instead of reaching for the light switch, she set one of the portable lights just inside and to the right of the entry and clicked it on. A wide, bright beam spread from its source across the dance floor, lighting it completely, their footprints still the only indications that anyone had been there in a very long time.

Ciara scanned it. No paw prints there, either, though at this point she hadn't expected any. Her crazy theory seemed less crazy with every new discovery they made. No one else noticed their absence, so she kept her observations to herself. If her friends weren't drawing ghostly conclusions, she wasn't going to be the first to voice them. They didn't have enough shared history between them for her to want to risk coming off looking like she'd lost her mind.

Using the first light as a guide, Kate set the second one down just outside the area behind the bar, so the narrow and heavily shadowed space was lit up as if it sat in broad daylight. Carlos aimed the third at the seating area, illuminating all the tables and chairs. He held up the fourth. "Where do you guys want this one?"

Ciara shrugged. They could see pretty clearly now, though she had to admit, the bright spotlights destroyed the feel of the place. She preferred the warm yellow bulbs, even the flickering ones, to this. They'd been a little creepy, but a lot more welcoming in general. She studied the setup: the cozy tables, the seats at the bar where someone could lean their elbows and pour out their sorrows to a friendly ear, the small, almost intimate dance floor. This was a place she would have enjoyed visiting, having a drink, letting off steam after a long workday.

"How about that little back room? We haven't been in there yet," Kate reminded them. She took the fourth portable from Carlos and walked behind the bar. At the end where it met the wall was another door. She tried the knob. "Not locked," she called, "but it has one, and I'm betting it takes the same key." This one opened inward, and Kate pushed it as wide as it would go, then set up the final light just inside and turned it on.

There wasn't room behind the bar for all of them, but they crammed themselves into the narrow space anyway, each trying to peer over the other's shoulder. "Anything interesting?" Jeremy asked, falling off his tiptoes and bumping the shelves of cobweb-covered bottles. They rattled, but nothing fell. "Oops, sorry."

"Hey bro, don't forget what those might be worth," Carlos reminded him.

"It's an office," Kate reported. "Desk, chair, filing cabinet." She glanced over her shoulder and made eye contact with Ciara. "There's a phone on the desk, but I don't see any numbers on it. Everything's really battered, and the filing cabinet's rusty, like all the money went into the bar, and this was an afterthought.

Given the nicer quality of what I saw out in the main room, I think this furniture was secondhand even before it sat here for a hundred years. There's also a small cot. Looks lumpy. My guess is the owner slept here sometimes, but no evidence that he lived here—no dressers full of clothes or toiletries, just some jackets and a spare shirt hanging on a rack. Hey, speaking of toilets, is there one? 'Cause if there is, I think we can discard the movie set theory. I could see them recreating a bar and even an office, but if there's an actual working toilet, we're probably looking at an honest-to-god speakeasy here."

"Right. Because people drinking would need to go to the bathroom. And they wouldn't want customers traipsing back and forth to the ones in the lobby because it would draw too much attention to their secret hideaway." Carlos backed out from behind the bar and worked his way along the walls.

"Also," Ciara put in, "if the owner slept here sometimes, he would need a place to pee." She joined Carlos and searched in the opposite direction. In the farthest back corner, past the tables and chairs where even the portable spotlights couldn't reach, her hand encountered a doorknob. "Hey! I think I've got it." The others gathered around her, using their phone lights for illumination.

"Much smaller door than the other one. No lock. Could be a closet, but . . ." Jeremy reached over and pushed the door open. "Yep, bathroom."

They stared at the single toilet with a pedestal sink beside it.

"It's a closet on the blueprints," Kate pointed out.

Jeremy stepped inside and rotated in a three-sixty, examining all the walls, the ceiling, and behind the door with his phone's flashlight. "I think it used to be one, and someone converted it. If my sense of direction is right, we're exactly two floors below the lobby bathrooms. Would have taken some doing, but yeah, they could have hooked this up to the existing pipes. And speaking of bathrooms." He started to swing the door shut with him inside.

"Wait! What are you doing?" Kate asked.

He raised his eyebrows. "You really want a blow-by-blow description? I've been drinking coffee all day at work. I'm taking a piss."

Kate stopped the door from closing with her work boot. "Not here, you aren't. Same problem as the lights. These pipes haven't been used in a hundred years. Let's make a quick check to be sure it's really hooked to the system and not a set piece." She reached around and twisted the knob on the cold-water side of the basin.

A groaning and screeching like they'd cracked open the gates of hell erupted from the wall behind the sink, echoing up into the ceiling and beyond. Four pairs of eyes tracked the sound, waiting for the ceiling to fall in on them. Then a trickle of brownish-yellowish water dribbled into the basin leaving a track in the inches of dust, mold, and grime that had formed there over a century. Kate turned the faucet off. The pipes continued rattling for another minute and finally fell silent.

"Well, I think that proves the speakeasy theory, and also says we shouldn't be flushing anything or trying to run the hot side. I'm not even sure that test was a great idea. If we burst a pipe, the owners will have our asses." Kate turned to Jeremy. "You'll need to run upstairs to use the bathroom. Actually, let's all go. I want to grab cleaning supplies from the maintenance closet."

"You want us to clean the bathroom? I mean, I know it's gross, but—"

"I want us to clean the entire place," Kate said, cutting Carlos off. "We can't see the details of what's down here because it's all covered in dust. If we want to learn the mysteries of this bar, we're going to have to, literally, uncover them."

They returned a half hour later carrying mops, buckets of soapy water, rags, and bottles upon bottles of cleaning solution. Setting everything in the center of the dance floor, they stopped. "Um, did someone move the lights?" Ciara's voice wavered as she spoke.

She wasn't wrong. The light covering the dance floor had shifted slightly to the left to encompass the outer end of the bar as well. The one aimed behind the bar was angled farther upward. The spotlight on the seating area seemed unchanged, but the one pointing into the office annex was completely switched off.

"I might have turned off the office one when I came to join you guys at the bathroom," Kate said, rubbing the back of her neck, her eyebrows drawn together. She didn't sound at all certain.

"We probably bumped into them moving back and forth," Jeremy put in. "I mean, I was in kind of a hurry to get upstairs. If I kicked the one by the dance floor, I doubt I would have noticed."

"Sure, that must be it." Carlos didn't sound sure, either. "I'll just set them back where they were." He moved to adjust the one pointing behind the bar.

"No, wait!" Kate pointed up to where the center of the beam now landed on a sign above the shelves of bottles. "Look!"

"Does that say, 'Mickey's Speak EZ'?" Ciara asked, squinting.

"Yeah," Kate breathed. "And EZ was the name on the collar you found, spelled exactly that way." Her eyes were wide.

Ciara nodded. The power of speech had left her.

"It could just be another—" Kate began.

Ciara found her voice. "Coincidence? How many 'coincidences' are we going to have before we start wondering if there's something weird happening here." There. She'd said it. Out loud. To her amazement, Kate nodded in agreement. "You've been thinking that, too? Why didn't you say something?" Ciara asked.

Kate gave a nervous laugh. "For the same reason you didn't. I was afraid you'd think I was out of my mind."

"Um, guys?" Carlos interrupted, arms outstretched, and palms turned upward. "Maybe you could deal us a clue card here, because Jeremy and I have no idea what you're talking about, other than it looks like the bar's owner was Mickey, and he didn't know how to spell."

"Okay," Kate said, passing out bottles of cleaner and some rags. "Let's start with one of the tables for four and some chairs, and we'll sit and explain what Ciara and I have discovered so far. Trust me," she added, forestalling any arguments about the delay, "you want to be sitting down for this."

Chapter 10

Tuesday, October 25, 2022

MICKEY WOULD HAVE given anything if her four unusual guests would stay.

Ever since the speakeasy door had opened and EZ ran out, she'd been alone. She worried about him, all by himself in the gray fog. Had it harmed him? Or was it the pathway to the afterlife?

That didn't feel right. Doors to heaven meant bright lights and welcoming loved ones, not swirling miasmas that caused fear.

Her parents had died when she was in her teens. Were they waiting for her in that fog? Was this some kind of test? She and Paul had gone to church every Sunday until she turned eighteen and could decide for herself. She thought of herself as a good person.

Except . . .

There was the whole loving women thing. It didn't matter to Mickey, and she didn't think it should matter to God, either, if He were truly the benevolent entity the preachers preached about. She'd stopped going to church because a significant portion of the congregation would not have agreed with her way of thinking on the subject, and even if they didn't know about her preferences, it bothered her to hear it, but still, she had faith . . .

So, no. This might be a test, but it wasn't a punishment. At least not from God.

Except, so far, she wasn't making the grade.

All she knew was she missed EZ terribly and hoped they'd be reunited someday. The little dog meant everything to her. Once she'd overcome the initial shock, she'd thought to go into the gray mist after him, terror be damned, but now she couldn't move at all.

Mickey thought only a couple of days had passed, but she had no way to measure time—no windows to let in sunlight, and the clock on the wall had stopped because of course she hadn't wound it in . . . days? Months? Years?

Decades?

Then the door reopened, and the quartet of visitors returned, and she watched them move around her place, picking up everything, studying, examining. They acted like they'd never been in a bar before. Who lifted and read the label of every whiskey bottle?

They couldn't see or hear her, and even more frustrating, Mickey couldn't hear them either. And whenever they walked behind the bar and passed *through* her . . .

Jesus, they're passing through me. I'm an honest-to-god ghost. Maybe it's a good thing I can't move 'cause I'd be a heap on the floor. But why am I still here?

. . . it caused uncomfortable tingles like that pins-and-needles sensation people had when they held their limbs in place for too long.

Almost like their contact with me is waking me back up, bringing me back . . . to life.

They brought the most incredible bright lights that *didn't need electricity* to operate. Of course, Mickey had used flashlights. The crew kept a number of them backstage for when the power inevitably went out during a performance for a short time. But these were so bright and maneuverable. The lighting team would have made great use of them.

They had little handheld lamps, too—small rectangular ones that emitted a much less powerful beam but weighed little and could be carried around with them. Mickey had never seen anything like those.

Grateful for the distraction and entertainment, Mickey watched. She wished she could hear their conversations. She wondered what they talked about, what they thought of the home she'd built for the outcasts of her era.

In particular, Mickey wondered what the brunette with the odd streak of blue in her hair was thinking.

In her lifetime, Mickey had never seen a woman make a pair of dungarees look that good. The denim material hugged every curve of her pinup-girl figure—rounded hips, firm bottom, trim waist. She must have had them tailored. Levi Strauss & Co. didn't make them for women, which didn't bother Mickey since her lanky frame more resembled a man's anyway, but they never would have fit the very feminine form now wearing them in her bar.

She wore a long-sleeved black shirt made of some stretchy fabric that molded to breasts so right for Mickey's hands that she could almost feel the soft skin against her calluses. The shirt color set off the bright blue in her hair, one strand of it curling down to brush the top of one breast in a teasing, tantalizing fashion.

Gah.

If she could've moved, Mickey would have shaken herself. *You're dead, stupid. This is not the time to make yourself aroused. Like you aren't frustrated enough with your situation already.*

But she couldn't take her eyes off her. And when they discovered the bar's tiny bathroom and then abruptly left, Mickey ached like a piece of her heart was being wrenched from her incorporeal chest, and in other more unmentionable places as well.

Then she felt it.

Another presence. Something with energy and purpose that vibrated the air around her, and yet, whatever it was, it wasn't like Mickey. It was different, less . . . cohesive? It brushed past her, and the tingles it elicited were far more unpleasant to the point of pain. She wanted to jerk away from its proximity, but of course she couldn't move.

EZ? No, too big. Whatever, no, whoever this was, it was human in size.

Icy digits . . . fingers? . . . so cold she could feel them through the fabric of her ghostly shirt gripped her shoulder in a vaguely familiar squeeze that may have been intended to comfort but instead caused only pain. The unseen hand released her immediately.

Like it knew what it had done to her.

Mickey's senses reached out, following the unseen entity around the bar as it approached several of the portable spotlights. It switched off the one leading into the office. Nothing to see there, she supposed. Then it shifted the one behind the bar to aim higher, and the one on the dance floor to focus on . . .

The exact spot where she'd died.

If she'd had the capacity to breathe, Mickey would have sucked in a sharp breath. She experienced the moment again, viscerally, the bullets piercing the skin of her back, tearing through her insides to mangle vital organs, and ripping their way back out of her abdomen to hit the bar.

She wished she could scream. She wished she could fall. She wanted to curl into the fetal position and try to hold in the pain.

Instead, this bizarre in-between existence held her rigidly upright, mute and vibrating with energy and agony she could not shed.

The other spirit . . . no, the other *something* returned to her side. It leaned in close, their two different energies mingling with a crackling sound she *experienced* more than heard.

I'm so sorry.

The shock of words resounding in her brain almost, *almost* chased the pain away. The voice was neither male nor female, too distorted to guess at gender.

I'm going to fix this. I promise. Somehow, I'm going to figure this out and make it right.

Before Mickey could attempt a response, though she had no idea how to do so, the other entity had gone.

Chapter 11

Tuesday, October 25, 2022

THEY POLISHED THE centermost table and four chairs to a shine and took their seats around it. While Carlos and Jeremy exchanged looks of concern, Ciara laid out all the strange and quirky things that had occurred over the past few days: the dog's arrival only about a week before they found the speakeasy, the dog dropping the key to said speakeasy where Kate would find it a few hours before Ciara bumped into the false wall, the dog being inside a room with only one exit which had been blocked, the hundred-year-old collar, the portable lights moving and turning off apparently by themselves, and the lack of pawprints in the dust.

"Oh, I hadn't caught the pawprint thing," Kate said when Ciara finished speaking. She stared over Jeremy's shoulder at the still dust-covered dance floor and entryway. "Good eye. I'm impressed. And yeah, that's seriously creepy."

Ciara sat up a little straighter in her chair and smiled, though it wavered a little. They were talking about a ghost, after all.

"Please. You can't be seri—" Jeremy began, but Kate cut him off with an upraised hand.

"Wait. There's a couple more." She ticked them off on her

fingers. "One," she said, "the dog's arrival coincides with the electrical and sound problems we've been having backstage. The spotlights flicker and go on and off, and the sound cuts out. Nothing too major. It never lasts very long, but we've gone over the equipment a dozen times, me and Jeremy, and we can't find a cause. And then there's two," she said, holding up a second finger. It shook.

Jeremy reached out and covered her hand with his own, pressing it down to the table's surface. Ciara understood his concern. Nothing shook Kate. She was the crew leader, the oil in the well-oiled machine, the rock that everyone leaned on when an actor missed an entrance or forgot a vital prop for the next scene, or the wrong spotlight came on or the curtain failed to rise. Kate always remained calm and steady and sorted everything out to get the show moving forward again.

And she was shaking.

"What's 'two'?" Carlos asked. He didn't look good, either. His tan complexion had gone pale under the spotlights, his eyes were wide, and he breathed a little faster than normal.

Kate took a slow breath and let it out, regaining her composure. She offered Jeremy a reassuring smile and slipped her hand out from beneath his. "Two," she said, holding up a second finger once more, "is that the lights didn't just shift randomly. That one behind the bar was intentionally raised to fall on the sign that named this place."

They all turned to look. Sure enough, the spotlight seemed centered on the "Mickey's Speak EZ" sign over the liquor shelving.

"Someone, or some*thing*, wanted us to make the connection between the dog and the bar," Kate finished, folding both hands on the table in front of her.

For several moments, they sat around the table without speaking, staring into space rather than making eye contact, their too-rapid breathing and the hum of the portable lights the

71

only sounds in the otherwise quiet room.

Carlos finally broke the silence. "Damn, I wish I could trust the liquor in those bottles." He chuckled softly.

It snapped the tension like a cut cord, and the others exhaled as one unit.

"I'll admit there's a lot of coincidences here," Jeremy said. "But we could still come up with logical explanations for most of them. I'm going to need something more tangible to buy into the ghost theory."

"Ghosts aren't tangible," Kate pointed out.

"Except EZ can pick up things like the key and the bar towels. And Antoine, the café owner next door. He touched EZ, shook his paw after EZ almost got hit by a truck." Ciara quickly recapped that event for her friends. "He's the only person I've ever seen manage to touch him, though. And he did seem to have an odd reaction to it." She shook her head. "Every time I've tried, EZ runs off."

"See?" Jeremy said. "There you go. Not a ghost."

"Or he's a poltergeist. They can move things. And Antoine might have some kind of special . . . affinity . . . for ghosts," Carlos suggested, earning a scowl from Jeremy for his input.

Jeremy pushed his chair back, squeaking it across the tile. The others winced. He stood and paced beside the table. "Lights and soundboards glitch all the time. There's another entrance to this place we haven't found yet," he said, waving at a shadowy corner of the bar. "We disturbed the pawprints and bumped the spotlights while moving around. The collar was in here all along. It doesn't belong to *that* dog. And *that* dog found the key in the theater somewhere and ran around with it until Kate yelled at him and he dropped it. He likes to take things. Coincidences *do* happen, you know. You all are reading too much into this." He stopped pacing, frowned, and glanced down at Kate. "It's really weird being the voice of reason."

She grinned up at him. "Yes. Total role reversal here." Kate met the gazes of each of the others. "But somebody needs to be or we're going to scare ourselves silly."

"So, what do we do now? Lock it back up and run away?" Carlos looked longingly at the open door leading to the other storage spaces.

The spotlight on the "Mickey's Speak EZ" sign flickered.

Kate gave a nervous laugh. "No, I don't think that's the right move." The light steadied. She pointedly shifted her gaze away from it and took a deep breath. "I think we continue what we were doing. We clean this place. We gather more clues about what happened to make someone hide the speakeasy more than it was already hidden. We *all* look for reasonable explanations for the weirdness, but we try to keep open minds. So far, nothing has seemed dangerous or threatening." She looked to the others for confirmation.

They nodded.

"The dog is cute and friendly, if a bit of a thief," Ciara felt compelled to note. She carefully didn't name him EZ, wanting to lend her support to Jeremy's much more plausible theories.

"And this place is amazing and cool," Carlos admitted. "This Mickey guy spent a lot of money and effort on turning basement storage into an inviting atmosphere. I'd love to work here."

"I'm up for staying if you guys are," Jeremy said, "since I don't believe in ghosts anyway."

"I'll keep trying to catch E—erm, the dog. I'll be more convinced that he's not a ghost if I can touch him, too. But later this week I want to do more library research. I don't know much about ghosts, or ghost theory as the case may be," Ciara added, giving Jeremy a smile. "But I want to know if other people have claimed to have been able to touch them, and when I tried online I got a million hits. For this I think I want to speak with an actual living human being, preferably someone who can tell me exactly where to look, even if they do think I'm nuts. I'll say I'm writing a book or something."

Carlos snorted in response.

"You should look into old payroll records, too," Kate put in, grabbing a bottle of cleaning solution and starting on the next table over. The others followed her lead, busying themselves in order to not think about strange things. Jeremy cleared webs off the liquor bottles, lifting and examining each and separating the already open ones from the ones that were still sealed.

"Why?" Ciara went for a mop, dunked it into a bucket of soapy water they'd brought down earlier, and erased their footprints from the dance floor, returning the wood to a glossy shine. Carlos started on the bar, squirting cleanser across the top and following up with a rag like he did with his own bar in the lobby before every performance.

"Well, I've been thinking," Kate said, wiping down a chair. "For Mickey to build a place like this, what with the location, wiring, plumbing, and all, he'd have to know the building really well. Maybe he had a job here. He certainly would have needed permission from the owners, and I'm betting most of the people who worked for the theater at that time knew about it and drank here."

"That's going to take some time." Ciara leaned on the end of her mop, considering. "You wouldn't believe the mess the old records are in. Going back that far . . . everything's on paper. No computers back then, obviously, and judging even from the more recent ones that I've seen, every bookkeeper seems to have had a different filing system, if they had a system at all. But I'll try."

"Hey guys?" Carlos said, catching everyone's attention. He'd already cleared the top of the bar and had been working up and down the outer side that faced the seating area, removing a hundred years of grime. Now he stood at the curved end jutting out toward the dance floor where the second spotlight now fell. "I hate to add more weird, but, well, I think you should look at these."

They clustered around him and stared at two neat holes in

74

the rounded curve at the end of the bar.

"They're hard to spot because they're just below the countertop, though the spotlight helped." He paused while they all remembered that spotlight had also apparently "moved" on its own, almost as if someone had wanted them to look there. Again. Carlos cleared his throat before continuing. "I also noticed them because the rest of this is in such good condition that any damage stands out. The few chipped spots I came across have been carefully repaired. So I'm thinking whatever made these holes occurred right before the place was closed up. Otherwise, Mickey would have fixed them, too."

Jeremy ran his finger around the edge of one of the holes, then abruptly pulled it back. "Your murder theory is starting to look a little more believable, pal. The question is, was Mickey the murderer or the victim?"

"Wait, what? What are you saying?" Ciara asked.

Kate looked at her. "Bullet holes. The boys think those are bullet holes."

Chapter 12

KATE YANKED A small flathead screwdriver off the toolbelt she always wore and dropped to her knees. "One way to find out." Trying to do as little additional damage as possible, she dug into the rightmost hole, working the head of the tool around in a circle. Chips of wood fell away as she widened the hole farther and farther. After several minutes, she pried free something small and metal. She held the bullet in her palm for the others to see. "I'm guessing the second hole is the same."

Carlos took it from her hand and studied it. "We need to call the police," he said, voice hushed.

"What for? Everyone involved would be long dead. No one to catch. No one even to provide closure for." Kate made eye contact with each of them. "I say we keep going as we are."

"I still want to know if Mickey did the killing or the dying," Jeremy said.

"Why do you think Mickey did either one? We don't even know somebody died," Ciara said.

Carlos shook his head. "Somebody died. And only the killer and the victim were here at the time."

"You can't possibly know that for certain," Jeremy said. "I

don't care if you are a television crime drama addict."

"Where's your proof?" Kate put in.

"I don't need proof. I have logic. Just go with it for a minute. Assuming the killer and the victim are the only ones here at the time of the murder, one of them had to be the owner because Mickey would have had to be on site to give anyone else access since he'd have the only key. Think about it." Carlos turned around to lean his elbows on the bar and dropped into a cop show detective voice. "If anyone else had been here during the incident, they probably would have contacted the authorities, speakeasy or not. You don't hide a murder to protect a bar, even if it's your favorite hangout. You just don't. You call the police and leave an anonymous tip. But the owner..." He straightened and walked behind the bar where Mickey would have frequently stood and stared out across the entire space. "The owner would have gotten rid of the body and not called anyone in, both to preserve the speakeasy and to avoid murder charges." He paused. "But he would also have fixed the holes and kept the bar going instead of hiding it, so..."

"So, Mickey wasn't the murderer." Ciara experienced an odd sense of relief at that conclusion. She didn't want Mickey to be a killer. Mickey had built this amazing place. He'd had a dog he cared about so much that he named the bar after him. That didn't paint a picture of a murderer for her.

"No," Carlos agreed, shaking his head. "He wasn't." He stared at the bullet holes for a long moment. "Mickey was the victim. And the killer got rid of the body, then built the façade himself if he had the skills or blackmailed some of the theater staff to help him if he didn't. I'm betting on the latter."

"Why?" Jeremy asked.

Carlos pointed at the floor. "It's black tile, but even so, I don't see any bloodstains, no sticky, tacky places."

"Little less detail, please," Ciara said, swallowing hard.

"Sorry. But yeah, why clean up if you're going to hide the

place by yourself? No, the killer needed help, so he or she scrubbed away the obvious evidence so the helpers wouldn't notice but didn't bother with the little holes. The helpers probably never knew about the murder. Threatening them with revealing they had a speakeasy in the basement at that time might have been enough to earn their compliance and silence. And unlike a death, a closed speakeasy wouldn't be a tale that got talked about years later and passed from employee to employee."

"I think the dog died then, too," Ciara said quietly. She eased the collar out of her pocket and cradled it in her hands. Since she'd found it, she'd been keeping it with her all the time. She wasn't sure why. She held it toward her friends and pointed at the darker stains. "I thought these were caused by age and fading. Now I think they might be blood."

"I wonder if that could still be tested. Something else to research," Carlos said. "I'll look into that one."

"Hey, could it have *only* been the dog? I mean, it discounts a lot of Carlos's theory, but while I'd hate to hear about an animal getting shot, I really don't want to think about someone being murdered here," Jeremy put in.

"Nah, the height's all wrong." Carlos waved a finger back and forth between the two holes. "I mean, maybe if EZ was a Great Dane, but otherwise, those shots would have gone right over a dog's head. However—" he moved to stand in front of the holes, then he looked down, "—if Mickey was a few inches shorter than me, this would put him at just about the right height for a couple of torso shots."

Ciara shivered.

"I'm not saying the dog didn't also die at the same time," Carlos said. "Or maybe that's the owner's blood on his collar. But Mickey pretty definitely did."

"So now the question is, *what* time did Mickey die, or at least on what day? If I'm going to start searching through old payroll records, a date would be really helpful in narrowing that down,"

Ciara said, unable to tear her eyes from the floor, imagining a body lying there in a fedora hat and a 1920s suit, blood pooling on the tile around him. For half a second, she swore she did see exactly that: grey pinstripe suit pants, matching jacket, black-and-white shoes . . .

Kate waved her hand in front of Ciara's face, breaking the illusion or hallucination or whatever it was. "That's easy. January 1924."

"Right, the calendar," Carlos said.

Ciara's breath caught in her throat. When they'd first opened the door to the speakeasy, two of the three working ancient bulbs had been over the end of the bar where the bullet holes were and the calendar. Kate was right. Some supernatural force *wanted* them to figure this out. Maybe the ghost of Mickey himself. But why? Why now? To catch a killer who had to have died decades ago?

Oh god, maybe it was to find Mickey's body. What if it was hidden in the theater somewhere? She really hoped that wasn't it, but the sooner she figured out who Mickey was and whether or not he had a death certificate, the better.

"I can narrow the date down even more than that," Jeremy said. He stood beside the small wastebasket behind the bar and held a crumpled ball of papers in his hands. Uncrumpling them, he revealed a 1923 calendar identical in theming to the one on the wall but from the previous year. "It was January first, New Year's Day." He frowned. "Shitty day to get murdered."

Kate reached over and smacked him on the shoulder. "Every day's a shitty day to get murdered, dimwit."

"How can you be so exact?" Ciara asked. "I don't actually need the day. The month and year are enough for searching through the record boxes, but I'm curious."

"Well," he said, mock wincing and rubbing his arm where Kate hit him, "I'm not a hundred percent positive. I'm guessing. But I'd bet I'm right, or at least within a few days." He turned to Carlos. "When do you throw out the trash at the lobby bar?"

"Every night at the end of my shift," he said, distracted, while he poked one finger in and out of one of the bullet holes.

Ciara imagined he was thinking about what that bullet did to Mickey's body. She knew *she* was imagining it.

"Right. And we do the same at the coffee shop. You don't leave garbage around when you're serving food or drinks. You just don't. Mickey tore that off on New Year's Eve or New Year's Day and tossed it in the can. Then he got shot before he could empty it."

They continued cleaning, finishing the floors, the tables, the chairs, and the bar itself, but the mood had shifted from excited to solemn. They were no longer having a great adventure. They were on a mission. They just weren't sure what that mission was, exactly.

At the end of the evening, they shut down the portable lights and left them in place. Then the four of them gathered outside the speakeasy's door while Ciara turned the key in the lock. "I have to do some actual work tomorrow," she said, "but once I'm finished, I'll dig into the old staff records and see if I can't find Mickey on the payroll."

"And I'll look up hundred-year-old stains and see if they can still be tested for blood, using something we'd have access to," Carlos added, eyes bright. He took the bullet they'd found from his pocket. "I can also research this," he said, holding it out. "If I can't identify the make and caliber, I have online friends who probably can." He was back on his crime show kick again.

"You have online friends who are ballistic experts?" Ciara asked, stunned.

"Oh yeah. There are entire websites and Slack channels dedicated to the real science behind the crime shows and how fiction keeps getting it wrong. Somebody there will know."

Kate exchanged a look with Jeremy. "I'm afraid we're off the sleuthing team for the next few days, but please keep us updated if you two find out anything else. Management has us building scenery and arranging lights for the annual Halloween bash the owners always throw." She turned to Ciara. "It's a blast. We turn the lobby into the courtyard of a haunted castle complete with lighting and sound effects."

Ciara's eyes widened. "That's what all those weird orders were for. I couldn't figure out which play we were doing that required dry ice, spray-on cobwebs, and glow-in-the-dark paint." She laughed. "Certainly not *Hamilton*."

"That would be an interesting interpretation, though. *Zombie Hamilton*. Someone should definitely do that," Jeremy suggested.

"You really are isolated in that office of yours," Kate said to Ciara, ignoring her boyfriend. "I can't believe you didn't know about it."

She'd known about it. Sort of. She'd overheard the ticket sellers discussing a party and some of the ushers talking about a "thing" on Halloween night, but she'd assumed it was a private gathering at someone's home that she hadn't been invited to. It hadn't bothered her. She preferred small groups to large crowds. Besides, over the past few days she'd had plenty of other distractions to occupy her off time.

"You're allowed to bring a plus one. Any prospects yet?" Kate asked.

"No." That did bother her. Because the answer had been no since she'd taken the job here months and months ago. She and her former—well, she wouldn't call her a girlfriend. More like a female companion with occasional benefits. They'd broken up when she accepted the offer and moved halfway across the country. Again. Neither had wanted to try to maintain a long-distance relationship. But that didn't account for the extended dry spell. She planned to stay here. She wanted to forge new bonds. She'd made some friends. What was stopping her from pursuing someone for more?

It wasn't like she'd dated dozens of women before Ellen. Ciara wasn't a natural flirt and didn't do one-night flings. But she usually had at least a passing interest in someone—the checkout girl at the grocery, the barista who made her coffee, but no. Not here.

Since she'd moved, there'd been no dates, no girlfriends, no women she had more than the slightest attraction to. Sometimes it felt like she was waiting for lightning to strike . . . but there weren't any storms on the horizon.

"Oh," Kate said, recovering from Ciara's curt response. "Okay. Not an issue. You'll have all of us to hang with. Anyway, it's a costume party, so think about what you want to wear. With everything that's been going on, I haven't even had time to look for one for myself. Have either of you?" Kate asked the guys.

Jeremy and Carlos shook their heads.

"You can come as anything you want. There's no set theme for the costumes, and they have a contest and giveaway prizes. Oh, and it's an open bar." Kate seemed especially happy about that.

"Which I have to work," Carlos groused.

"You get paid overtime since it falls on a Monday this year," Jeremy reminded him.

"Yeah, there's that."

They were halfway up the stairs when Ciara had the best idea. "Oh! I know what we should do for costumes." She gripped Kate's shoulder ahead of her. "You and I should be flappers. And the guys can be gangsters or bootleggers or something else from the time period. I mean, we've been practically living in that history for days now. And hey, maybe it'll put us in the right mindset to solve this thing!" Her mind danced with possibilities: fishnet stockings, a glittery headband with a feather, a tight-fitting dress with a fringe at the hemline . . . blue to match her hair. Yes.

"That's perfect!" Kate said, nodding. "I love it." She slipped an arm around Jeremy's waist beside her. "Hey, can I be your gun moll?"

He leaned over and kissed her. "Sure, doll face," he said, speaking out of the corner of his mouth. "Whatever my baby wants."

"And Renaldo will drool over me in a pinstripe suit." Carlos put one hand to his cheek. "Oh, I need to go shopping, ASAP."

"Vintage clothing stores, here we come." Ciara hoped to find something appropriate and affordable. She needed to look her 1920s best. She wasn't sure who for, but it felt . . . important.

Ciara laughed quietly at herself, the sound lost under the chatter of the others. Plenty of eligible women would be attending the party. Maybe she expected that lightning to strike.

Chapter 13

Wednesday, October 26, 2022

ON WEDNESDAY, CIARA worked from nine to one emailing QR codes for extra tickets to local business owners and city government officials who'd made sizable donations to the theater. They were doing well, all things considered, but some maintenance projects loomed in the near future: the exterior needed painting, which would cost tens of thousands, and some of the decorative filigree on the roof required repair, along with a number of other smaller things like the replacement bulbs for outside lighting so old they had to be ordered from a specialty shop in Italy. Donations made those possible, and the least the theater could do was give the donors some additional free tickets for performances that weren't sold out on top of their season passes. That way they could bring family and friends, which meant more butts in the seats and greater concession sales.

Once she had that sorted, she figured it wouldn't be dishonest to start searching through the old employee payroll files. After all, she'd been hired to organize things, and the old records certainly needed organizing.

She used her key to unlock the bookkeeper's storage closet at the rear of her office—a long but narrow space that began with file cabinets on either side but gave way to stacks of simple cardboard boxes at the far end. Flipping the overhead fluorescent lights on and squinting into the glare they created, Ciara studied the labels on the metal cabinets.

Even these had been here a while, though someone had taken the time to mark each one with the correct years beginning in the early 1990s and going back to the 1950s. Everything more recent than those was on disks, thumb drives, and now the cloud. Ironic that she'd have a harder time trying to pull something off a 1995 floppy disk than she probably would digging up a physical form from 1954, but the bottommost drawer of her desk, which looked like it had been in that office since the theater was built, contained a plastic box full of the damn things. She hoped she'd never need to look at one.

The walking space between the cabinets was so narrow Ciara had to turn sideways, but she slid her way between them, watching as the years went by. Handwriting changed, but the ordering of the labels didn't. Year first, then beneath it the type of forms: payroll, taxes, insurance, employment contracts, and miscellaneous.

However, once she hit the 1940s, things got messy. Whoever had been in charge then had the bright idea to label the tops of the storage boxes and one of the sides, but it wasn't always the side facing outward. And the boxes went from floor to ceiling. Ciara had to leave and fetch a stepladder from maintenance to reach the top.

She skipped the first couple of stacks figuring they would be too recent for her search. The third was still the 1930s, but two more deep and she hit the era she was looking for. She pulled down box after box checking the dates and contents and shoved them toward the entrance, effectively cutting off her only pathway out of the closet, but there was nowhere else to put them, and she didn't feel like carrying each one all the way out. God help her if there was a fire.

When she finally hit 1924 Payroll, she gave a little whoop and prepared to carry it to her desk, only to realize she'd blocked herself in, so she sat down on a couple of other containers, set the box in front of her, lifted the top . . . and groaned.

All the forms were loose and piled one on top of another. No actual files separated by month or employee, just single page after single page. She separated the first one and held it up. The ink had faded badly over the years. She could barely make out the words, but if she strained her eyes, she could manage it. She studied the page in front of her and . . .

This wasn't a payroll form.

It was insurance for some guy named George Rodriguez. And the next was an invoice followed by an honest-to-god inner-office memo about toilet paper use.

Ciara dug a little deeper and found more of the same. The box might have said *Payroll*, but it was a mix of everything paper that had come through this office that year, all thrown haphazardly into this one container.

She blew out a frustrated breath, shifting her blue hair across her forehead, and listened to the faint jazz music carrying through the wall from someone else's office—maybe maintenance down the hall, though they usually preferred hard rock. Ciara tried to look on the bright side. At least the year was correct. Any form that actually had a date on it did say 1924. Well, if she was going to have to go through it all, she might as well do what they paid her for and sort it out.

An hour later, she'd arranged the single box of papers into six piles by form type and read through every payroll list for that entire year.

No Mickeys.

Also no Michaels, Mikes, or Micks.

There was a Mitchel, but that didn't feel right. That would be shortened to Mitch. So maybe Mickey hadn't worked for the theater after all. Or maybe he'd worked there during an earlier year. The distant jazz music had faded away to be replaced by big band. Only now it seemed to come through the opposite wall from the jazz.

There were no offices on that side, just the lobby.

She pushed away a shiver, chalked it up to Carlos or one of the other staff members exploring their musical options, and tried to focus.

Not bothering to organize this time, Ciara scrounged through 1923 and 1922, both just as disorganized—and judging from the handwriting, probably stored by the same employee. Nothing.

She kicked the nearest box, then kicked it again. If Mickey were merely a friend of the theater owners at that time, she'd never find a record of him here. And Mickey deserved to be found.

Ciara stopped in the lobby just long enough to tell Kate and Jeremy the bad news, then headed around back to check the dog bowls again. Instead of going through the house where a rehearsal was in progress, she exited through the front doors and used the side alley. Turning the rear corner, she froze.

So did the little brown and white dog, his head jerking up from where it had been half-buried in the food dish. So, it did eat.

They were only about ten feet apart, and Ciara didn't want to spook him.

Heh.

She crouched down, then seated herself cross-legged on the asphalt and waited. Her heart rate jumped when the animal immediately trotted over and sat in front of her, just out of touching range. No collar, which didn't prove the tattered red one was his, but . . .

"EZ?" she tried, then held her breath.

He barked.

Ciara exhaled. "That's your name, isn't it? EZ?"

The dog barked a second time.

Wishing she had some treats, she held out a hand, palm up, for him to sniff. "Come here, EZ. It's okay. I won't hurt you. I saved you, remember?"

EZ looked from her fingers to her face and back again. Stretching his neck forward, he let his snout come so close to her fingertips she could feel his warm doggy breath on them. He gave a little whine, and his whole body trembled. Ciara tried leaning toward him. EZ backed away.

"Okay, I'll stay put," she promised. "Let's try something else. Um, do you know any tricks? How about 'sit'?" She'd seen him sit the day she saved him from the truck, but not on command. "Can you sit?"

The dog's butt hit the ground.

"Good boy," she cooed in a tone reserved for animals and small children. "How about 'shake'?"

He waved a paw in the air, but when she tried to take it like Antoine had, he set it down. Ciara pouted at him. "What, I'm not good enough to shake paws with?" She pointed at the dog bowls. "I'm the one leaving food for you there, you know."

EZ barked at her, turned in a circle, and sat back down, his tongue lolling out the side of his mouth.

"Laughing at me again, are you? Okay. What else? Speak? Speak EZ, speak!" She stopped and chuckled, realizing what she was saying. EZ's owner had been a man with a sense of humor.

The dog barked three times.

"You're really smart. Such a good boy. Mickey trained you very well."

At the sound of the bar owner's name, EZ's entire demeanor changed. His stubby tail ceased its frantic wagging. The pointy ears drooped, and he dropped to his belly, his head resting on his paws, and looked up with the saddest puppy eyes she'd ever seen. Then he whined, long and low and so heartbreakingly mournful Ciara's own eyes welled up.

"Aww, baby, I'm sorry. You miss him, don't you? I'm so very, very sorry." She couldn't hold back any longer and reached to stroke EZ's head, but the dog scrambled away. "Hey, wait!"

No use. He turned and ran, past the mostly empty food dishes, past the backstage door, and out of sight around the far corner of the theater.

"Damn," Ciara whispered. She stood and brushed off her slacks, then unlocked the stage door and reached inside to where she kept the bag of dog food and a thermos of water. Once she'd filled both bowls, she made a final check for EZ, but the dog was long gone.

Ciara struck out at the vintage clothing store. The handful of 1920s pieces they had in stock were either too expensive or not her size. However, the saleswoman suggested a couple of online retailers who made reproductions. If she paid for expedited shipping, she'd get what she needed in a couple of days.

Eventually, she settled on a knee-length, short-sleeved, deep blue flapper dress with black beadwork throughout and black fringes at the hemline. The blue matched the streak in her hair perfectly, which was good since, anachronism or not, she didn't plan on redyeing it for one night, nor did she intend to cut it to the short length that had been fashionable in the twenties. She already owned black heels, but she sprang for black satin theater gloves, a long faux pearl necklace with a matching bracelet, and a headpiece of black beads with a blue feather that would complement the dress. Fishnet stockings with garters completed the look—she'd always wanted to try them; they seemed so sexy—and she escaped the checkout having spent a little over a hundred dollars—more than she'd wanted to invest in a Halloween costume, but less than she'd expected, and far less than a period piece.

Besides, with speakeasies as popular as they currently were, she was sure she'd find another opportunity to wear it.

Chapter 14

Thursday, October 27, 2022

CIARA STOOD OUTSIDE the downtown library's main entrance after work, trying to decide how to play this. "I'm an author doing research" wasn't going to cut it. Someone inevitably would ask what her book was about, and she'd never tried to write anything in her life other than school essays and grant applications.

Every other excuse she could think of made her sound like a flake.

At the end of the day, though, did she really care what these people thought? She'd never done any sort of research at the library prior to this week. She usually used the internet. She'd only come in to check out some Sapphic romances when she got lonely. She was unlikely to need the nonfiction sections again, and after a few months, no one would remember she had ever been there.

Besides, she could look up anything she damn well wanted to.

Ciara pushed through the huge glass doors on their brass hardware, the library as old as the theater but with a stateliness rather than that touch of ostentation the theater possessed. No one stood behind the lobby's heavy oak general assistance desk, the gouges and worn-smooth places resulting from a hundred-plus years of dependable use. She waited around for a few minutes in the echoey, high-ceilinged space, murmured conversations from adjacent areas carrying along the corridors, but when a librarian didn't appear, she figured one wasn't coming. Staff shortages were still common everywhere.

She spotted some public touchscreens she could use to tell her where to start looking, but her questions were so specific, that would probably send her on a wild ghost chase. Instead, she took the elevator to the top floor where the archives were.

Ciara recognized Claudia Waters right away with some relief. The older librarian stood between two of the rows of shelves. It looked like she was reshelving misplaced books. The rest of the floor was empty of people.

Claudia glanced up and smiled at her, then nodded at the book with a maroon cover in her hand. "People need to put returns on the carts and leave the shelving to the librarians. I swear half the hours I put in are spent correcting others' mistakes. They don't understand the organizational system we use. They just stick anything anywhere it fits." She tugged another book free with a bit of effort and chuckled. "Or doesn't fit, as the case may be." Setting both books aside, she put her hands on her hips. "Well, enough of my complaining. People start following the rules, and I could find myself out of a job I love. What can I help you with today? More 1920s?"

"No, actually I . . ." Ciara cleared her throat and focused on the rows and rows of multicolored bindings. "I'm guessing it isn't your area of expertise if you work in the archives, but there wasn't anyone at the desk downstairs and . . ."

The librarian frowned and came closer. Ciara noticed she smelled of baby powder, roses, and a slight mustiness that must come from spending so much time around old books and wasn't the least bit unpleasant. "Just spit it out, dear. I know this facility from top to bottom. I'm sure I can point you in the right direction, and people research the strangest things. There's nothing you can ask for that will shock me. I've heard requests for books on everything from devil worship to orca mating habits to how to cook goats' balls."

Ciara sputtered and laughed, then met the older woman's eyes. "How about ghosts?"

To her credit, if Claudia was surprised, she didn't show it. Instead, she headed for the study tables, waving a hand over her shoulder for Ciara to follow. They sat across from each other at the center table. "Does this have something to do with your hundred-year-old dog collar?"

Ciara considered lying, making it a more general request, but the look in the librarian's eyes said she'd see right through her. "Yes. I . . . I know it sounds crazy, but . . . I think the stray at the theater might actually be a ghost. But I don't know much about ghosts, and it doesn't fit with what I thought I did know. The dog can touch things, move things, and sometimes he lets people touch him. But he shows up in places he shouldn't be able to get to, and he responds to the name of a dog that lived a hundred years ago. I know it sounds completely insane—"

"Oh no, not at all." The librarian stared off into a corner of the archives. "The world is full of mysterious and unexplainable things. Look around you." She swept out an arm to encompass the shelves and shelves of books. "Humanity has written all these and millions more to quantify human experience, but the books keep coming. We'll never know it all."

"Well, I'd like to find out what we do know. I've heard stories about ghosts that move things. But can some ghosts touch people? And is it common for a ghost to be seen by so many? Most of my coworkers have had run-ins with this dog, as well as the owner of the restaurant next to the theater."

"Hmm." Claudia remained silent for a long moment. "I think I can get you started. Lucky for you, ghosts have recently become a special interest of mine."

"Oh, have you seen one?"

The librarian laughed. "Not exactly. But let's say I have a personal stake in their existence and what they're capable of."

Ciara wondered if Claudia Waters had lost someone recently, a spouse or sibling perhaps. Or maybe, like many elderly people, she hoped for evidence that she might continue in some form after her death. Either way, it seemed impolite to ask, so she didn't.

The older woman stood and fetched a piece of paper and a pencil, then jotted down several titles and authors from memory and slid the list over to Ciara. "You'll find these in our parapsychology section, third floor to the left of the elevator. We don't have a lot on that subject compared to other areas of interest. Remarkably there isn't much call for it. But these should, if not provide the answers, give you new ways of looking at the questions." She tapped one of the titles three times with a wrinkled finger. "Pay particular attention to this one. I recall something like what you've described in there."

Ciara took the paper and slid it into the pocket of her jeans. "Thank you so much." She stood and held out her hand.

The librarian stood as well, but held up both hands, palms out, warding off her offer of a handshake. "Sorry, dear. Let's just do this." She gave a friendly wave with her fingers. "I'm afraid I'm still not comfortable with handshakes since the pandemic. And I'm 'of a certain age' so especially vulnerable to it, you know."

"Oh, yes, of course." Ciara mimicked Claudia's ten-fingered wave. "I'm sorry."

"Please, don't be." She escorted her to the elevator, and Ciara pushed the call button. Claudia indicated the now-empty tables and chairs of the archive floor. "If it weren't for you and your friend the other day, I'd have no reason to be here."

The elevator opened and Ciara stepped inside.

Claudia Waters bid her farewell.

The doors closed.

In the parapsychology section, she found the three books and spent the hours until the library closed poring over them. Ninety percent of the contents were speculation and hearsay, as she'd expected—stories of sightings and encounters with spirits that were repeated almost down to the last detail by different people at different times but all apparently coming into contact with the same ghosts.

In the end, Ciara gained several takeaways. One, yes, multiple people might see the same spirit, both at different times and at the same time as a group. Two, poltergeists were regularly reported to move things around. However, they did not tend to be seen while doing so. EZ dropping the key would be a very unusual sighting. Three, some spirits were believed to be strong enough to maintain physical form and even touch the living, though people who said they'd been touched by spirits mostly described the experience as "cold," or "tingly," and not at all like physical contact with a living person, or in this case a live dog.

One description in particular caught her interest, and she wondered if it was what Claudia had wanted her to find:

"Many theories exist regarding connections between the dead and the living. A recent hypothesis, 'Energy Transference Aptitude,' suggests that certain corporeal beings with a strong affinity for either the spirit world in general or a particular spirit might intentionally or unknowingly transfer some of their 'life force' to the noncorporeal entities with which they come in contact, thereby increasing their strength and substance."

Everyone at the theater adored EZ. Had they all been accidentally "enabling" the ghost dog to manifest more frequently and substantially? And Antoine had been angry at EZ. Anger still created an emotional bond between the giver and the recipient. Was that why Antoine had been able to touch the dog? Had the café owner given EZ the energy to become solid enough, at least for a moment? Or was something else going on entirely? Too many questions.

She definitely wanted to stop by the café and speak with Antoine about what he'd felt when he touched EZ's paw.

While the encounters at the theater bore some similarities to sightings described in the books, nothing reported in those pages came close to explaining the frequency, clarity, and consistency of EZ's appearances with the exception of the "Energy Transference Aptitude" theory. What was going on in the Big City Little Theater Company was extremely unusual and spoke of something beyond the spirit realm, something that defied description, taking place there. The closest other comparisons involved ghosts of people who kept returning to the locations of their death because they had unfinished business there.

But what unfinished business could a dog possibly have?

Chapter 15

Friday, October 28, 2022

DURING HER LUNCH break on Friday, Ciara decided to take Antoine's advice and invite her friends to join her at the café next door—an adorable little French place with crepes and quiches, indoor/outdoor seating, and fancy little touches like colorful umbrellas over each outside table, white tablecloths, and real napkins, all of which still didn't bring up the menu prices. Carlos had wanted to meet up anyway since he had some information about testing old stains for blood and also the bullet they'd found.

The two of them took a table out front and perused the menus until Kate and Jeremy joined them a few minutes later. "Sorry we're late," Kate said. "We had to secure the party setup in the lobby and cover everything with tarps before tonight's first show. Don't want the customers tripping or pulling anything down."

"I'm just glad this is the bosses' idea, because the lobby looks like a disaster area. It'll be great on Monday, but the weekend audiences won't be impressed by the mess," Jeremy added. "You guys get costumes yet? I lucked out. My grandmother had some of her father's clothes from the twenties, and we were about the same size. I got a suit and a hat. The shirt won't be quite as authentic though, and I have to wear my own shoes. Dang that man had big feet."

"I picked up a gangster getup at the costume shop over on Third Street," Carlos said. "It's a rental, so it's better quality than the stuff they sell for single-night use. Renaldo will love it. He's coming as a cop from that time period."

"Match made in heaven," Kate said. "I dug into the costume storage and came up with one of the dresses we used when we put on *Chicago* a few years ago. Black with silver sequins. What about you, Ciara?"

"Guess I'm the unimaginative one. I couldn't find anything at the vintage store, so I ordered from an online shop, 'Timeless Treasures,' and had it rush delivered. It arrived yesterday, and it looks good."

"I'm sure it'll be stunning," Carlos said, patting her shoulder.

The waitress arrived to deliver glasses of water and take their orders. The specialty of the house was the crepes. Ciara had hers with chicken in a cheese sauce, along with a small salad. The others ordered crepes as well. "Be sure to save room for dessert," the attractive redhead warned. "The strawberry with chocolate sauce ones are delicious." She collected their menus and hurried away to put in their orders.

Ciara followed her with her eyes as she disappeared through the café doors. Most of the interior tables were full, as were several of the ones on the front patio. She didn't spot Antoine behind the counter, but as busy as they were, he was probably in the kitchen. She did notice a "For Sale" sign in the corner of the glass door.

"Oh, damn," she said, pointing it out. "Looks like Antoine is retiring. He mentioned something about that a few weeks ago. Said he'd been slowing down lately, though he wasn't very slow when he was chasing EZ." Ciara frowned. "I hope it's changing hands and not going out of business entirely. This is my favorite lunch spot."

"I can't imagine they'd close," Kate noted, "not with the solid business they're doing. And yeah, I come here for dinner after work sometimes. I'm sure they'll find someone to take it over. Okay," she said, rubbing her hands together. "Let's debrief. Carlos is practically bouncing out of his seat, and I think Ciara said she has new information. Unfortunately, Jeremy and I have nothing. We've been neck-deep in Halloween party décor."

Jeremy nodded his agreement.

Carlos and Ciara looked at each other. "You go first," they said in unison, then laughed.

"Ladies first," Carlos insisted.

"Okay, thanks." Ciara gave a quick recap of her unsuccessful payroll search followed by her latest encounter with EZ.

Jeremy raised a hand to stop her. "Maintaining the voice of reason," he said with an apologetic smile, "dogs generally respond to tone. The fact that he barked when you called him EZ doesn't necessarily mean that's his name or that he's a ghost. Same with his reactions to the owner's name. We're attributing human responses to an animal here."

"Dogs have feelings," Ciara said. "I'm not arguing your point about the name, but you should have seen him. I wanted to cuddle him so much when I mentioned Mickey. That dog is mourning a loss."

"But you didn't cuddle him," Jeremy pointed out. "You still haven't touched him. Pass a hand through him and I'll definitely be on Team Ghost Dog, but until then, I'm staying with Team Reality Check. Sorry."

"That's my guy, always sucking the excitement out of everything," Kate said, slinging an arm around his shoulders. "Got anything else?"

Ciara nodded. "I went back to the library and did some research on encounters with ghosts. *If* that's what's happening here," she said with a nod to Jeremy, "I have to admit, it's extremely

99

unusual and doesn't completely match up with anything I read about. I mean, some elements are in synch, and there are some way-out-there theories to experiment with, but our sightings are very frequent and the number of witnesses is much higher in our case compared to any of the others I skimmed through. I want to talk to Antoine at some point, and I still think EZ is a ghost, but I also feel like there's something additional going on."

"Like the flickering spotlights and the way they seem to point at certain things?" Kate asked.

"No, that still feels . . . ghostlike," Ciara said. "There are lots of examples where light sources flicker to attract attention or at least indicate a ghost's presence during a haunting. I just . . . I don't know. I think there's more to it. Like, EZ behaves like a dog. A really intelligent dog, but still, a dog. He steals things and plays with them. He does tricks. But the lights . . . that seems like it has a human intelligence behind it. It's too high a concept for a dog to use lighting to get our attention on specific things." She glanced around the table at her friends' expressions, a mixture of thoughtful and bemused. "Does that make any sense?"

"Maybe we're dealing with a second ghost," Carlos said. "You think the lights might be Mickey trying to tell us something?"

"Yes," Ciara said, nodding. "That's exactly what I think. I just wish I knew what it was he was trying to tell us." She spread her hands wide on the table. "That's all I have."

The waitress arrived at that moment with a tray of crepes. She set them down in front of each of them, refilled their water glasses, and rushed off again.

"Okay, my turn," Carlos announced around a mouthful of ham and cheese crepe. "Mmm, this is delicious. Good choice of restaurants, Ciara."

Kate circled her hand in the air, the universal signal for *Get on with it,* chewing a bite of her spinach and mushroom crepe.

"Right. So, I've got good news and bad news. The bad news is the stains on the collar are too old to determine if they really are blood or not, and also too old to figure out if it's dog blood or human blood. I mean, there might be some really scientific tests they could run, but it would require a lab and high-tech equipment we'd neither get access to nor have the training to use." He took another bite of his crepe.

"So, what's the good news?" Ciara asked, savoring her own lunch, and hoping they wouldn't close the café. The food really was wonderful.

"My ballistics expert friend came through." Carlos pulled out the bullet they'd found and set it in the center of the table where it rolled back and forth on the glass surface for a moment before lying still. "This is a .357-caliber bullet and was most likely fired from a .38 Special Smith and Wesson revolver since that was an extremely popular gun in this area at that time."

"I thought all the bad guys had tommy guns," Kate said.

"Yeah, those were around, too. But if you wanted a revolver and not a machine gun, this is what it fired. Bad guys used them. So did civilians. But what's interesting to note is that the .38 was the handgun of choice for the police around here during the twenties." Carlos took a sip of water from his glass.

"Weren't police issued a specific type of gun?" Jeremy asked.

"Nah. That wasn't until later, the thirties, I think. In the twenties, they chose and bought their own weapons, and they usually had to pay for their own ammo. Times have definitely changed there."

Ciara sat up straighter in her seat. "So you think the police shot Mickey? Like maybe during a raid of the speakeasy?"

Carlos shook his head. "I thought of that, too. But it doesn't really work. If it was an official act, sanctioned by the police department, they would have arrested him, not shot him." He paused, thinking. "Unless he was armed himself, maybe. We didn't find a gun while we were cleaning the bar, and there weren't any other bullet holes to suggest Mickey might have fired first, say, at a police officer."

Jeremy held up his hand again. "Nothing says it was definitely a cop. It could have been anyone with a common gun like that. Also, we haven't gotten inside the cabinets yet. We only cleaned surface areas. There might be a second weapon involved. And we weren't looking for other bullet holes, either. When we go back down there, we should check the wall around the door. That would have been opposite to where Mickey was apparently standing."

"Well, one thing's for sure," Carlos said. "If Mickey did get off a shot, he's got terrible aim because his killer must have survived it. Someone had to live to get rid of the body and hide the bar." He polished off his last bite of crepe and waved toward the window of the café to get the waitress's attention. "Who's up for dessert?"

The waitress returned with her order pad in hand. Before they could give their dessert choices, Ciara asked, "What's with the 'For Sale' sign? Is Antoine retiring? Also, I haven't seen him today. I wanted to ask him something."

The perky smile dropped away from the young waitress's face. "Oh, I guess you haven't heard. I thought everyone already knew."

Ciara's stomach dropped while icy fingers worked their way up her spine. She had a terrible feeling. "Knew what?" she managed, breath catching in her throat. Her friends exchanged nervous looks, their thoughts running in the same direction hers had.

"Antoine passed away a couple of weeks ago. Heart attack." She brushed a tear from her cheek with the back of her hand.

"A couple of weeks. Are you sure?" Carlos asked, a tremor in his voice.

"I found him," she confirmed, giving a little shiver. "He was lying in the back alley when I came in for work. Must have been taking out the garbage. We all miss him around here." She cleared her throat. "Sorry. Can I get you anything else?"

Carlos shook his head. Kate had gone pale. Ciara's hand trembled when she lifted her water glass to take a sip, sloshing the liquid about. Even Jeremy was breathing faster than he had been a moment before.

"Just the check," Carlos managed.

The waitress left to retrieve it.

"You said you talked to Antoine on Sunday. You're absolutely certain?" Jeremy asked.

Ciara couldn't find her voice. She nodded instead.

"Well, now we know why EZ let Antoine touch him," Kate said. "Antoine was a ghost himself."

Ciara exhaled. "And now we have three."

Chapter 16

October 31, 2022

THE REST OF the weekend passed in a blur of performances and last-minute Halloween party preparations. Though she'd been desperate to return to the basement, Ciara barely had a minute to escape her office, and when she finally did, an usher begged her to pitch in with the matinee because a couple of the regular staff had called in sick.

Off at an early Halloween celebration more likely, given most of the ushers were college students.

Two of the backstage crew reported new EZ sightings phrased as complaints about "that really cute but annoying dog she needed to hurry up and catch and take home with her." Other than her friends, no one else was calling him a ghost. Probably just as well. The last thing the theater needed in these difficult financial times was rumors of being haunted by a spirit canine.

Then again, given the season, that might bring in more business than it chased away.

So, when Monday evening rolled around, Ciara was almost surprised. She'd spent the day at home, re-dyeing the blue streak in her hair a brighter shade, doing her makeup, painting her nails, and finally slipping into the sheath-like flapper dress, fishnet stockings, and heels.

Okay, not the heels. Those she carried in a soft cloth bag to protect them, instead tying on her sneakers for the walk of several blocks to the theater while dodging trick-or-treaters, evening revelers, and the increased police presence clogging the sidewalks. She'd swap out the shoes when she arrived and ditch the sneakers in her office.

The weather held for the holiday. Clear skies with a full moon and a scattering of stars visible despite the city's light pollution. The chilly nip in the air had her grabbing a black shawl at the last moment, and Ciara was glad she did. When the slight wind blew between buildings, she tugged it tightly around her.

While Halloween had been her favorite holiday growing up, she still experienced a sense of melancholy as couple after couple preceded her toward the lobby. It seemed as if everyone had a date for the staff party, even eighty-five-year-old Esther from costuming who swore she'd "never put her faith in a man again" after divorcing five different husbands.

"Ciara! Hey, come on!" Kate waved to her from the glass doors, the fringe at the hem of her own flapper dress blowing in the breeze. Jeremy stood at her side in full gangster attire right down to the realistic-looking tommy gun he held. They made an adorable pairing.

With a sigh, Ciara joined them, and they stepped inside the darkened lobby.

Loud dance music beat against her eardrums, along with happy chatter and laughter. Strobe lights flashed to the rhythm. Glow-in-the-dark cobwebs covered every available surface. They'd hung strings of orange and purple bulbs along the bar where she could barely make out Carlos juggling a pair of bottles before tipping one to pour into a shot glass.

The "haunted" castle set surrounded the open space on three sides, turrets of black and gray foam "stone" climbing to the ceiling in the corners. Dozens of bats on strings hung from the overhead lights. The lounge furniture and area rugs had all been removed and stored in the aisles of the main theater area in order to make way for an expansive temporary dance floor now writhing with bodies. It looked like everyone who had ever worked or performed here was in attendance tonight, along with some of their wealthier patrons who had received special invites.

"Amazing decorations!" Ciara shouted into Kate's ear to be heard over the bass line. "Your team did an incredible job."

Kate nodded. "Thanks! It was Jeremy's design a few years back, and so popular we've been using it ever since."

Jeremy grinned and leaned down toward Ciara. "What she means is, this thing was so expensive to construct, we have to reuse it to get our investment out of it, but it's durable and holds up well. We replace the stuff that doesn't last, like the webs, and refresh the glow paint. Come on, let's get a drink."

Ciara followed them to the bar, squeezing between a clown and a blood-covered zombie. When she reached the counter, she switched shoes and put the sneakers and her shawl in her bag. "Can you store these somewhere back there for me?" she asked, holding it out to Carlos but keeping her purse on her shoulder. "I'm never going to make it to my office."

"Sure thing." The bag vanished behind the bar. Carlos poked one of the other bartenders who was wearing a Bride of Frankenstein getup. "I'm gonna grab drinks for these guys and take a break. You got this?"

She nodded. "Send Bella back when you see her, though."

They had three bartenders working at the moment, but Ciara had spotted Bella out on the steps smoking a cigarette when she came in. With drinks in hand, they all wandered to one of the hallways where the music wasn't quite as loud.

"Where's Renaldo?" Jeremy asked.

Carlos straightened the jacket of his pinstripe suit. It really did look fabulous on him. "Coming late, after my shift ends." He pulled his phone from a pocket and glanced at it. "Couple of hours from now."

They chatted a while, but the noise level made meaningful conversation impossible. Eventually Carlos returned to the bar, and Kate dragged Jeremy onto the dance floor for a slow song, leaving Ciara to prop herself up against a bare spot of wall and people watch while she sipped her glass of . . . something purple. Carlos had called it a Purple People Eater with vodka and blue curacao, along with sweet and sour, grenadine, and cranberry juice. Delicious, and definitely more her thing than the Electric Smurf Kate had been drinking, though that one would have gone better with her hair.

When the beat picked up again, she joined her friends on the floor. It was fun, but didn't stop her from feeling like a third wheel, so after a few songs, she retreated to the sidelines once more, had a soda, and enjoyed the vibe.

With so much movement and all the blinking lights, she didn't know how she spotted him, but she did—EZ.

The little dog sat beside the stairwell entrance. Someone had propped the door open, probably for airflow since the basements were always freezing and the heat of so many bodies in the lobby had raised the temperature to sweltering levels. Ciara would have sworn EZ stared right at her. The dog's mouth opened and closed once in a bark she couldn't hear over the noise. Then he turned and disappeared down the stairs.

"That is a Lassie move if ever I saw one," she muttered. Ciara scanned the room for her friends, but Renaldo had arrived and was leaning on the bar chatting with Carlos, and Kate and Jeremy had their arms around each other and were swaying to the music, completely lost in their own world. "Well, crap."

Halloween night. Cold stairs. Creepy basement. Ghost dog and at this point who knew how many other spirits hanging around. Seemed like everyone she encountered these days was dead.

No wonder she couldn't find a girlfriend. Dead people made for poor dating options.

The last thing she wanted to do was follow EZ by herself, but with an eyeroll and a sigh, Ciara stepped into the stairwell.

Not as alone as she thought. Several couples had taken refuge on the first flight down and were making full use of the dimmer light and relative privacy to make out. She slid past them, mumbling apologies and asking if a dog had run past. One guy in a blood-spattered tuxedo didn't bother to break his liplock with his date but pointed down the stairs.

Averting her eyes, Ciara hurried down.

She passed the open door to the main basement where a second more intimate party was going on. No music, though the sound trickled down through the ceiling. Just small groups talking and drinking. Once she figured out what EZ wanted she'd have to come back here. This was much more Ciara's speed.

Her heels clicked on the concrete steps as she continued to descend. No more couples. No sign of EZ. Several of the overhead bulbs had burned out. She'd need to tell Kate to replace those. Someone could fall and hurt themselves.

By the time she reached the subbasement, she was mostly in the dark and completely alone.

It made sense. As far as she knew, she had the only key to both the secondary basement and the speakeasy. The subbasement door was closed and locked. As she fished around in her purse for the keys, Ciara froze.

The stairs ended at the door. She could have failed to spot EZ in the main basement a few steps above. There'd been a lot of activity there. But surely someone would have exclaimed at the presence of the dog. He hadn't gone back up. She definitely would have seen him then.

Nope. EZ had done it again. He'd gotten into a locked room.

Ciara swore the temperature in the stairwell dropped another five degrees, and she shivered. Goosebumps rose on her arms and legs. She found the keys, unlocked the door, and pushed it wide open.

The overhead lights were on, illuminating the open area between the stairs and the storerooms, and sitting in the dead center wagging his stubby tail was EZ.

Ciara stared at the dog.

The dog stared back.

Breath coming hard and fast, she took a step forward, then another, and crouched down. "Okay," Ciara managed, her voice a mere squeak. She cleared her throat and tried again. "Okay. We're going to settle this once and for all." Though she wasn't sure what there was to settle. She knew. She knew exactly what EZ was.

After their last encounter in the alleyway, Ciara had come prepared with a package of treats in her purse. She rustled around in the handbag, the cellophane packaging crinkling while she fumbled to open it and withdraw a "tasty beef chew no dog can resist" according to all the commercials. She held one out in an open palm, her whole arm shaking.

Clearly Bow Wow Bites' advertising department hadn't done product testing with ghosts.

EZ extended his neck forward and sniffed, then *whuff*ed quietly at the offering. He glanced from Ciara to the speakeasy's closed door. His message was clear.

"Nope. Not going in there. Not alone."

She considered the situation and revised.

"Not unless you come here and let me pet you. Or, you know, pass a hand through you, or whatever." Yeah, she was trying to negotiate with a dog. But as she'd told the others, EZ was no ordinary dog.

EZ gave one more forlorn look toward the speakeasy, barked once, and *trotted right toward her.*

Ciara almost broke and ran. All the hairs stood up on the back of her neck. She held herself in place, muscles rigid. She'd clung to some doubt before the second door incident, but EZ had to be a ghost. There was just no other explanation.

Holding the palm with the treat on it as steady as she could, she waited until EZ was close enough, then reached with her other hand . . .

And stroked his warm, solid body.

Chapter 17

October 31, 2022

"YAHHH!" CIARA SHOUTED, jerking her hand away as if burned. She overbalanced backward, landing on her butt, and scrambled away like a crab—not an easy thing to do in a flapper dress.

For his part, EZ appeared equally startled, turning tail and skittering away to cower against the speakeasy door. He shivered from snout to tail, ears down, hunched in on himself. A mournful whine escaped his throat. The treat lay on the concrete floor between them, and EZ stared at it, then at Ciara, as if accusing her of betrayal.

"Oh geez," Ciara breathed, taking a moment to compose herself. She twisted her body until she rested on her knees and studied the dog. "Geez," she repeated. Ironic that she'd been completely prepared for her hand to pass through the dog, and utterly, entirely freaked out when it had not.

But what did this mean? Was EZ not a ghost after all? And if not, how had he gotten into both the locked speakeasy days before and the locked subbasement tonight?

"If you're a spirit, you're a very unusual one," Ciara said, calming her tone.

Jeremy would love this turn of events. Even with all the other weirdness going on, he'd be twice as hard to convince of a haunting now.

"I'm sorry. I didn't mean to frighten you. Come back over here. I promise not to shout again. Look! There's the treat." She pointed at it. "You can still have it, and I've got more." Her purse had fallen to the side. She snagged its strap with one finger and drew it to her, then pulled a few more doggy snacks from the pouch and lined them up on the floor in front of her knees.

EZ barked once and edged toward the single treat in the center of the room.

"That's it. Come on. I really am sorry. Such a good boy. And you're so soft. Come let me pet you again."

The dog inched forward, extended his nose to the treat, and gave it a good sniff. Then he snapped it up and ate it in one bite. His eyes focused on the other snacks near Ciara. She stayed quiet, letting him make up his mind. A few moments later, EZ approached, cautious, gaze darting between the treats and Ciara's face.

When he finally engaged in eating them one by one, she reached out her hand again and laid it gently on the top of the dog's head. For a second, he paused, stiffening, then relaxed and continued eating. She let her hand stroke down EZ's neck and along his back to the base of his tail.

Warm, soft, and solid. He had a slight but not unpleasant doggy smell, and the roughness of his tongue tickled when he licked her hand in thanks.

The last treat consumed, EZ surprised Ciara by climbing slowly onto her lap, placing each paw delicately and carefully as if worried he might damage her dress, then curling up on her thighs. She continued to pet him, and he reveled in it, wriggling under her touch. When he rolled onto his back for tummy rubs, Ciara laughed and obliged him.

"Why do I feel like it's been a long time since someone

petted you?" she murmured.

Tongue lolling out of his mouth, EZ stared up at her in adoration.

They remained that way for several minutes until some thumps from the partygoers on the floor above startled EZ from his relaxed pose. He scrambled to his feet, stretched, and gave a wide yawn, then trotted back to the speakeasy door. Sitting, he stared at Ciara.

"Back to Lassie again, I see," she said, and pushed to her own feet. "Well, I did promise to go in there if you let me pet you, though I think you got the better end of that deal." She walked over to join him at the door. "What, you can't walk through this one again?"

EZ barked.

Ciara frowned. There had to be rules governing what EZ could and couldn't do. Random didn't make sense. She merely had to figure them out.

Digging into her purse once more, she came up with the key ring and inserted the appropriate key in the lock. The speakeasy door opened on creaky hinges. *Great.* "Nice and creepy. Perfect for Halloween." The interior was dark. They'd shut down the spotlights when they left the last time. The musty scent of the abandoned space, mixed with the cleaning chemicals they'd begun using, wafted through the doorway.

EZ brushed past her legs and scampered into the darkness, toenails clicking on tile. He vanished in the shadows.

"Hey, wait! Don't disappear on me again." She stepped forward, crossing the threshold.

The door slammed shut behind her.

"Shit!" Ciara jumped in the pitch dark, almost falling in her heels. Instead of trying to fumble around on the floor to find the spotlights, she instinctively reached for the light switch she knew was on the wall beside the entry. Her hand found it, and she flipped it on with a *snap* that seemed to echo in the bar, then braced herself for the potential consequences of her actions.

Fewer bulbs lit up this time, the same three that had remained steady during her first visit with her friends: one over the calendar, one over the radio, and one over the end of the bar. Nothing bad happened. Nothing crackled or sparked or showered her with broken glass.

She turned and tried the doorknob, not terribly panicked since she had the key, but still wanting reassurance. It twisted. The door opened when she pulled. No one occupied the open space beyond. The rest of the subbasement was empty. She waved a hand outside the doorway feeling for . . . what? An unseen presence? A draft she hadn't noticed before? Something that might have caused the door to slam? Nothing.

Except . . . an odd heaviness when she pulled her arm back to her side, like the air in the speakeasy was somehow *thicker*? *weightier*? than the air outside it.

So freaking weird.

Ciara shut the door. She opened it again. Shut it again.

And left it shut with herself inside.

"Okay Ciara. This is why all the characters who investigate in horror movies die. You know that, right? You should be running away. What the hell are you doing?" But she wasn't trapped. The door worked, and this reassured her enough to continue to remain inside.

She let out a long breath and glanced at the seating area, now nothing but shadows since all the bulbs above it were out. A soft *woof* coming from the office doorway behind the bar drew her attention. So that's where EZ had gone.

When she turned back toward the bar to look for him, someone was standing there.

Ohfuckohfuckohfuckoh—later, she'd be very proud of herself for not screaming, though the only reason she didn't was because her breath had frozen in her throat. Her knees locked; her muscles went rigid. She couldn't move, couldn't run.

"H-hello?" she forced out. "I, um, didn't see you there."

That's because he wasn't *there a second ago, dumbass.*

Her subconscious was right. Dim lighting or not, there had absolutely *not been anyone there* when she first stepped into the bar.

The figure didn't move, didn't respond to her wavery greeting. In fact, he did nothing at all but stare out across the speakeasy, a faint smile on his lips.

Ciara drew a long breath. *Okay, think logically.* Maybe the handsome figure in the pinstripe suit and fedora had slipped out of the office when she was looking the other way. Right. Sure. How had he gotten in there in the first place?

And still, he didn't move a muscle or speak a single word or even glance in her direction.

Ciara walked toward him as if pulled, approaching from the end of the bar. When she was within reach of his arm, she stopped and studied him further, sucking in a sharp breath when she realized the "he" was actually a "she." Slight curves stretched the chest panels of the suit jacket she wore. And the thick eyelashes and full lips softened an otherwise sharply angled face and firm jawline. Broad shoulders, a casual but in-control stance, and a height a couple of inches greater than Ciara's own, rounded out the picture.

God, the woman was gorgeous.

But what *was* she? Another ghost? Something else entirely? Ciara watched the woman's chest for a long moment but detected no rise and fall to indicate breathing. The eyes—deep blue, swoon-worthy eyes—remained open but fixed on the seating area.

"Hello?" Ciara tried again. "Can you hear me?" She reached out to touch the jacket sleeve but thought better of it and waved her hand in front of the woman's face instead.

No response.

Something pawed at Ciara's leg, and she looked down to

see EZ wagging his tail and staring up at her. "This is Mickey, isn't it?" she whispered, unsurprised by EZ's affirmative bark. No wonder she hadn't been able to find the bar owner's record of employment in the theater's files. She'd been searching for a man.

Thinking back, she recalled a Michelle . . . Mc-something-or-other . . . in the boxes of documents from that decade. This had to be her. Michelle, who presented as a very handsome butch and referred to herself as Mickey. Of all people, Ciara should have thought of that possibility, but because it had happened in the 1920s she'd assumed . . . duh. Of course, there were lesbians in the '20s. There were members of the LGBTQ+ community in every era if you knew how to look.

Well, she was looking now. And, with a start, she realized she recognized her.

Mickey was one of the women from the black-and-white photograph in the hallway outside Ciara's office, the one with the backstage crew gathered around a stepladder, all of them in overalls and rumpled shirts.

Damn, Mickey cleaned up well.

Unable to stop herself, Ciara raised her hand to cup Mickey's cheek in her palm.

Her hand passed through the other woman's face.

Chapter 18

EZ! EZ's okay!

Mickey's heart wanted to leap from her chest at the sight of the little dog. Well, that is, if she still had a beating heart. But her joy and excitement were the same.

She watched as EZ sped across the dance floor, skidding and scrabbling like he always did on the polished surface, past where she invisibly stood behind the bar, and into her office as if he was searching for her. Her joy faded. He couldn't see her, couldn't even smell her presence with his heightened doggy senses.

Because you aren't alive, she reminded herself, disappointment and depression fighting for dominance, along with a more than healthy dose of frustration.

She remained frozen behind her bar, unable to move, unable to interact with anything, but somehow she could see what went on in her abandoned establishment. In her peripheral vision, she watched EZ hop up onto her cot, twirl around a few times, then lie down with his head on his paws, as dejected as she was.

But he was here. He was okay. And he looked . . . alive.

She focused on the rest of the Speak EZ, run-down, dirty despite the perfunctory cleaning her earlier guests had performed, the endeavor of her heart and soul beaten and broken and lost to time. The bar had died, but EZ was alive.

How?

More movement at the entrance drew her attention away from her beloved pet, and Mickey's pleasure returned.

She came back. When the fog outside the entrance dissipated, the beautiful woman with the blue streak in her hair stood there, framed by the entryway, staring into her bar.

And oh, sweet baby Jesus did she look incredible this time around. Instead of the dungarees she'd worn on her last visit, she sported one of those "flapper" outfits the ladies favored in the trendier joints around the city.

The woman turned on the lights, most of which no longer worked to Mickey's dismay, then messed around opening and shutting the door, though Mickey didn't think she could see the fog like Mickey could.

Mickey let her gaze trail upward from the black high heels that accentuated shapely calves, over the fishnet stockings, lingering just above the woman's knees where black fringes teased a peek at her thighs and oh! Garters. Just the barest glimpse, but it set her pulse (or whatever passed for her as a pulse) racing. Mickey had always had a thing for women wearing garters. The blue dress had a plunging V-neckline, ample cleavage hidden only by a long string of white pearls. Long, satiny theater gloves drew attention to her well-toned arms, and tasteful makeup highlighted full lips and deep brown eyes.

She'd never gone for girls who followed trends before, but at that moment Mickey wanted nothing more than to engage her enchanting visitor in flirty conversation and see where the night might lead.

If only she could speak.

Or be seen.

Or do *anything* to get the woman's attention, dammit.

Determination seeped in, driving out the sadness and

loss, the frustration and confusion. This was *her* body or spirit or whatever she was. This was *her* place, *her* bar, her home and her sanctuary. Paul might have had some control over her in the house they'd shared. Society might dictate her actions on the street, but no one told her what she could and couldn't do here. Mickey *willed* herself to find some way to connect. When EZ's jaws opened and closed in a silent bark and he ran straight toward her, she knew she'd accomplished something, though she wasn't sure what until her visitor *looked right at her*.

Mickey couldn't turn her head, couldn't meet her gaze, but she knew she was being stared at, knew the beautiful woman was seeing her. Knew from the look of astonishment and no small amount of fear that her guest recognized she was experiencing something extraordinary . . . and so was Mickey.

The lovely lady said something to her, maybe "hello" from the motion of her lips, but of course Mickey couldn't respond. She hated that she had frightened her visitor. That hadn't been Mickey's intention at all. But what else had she expected? She was a ghost. People feared ghosts.

And yet . . . the woman approached, one small step at a time, but she kept coming until she stood directly in front of Mickey, staring up into Mickey's eyes.

Even though she couldn't adjust her angle of vision, Mickey still tried to take in every motion, every nuance in the woman's expression, noted the moment her eyes widened further as if something even more astounding than ghosthood had surprised her. She had no idea what that could have been. What could be more startling than standing toe to toe with a spirit?

The woman said something else, probably "hello" again, then waved a hand in front of Mickey's face and finally had a brief conversation with EZ. At one point, she thought the woman said Mickey's name. Had she put together that the sign over the bar, "Mickey's Speak EZ," was referring to her?

Pretty and smart. And so very feminine. Exactly Mickey's type.

And then the woman touched her. Or, well, her hand passed through Mickey's cheek, a failed attempt at a very intimate gesture.

Ohhhh . . . god . . .

Unlike every other living person who had passed through her unseen form, a touch from this particular woman sent heat coursing throughout Mickey's entire being. More sensual than satin, more intoxicating than an entire bottle of gin, more exhilarating perhaps than orgasm itself. Half of her wanted to writhe and squirm away while the other half begged to get closer, immerse herself, bathe in this one brief contact that ended so painfully fast and yet seemed to go on forever.

The surrealness of the moment was too much for the woman, whose eyes rolled up as her knees went weak, and she sank to the floor in a faint. But for Mickey . . .

In those few seconds, Mickey felt *alive.*

Her own world whited out, for how long she couldn't tell, but when Mickey returned to herself, her field of vision had shifted.

She was looking down—down at the woman only now regaining her senses. Their eyes met, really met. The woman mouthed something Mickey couldn't make out, then scrambled to her feet and raced from the room. EZ gave Mickey one last forlorn glance over his shoulder and followed her. The door to the bar slammed shut.

Don't go! Mickey tried to shout, but her mouth remained closed. She had to come back. She had to.

When that woman touched her, Mickey had moved. She'd managed to turn her head. Whatever it was that had happened between them, for that one moment it had given Mickey back her connection to the world.

Chapter 19

November 1, 2022

"HE'S A SHE. Mickey, I mean, is a girl, well, a woman, and a ghost. And he's . . . *she's* . . . in the Speak EZ right now. And she's hot. I mean, really hot, and—"

"Whoa! Whoa, girlfriend, slow down." Carlos held up both hands, palms forward, fending Ciara off. "One piece at a time. You saw another ghost?" He picked up the bottles he'd set aside and mixed another drink for one of the set crew.

Ciara bounced on the toes of her shoes, all the fringes on her flapper dress flying back and forth and up and down while she waited for the guy to leave and head back to the dance floor. Then she leaned over the bar, close to Carlos's ear. "Mickey's a woman. And her ghost is in the speakeasy, and she *looked* at me. Oh, and EZ is a live dog, but he was Mickey's, so he must have died, but he's alive again. I petted him!"

"O . . . kay . . ." He glanced over Ciara's shoulder and waved at someone behind her. Well, a couple of someones because Kate and Jeremy appeared on either side a moment later.

The party was still in full swing, though not as crowded since it was after midnight. She'd checked her phone as she ran up the basement stairs. Her faint had lasted maybe five minutes. "Hey guys, you gotta hear what just happened to me!" She repeated her story for the rest of her friends.

Carlos cocked his head from side to side, examining her from every angle. "She's not drunk," he said. "Believe me, I know drunk. I'm a bartender."

Jeremy frowned, eyebrows drawing together. "The dog is alive. Mickey is a woman. She's still dead. Your hand passed through her. Am I getting all that right? But then she looked at you, so she's *aware*?" He weaved a little where he stood.

Kate laughed and steadied him with one hand on his shoulder. "*You*, however, *are* drunk, loverboy. Good thing I'm driving." She turned to Ciara. "Do you think she's still there? The ghost? I mean it's one thing to encounter a ghost when you don't know it is one. It's totally different to go meet up with one intentionally." She considered for a moment, nodded once, pivoted on her heel, and marched toward the basement steps.

"Wait! Where are we going?" Jeremy raced to catch up with her, Ciara trailing close behind. Carlos tossed his bar towel to his assistant and took another break to follow them.

"To introduce ourselves to Mickey," Kate stated, ever direct. She started down the stairs, staying to one side to avoid the lovers still lingering there. "We can ask her who killed her. Short, sweet, and to the point. Case closed. Make it public, get her justice, problem solved. That might fix everything."

"I'd be happy if it would just fix the issues with the lighting system. Angry ghosts aren't good for electronics," Jeremy groused, his words slurring a bit. The fake Tommy gun he carried bounced against his hip as he descended the stairs.

"But what if... what if I don't want—" Ciara broke off when Carlos reached the same step she stood on, a few hops down from the last in a line of couples making out.

"Hey, girlfriend," he said gently while the others drew farther away, oblivious to their pause. "Hot or not, she's a ghost. Not exactly partner material, right?"

Ciara leaned against the cinderblock wall, the chill of the stone raising goosebumps between her bare shoulder blades. Of course, he was right. What had she even been thinking? Except . . . there'd been a connection. She'd felt it. Though what *it* was, she had no idea. Attraction for certain, and it seemed to run both ways judging from Mickey's gaze.

She wanted to get to know that woman. Even if it meant nothing, which of course had to be the case. Wishing for anything more was self-destructive and selfish in the extreme.

Mickey was dead. Mickey's spirit was somehow trapped in the theater. It was Ciara's and her friends' responsibility to help her move on.

"How do you know me so well?" she whispered, embarrassed.

Carlos grinned. "Because besides drunk, I know lonely when I see it. Because before Renaldo came along, I was having the longest dry spell of my young and handsome life." The grin faded. "But I also know lost causes, and sweetheart, this is about the most lost of any cause I've ever seen."

Ciara managed a small laugh, but it fell flat. "You're right. I know. But she appeared to me. I want to understand why me and why not sooner."

Crooking his arm at the elbow, Carlos shifted away to face down the stairs. "Well then, let's find out."

She took his arm and let him lead her down the stairs, grateful for the support. She hadn't realized it until now, but her knees still shook from the earlier encounter. She stopped again. "Where's EZ?" Ciara looked up the stairs, then down them again. "He followed me out of the bar. I'm sure of it. I remember hearing his toenails on the stairs. Did you see him come out into the lobby?"

Carlos shook his head. From about a dozen steps down, at the bottom, Kate glanced back over her shoulder at them. "There were a lot of people milling around, and between the dim overheads and the strobes a little dog would have been hard to spot. I'm sure he's around."

As if on cue, the overhead bulbs flickered, making Ciara wonder if EZ had returned to his ghost-dog status. "Hmm." But Carlos pulled her along, and they joined the others inside the main space on the subbasement level. The door to the speakeasy stood shut.

"Um, I didn't close that door." Her voice came out as a scratchy whisper. She remembered running, and EZ chasing after her, and then a slam. But she hadn't done that, and Mickey was neither mobile enough nor tangible enough to have shut it behind her. Again, she had the oddest feeling there was something more going on here, another presence at work beyond Mickey and EZ. The killer maybe?

Ciara shook her head. Answers weren't going to reveal themselves. She needed to find them. Determined, she marched across the open space and wiggled the doorknob. It was unlocked.

"I didn't stop to lock it either," she admitted as her friends gathered with her.

"Understandable given the circumstances," Carlos said.

She opened the door.

The four of them crowded into the entryway and peered into the speakeasy. The lights glowed warmly over the bar and dance floor areas, not a trace of flicker, though the ones over the tables remained out. There was no sign of Mickey's ghost. They let out a collective breath.

"You've been using the original lighting?" Kate asked, a trace of admonishment in her tone.

"It feels right," Ciara said without apology. "And the ceiling bulbs are harder to shift around," she confessed. "While I appreciate the clues, I'd rather not have the startle factor. There haven't been any sparks, shattering, or smoky smells. I promise."

Kate frowned but nodded. "Fine. But at the first sign of problems, switch them off and go with the spots we brought down. We do not need a fire down here." She stepped farther into the room.

"So where is she?" Jeremy asked, stepping inside and wandering around, though Ciara noted he avoided the shadows.

She shrugged. "Gone. But she was standing right there." Ciara pointed at the end of the bar and shuddered when she realized exactly where *there* was. "Where we think she died," she finished in a whisper.

"Makes sense," Carlos said, going to stand in that exact spot without hesitation. He was using his investigator voice again. He stared at the floor, then looked at Ciara. "You said she was all dressed up? Like for a special occasion?"

Ciara let the tantalizing memory of the striking figure Mickey had cut in that pinstripe suit wash over her. When she described Mickey's appearance, Ciara's skin tingled. Her cheeks flushed with heat.

Kate waved a hand in front of her face. "Earth to Ciara!" She laughed. "Well, we've solved one mystery anyway. Now we know Ciara's type, that's for sure—handsome well-dressed butch."

"And dead. Let's not forget dead," Jeremy chimed in. He belched.

Kate rolled her eyes. "While I'm apparently into semi-cute guys who have no manners."

"*Semi*-cute?"

"I never was before," Ciara said softly, cutting off the impending squabble.

"What was that?" Carlos dragged his shoe through the dust covering the dance floor making a wide arch, then strolled to her side. Ciara blinked. They'd mopped it only a few days ago. How had it gotten so dirty again so soon? She discarded the thought. Erasing a hundred years of grime would take more than a cursory brush with a Swiffer Wet.

"I said that handsome butches weren't my type . . . until now," she admitted. "My last three girlfriends, well, my only three girlfriends, they were all femmes."

125

"Huh," Kate said, musing. "Maybe that's why they're your exes."

"Or maybe someone slipped her a *Mickey*!" Jeremy hooted with laughter at his own joke, carrying on far longer than the one-liner warranted.

Kate shook her head. "You've been waiting to drop that one since we were upstairs, haven't you?" She paused. "Seriously though. You don't think this spirit cast some kind of spell on you, do you?"

Ciara met her eyes. "No, I don't. The ghost could barely move, couldn't speak, and I don't think she could hear me, either. If she had the power to control me, I doubt she'd be in this situation in the first place."

"And speaking of this situation," Carlos announced, raising his voice, "I was trying to make a point."

"Oooh, I'm sorry, Detective. You may now continue cracking the case." Jeremy gave a slight bow from the waist, almost toppling over in the process. Kate righted him with a firm grip on his shoulder.

Unperturbed, Carlos continued. "Whereas we only had a working theory that Mickey was killed on New Year's Eve, we can now add more credence to that assumption."

Ciara cocked an eyebrow at him. "You know, your vocabulary increases when you're in private eye mode."

He waved his hands in the air as if dispelling smoke. "Whatever. The point is, you said Mickey was wearing a full suit, jacket and pants, dress shoes, and that she looked . . . How did you put it? Oh yes, hot. Really hot."

Ciara covered her face with her hands. "Yes." Her voice came out muffled.

"She was dressed up for a special occasion. New Year's Eve."

Without warning, the calendar on the wall dropped from the hook that had held it a hundred years and slapped onto the tile floor. The bulb above it flickered and went out.

· Kate folded her arms over her chest. "It's like someone's telling us we've learned all we need to from that clue. Like, 'move on.'"

The bulb over the end of the bar brightened, then dimmed. It too went out, leaving the one over the radio as the only remaining light in the room. "We've identified the location, too, at the end of the bar. We don't need that one anymore, either," Ciara confirmed.

As one, the quartet turned to stare at the radio.

Chapter 20

November 1, 2022

WITHIN TWENTY MINUTES, they'd tried everything. With Kate standing by ready to do who knew what, Ciara snapped the dial of the radio into the on position. Nothing. Jeremy peered into its depths through one of the speakers using his phone's light. "There're tubes in there. Honest to god tubes. I haven't seen those since I tried to repair my great-grandparents' television set. If it was working, they'd light up. This thing's as dead as Mickey is."

Kate elbowed him in the ribs. "Show a little respect, dumbass. We don't want the strapping butch ghost angry at us."

Ciara considered that. Mickey had possessed some impressive biceps and abs from what she could see through the jacket and shirt. Running lights all day and a bar at night must have kept her very fit. She knew Kate was in great shape, and she held only one of those jobs.

Jeremy eyed the single working lightbulb overhead as if waiting for it to shatter. "Nope. Nothing. Mickey has a thick skin. I mean, if she still has skin." This time Ciara elbowed him.

Carlos held out both hands in a calming gesture. "All right, what else can we try? Are we sure it's plugged in?"

Ciara felt around behind the radio, squeaking a little when she encountered some dead spiders and a lot of dust. She traced the cord to a wall socket where its round head was inserted. "Yep," she called over her shoulder.

"Welp, that's it then." Kate turned on her phone and checked the time. "One thirty. We have work later today. Let's call it. I'll ask some of the crew if anyone knows anything about old radios. Maybe someone's an enthusiast."

"Can't you fix it?" Carlos asked.

"I'm a tinkerer. I mess around with old tech until I get lucky with it. I don't want to leave something this important to trial and error. I could end up damaging it beyond repair if it isn't already."

Ciara paused en route to the door. "We don't want to bring anyone else in on this, though, right?"

Kate nodded. "Right. If someone comes forward, I'll just say I found it on eBay or in a thrift store or something and see if they can fix it for me. Or we can always take it to an expert." She squinted at the ceiling. "And I'll bring some replacement bulbs for the ones that blew. We really need more light in here."

Jeremy sneezed, then waved his hand in front of his face. "And more cleaning. Definitely more cleaning. I swear the dust bunnies are reproducing like . . . well, bunnies. Yeah, I'm officially wiped out. That was a terrible joke. See you guys later." He squeezed past Ciara into the outer space with the doors to the other storerooms. Carlos followed. A moment later they heard the guys clomping up the stairs.

"Let me take care of the bulbs," Ciara said when Kate moved to leave. "I saw some old-timey ones online when I was looking at 1920s fashion. Pretty much anything and everything 1920s style came up in that search." She glanced at the ceiling and around the filthy but lovingly appointed bar. "We should try to keep this place as authentic as possible. Mickey would want it that way."

"And since when do you know what Mickey would want?" Kate said gently, then waved her comment away. "Go for it," she said. She was halfway to the stairs when she stopped again. "You coming? I gotta run if I'm gonna stop Jeremy from driving himself home."

Ciara shooed her with both hands. "Just need to check the wattage for the bulbs. There's at least one I can reach without a ladder. I'll lock up."

The expression on Kate's face spoke of uncertainty, but she gave a curt nod and took off up the stairs behind her boyfriend.

For a long moment, Ciara stood in the doorway of the speakeasy, waiting for she didn't know what. The bass music drifting down from the upstairs floors abruptly stopped, the party ending. She and her friends weren't the only ones who had to work later today. A few more footfalls sounded on the stairs as the make-out couples grumbled their way to the lobby.

She was alone. A shiver passed through her. Or was it more a tingle of anticipation? Yes, she'd screamed when Mickey's ghost moved and looked at her. Yes, she'd run. But those actions had been more out of surprise than fear. She'd sensed no malice, no threat in Mickey's expression, only concern. Concern for her, lying on the floor at Mickey's feet.

Her cheeks flushed when she thought about what she'd rather have been doing at Mickey's feet. Exasperated with her runaway emotions, she shoved those feelings away.

Mickey was dead, her spirit trapped for a hundred years. Ciara couldn't imagine a lonelier, more frustrating, more horrible fate. And yet the bar owner had been worried about Ciara.

She stepped inside the speakeasy, almost expecting Mickey to reappear in the spot where she'd died, but nothing changed. The tables and chairs, bottles and glassware sat silent and still as they had since the day the door had been hidden behind the façade.

While she didn't really believe it, a small part of her did

have to question whether tonight's events had been some sort of dream or hallucination. Could she have imagined what occurred between her and EZ? Between her and Mickey? She hadn't had that much to drink, but, all bad puns aside, someone could have slipped her something. Her fascination with the photo of the set crew in the hall outside her office might have played on her mind. She wished she knew where EZ had taken off to. Having him here now would have gone a long way toward making the night's events real.

She crossed the room to the wall calendar and stared up at the bulb hanging above it. Unlike the others, this bulb had been set into an upside-down wall sconce sort of thing, positioned intentionally to illuminate the calendar or any other decorative piece Mickey might have chosen to hang there.

She glanced at the calendar itself, folded in half on the floor, the January beauty grinning up at her from the past, and laughed. The bar owner had created a warm and inviting environment in the Speak EZ, but her taste in art left something to be desired. Couldn't she at least have hung a painting of dogs drinking whiskey and playing poker or something? Still, it had been Mickey's choice, and it didn't belong where it was, even if Mickey's ghost had knocked it down.

She found the nail it had hung on lying by one of the tables and set it back in its hole. Looking around, she searched for something to bang it in with, but she didn't want to damage any antiques. Ciara settled for the bottom of her shoe, pounding in the nail until she couldn't wiggle it with her fingers. She set the calendar triumphantly back in its place. Now to the job she'd really come for.

Even in its lower position, Ciara had to drag over one of the bar chairs and kneel up on its seat in order to reach the bulb. She untwisted it from its socket carefully, not wanting to break it off in the holder. With it safely in her palm, she scrambled down, tucked it into her purse, and headed for the door which she'd left wide open. Just in case.

Except, she didn't want to leave. Something unseen and intangible tugged at her, urging her to stay a little longer. And Ciara had a pretty good idea what that something or *someone* might be. And yes, it did occur to her to wonder if giving in was a healthy move, but she shifted direction and seated herself cross-legged in the spot where Mickey's body had fallen.

Closing her eyes, she tried to picture the handsome butch. It wasn't difficult. Every sensuous detail had been etched into her brain. She opened her eyes, again expecting her to appear, but she remained alone. It had to have happened. There'd been too many other weird occurrences like talking with Antoine after his death. And lots of people had encountered EZ.

But why had Mickey appeared only to her? And why wouldn't she come back if everything inside Ciara told her Mickey wanted her here?

Maybe the ghost had limits. She clearly had restrictions on her movement. Could Mickey have used up some sort of ghostly energy in turning her head to check on Ciara? Was that why she hadn't returned?

Stretching her legs out in front of her, Ciara drew lines in the dance floor dust with the heel of one shoe. The disturbed specks danced like fireflies in the light of the remaining bulb, then resettled. When nothing further supernatural occurred, she finally stood and gathered herself to go home.

Checking to make sure she wasn't leaving anything, she realized her wandering thoughts had caused her to trace a message across the square of parquet wood flooring.

ARE YOU REAL

Ciara bent over and added a proper question mark to the note, smiled faintly to herself, turned out the light, and left the bar. It didn't surprise her at all when clicking toenails trailed behind her as she headed up the stairs.

Six hours later, sleep-fogged and bleary-eyed, Ciara returned to the theater, EZ on her heels. When she encountered Kate in the lobby, she didn't know which of them was more startled—Kate, who jumped back three feet when she spotted the dog, or Ciara, who expected to have a few hours to herself before the rest of the crew staggered in at the delayed start time that the bosses had sympathetically set for today.

Kate had a wrapped bundle in her arms—a bundle about radio-sized. She juggled it precariously before regaining her balance and eyed the canine. "You found him, I see," was all she said, though her voice held a slight tremor and her cheeks had lost some color. Even when she wasn't in control, she pretended to be.

Unable to resist, Ciara scooped EZ into her arms. The dog went willingly, licking her cheek when held close enough. He'd spent the night on her bed, curled against her back. She'd need to invest in a leash, collar, and some other doggy necessities at some point, and she needed to take him out to the alley where she'd left his food, but for now she thrust him toward Kate. "Yep! Wanna pet him?"

"Yaaaah!" Kate backpedaled farther, using the radio as a makeshift shield. "No. Um, no. Hands are full." She nodded at the antique in her arms.

Taking pity on her, Ciara cuddled EZ to her chest. "He's just a dog, Kate. Any luck with that?"

"One of my team recommended a guy. I'm walking it over there now." She started for the front double doors, then stopped. "You left the bar unlocked, by the way. Be more careful. I've told the rest of the staff that the subbasement is off-limits, but we don't want someone poking around down there."

"Oh! Right. Sorry." Ciara thought back to the night before.

No, she didn't think she'd locked up like she'd promised. "Guess that's something Mickey and I have in common. I won't let it happen again."

Kate cocked her head. "What do you mean? What do you have in common?"

Ciara hesitated. What *had* she meant? The words had tumbled out without her thinking. "I guess I figured Mickey must have accidentally left the door unlocked the night of her death, and that's how the killer got in. Though now that I think about it, I suppose she might have known her killer and let him or her into the bar herself." But somehow that didn't feel right.

"Well, however it happened, the killer either took the key off Mickey after shooting her, or already had a copy, because the bar was locked when we first found it."

"Then how did EZ get it?"

The dog barked at the sound of his name but wasn't forthcoming with answers.

Kate eyed him. "Who knows? Maybe the killer threw it away after hiding the bar, and EZ found it. Or again, maybe there were two keys and EZ had one of them while the killer had the other." She shrugged. "Oh, hey, what's up with that weird note you left in the dust? That was you, right? We aren't receiving written messages from beyond now, are we?"

Ciara laughed. "Nope, just mind wandering and doodling while I thought things through." Though she wondered what was so weird about "Are you real?" Seemed like a reasonable question to write under the circumstances.

"Huh, almost a shame, that. This whole thing would be a lot easier to solve if we could ask Mickey who killed her." Kate backed her way through the double doors, descended the front steps, and headed off down the street.

Ciara placed EZ on the floor and wandered to the subbasement with him right behind her. Since she had the only key (that was available anyway), the door to the bar remained unlocked. Stepping inside, she flipped on the one remaining bulb and added a couple of spotlights to the mix until her online special order could arrive tomorrow.

The modern lighting destroyed the warm ambience of the speakeasy, casting everything in harsh glaring white, but it couldn't be helped. She needed to see if she was going to continue investigating.

Her sneakers squeaked across the tile as she made her way behind the bar and laid her palms flat on its surface. Standing there, she tried to view the place as Mickey would have, and a sense of pride suffused her—channeling Mickey? Or mere empathy? She had no idea.

"Dammit, I could use another clue while Kate gets your radio working," she murmured, letting her gaze rest on the tables and chairs, the door to the tiny bathroom, the dance floor . . . "Oh. Um, thanks."

There, in the dust, someone had erased the word "real" and added an underscore, leaving the message as:

ARE YOU   ?

Well. This changed things. Communication was possible, though apparently about as limited as the spirit's movement. In fact, it was probably limited *by* the spirit's movement. Instead of writing a whole new question, Mickey had used as much of the existing message as she could to minimize how many lines she had to draw in the dust.

So much for cleaning. Ciara wasn't touching a single speck on that dance floor. Instead, she plunked herself on a barstool and tried to come up with how she wanted to ask a hundred-year-old ghost who her murderer was.

Chapter 21

????

MICKEY HAD NO idea how much time had passed between last seeing the beautiful woman in her bar and opening her eyes to the second message scrawled in the dust on the dance floor. With the first one, one moment it was clean, polished by a brisk mopping she guessed had been done by the strangers who had begun wandering in and out. The next, dust had blanketed it once more—unnatural dust, it seemed, since it appeared so quickly. Then again, as she'd already realized, she was currently a terrible judge of the passage of time.

She had the distinct impression things happened all around her while her transparent and, more often than not, invisible body froze and her mind along with it. In fact, she suspected she'd been in some kind of limbo for a very long time before the quartet of friends rediscovered her safe haven and initiated her reawakening.

But now she had a new impetus—hope. First, she'd watched them, consciously watched. Then she'd managed a brief appearance and a shift of her head and eyes. The writing had proven more difficult. It had taken hours to figure out how to solidify her palm enough to wipe out the "real" and underline the "you," and hours more to shift herself, inch by torturous inch, into position to actually do it. But Mickey would take hours. It beat the hell out of days or weeks.

Or years.

She could move. If she really put her mind to it, she could move. The touch of that gorgeous woman had shown her the way to focus her thoughts and move. And she felt that if she were touched again, it might become easier. Except they kept missing each other. Mickey would appear and find the bar empty, but signs of visitors remained.

And Mickey didn't know why.

But now there was a new message, and that had Mickey's full attention because it confirmed everything she thought she remembered.

WHO KILLED YOU?

The only problem, of course, was the movement required for her to respond. Damn, why did everything have to be so hard? It took the better part of what she thought was a day for her to wipe the words away and add two more question marks to the first.

Because she had no idea.

When Ciara found three question marks waiting for her in the dust, she groaned. Clearly, Mickey couldn't identify her killer. Worse, this wasn't working. She could write paragraphs about herself and her friends and their efforts to help. She could even leave an actual printed note on paper. But if Mickey couldn't communicate back more than a letter or symbol or two at a time, it became useless.

Still, she made the effort and typed up an accounting of all that they'd figured out so far. She introduced herself and her friends. She explained what she knew about EZ somehow coming back to life and that they were trying to find a way to get Mickey unstuck, though whether or not that meant Mickey would end up in her own time, or Ciara's time, alive, or somewhere in the afterlife, whatever that may be, Ciara admitted she didn't know. But it stood to reason that if EZ had found a way to escape death, maybe Mickey could, too.

Some combination of supernatural events had let the dog have the life he deserved. There had to be rules, a method, a path, maybe certain actions they had to perform in a specific order. They just didn't know what they were.

"It's like one of those escape rooms," Jeremy had commented, referring to the current craze sweeping the world where people allowed themselves to be placed in what amounted to a room-sized puzzle box and they had to overcome a variety of mental and sometimes physical obstacles in order to get out.

He wasn't wrong.

The one thing Ciara left out of her note, however, was exactly how much time had passed. Ciara didn't think Mickey had figured that out. There was no reason she should have. The speakeasy had no windows, no working clocks, and no access to the outside world. And Ciara didn't want to be the one to break it to Mickey that everything and everyone she'd known, with the exception of EZ, were gone.

If she knew that, Mickey might prefer to try to remain in 1924. If it was even possible.

In the meantime, Ciara had continued her research in the old files to see if they led to any clues as to who Mickey's murderer might have been, but she'd found very little: an unclaimed January 1924 bonus check, some memos going back and forth between the bookkeeper and the managers of that time discussing letting Mickey (Michelle) go since she hadn't been showing up for work even though she'd always been an exemplary employee, and records documenting their attempts to contact Mickey's brother, Paul (listed as Officer Paul McFadden)—which gave them a new trail to follow.

Kate and Jeremy were working on getting the radio repaired. They'd taken it to three different people so far. So she turned her new lead over to Carlos.

"I think I've got something here," Carlos called from his sprawled position across one of the theater lobby's couches.

The four of them had settled into a routine. For the past two days, they'd brought their laptops with them to work. During lunch breaks, they met up in Ciara's office where they could access the building's public Wi-Fi and have privacy. After work, they'd migrate to the lobby and its comfortable seating to continue their searches.

The others stood to crowd behind Carlos on his chosen couch so they could see his screen.

"There isn't much. A copy of a birth certificate. She was born in 1894 in New York City. At some point, probably around 1899, her family moved because they appear on later census records as living here. The census lists her parents, Sean and Elizabeth, and a brother, Paul, who's two years older than Mickey. Then, there's a whole lot of nothing until a notice of her parents' deaths in 1910 during a flu epidemic."

He looked over his shoulder at the others. "Damn, that must have been tough, losing both parents at sixteen. I'm guessing her brother finished raising her. He would have been old enough at eighteen and viewed fully as an adult at that time. After that, she disappears until a brief mention in a list of the crew and other staff on the theater's opening day in January 1915." He glanced at Ciara. "You'll have better luck finding more on her if you continue to dig through the physical files in those dust-covered boxes. Sorry. Today, everybody records everything. If she were from this generation, I could probably tell you what she had for breakfast five years ago. But for any records to have survived on someone from the 1920s, they would have had to have done something remarkable that someone saw fit to preserve and eventually scan into a computer."

"Yeah, that makes sense," Kate put in. "She's a trailblazer in her actions with running a speakeasy and her appearance, but she's a quiet fighter. Her protesting the status quo took the form of surreptitious accomplishments. I'm sure she had an impact on the community, but it was all behind the scenes." She laughed. "Just like her day job working set crew and lights for the stage."

Carlos nodded. "Right. But look at this." He clicked a different open tab displaying a scan of a creased and yellowed time sheet. "You said Mickey's brother became a cop, and I think I found him." He pointed at the screen. Ciara squinted. Time had faded the inked names and numbers in some places and erased it entirely in others, but piecing bits together, she could figure out it was a copy of police shift rosters from 1924. About a third of the way down, Carlos had highlighted the name Paul McFadden in yellow. He worked the night shift, at least during the month of November 1923.

"Wow, that's an incredible find," Ciara praised him, leaning in farther. "Is there really nothing else on him or Mickey, though?"

Carlos held up a hand to forestall her whining disappointment. "Don't give up all hope just yet. I've only gone through the official databases, and even then, only the ones that are open to public access. I haven't tackled newspapers. I'll start on those tomorrow. Maybe one of the siblings did something noteworthy."

She nodded, and they all sat in silence for a moment. It had been an incredible couple of weeks. Ciara broke their reverie. "I wonder what her brother was like."

Ciara. Mickey let the name flow through her thoughts like a melody carried on a spring breeze. *Her name is Ciara. And she is trying to save me.*

The rest of the lengthy letter faded into the background with the discovery of the beautiful woman's name. She forced herself to focus, taking in all the information, as well as the thoughtful way in which it was delivered to her.

Ciara had somehow typed paragraph after paragraph of details about herself, her friends, and what they were doing and had done so far in very large letters, then spread the pages in neat rows across the tile floor right in front of the spot where Mickey found herself appearing—the spot where she'd died. Mickey tried to envision the size of the typewriter that would have produced such printing and failed. How had she done this?

She brushed her curiosity away. Not important right now. Funny how, when you were dead, a lot of things lost their importance. Living was what mattered because not only did she know now from EZ's success that it might be possible, but she also had encountered a woman who made her feel more than any other woman had. She desperately wanted to meet her, and she was determined to find a way to reclaim the life that had been stolen from her.

The size of the print and the way the pages had been placed meant Mickey merely had to incline her head downward to read all of it. So Ciara understood Mickey's limitations. Good. It had become so tiring trying to draw letters in the dust. She didn't want to waste the energy she had.

Once she'd finished reading, however, her melancholy returned. They knew so little. *She* knew so little. Mickey had few people who disliked her, let alone hated her enough to kill.

Sure, she squabbled with the other members of the set crew sometimes, had to escort an unruly customer upstairs and send him home, fought with her sibling over stupid things like her short hair and mannish clothes, broke up with Annie ... though Annie had broken up with her. It had been Annie's choice.

Except . . . Annie had been hanging around the bar for a few months before New Year's, trying to get Mickey's attention again. Mickey had ignored her, but . . . something new had happened between them, hadn't it? A shouting match over . . .

Mickey wanted to blow out a breath or shake her head in frustration at her patchy memory, but of course she could do neither without more effort than she wanted to expend. And there'd been another altercation, too.

She studied the rows of liquor bottles on the shelves behind the bar, barely within range of her peripheral vision. Her alcohol supplier, or more accurately her alcohol smuggler, had stopped in before Christmas. They'd disagreed—over shipments? Prices? She couldn't remember.

Why couldn't she remember? How long had it been?

And why had Ciara left that very important detail out of her lengthy note?

Unless it had been a very, very long time.

Chapter 22

November 7, 2022

"THERE'S NOT A thing wrong with it," Kate stated, standing in Ciara's office doorway with her hands on her hips.

EZ lifted his head from where he lay curled on the dog bed Ciara had set in the corner, yawned showing all his teeth, and lowered it again. He closed his eyes, uninterested in human drama.

Ciara set down her coffee mug, the one that had a rainbow on the side with the words "So Over It" printed beneath. Let staff and investors interpret that as they would. "Wrong with what? The lightboard? And it's your day off." They'd had the manufacturer's repair guy in to look it over when the lights continued to turn on and off and flicker at inopportune moments during performances. There'd been an uptick in glitches since she'd encountered Mickey on Halloween.

She and Kate and Jeremy knew exactly what was going on. Mickey or whatever other spirit had been active in the speakeasy was growing impatient. But they had to call in the big guns for a cover story. Otherwise, it would have seemed odd for them not to and might have warranted a visit from the owners. And they didn't need that.

"It's your day off too and, no, not the lightboard. Well, not *only* the lightboard. That, too," Kate grumbled, stepping inside. She perched one hip on the edge of Ciara's desk. "Damn repair guy took the whole board apart and had to scramble to get it back together before yesterday's matinee. Stayed into overtime to do it. Worked a Sunday morning. Guess I can't fault him since he did that. But it all checked out. He blamed the wiring in the walls of this 'ancient artifact' as he called our theater."

She frowned. "No, I'm talking about the radio. Three antique radio experts in this town. Jeremy and I took it to all three. Nothing wrong with it. They checked every part, didn't even need to replace anything." She stood again and puffed out her chest. "Don't make 'em like this anymore," she said in a lower voice. "Each of them plugged it in and picked up local stations, though the speakers are kind of tinny, but every time I'd bring it back and try it downstairs, 'cause you're always leaving the darn door open." She paused to glare at Ciara who blushed. "And it wouldn't turn on, and I'd have to take it to the next guy. None of them could explain why it wouldn't work here."

"That's really weird." Ciara picked up a pencil and twirled it between her fingers. "Then again, everything is weird around here."

Kate shrugged. "Anyway, I put it back in the bar. Didn't want you freaking out when it appeared there. And also, you left the door unlocked again."

"Oh! Sorry. I was distracted." She had been, too, sitting on one of the stools and daydreaming about what it must have been like to sit there and sip a drink and chat with Mickey the way normal people would instead of trying to communicate with printouts and dust writing.

Kate poked her gently in the shoulder and grinned. "Yeah, I bet you were. Gotta run. No other updates, and Carlos said to tell you he hasn't found anything new, either." She slid off the desk and left the office.

A glance at her phone told her it was lunchtime, so Ciara headed down to the subbasement with her brown paper bag and a can of Coke Zero from the minifridge she kept in the corner opposite EZ's new bed. As if he knew where she was going, EZ jumped up and followed.

Or maybe he was hoping for scraps of her bologna and cheese sandwich and chips.

She grimaced. Not nearly as wonderful as Antoine's café, but she hadn't been back *there* since she'd found out about Antoine's death. The thought of eating in a haunted restaurant ruined her appetite.

And that made her stop halfway down the stairs and lean against the cinderblock wall because she was laughing so hard she had tears rolling from her eyes. Because at that very moment, she was taking her lunch to eat in a haunted speakeasy.

Well, Mickey's ghost was a far sight cuter than Antoine's.

She pushed off the wall and continued down, her sneakers squeaking on the concrete stairs and the floor below. EZ danced in little circles around her, almost tripping her as she crossed to the hidden door. Kate was right. It was unlocked.

She really needed to be more careful about that.

Once she and EZ were inside, she flipped on the lights with the replacement bulbs she'd installed, shut the door behind her, and locked it with the key from her jeans pocket, then took her regular seat at the bar. The view hadn't changed from the last five days she'd done exactly this: bar, bottles, glassware, the tables and chairs reflected in the mirror behind the shelves. Only now the empty spot where the radio sat had been refilled, the dormant piece of ancient technology dark and silent.

Now that all the fixtures worked, the speakeasy felt even more warm and welcoming. No more dark corners and shadowy spots. But it also meant no more tricks of the flickering lights, movement where there should be none, hints that another thinking, feeling being might be present.

Ciara was alone. Ciara missed Mickey.

How could she miss someone she hadn't even properly met?

Her hands stilled with the bologna sandwich halfway to her mouth. She didn't even remember unwrapping it from the plastic.

Something *was* moving. *In the mirror.*

She'd been so fixated on the radio, she'd missed it at first—shifting forms, blurs and blobs more than distinct shapes, floating first around the entry to the speakeasy and then between the tables and chairs, weaving their way ... to the table closest to the bar where she sat.

Ciara whirled around on the stool so fast she nearly slid off. Her sandwich went flying, the layers separating in midair to land scattered across the black tile: bread, meat, cheese, bread. EZ scrambled from his spot by her seat, going for the cheese first and foremost, wolfing down the cheddar like she never fed him even though she always kept his bowl full.

She stared across the seating area, balancing herself upright with her spine rigid against the bar's edge.

There was no one else in the Speak EZ.

Ciara spun back. Yes, the figures still moved about in the mirror, only they'd resolved themselves into discernible people— Mickey, and some tall, broad man, both carrying what looked like crates full of bottles, which they set on one of the larger tables. Ciara's head swiveled back and forth between the real room and the reflected one so fast she made herself dizzy. The two separate but distinct realities utterly confounded her.

And they *were* realities. Both of them—the bar in 2022, and the bar in ... 1923? Had to be before Mickey's death. The colors of the people in the mirror were vibrant, lifelike ... no, *alive*, not washed out like Mickey had seemed when Ciara encountered her on Halloween. And animate. Very animate. Handsomely animate. She admired the ripple of Mickey's biceps when she eased the heavy crate onto the round wooden surface, the way her trousers stretched over a firm backside when she bent at the waist. She'd rolled her sleeves up to the tops of her shoulders, so Ciara could view every flex and release, though she heard no sound.

Like watching a silent movie.

The two figures paused for a moment, the man reaching into a pocket of his overalls to remove a rag and mop his forehead while Mickey barely seemed winded by all the exertion. Then they faced one another across the table.

Ciara climbed off the barstool, rounded the end of the bar, and approached the mirror slowly, cautiously, wondering if they could see her the way she could see them, but they weren't looking in her direction, so she couldn't tell. No, they were very focused on one another, and judging from their postures, sharp hand gestures, and the rapidity of the movements of their mouths, they were having an argument.

Mickey waved an arm at the bottles in the crate. She indicated one with a green and gold label. Then she pulled out another with a bright blue label and a fancy red cork, held it up, and pointed at the wording printed on its surface. Meanwhile, the man drew a sheaf of papers and a pen from another pocket. He flipped the sheets back and forth in front of Mickey's face like an angry fan and slapped them on the table. She shook her head, dropped the bottle back into the crate, snatched the pen from him, and crossed out several things Ciara couldn't make out from that distance, then threw the pen down. He slapped his palm on the back of the nearest chair, sweeping the papers off the table's surface to scatter into the air like giant moths. They got caught up in the breeze from one of the standing fans—the ones that still stood in the bar. Ciara hadn't had the courage to try turning one on yet. This blew the papers all over the place, across tables and empty chairs and the tile floor.

One slid under the bar through the narrow crack between its base and the floor. Mickey didn't seem to notice.

The argument continued for several minutes, one pacing away from the table, then the other, and back again. Mickey with her arms crossed over her chest, staring the man down. It was all like watching an elaborate pantomime, the meaning of which the audience was challenged to interpret for themselves.

"Well," Ciara murmured, glad to hear any human voice, even if it was only her own, "this sure beats Netflix all to hell. Wish they'd turn the volume up, though."

EZ barked once in agreement.

The figures in the mirror gave no indication they'd heard so at the very least Mickey and the man couldn't hear EZ and herself. She still didn't know if they could see her, though. They hadn't once looked in her direction.

The posturing and apparent shouting went on until the man reached in a different pocket, this one low on his right hip, and Mickey froze in place. He never removed whatever he'd been reaching for, but Mickey slowly shook her head, reached for the pen, gathered whatever papers were still in reach, including picking up a couple from the floor, and signed them one by one. Ciara would swear she could imagine the harsh scratch the pen made against the paper from the way Mickey's arm jerked through each signature.

Mickey thrust the collection of forms back at the man's chest. He removed his hand from his pocket, empty, and took them, sorted them into a neat pile, and tucked them away. With a self-satisfied smirk, he turned and left through the entry door.

Chapter 23

"THIS ISN'T GOING to work," Carlos said, standing in the center of the dance floor, watching Jeremy slide an unbent coat hanger into the space beneath the bar while Kate and Ciara knelt on either side of the bar watching for the paper's emergence.

"Of course it is," Jeremy said. "It was my idea."

"Would paper even last that long?"

Ciara glanced up from the inch of space on her side and glared at Carlos, though she knew her glare lacked effect. Raising one hand she pointed from the calendar they'd hung back on the wall to a stack of dusty napkins on the shelf behind the bar to the open office doorway leading to a desk covered in notes and memos. On paper. Carlos had the good grace to look sheepish.

"Okay, so it might still be there. But—"

Something rustled and crinkled beneath the bar as Jeremy swept the extended hanger back and forth, the metal scraping and squeaking like chalk on an old-fashioned chalkboard across the tile. A moment later, something flat and yellowed slid into Ciara's hands.

"Got it!" she called, scrambling to her feet with the treasure held gently between her thumb and forefinger. Carlos reached down a hand to lift her by the elbow, then moved with her to the closest table—the same one Mickey and the burly man had been arguing over.

Ciara laid the single sheet in the center of the table's surface while Kate shook her phone twice to activate its flashlight since the overhead bulbs were warm but dim like a bar's would be. The result was disappointing.

Jeremy shook his head. "Most of the ink's faded away. Not a surprise, but I thought maybe with the room sealed—"

"Time is time," Kate said. "Things wear away. This isn't a tomb."

"Well, it sort of is," Carlos muttered. Ciara smacked him on the arm. He grimaced and shut up.

They stared at the gridded sheet, clearly an invoice of some kind, with a list of items that were no longer legible, though Ciara thought she could make out the word "rum," and another squiggle looked like "vodka" misspelled as "vokda." The paper was thinner in some places, and scratch marks were evident where Mickey had angrily crossed several items out. There were even a couple of spots where her pen had gone through, leaving jagged holes.

Mickey had been really mad at her visitor.

"Whoever wrote this out had the penmanship of a third grader," Kate commented. "It would be hard to read even *without* the years fading the ink."

"Look! There's Mickey's name!" Jeremy exclaimed, pointing to the second line down and a blob that might have read "Mickey McFadden" printed not signed. Mickey had never signed this invoice. He cocked his head at Ciara. "You really saw all this happen in the mirror?"

They turned as one toward the glass, but of course they saw only themselves. Carlos waved to their reflections. Jeremy waved back. Kate smacked them both.

"Yes," Ciara breathed, exhausted. It was late, around seven.

150

She'd had to text them all. Kate had already gone home, and the others came in from wherever they had been, Jeremy smelling like coffee as usual for a Monday. They'd ordered in Chinese—no one else wanted to go back to Antoine's, either. She'd told them what happened over kung pow pork and fried rice and egg rolls, and they'd wanted to find the lost page.

"Nothing there now," Kate mused. "Any idea what time of year it was?"

Ciara closed her eyes, reviewing what she'd seen. "Cooler weather," she said as if retelling a dream. "Mickey had on long sleeves rolled up to her shoulders." Her voice grew more distant. "Nice shoulders." She was next to get smacked.

"Focus, Ciara," Kate scolded her.

"Right. There was a long black coat thrown over one of the chairs. Manly looking, but it still could have belonged to either of them. So, I'm guessing not summer."

"Anything else? Hey, did you see the calendar?" Carlos moved to stand beside the January, 1924 image, the brunette smiling down over his shoulder.

Ciara concentrated. Had she looked at the wall? She'd been so focused on the two people . . . mostly Mickey . . . "Wait. Yes! It had a woman holding a huge, cooked turkey on a platter in front of her even bigger boobs."

"Mickey's a bit of a dog, isn't she?" Carlos muttered.

"November, then," Kate stated, ignoring him. "Probably November of 1923."

"Why are you so sure?" Jeremy asked.

"Because someone or something is trying to help us figure this out. We've been directed to EZ's collar, the bullet holes, the calendar, even the ghost of Mickey herself. If this entity showed you that particular moment in Mickey's life, it meant something." Carlos paced across to the bar. "We just need to figure out what it is."

"Well, one thing is for sure." Jeremy picked up the piece of paper and held it in front of his face so he could look through the gashes Mickey had made in it with her pen. "Whatever is on this, it seriously pissed Mickey off."

A few Zoom conferences between Carlos and his cop-show-fanatic friends revealed some exciting information: faded ink could be restored, given the right chemicals, available at any drugstore, and the right type of lighting—black light to be exact. It took two days to gather the materials, including a trip to Spencer's Gifts for the light, but by Wednesday afternoon they had what they needed.

Carlos carried out the procedure, with his Canadian buddy, Pierre, on standby via the computer if anything went amiss, but it didn't, and Carlos disconnected with a final, "Thanks, *mon amie*," and blew a kiss at the screen.

"Renaldo will be jealous," Ciara cautioned, referring to Carlos's on-and-off boyfriend in the makeup department. While Carlos had a definite thing for Renaldo, neither was known for maintaining monogamy.

"Pierre is straight," Carlos said. "Now, let's see what we have here, and why it made Mickey so angry."

They were gathered in Ciara's office for the better lighting. Kate took all the chemical bottles and the black light and set them on top of one of the old filing cabinets in the storeroom so they would be away from EZ's pilfering, and they crowded around the desk where the paper lay, fully restored except for the holes.

"It's an invoice for different kinds of alcohol," Jeremy said, sounding disappointed. "Like, duh, of course a bar would have invoices for alcohol, and some big brute of a guy would deliver it."

"That doesn't explain the anger," Kate said, tapping a

finger against her chin. Her eyebrows rose. "Hey, look here!" She pointed at three columns of numbers labeled September, October, and November. "The numbers are prices per gallon, I think. Four dollars, five, six. Geez, that would be . . ." She pulled her phone out and typed a question into the internet search bar. "About seventy dollars a gallon in today's money. That's insane!"

"Mickey's supplier was raising the prices by a dollar each month. And with Prohibition in place, she probably had few options for obtaining alcohol, all of them illegal. She would have had to pay or risk, well, everything—her secret business, her freedom." Carlos looked angry on Mickey's behalf.

"Maybe even her life," Ciara said in a soft whisper. The others turned toward her. "I don't know what the guy was reaching for when Mickey suddenly gave in, but it scared her enough to quit fighting him and sign the other documents. Maybe by December or January she decided to call his bluff."

"And found out he wasn't bluffing. You think the booze supplier killed her?" Kate asked.

They all stared in silence at the paper on the desk.

"There has to be more. You don't kill your customers. You negotiate. Otherwise, you run out of customers. Besides, her brother was a cop. That would have been a really stupid move, even if the seller was mob, like most of the bootleggers of the time were." Ciara ignored the others' stares. "I've been doing my research," she said. "And then there's the whole label thing. Mickey was pointing at the labels on some of the bottles. What's that all about?"

Her friends shook their heads or shrugged or both.

"Well then," Kate said, clapping her hands once with her usual take-charge authority, "let's go figure it out."

They proceeded down to the subbasement like a train with Kate as the engine and little tail-wagging EZ trailing behind as the caboose. Ciara even made a couple of chug-a-chug noises to which Jeremy and Carlos blew train whistles that echoed up and

153

down the staircase.

"You all are nuts, you know that?" Kate said, but she was laughing.

When they reached the bottom, Ciara sobered. "It isn't really funny. Mickey's life or, erm, afterlife is at stake here."

Carlos rested a hand on her shoulder. "Gotta keep this light, girlfriend, or we'll all lose our minds. This is some crazy *caca* we're dealing with. Don't worry. We want to rescue Mickey or release her or whatever just as much as you do."

"Well, maybe not *quite* as much," Kate mused. She strode across the open space before anyone could smack her but had to stop at the speakeasy door. "*Now* Ciara remembers to lock it. And here I thought I'd toss off that quip and make a hasty escape."

Ciara rolled her eyes, unlocked the door, and let them all inside. EZ went straight to the spot where Mickey had died and curled up on the tile, lowering his head to his paws with a soft whine. "Soon, baby, soon," Ciara tried to reassure him. His tail wagged once in response.

Kate stood in front of the shelves of bottles, head turning from side to side as she took them all in. "Okay Ghost-Whisperer, which ones was she all kicked up about?"

Ciara joined Kate while the boys hung back by the dance floor. She studied the alcohol offerings. "Problem is, they're all faded, like the invoice. The ones that upset her were green/gold and a blue one with a red foil cork top."

Though they'd cleaned some of the bar while searching for clues, they hadn't gotten to the liquor collection, so they had to clear away decades of dust and cobwebs to even begin telling one color of label from another. "There!" Carlos pointed, indicating the highest shelf, well above Ciara's head. "That one has some gold printing on it."

Ciara squinted. Sure enough, the light over the shelving, the one that also illuminated the radio, glinted off some metallic wording on the centermost bottle. The label itself might have once been dark green, as she'd seen it in her vision from the past. Now it merely looked blackened to her.

"Slide over," Carlos said. Ciara obliged, and he reached up on tiptoe to take down the bottle in question. Using one hand, he brushed away the collected grime, revealing a hint of green.

"That's it . . . I think," Ciara said. She peered closer. "What language is that?"

"Polish," Carlos said. "The printing on these survived better than on the paper the invoices were printed on."

Jeremy raised his eyebrows. "You speak Polish? I'm impressed, bro."

"Nah, I recognize this brand." He pointed at the name of it, which included some letters Ciara didn't recognize in the English language. "It's very famous. High quality vodka. Excellent bottling to preserve the taste. I've only ever held one other bottle of this. The distillery went under around 1925. This one bottle, since it's unopened, would probably bring in thousands, if not tens of thousands of dollars if sold on eBay or some such. Even back in 1923 it was highly respected, and Mickey understood its worth, because she had it on the topmost shelf and centered. It's what bartenders do with the good stuff, since there isn't a lot of call for it."

They set the bottle aside and continued searching for the blue and red one. It wasn't on the shelves. It wasn't in the cabinets under the shelves or under the bar, either. "If that flashback took place in November, maybe it got used up and tossed out," Kate suggested.

"Maybe . . . Let me check her office. I think I remember spotting a few bottles back in there." Ciara squeezed past Kate and entered the back room of the speakeasy. She turned on the desk lamp, which also worked, as well as the portable spotlight to make things brighter. Cot, desk, chair, clothes rack. There. Behind the men's-style coats hanging on the rack, one of which actually appeared to be the one she'd spotted in her vision.

Ciara went to push the overcoats aside, then froze with her hand on the sleeve of the one she recognized. A shiver passed through her, followed by a wave of oddly comforting warmth. Mickey had worn this.

She had the strangest, strongest urge to wrap it around herself like an embrace.

Shaking it off, she reached behind the garments and pulled out a collection of bottles one by one. They came in a variety of shapes and sizes and glass shades, and they had labels in different colors, and sure enough, the one with the blue label and red top was among them. When she went to grab the final of the five back there, her hand brushed something paper—a small notebook with a black leather cover.

"Got it!" Ciara called through the still open office door. "And I found something else."

The others squeezed into the tiny room with her. Carlos and Jeremy sat on the lumpy cot while Kate took the squeaky desk chair.

"Do we need to go get the chemicals from upstairs?" Jeremy asked, eying the notebook.

Ciara opened it and flipped through the yellowed pages with neatly printed notes clear as day all the way through. "Nope. She wrote this one in pencil. It's totally legible." She scanned several pages. "And from what I can tell, she was translating the labels from Polish to English. I wonder if . . ." She broke off and knelt down again, then felt around behind the coats some more until her fingers grasped another book. Pulling it out, she read the title embossed on the leather cover. "Polish-English Dictionary. Yep, thought so."

"But why?" Carlos asked. "And why keep those specific bottles back there when she could be selling the contents in her bar? She certainly had to pay an arm and a leg for them."

Ciara tuned out the others' speculations while she continued to skim through Mickey's notes. Her eyes widened. "Hey, listen to this. 'bouquet rose and crayon, flavor of meat warm, aged two centuries.'"

"Um, what?" Jeremy shook his head. "That's nonsense."

"Right. It is." Ciara picked up the blue and red bottle and studied the label. "But that's what this says in Polish. Nonsense. Complete nonsense. The label is a fake. And that means the contents are probably awful, even though this claims to be a bottle from the same famous distillery as the other one from her top shelf. No wonder Mickey was furious." She blew out a breath, then took a calming one as she felt her own anger rise. "Not only was that guy charging her more and more for her liquors, but he was selling her imitations. And she knew it."

"And she refused to serve it to her customers, even though she still had to pay for it. Some serious integrity there," Kate commented.

Ciara's insides warmed at the compliment, even though it wasn't for her. It gave her one more reason to find Mickey attractive beyond her stunning looks.

"So maybe we've cracked the case!" Jeremy announced. "She figured out the bootleggers were counterfeiting labels and threatened to expose them to, I don't know, their other customers, and they killed her."

Carlos shook his head. "Nope. If she exposed the bootleggers, the bootleggers would just expose her and her secret bar. They'd all get arrested. It doesn't work. They both had something on the other. There's got to be more to it."

"Besides," Kate put in, "if we have solved the mystery and identified the murderer, wouldn't something have . . . changed around here? Some indication that Mickey's situation has been resolved?"

All four of them looked around the office, then wandered back into the main room of the Speak EZ. Nothing appeared or felt different.

If Mickey had moved on, would Ciara even know? Would Mickey have any way of saying goodbye?

Something about that made Ciara very sad.

Chapter 24

November 14, 2022

ANOTHER DAY OFF spent in the subbasement. "My social life needs an uplift," Ciara muttered, chin in her palms, elbows on the bar. She stared at herself in the mirror behind it, willing something to happen, someone to appear.

Who are you kidding? It's only Mickey you want to see.

On the floor beside her, EZ barked. Ciara glanced down at him. "Where is she, boy? Why hasn't she come back? Did we figure it out, after all? Is she gone?" In addition to the now perfectly normal mirror, there'd been no sign of Mickey's ghost, either.

The dog had no answers for her except to stand and run in three circles over the spot where Mickey had died and lie down again.

The low chime of a clock, the one hanging near the door to the bathroom, nearly startled her off the stool. *That* actually worked once she'd figured out how to wind the old wooden timepiece. Lovely workmanship with little carvings of sheep on either side of the face. She'd run the manufacturer's name through Google and discovered it came from a little clockwork factory in Ireland. Ciara wondered if it had been a keepsake from

Mickey's parents after they passed away in that flu epidemic.

She'd probably never know. Either way, it was now 3:22 p.m.

Wait. Why would chimes be sounding at 3:22? And it had only *bonged* once.

Maybe it didn't work so well after all.

"Damn it," she muttered, climbing down off her seat and striding over to it. Hands on her hips, she stared up at the clock, the pendulum swinging back and forth lazily below the main housing. The hands read 3:23. Huh. Nothing wrong with the time it kept, at least. "Maybe I should take you to a repair shop, too."

And now she was talking to dogs *and* clocks. *Sorry potential girlfriends. My social calendar is* full.

Bong.

Ciara jumped backward, banging her tailbone into the edge of one of the tables. Thank goodness it was rounded and not square. "Don't do that!" she shouted at the clock. Then, "Oh my god, I'm losing my mind."

Bong.

She sighed. "The radio doesn't work, but it's supposed to. And the clock works too often."

Something brushed her ankle. EZ had joined her. He sat on the tile, all his attention focused on the clock.

"Sorry, boy. I bet that noise hurts your ears. It scares the crap out of me. Did Mickey really like this thing? It's pretty, but it doesn't match the rest of the décor."

Ding ding.

Great. Now she had *bonging* and *dinging*. If it started talking back to her, she was so out of here.

Wait.

Feeling ridiculous or stupid or both, Ciara slowly turned her eyes from EZ to the clock. "Um, Mickey?"

Ding ding.

"Oh, holy shit. For real?"

160

Ding ding.

"*Bong* for no, *ding ding* for yes, is that it?" she said, barely containing her excitement. Her pulse pounded and her breathing came a little too fast. Finally, some real communication.

Ding ding.

"Yes!" She fist-pumped the air while EZ twirled in circles.

Ding ding.

"Oh! No, I mean, 'yes' like, as in 'yes, we're getting somewhere.' I wish you'd figured this out sooner." The clock hung silent, the only sound the ticking of the mechanisms within. "Oh, I'm not criticizing you. I promise. Actually, you probably couldn't do anything with it until I figured out how to wind it, right?"

Ding ding.

"But that was five days ago, and I've been here lots of times since then. Why didn't you—?" She cut herself off, measuring the distance between where Mickey died and the clock by the back corner next to the bathroom. "Oh. Wow. It took you that long to cross the room. Didn't it?"

Ding ding.

"I'm sorry. But this is still awesome. So, let's talk."

They worked out a system to broaden Mickey's possible responses at least a little bit. In addition to "yes" and "no," *ding bong* became "maybe" and complete silence meant "I don't know." Starting with casual information first, they sorted out the basics through process of elimination.

Favorite color: red? *Bong.* Blue? *Ding ding.* And so they continued, covering foods (Italian, *not* Irish as Ciara would have guessed), music types (jazz), and other minutiae of their likes and dislikes with Ciara giving her own answers for each of Mickey's.

The *bong, bong, bong, bong* in response to Ciara's shyly asked question about whether or not Mickey was enjoying their interaction almost made Ciara stop the conversation altogether.

Until she realized it was four and the clock was behaving as it was designed to in that moment.

Ciara laughed until her sides hurt, and tears ran down her face.

Ding ding.

"What? You thought it was funny, too?"

Bong.

What then? In that moment, Ciara really wished she could ask something other than a yes or no question, and she said so out loud.

There was no response to that, of course.

Out of chitchat, Ciara cautiously guided the discussion onto riskier pathways. She asked if Mickey was in pain, anxiety tightening her throat until Mickey said she wasn't. She confirmed that Mickey didn't know her killer, and when she put forth the bootlegger as a candidate, received a "maybe" in response. "Are you lonely?" got an answer of yes, and Ciara reached to touch the side of the clock with her fingertips, imagining covering Mickey's own hand and offering what comfort she could.

When she asked if Mickey was scared, there was a long silence before Mickey responded "maybe."

Save me from tough butches.

There were other questions, too, that she really wanted answers to but couldn't bring herself to ask. Did Mickey like her? Had Mickey had a boyfriend (or better yet, a girlfriend) back in the 1920s? (That would have been especially cruel given any relationship she'd been in would be quite literally dead.) So many more inappropriate and overly personal things she did not ask.

Biting her lower lip, she tried a less direct approach. "I like your style," Ciara ventured, feeling her way. "The bar. Your clothes. I like the choices you've made."

Silence. Well, she hadn't really asked a question.

"I was ... wondering ... if you liked mine." *God, I'm a twelve-*

year-old passing a note to a cute girl in her math class. Do you like me? Check "yes" or "no." How childish can I—

Ding ding.

And just like that, Ciara's stomach was doing backflips. It wasn't confirmation, but given those style choices, the calendar on the wall, and the way she'd seen Mickey carry herself in the vision, her lesdar was pinging like mad. And Ciara's heart danced with joy.

They went on for another hour until several of Mickey's "yes" responses came with the dings very far apart. "You're getting really tired, aren't you?"

Bong.

"Lying to me already?"

Bong.

Placing her hands on her hips, Ciara glared into the space beside the clock where she imagined Mickey's ghost to be.

Ding . . . . . . ding.

"Okay," she said, a note of regret in her voice that she couldn't help. "Let's stop for today. I promise I'll come back tomorrow, or sooner if we figure out anything new."

She gathered her purse from the top of the bar and called EZ from where he'd been hanging out in the office while they talked. They were at the door when she glanced back at the clock.

"Oh! One last question. Do you have any idea why the radio won't work? The repairmen said there's nothing wrong with it."

Ding . . . ding.

"Well, great. Maybe we can narrow that down tomorrow. Good night, Mickey. I really enjoyed talking to you."

The last thing Ciara heard as she locked the speakeasy door behind her and the dog was the clock dinging twice more.

The lights in the bar went out, and Ciara closed the door behind her and EZ. A moment later the key turned, and the lock clicked and Mickey was alone in the dark. She never had much trouble seeing, even without light, though the bar's furnishings appeared to her sight outlined in hazy gray until someone turned the lights back on.

No, it wasn't the dark that depressed her. It was the aloneness.

However, tonight . . . tonight she didn't mind so much.

She'd *talked*! She'd talked to *Ciara*! And Ciara had told her she liked Mickey's "style," whatever that meant.

Of course, she understood the word, but when she tried to apply it to herself, she didn't entirely grasp the context. Staring down at her shimmery image standing beside the clock, she considered what Ciara had really meant. She'd said her clothes and the way she'd decorated the bar. So, maybe she was referring to Mickey's "taste"?

Mickey's taste had always run toward the masculine. Did that mean Ciara liked men? Or did it mean Ciara liked women who preferred a masculine style?

Gah. What was wrong with her? She was behaving like she was a teenager again—liking a girl and mooning over her, all awkwardness and confusion and embarrassment, terrified of being found out but a tiny part of her wishing she would be, on the even tinier chance that the girl might feel the same.

And who was she kidding? Her current situation made everything even more hopeless. Relationships weren't built on "yes," "no," and "maybe."

And she was dead. Despite what EZ had accomplished, she didn't believe there was a way around that little obstacle.

But when Ciara had laughed, when the clock's own chiming had startled her and she'd laughed and laughed, Mickey had felt lighter, warmer than she had since she'd last been alive. She'd been so overwhelmed with the pleasure of hearing that laughter that she'd chimed "yes" and confused Ciara even more, but it had been worth it.

If there was any way for her to get back, to get to Ciara and make her laugh again, for real, in person, Mickey was determined to find it.

For now, though, she needed to rest. Exhaustion slowed her movements even more than the near crawl she'd managed to cross the bar, and she'd been proud of that. Now she was proceeding by inches back toward the dusty dance floor because what she needed to explain about the radio couldn't be done with a yes or a no.

Ciara must have momentarily forgotten her limitations. She'd said she'd return tomorrow, but there was no way Mickey could be in place by that time. She'd been ecstatic when her idea of using the clock for communication had worked out, when she'd managed to materialize just enough of one finger *inside* the clock while the rest of her remained incohesive so that she could put all her energy into tapping the two different chimes as needed. But the effort had drained her.

Her heart sank, and she hoped Ciara would wait for her to reach the floor.

She hoped Ciara would wait for *her*.

Chapter 25

November 20, 2022

CIARA'S ANXIETY ABOUT Mickey moving on had begun to build again when the message in the dust finally appeared. She'd known, of course. If it had taken Mickey an entire week to cross from the bar to the clock, it would take her almost as long to cross back to the dance floor. But she'd hoped that maybe Mickey might learn how to increase her speed of motion the more she did it or . . . something.

And then there was the guilt. She *wanted* Mickey to be able to move on, didn't she?

No. You want her alive again. Like EZ.

Maybe you should consider finding out what Mickey *wants.*

Do you want to go to the afterlife might be the mother of all yes-or-no questions.

And it could wait. Because after six days, there was a new word scrawled in the dance floor dust: "fuse."

"Fuse. Seriously?" she said out loud, turning in a circle on the dance floor but out of reach of the writing. For some reason, she never wanted to erase Mickey's words. Sometimes she had to, to make room for her printouts, or EZ scattered the dust with his paws and mucked it up, but she hated when that happened.

It was her one example of semi-tangible proof that Mickey was *real*.

After all these weeks, her friends still hadn't seen Mickey, and they hadn't been present during the clock conversation, though they thought that was about the coolest thing ever. "It confirms that she's still a thinking, feeling individual, and not a shell or mere shadow of herself," Ciara said, then blushed. "I've been talking with Ms. Waters . . . um, Claudia, at the library," she'd admitted over coffee the day before. "Always makes me feel weird to call her by her first name, like I'm disrespecting an elder, but she keeps insisting. Anyway, according to her research, most ghosts are incapable of anything more than fading in and out and maybe moving something small. But she said there are exceptions."

"Sounds like Ms. *Waters* is a real *fount* of knowledge," Jeremy quipped, but Ciara ignored him.

"Mickey's unique. At least as far as my own reading can tell me." Carlos indicated the laptop on the table beside him. "Real ghost hunters would have a field day with her."

"And that's exactly why we aren't bringing anyone else in. She's been through enough," Ciara said, taking a sip of her latte.

"An expert might be able to help," Kate suggested. She tossed back the last of her cafecito.

Ciara had never understood drinking those Cuban coffees, even though they were delicious. It was like doing whiskey shots. Yeah, you got all the impact of the alcohol, or in this case the caffeine, in one quick burst, but the enjoyment was so short-lived. Her mind wandered. She wondered if Mickey had ever had Cuban coffee.

"We're kind of at a standstill here," Kate finished, dabbing her lips with a napkin.

"Yeah," Carlos inserted himself again. "I haven't had any luck searching the newspaper archive sites or anything else I could worm my way into. Mickey and her brother weren't that notable. And, I've been hesitating to say this, but I worry we might be running up against a deadline."

Ciara cocked her head. "What kind of deadline?"

"A literal one. The first time you saw her in the bar it was Halloween night. Maybe not for her, but for you. Then your vision . . ." He paused, gathering his thoughts. "November according to her boob turkey calendar pinup."

Jeremy snickered. Kate shushed him.

"Look, I don't know anything for sure. Heck, none of us know anything for sure. We're all feeling our way with this. But pay really close attention the next time you 'get together.' I know where your focus will be." Carlos winked at Ciara. She blushed. "But try to note the date, okay?"

Ciara froze with her coffee cup halfway to her lips. She felt the blood drain from her face. "Her death date. You think that's what we're leading up to, don't you?"

Kate gave a small gasp—a massive display of emotion for her—and Jeremy shifted in his seat, but they didn't disagree.

Carlos held out both hands and wrapped them around Ciara's on her cup. "I don't know, girlfriend. I really don't. This isn't my area of investigation. I'm all about how people die the first time around, not what happens if they do it again. But the progression of dates is concerning. And if we don't figure this out before we hit New Year's, and she has to relive that night, well, I'm worried about how it will affect her. And you. That's all."

Ciara pushed the memory from the day before out of her mind and stared at the single word "fuse" written in the dust. The frustration rose again. "It can't be a fuse. The repair guys all had it working in their shops . . . oh. Of course. But doesn't the bar run on the same power as the rest of the theater?"

She didn't expect an answer and she didn't receive one. They really needed more ways to communicate.

Honestly, Ciara didn't quite know why she was so hung

up on getting the radio to work. Except one of the spotlights had shifted to it, and if that wasn't about the bottle of expensive liquor on the top shelf, then it had to be another clue somehow.

As if on cue, the bulb above the shelf where the radio sat began to flicker wildly, then stopped.

Yes. She needed to fix the radio.

The four of them had examined most corners of the bar, and they hadn't come across a fuse box of any kind. The bathroom seemed like an unlikely location for such a thing, but Ciara went over it again, which didn't take long considering the tiny space. That left Mickey's office.

Though the Speak EZ was clearly an expression of Mickey's ideas of hearth and home, the little office always felt more personal to Ciara whenever she went in there. For one thing, Mickey had slept on that cot, which on one level was a bit arousing, and on another made her wonder what Mickey's relationship with her brother had been like. Why sleep at the bar on a tiny, lumpy cot when you had a bed at home to go to? It could have been that Mickey worked extra late some nights and needed to be at the theater at an early hour, so the spare bed saved her time.

Or it could be that she didn't get along with her police officer brother very well. A police officer who would have been very angry to discover Mickey operating an illegal bar during Prohibition.

Maybe instead of searching for records on Mickey and her brother, Paul, during their lifetimes, Carlos should start looking at events taking place shortly after Mickey's death. Ciara typed that information into a group text that would be sent as soon as she stepped outside the speakeasy and had a signal again.

In the meantime, she poked in every corner of the little office, lingering around Mickey's desk where she came across a few more invoices that weren't quite so faded. And, yes, the liquor supplier's prices had been steadily increasing since Mickey had opened the bar a couple of years before her death.

She also gave in to her urge to pick up the rotary-style phone's receiver and hold it to her ear—dead of course. Any phone line Mickey had installed down here would have been cut off for nonpayment fairly quickly after her demise and the closing and hiding of the speakeasy. Ciara did, however, figure out which number on EZ's collar tag was the number to the bar and which had probably been Mickey's home number—top one was bar, bottom was home. The number for the bar's office was penciled on a small white card barely still attached with yellowed tape and hidden beneath the receiver. With a sigh, she set it back on its cradle.

Next, she moved the entire clothes rack, stirring up a cloud of dust that set her sneezing. When the air didn't clear, Ciara flipped on the desk's tiny fan, forgetting any worries about electrical problems. To her amazement, it worked, the blades whirring and creaking within a metal cagework. But it got the dust whirling even more so she turned it off.

Nothing behind the hanging coats, a pair of black trousers, and a yellowed but once white button-down shirt. Unable to resist, Ciara buried her nose in the shirt's fabric, imagining Mickey might have worn cologne and hoping for a hint of Mickey's scent, but no perfume lasted a hundred years. All she detected were must and mold that instigated more sneezing for her trouble. Then she considered the fact that Mickey's invisible ghost might be watching her at that very moment and released the clothing as if it were on fire, blushing to the tips of her ears.

Well, if Mickey hadn't already figured out she liked girls and if she was watching, she certainly knew it now.

Fanning her face to cool some of the heat, Ciara considered what was left to search. She supposed the fuse box could be behind some piece of furniture in the bar proper, maybe even inside the glassware cabinet beneath the shelves of bottles, but that didn't feel right. She straightened her shoulders, grasped the legs of the cot, and pulled it away from the corner where it rested.

Two things happened at once. The left end leg of the ancient metal frame gave way, toppling the cot sideways but at an odd angle. And something wooden and heavy rolled from under the threadbare pillow and *clonked* onto the floor.

It took Ciara a long moment of holding the elongated shaft of polished wood with the rounded tip in her hands before she figured out what it was, and when she did, her face flamed all over again.

Oh.

But had Mickey used the crude but effective dildo on herself? Or had it been for . . . overnight guests?

"Mickey's a bit of a dog, isn't she?" Carlos's observation came back to Ciara in a rush.

The flash of jealousy surprised her, as did the somewhat intense burst of arousal in the pit of her stomach.

Mickey's an adult, she reminded herself. *What, did you think she'd be a virgin? It was the Prohibition era. Booze was out, but everything else was waaaay in. Get a grip, Ciara.* She glanced down at the sex toy in her hands. *But not on this.* Too personal. Way too personal. Averting her gaze, she slipped the dildo between the sheets by feel, tucking them in farther so it wouldn't fall out again even with the frame at an angle.

Wondering if she could possibly embarrass herself more, she straightened . . . and spotted the fuse box in the corner of the wall behind where the bed had been.

Chapter 26

November 20, 2022

OH GOD, KILL me now, Mickey thought, watching Ciara from the bar through the doorway leading into her office. Then, *Oh yeah, too late.*

It had taken a tremendous amount of energy to turn her head enough to see what Ciara was doing in there, and once she did, she wished she hadn't. First, the beautiful brunette with the streak of blue had smelled the clean shirt she always left hanging in case she needed to stay overnight. Not so clean after however long it had been—and yes, she'd noticed that Ciara had again conveniently not given her that information. The changes in styles and technology worried her. How many years had passed?

Those worries fell on the back burner, though, when Ciara inadvertently engineered Mickey's single greatest moment of mortification. She'd found Mickey's . . . plaything. One of them, anyway. She'd owned several different types and stored them in various locations around the office/bedroom for convenient use, mostly with Annie, occasionally with a one-nighter, though those got tricky since any one-nighter would be a customer and her customers were all friends or friends of friends. And in her greatest moments of frustration and loneliness, by herself.

The one Ciara had stumbled upon had been new, a late Christmas gag gift from Bess, another masculine-presenting lesbian she worked the sets with who liked to drink at her bar. "There's dry spells and there's total drought," Bess had said when Mickey unwrapped it and then had to quickly tuck it back in the box so no one else would see. "It's been over a year since Annie dumped you, and a month since one of the other girls stayed past closing time. Don't know if that's your kind of thing or not." She indicated the contents of the box. "But desperate times and all that."

They'd both laughed, and Mickey slid Bess a drink on the house to distract her from how forced that laugh had been on Mickey's part. She'd never been much for penetration, but maybe that's what she needed to ease the constant ache inside her. She'd discarded the box and tucked the toy beneath her pillow for later use. Except she'd never gotten a chance to use it.

Because someone had shot her that very night.

Mickey wondered what had happened to Bess. Hell, she wondered what had happened to Annie. Did they still work at the theater? Were they ancient? Were they even still alive? And her brother. What had happened to him?

For once very glad Ciara couldn't see her, Mickey watched for her reaction to what she'd discovered—embarrassed, definitely. Mickey hadn't realized a person's skin could achieve that bright a shade of red. But as Ciara continued to hold it in her hands, turning it over and running a palm along its length, she thought she could see something else, too.

Arousal.

Between those two actions with the clothes and the toy, Mickey had a pretty good idea where Ciara's preferences lay.

The burst of joy at that discovery was short-lived.

You're dead, you idiot. You don't know what EZ did to come back. Stop wishing for things that will probably never be.

But the tiniest flickers of hope and want refused to fade.

173

Ciara put the dildo between the cot's sheets, took out that small, square flashlight she'd used on her early visits, and opened the fuse box behind the bed. Except she didn't turn the flashlight on. She held the flashlight up to the box and . . . it flashed its light once. Almost like a smaller version of what Mickey had encountered when a photographer had taken a portrait shot of her brother the day he graduated from police training and when the archivists had come to document the theater's early history and its employees.

Could that tiny rectangular box also be a camera?

Jesus, what year is it?

Ciara slipped the camera/flashlight back into the pocket of her dungarees, left the office, and *walked right through the heart of her* on her way out the door.

And for a moment, Mickey's body shimmered into existence.

Ciara turned to call out her usual, "Goodbye, Mickey! I'll be back later, promise!" when she froze and stared at the spot where Mickey stood. Mickey willed her neck to turn so she could face her, and it was *easier* this time. "Mickey?" Ciara said, taking a step back toward her.

EZ barked and barked, running circles around and around Mickey's suddenly visible legs.

Mickey opened her mouth to respond . . . but she'd already faded away.

It had lasted only a few seconds, so brief Ciara wasn't certain she'd seen it, but she thought Mickey had been standing there beside the bar, watching her leave. Which meant she had probably seen what went on in the office as well.

Was it possible to implode from embarrassment?

Shaking it off, she continued out the door and stood with EZ in the open space beside the stairwell entrance. She didn't bother to lock the speakeasy. Ciara didn't intend to be away long. She had a direction now, a path to follow.

First, she texted the photo of the fuse box to Kate and Jeremy, along with the short version of what she needed and why. They'd be her best bet for figuring out how to fix whatever had gone wrong. She glanced at the clock on her phone. They were between the Sunday matinee and the evening performance, so one of them would get the message.

Next, she sent her thoughts about what time period to research over to Carlos. He responded in seconds saying he'd get on a search later tonight for Mickey's brother in the years after Mickey's death.

She trudged upstairs and settled in at her desk, determined to get some work done. It wasn't that she was behind. Most of her visits to the speakeasy had been after hours. But she'd been constantly distracted, and if she didn't double-check everything, she made careless mistakes.

And someone was playing that damn jazz music again in one of the other offices. She glanced at the overhead vent and sighed. It wasn't overly loud. They had a right to listen to whatever they wanted as long as they kept it to a reasonable volume, which it was.

Several hours later, after the evening show, Kate and Jeremy appeared together in her doorway. Kate held up something squarish and metal, a look of triumph on her face.

"It's a fuse," Kate explained at Ciara's single raised eyebrow. Kate's grin spread farther. "From the 1920s."

Ciara's mouth dropped open. "How—?"

Jeremy shrugged. "The crew here never threw anything away. We found a box in the backstage storage room labeled 'fuses' a few months ago. That was one of the first places we cleaned out during that inventory push that let us find the Speak EZ."

"I thought maybe I could make something for the charity fund by selling them on eBay, like I did with those old lights,"

Kate said, taking up the tale. "But then Mickey came along, and I never got around to it."

"Good thing." Ciara pushed up from her chair and hesitated. "You have time now? I don't want to deprive you of dinner."

Kate was practically bouncing in place. "Are you kidding? I want to make that radio work. I think it's another clue. And I'm hoping to see Mickey in the . . . well, not flesh exactly, but you know what I mean. Why should you get all the cool experiences?"

Ciara thought about her most recent "cool" experience and her face flushed.

Kate peered at her. "What? Did something new happen?"

"Nope. Not a thing. Let's go."

They followed her out, Carlos joining them at the stairwell door and EZ trailing behind them. Once inside the speakeasy, Ciara took a quick look around, but there was no sign of Mickey so they entered her backroom office. She pointed out the fuse box to Kate who wasted no time in shining her phone light inside, searching until she came up with one darker and cloudier than the rest. She pulled it and tossed it to Jeremy. "Souvenir," she said.

A quick rummage through the storage box resulted in her finding one that seemed to match but without the damage. It took no time to insert it in the empty space.

"Is that it?" Carlos asked.

"Should be." Kate dusted her hands off on her jeans. "Let's try it out."

When they returned to the main room of the bar, they were surprised to see tiny lights lit up all around each of the shelves of bottles. Even with the dust, the glow lit every bottle from beneath, all the different colored glass shining like holiday ornaments on a tree.

"Those must have been on the same circuit," Jeremy said.

"Oooh, pretty," Carlos put in. "Maybe I should install lighting like this at the bar upstairs. I love the effect."

"Ahead of her time, I bet." Kate stepped forward and examined the installation. She nodded. "These kinds of bulbs weren't ordinarily used this way in the '20s. But she worked with the light crew in the theater, so she probably picked up a few tricks. Clever."

Ciara didn't know why, but Kate's praise for Mickey made her warm inside. She reached for the radio. "Ready?" At her friends' nods and a bark from EZ, Ciara turned the dial. It made an audible *click*.

A low hum resonated from within the casing. Then a soft glow became apparent through the speaker holes. Jeremy leaned down to peer into it. "Yep. Tubes are warming up."

The overhead lights flickered, then flickered again.

"Um, guys?" Carlos shot Kate a nervous look. "Should that be happening?"

"Are we about to get that interior wall fire you warned us about?" Ciara asked, stepping away from the nearest wall's surface.

Kate shook her head, but she kept her gaze on the ceiling lights, which continued to flicker more and more rapidly. "We've been using the electricity in here for weeks now. While it isn't out of the question, there's no real reason to think turning on the radio and shelf lighting would be any more risky than anything else we've done. Except . . ." She trailed off.

"Except it blew the fuse," Jeremy finished for her.

"But we already know the radio and shelves aren't on the same fuse as the rest of the bar's lights. How is one triggering the other? Or is this a coincidence?" Ciara no longer believed in coincidence. Not after the past weeks.

A hissing sound replaced the humming from the radio. The bar lights dimmed. The mirror behind the bottle shelves began to *glow*, and not only from the mood lighting Mickey had installed there. Everyone stared into the reflective surface as their own images vanished and other figures appeared in the bar behind them.

Twenty people or more, all in 1920s garb with 1920s-style haircuts, all milling about the tables and chairs, some dancing on the small square of polished wood, others sitting on the barstools sipping drinks. And one figure hurrying behind the bar wearing a pressed white button-down rolled up to the elbows and black trousers, her short brown hair a tousled but still-sexy mess.

Ciara's breath caught at the sight of Mickey, dashing and handsome as always. The figure turned to face away from the mirror and grabbed a pair of bottles from the bar to toss around a couple of times before she poured some of their contents into glasses.

Show-off, Ciara thought. But she smiled, impressed.

"Show-off," an unfamiliar male voice muttered, echoing her thoughts.

Kate, Carlos, and Jeremy stopped swiveling their heads back and forth between the mirror and their own otherwise empty 2022 version of the Speak EZ and stared at the radio.

"What the actual fuck," Jeremy whispered.

"You perform Hamlet in Shakespearean English and never miss a line. Who's showing off?" The owner of the second unknown voice chuckled in a warm alto and passed over the first speaker's drink, sliding it along the bar with a perfect push of momentum to stop it directly in front of him.

Ciara inhaled sharply. It was the first time she'd ever heard Mickey speak.

Chapter 27

November 20, 2022

"CAN THEY . . . HEAR us?" Carlos whispered, his chest pressed against Ciara's back. The four of them were crowded behind the bar again, Ciara and Kate right up against the counter with the bottle shelves above it, right next to the radio where the voices were coming from. Carlos and Jeremy stood behind them since they were taller and could see over their shoulders with ease.

"One way to find out." Jeremy leaned over and spoke directly into the radio's speakers. "Hey! Dead people! Over here!" Carlos contributed by waving his arms in the air over their heads.

"Shhhhh!" Ciara ordered, her whisper almost as loud. Kate reached back to smack all three of them.

There was no reaction from anyone in the mirrored past. Ciara wasn't sure if she felt disappointed or relieved about that, but disappointment won.

Mickey's voice . . . Dear god, she never knew a woman could sound that sexy. Deep, warm, rich. Ciara ached to have that voice speak to *her*.

Preferably in bed.

Kate whipped her phone from her back pocket, turned

on the camera, and aimed it at the mirror to begin recording what they saw. Damn, why hadn't Ciara thought to do that? Kate caught Ciara's incredulous look and grinned. "You were too distracted by . . . *that*." Her wave indicated Mickey. Or maybe Mickey's firm ass since the bartender was still facing away from them. "Even though I'm straight, I can definitely see the appeal. She's smokin' hot. Geez, she practically exudes fuckability."

"Should I be worried?" Jeremy asked, grinning. "Better yet, can I watch?"

"Shut up, dimwit. I'm with you and only you." Kate pointed into the mirror image. "Hey, note the date. Still November there."

They followed where she was pointing to the big-breasted turkey-holding woman in the pinup calendar on the wall. Glancing around, Ciara also noted coats and jackets thrown over chairs, fall colors in the clothing: oranges, yellows, browns, and reds, and little clusters of fake fall leaves at the center of each table.

"The decorations weren't there the last time I saw something in the mirror," Ciara whispered, still unwilling to raise her voice whether they could hear her or not. It felt wrong somehow. "I wonder why the extras."

In the mirror, there was a rhythmic rap on the Speak EZ door. EZ the dog pawed at Ciara's leg and barked at the sound, echoed almost instantly by an identical barking from the glass. They stared, wide-eyed, as *another EZ* ran out of the back office in the mirror and over to the entrance, bouncing on his hind legs beneath the doorknob.

"Wow, that's—" Carlos began.

"Freaky," Jeremy finished for him, glancing from one dog to the other.

Grinning, Mickey strolled from the bar to the door, unlocked it with her key, and threw it wide open. A jovial-looking man stood on the other side. He stepped in and held out his arms, wrapping Mickey in a hug. "Happy Thanksgiving, kiddo!" he announced.

Well, that explained the decorations. It also made Ciara uneasy. Time was passing. The gap between Thanksgiving and New Year's wasn't a wide one. Carlos's warning shrieked in her head.

"Thanks, Jimmy. Always good to see you," Mickey said, her voice carrying over the noise of the other patrons also sending their greetings. Seemed like Jimmy knew everyone, which Ciara guessed made sense. A speakeasy would have a regular and selective clientele. Everyone there likely knew everyone else. "You made it just before last call."

"Had to close the restaurant down," Jimmy said while passing over the bag he'd brought with him. "Plenty of leftovers in there. Turkey, stuffing . . . all the trimmings. You deserve a Thanksgiving feast too, Mickey. Paul working a shift tonight?"

Mickey took the bag and nodded. "He always signs up for holidays. Says he should let the guys with families have those nights off." Her smile turned forced.

Ouch, Ciara thought. Never mind his own family, his kid sister. Well, that said a lot about the cot in the back room.

She studied the other customers. Nothing too out of the ordinary, except for the occasional individual wearing all black who had probably come straight from working the set crew, and a few still in stage makeup. And yet, something niggled at her. She couldn't quite put her finger on it.

"What are they all doing there on Thanksgiving?" Jeremy wondered out loud. "I mean, Mickey's asshole brother aside, wouldn't some of them have families to spend the holiday with?"

Huh. Was that what bothered her? No, but it did seem odd. Ciara let her gaze rove over the room again.

Kate nudged her with her elbow. "You haven't figured it out yet, have you? I'd think you would have noticed it first."

"I certainly got it," Carlos put in. "And more power to her."

What were they talking about?

She looked again. Two guys by the bar, chatting amiably. Two women at a table in the back. Two more women standing beside the dance floor watching . . . two men on the dance floor holding one another in a tight embrace as they swayed to faint jazz music that must have been coming from the radio on the other side of the glass. Oh.

Oh.

"It's not just a speakeasy. It's an LGBTQ speakeasy. Oh, wow!" Ciara exclaimed. Mickey really was a trailblazer, taking a double risk like that.

"Well, that answers my question," Jeremy put in, tone sobering. "They probably didn't have family to go home to. This *was* their family gathering."

Kate lowered her phone, flipped it over so she could see the screen and fiddled with it a bit, then blew out a frustrated breath. "Figures. Nothing we're seeing in the 'magic mirror' is getting caught on camera. It's only showing our reflections."

"That's super creepy, you know," Ciara said.

"That's super awesome, you mean," Jeremy put in.

"Yeah, but no evidence." Carlos sounded disappointed.

Ciara rested a hand on his shoulder. "It's not like we really planned to tell anyone. People would still think it's a hoax, and our private lives would be over, not to mention Mickey's."

"Mickey's not alive," Jeremy reminded everyone.

But EZ is. Somehow. And Mickey could be, too.

"Hey, something's up." Kate pointed at the mirror.

The two women at the table in the back had stopped talking. One of them stood and faced Mickey across the room. When she approached the bar owner, her smile was predatory.

Mickey wasn't smiling at all.

Ciara tried to parse what Mickey's expression actually was—a combination of anger and . . . hurt, maybe? But the two women stood facing sideways to the mirror, so it was difficult to read her at all.

"Hello, Mick," the blonde said, tossing long, wavy strands over one shoulder. "Happy Thanksgiving." She moved as if to embrace Mickey, but Mickey took a step backward and crossed her arms over her chest.

"Happier than last year's, that's for sure. Would be happier still if you hadn't shown up out of the blue. For god's sake, Annie, it's been a year. To the day, even. You made your feelings about us very clear that night, when you broke up with me." Then a little softer, "Even when I begged you to stay. I thought you didn't like celebrating your holidays in the dark."

Oooh, double ouch. Poor Mickey. Two hits in ten minutes—the brother comment and now her ex. Ciara's heart ached for her. This had to have been the worst night of the year for her. Well, except for New Year's.

"Bitch broke up with her on Thanksgiving? Wow, she's a real dream girl, that one," Jeremy said while the others murmured their assent.

Gone was all the warmth in Mickey's tone, replaced by brittle ice backed with steel. Anyone with half a brain would have known to back off, but from the way "Annie" swayed on her low heels, she'd had too much to drink to read the warning signs. In fact, if Ciara had to label the look in Annie's eyes, she'd have to call it "hopeful."

Judging from Mickey's expression, that hope had a rat's chance in a cat shelter.

Seated at Mickey's feet, the other EZ growled low in his throat. Yeah, he didn't like Annie, either.

Annie pouted. She reached for the edge of the bar, misjudged the distance, and almost fell over before Mickey instinctively grabbed and steadied her. She took quick advantage of the contact, wrapping both hands around the arm Mickey had extended and not letting go even when the bar owner attempted to move away.

"Should have let her fall," Kate said.

"She's too much of a gentleman for that." Carlos tilted his head toward the mirror. "Kudos to her, but now she's stuck."

Ciara had her own suspicions that Annie hadn't "fallen" at all, that it had all been an act. After all, it looked like most of the customers worked in the theater. She bet Annie was quite the actress on and off the stage.

"So, what's a lady gotta do to get a drink around here?" Annie giggled as Mickey led her to an empty barstool and helped her onto it, then extracted herself and put the bar between them.

"Don't see any ladies around here," Jimmy, also seated at the bar, commented, none too quietly. He shot a pointed look at Mickey, then refocused on Annie. "You've been with two different men at the restaurant this week. Dangerous game you're playing. Matches and fire dating a cop and a bootlegger. Anybody here'd have to be a fool to jump into that mix. Again."

Bootlegger. Was Mickey's ex dating her alcohol supplier? The one she'd had that argument with over his prices? Was Annie about to convince Mickey to start seeing her again? Would one of Annie's other lovers find out? Jealousy made a fantastic motive.

"I think we have a lot more potential suspects for Mickey's murder here," Carlos said, voicing Ciara's thoughts.

Kate barked a laugh as Mickey pulled a bottle from beneath the bar, out of her customers' sight, and poured some of its contents into a glass for Annie. "Look what she's pouring for that floozy."

The bottle had a blue label and a red top—one of the fakes. And judging from Annie's face when she took a sip, it was awful.

The blonde grabbed a napkin and spit into it, then wiped her lips, leaving a red smear across the paper. "This tastes like paint thinner."

"Complain to your boyfriend," Mickey told her and turned away.

Well, that answered that. Mickey's supplier *was* one of Annie's lovers, and Mickey knew it. When she turned from Annie, she was facing the mirror. The pain etched in her features tore at Ciara. This encounter was costing Mickey dearly. She reached blindly for a bottle on the shelf, uncapped it, and sloshed some dark brown liquor into the first glass she could grab. She downed it in one long swallow.

"Oh, that's not good," Carlos said in a knowing tone from behind Ciara's shoulder. "That stuff's strong. She'll be drunker than drunk if she does a few more like that."

As if on command, Mickey poured another whiskey and chased the first with it.

"Like watching a train wreck," Kate murmured.

It all felt like an invasion of privacy to Ciara. They shouldn't be seeing this at all. They had a window into Mickey's soul, and they were peeping through it without her permission. But someone or something wanted them to watch, was giving them clues if they could interpret them correctly.

So, they watched . . . and waited for the inevitable collision.

Chapter 28

November 20, 2022

"AWW, BABY, YOU knew I'd come back sooner or later. No man could ever take your place."

Beside Annie, Jimmy grumbled something under his breath and shifted on his barstool to face away from them both.

"And you, hush," Annie said to him. "No one wants to hear anything else from you. Especially me, ever." She leaned over the bar behind Mickey, giving Ciara's group a clear view down her low-cut dress, but Mickey didn't turn around to face her.

The muscles in Mickey's jaw tightened, and the corner of her eye twitched. Ciara could see how she was physically holding her emotions in check.

"It's not like you're seeing anyone else," Annie continued, her focus on Mickey renewed. "Rumor has it you've been keeping to yourself for a whole year. Pining away for me?"

Ciara hated this woman—a woman she'd never met, never *would* meet. A woman long dead, but a woman who'd broken Mickey's heart if Mickey's stricken expression was anything to go by. But she also hated herself a little bit, for the brief surge of joy she felt upon hearing Mickey had been seeing no one for a long time. She pushed the reasons for that into a box in the corner of her head and locked the lid down tight.

Another two fingers of whiskey went into Mickey's glass. Her hand shook when she raised it to her lips and downed it in four swallows. Her breath came heavily enough to fog the glass; she was struggling so hard for control. This was her bar. She was the boss. Ciara knew what it was like, trying not to lose it in front of friends or, worse, customers.

But Mickey was rapidly reaching her breaking point.

Jeremy reached to wipe off the condensation made by Mickey's strained exhalations, but of course, it was on the other side of the glass. They waited as it faded away.

Annie checked the watch on her wrist. "It's closing time. How about I stick around, and we see where the rest of the night leads us?"

Mickey slammed her empty glass down on the back shelf so hard the base of it cracked. All the bottles on the shelves above her rattled with the impact. One rocked precariously—the one with the green and gold label—and fell from the top shelf. Half-drunk or not, without even looking, Mickey's arm shot out to the side. The bottle smacked into her open palm. Taking the utmost care, she set it beside the broken glass.

"Whoa, seriously badass," Jeremy whispered.

Ciara stared, wide-eyed. She couldn't agree more. And she had never, ever wanted a woman as much as she wanted the owner of the Speak EZ.

Her shoulders tense, her jaw tight, Mickey slowly pivoted to face Annie. With the exception of the jazz still drifting from the other side's radio, the entire bar had fallen silent when she broke the glass. Every eye in the room was on the two of them.

"When you decided we were done, I wasn't angry," Mickey began, voice low and even. "I couldn't blame you for wanting more than I could give in this world, couldn't fault you for needing a normal life." Without breaking eye contact with Annie, Mickey reached beneath the bar and drew out an unbroken glass, then poured herself yet another drink.

Ciara didn't envy the hangover Mickey would have. Or had. Or . . . right. Moving on.

Mickey sipped whatever she'd poured, another stall to regain a firm grasp on her composure, Ciara suspected.

"But now you're back. You're back, and you're playing with me."

Annie opened her mouth to interrupt, but Mickey held up a hand to stop her.

"Shut it, Annie."

Annie's jaw snapped shut.

"You're seeing Bobby. I knew before Jimmy said anything. Bobby likes to brag while he's carrying in the crates of whiskey bottles all about the women he screws in the alley. Of course he didn't know our history. Guess that doesn't count as 'the shadows' to you, huh?"

Annie's face flushed deep red, though Ciara couldn't tell if that was from embarrassment or anger.

"But he's not the only one. Right? What, you couldn't stay with me so you went for the next best thing?"

Her friend, Jimmy, seated at the far end of the bar, held out a hand toward her. "Mickey, I was gonna tell you—"

"Of *course* you were," Annie said, rolling her eyes. "Why you ever thought I'd be interested in—"

"It's okay, Jimmy," Mickey said, cutting Annie off. "I already knew. Night shifts aren't the only reason I'm always coming home to an empty house." She didn't sound as angry anymore, just tired. And sad.

But what was she talking about?

"Is she saying what I think she's saying?" Kate asked, always faster on the uptake.

"What?" Ciara asked.

"I think . . . this Annie chick slept with Mickey, and now she's sleeping with Mickey's alcohol supplier *and* . . . Mickey's brother."

188

Jimmy had mentioned a bootlegger and a cop. Oh god, Kate was right. And Mickey had to be devastated. And furious.

"It's a freaking soap opera," Jeremy put in. "Wish I'd brought popcorn."

Ciara fixed him with a glare. "It's Mickey's life, Jer. And I feel like an invader." But that didn't stop them from continuing to watch.

In the mirror, it became clear Mickey had had enough. "Annie, I think we're done here," she said. "And when I say 'we,' I mean everything that comes with me." She gestured around the bar and its patrons, most of whom were still gaping at the scene the two of them were causing. "This place wasn't built for you. It was built for folks who appreciate the refuge the Speak EZ provides rather than criticizing it. It was built for my friends. Friends who've become family. A family that no longer includes you. Go home, Annie. And don't come back."

Annie's eyes went wide. She scrambled off the barstool, knocking over the remainder of her drink in the process. The liquid ran down the length of the bar and dripped off the end, but no one made a move to clean it up. People seated at the tables and standing near the dance floor whispered and murmured to each other.

Ciara got the impression excluding someone from the Speak EZ was something Mickey had never done before.

"You think you can throw me out?" Annie's voice had risen to a screech of indignation. She wavered again on her heels, but no one made a move to steady her this time. "I'll tell everyone about this place. Everyone! You'll all be arrested."

At her pronouncement, the conversation that had started up again in the bar went silent. The stares shifted from fascination to hard, cold anger. A few stood, chairs screeching on tile, their former occupants ready to take action, though exactly what Ciara had no idea. By the scowls on their faces, it wouldn't be pleasant for Annie. Annie's friend from the table in the corner arrived at that moment to lay a calming hand on her shoulder, but Annie jerked away.

"You'll be sorry you didn't wait for me to come around again, Mickey McFadden. I promise you that."

Mickey's muscles tensed, but Ciara couldn't see her expression. If Ciara had ever doubted Mickey's willingness to openly fight for her rights and beliefs, that doubt fled now at breakneck speed. The bar owner stepped away from the mirror, around the end of the bar, moving into Annie's personal space before the overly emotional woman could blink or retreat. Several inches taller, Mickey leaned down until they were almost nose to nose.

Now Ciara could see her face, and the look on it sent a shiver through her.

Mickey's voice rumbled like Cerberus at the gates of hell, gravelly and low. "You will tell *no one* about this place," Mickey said, "or so help me God, in addition to telling anyone who'll listen what a two-timer you are, I will *out you* to the world, Annie, and every betrayed patron of this establishment will back me up on it. No woman will ever trust you. No man will ever want you, including whichever of those two foolish bastards you're cheating on by being here tonight."

Annie blinked, her mouth gaping open like a fish out of water. Mickey had absolutely hit the mark with that shot.

"You won't just be celebrating your holidays in the shadows. You'll be forever *living* in them," Mickey finished, driving the final nail into the coffin. She stepped to the door, fished the keys from her pocket, and unlocked it, then held it open. "Now. Get. Out."

Annie stared at her, eyes wide, for a moment long enough Ciara feared she might not obey. Then she spun on her heels, almost falling in the process, seized her friend by the arm, and they both hurried out.

"Beth!" Mickey called after the second woman as she was crossing the threshold.

Beth turned with a chagrined expression on her young, attractive face.

"You're still welcome here. Just don't bring *her*."

She pressed her lips together in a thin line, but nodded once, then shut the door behind her.

A full minute passed and no one spoke. No one moved. Mickey faced the door, then turned to face the rest of the room. "I'm not angry at anyone else," she said. "I love each and every one of you, but consider the bar closed for tonight. I'll collect on the tabs tomorrow."

People nodded and gathered their things, heading for the door. They made their way out, many pausing to offer Mickey a touch or a few words of encouragement. She didn't meet anyone's eyes.

Jimmy held back so he was the last to leave. "Can't reason with someone like that. You did the right thing, Mick."

"No," Mickey said, voice hoarse. "I don't think I did."

Jimmy clapped her on the shoulder. "Come on. Don't lose sleep over it. I'll walk with you to your place. Don't forget the leftovers I brought you."

"Thanks, Jimmy, but no. I'm spending the night here. Really don't wanna see my brother tonight. I'll eat the leftovers when I wake up."

He studied her face, assessing, then nodded once. "All right then. But lock up behind me. I'll see you tomorrow." He swung open the door and disappeared through it.

Mickey closed and locked it, then heaved a heavy sigh. She snapped off the radio on her side of the mirror and went into her office, alone.

The glow in the mirror faded away, and as Ciara and her friends stared at it, their own reflections reappeared in the glass surface, and everything was as it had been before the window into the past had opened.

Almost.

Chapter 29

November 21, 2022

"LOOKS LIKE THE show's over," Jeremy commented, reaching both arms over his head to stretch. He caught himself and made eye contact with Ciara. "Not a show. Sorry. Her life. But she's gone to bed." Their side's radio had fallen silent, a faint hiss the only indication it was still functioning at all.

"I don't envy her that cot," Kate said. "I bet it was lumpy and uncomfortable even then." She pulled her phone back out of her pocket and checked the time. "Geez, it's after midnight. I'm out. This has been . . . an experience. But I need to process all this, and to do that I need sleep." She slipped out from in front of Carlos and Jeremy and headed for the door. "You all coming?"

"Right behind you," Carlos said, rubbing his eyes. They'd all been staring into the glass for over an hour and a half. The two guys joined Kate by the entrance. "Ciara?" he called, noticing she hadn't followed them.

"I'm . . . going to stay a bit. I think better in here. The atmosphere helps with the right mindset." Her explanation sounded less than believable even to her, but the others, tired and overwhelmed, bought it.

Once she was alone, she took a seat on one of the stools at the bar, propped her elbows on the wooden surface, and rested her chin in her hands. EZ curled up on the floor beside her, assuming a similar position with his head on his paws, which made her laugh. "You saw it too, right?" Ciara asked the dog.

EZ cocked his head at her and raised one ear.

"Mickey was really upset. With herself. Maybe Jimmy didn't realize it, but I did. And whether that past version of her knows I'm here or not, I'm not leaving her alone."

Besides, her friends hadn't noticed it, but while the glow had faded, and they could see their own faces in the mirror again, the bar's overhead lights had remained dim. The radio still hissed, rather than hummed as it had before everything had gotten weird.

And a few seconds later, the glow reappeared, and Ciara's image vanished from the glass.

"Episode two," she murmured, then grimaced. "Right. Not a television series, no matter how much this is like watching a melodrama on a widescreen TV."

Mickey opened the office door. She'd changed out of her clothes into what looked like cotton undershorts and a white short-sleeved undershirt. Mickey crossed to stand facing the bar and poured herself another drink. Her hand shook, and she sloshed some of the whiskey out of its shot glass. And when she downed that one, she began to pour another.

"Shit," Ciara said, standing and moving to a position in the exact spot Mickey occupied on the opposite side. "Come on, Mick. You're going to make yourself sick . . . or worse, give yourself alcohol poisoning. That's enough." Of course, Mickey couldn't hear her. And Ciara knew that the bar owner wouldn't succeed in killing herself with too much to drink. History already told her how Mickey would die, and it wasn't that night. But it was hard to watch the strong woman in the mirror coming apart swallow by swallow.

Frustrated, Ciara banged a fist on the glass. The bottles in contact with the mirror on her side rattled against each other.

The bottles on the other side did, too.

Oh my god.

In the mirror, the bar owner's body stiffened. She cocked her head to one side and turned sideways so Ciara could view her in profile. A single tear ran down Mickey's cheek before she swiped it angrily away.

Ciara leaned in closer, so close her breath fogged the glass. Rolling her eyes at herself, she wiped the obscuring condensation away, then used her knuckles to knock once, twice on the mirror. "Hello? Can you hear me?" The knocking caused the lights encircling the shelves to flicker . . . *on both sides of the glass.*

Mickey set her drink aside, placing it carefully on the bar as if she feared dropping it.

Then she turned fully around . . . and *looked right at her.*

The fathomless blue eyes met Ciara's and widened in shock. Mickey jerked a glance over her shoulder, searching for Ciara in the bar, but of course she wasn't there. She was here. In an empty, ancient, disheveled Speak EZ a hundred years away.

Mickey shoved the row of bottles on the counter to either side in order to get a better look at Ciara in her entirety, or at least to her waist where the glass ended, and the wooden counter and shelves began. Ciara did the same on her side of the mirror to see Mickey more clearly. The end bottle on Mickey's side dropped off the edge onto the dance floor. Mickey made no move to catch or retrieve this one. It hit the tile with a *thunk*, and rolled away, luckily without breaking.

Ciara didn't think Mickey had even noticed.

They stared at each other.

Mickey's mouth moved, but Ciara didn't read lips well, and whatever Mickey said was too long for her to figure out. Ciara pointed to the radio on her own side of the glass and pantomimed turning it on. Moving slowly, never taking her eyes from Ciara's, Mickey did so, and the radio's hiss increased in volume.

"Who *are* you?" Mickey said, hesitant and unsure. "How?" Then she laughed at herself. "Damn, I'm really very drunk."

Yes, she was. Her words slurred a bit, and she wavered a little on her feet. It made Ciara want to reach out, comfort her, hold her. Tonight's events had really upset Mickey, though she seemed more undone by the whole scene with Annie than Ciara could understand. A whole year had gone by since their breakup. Wouldn't Mickey be getting over her by now?

Ciara didn't quite know how to answer Mickey's question, either. This Mickey was still alive, from over a month before her death, and a hundred years prior to encountering Ciara in the present day.

She went with, "I'm a friend. Someone you can talk to. And you look like you need both of those right now."

Mickey leaned back, resting her elbows on the bar behind her, and giving Ciara a better view of her toned body. In the shorts and undershirt, Mickey's muscles were well-defined—the product of heavy lifting behind the scenes while working sets and lights, not to mention carrying crates of bottles down to the subbasement bar.

Ciara leaned farther forward, hoping to get a view all the way down the firm thighs and calves, and ended up bonking her forehead against the glass.

She rubbed it with one hand and looked up to find the bartender silently laughing at her. God, the woman was stunning.

Except she was reaching blindly for another bottle, not caring which one her fingers found. Without taking her eyes off Ciara, she fumbled for her discarded glass and sloshed some clear liquid into it, then took a swallow and grimaced.

"Straight gin really does taste like garbage," Mickey muttered. "Or maybe it's just this awful label."

"So stop drinking it. Really, please stop. You're more than

halfway to blackout, and you're going to be so sick tomorrow."
Ciara pressed her palm to her side of the mirror in a pleading
gesture. "Come on. It can't be that bad, even if Annie was a total
bitch."

That comment earned her a raising of eyebrows and a barked
laugh. "This is really bizarre, you know," Mickey confessed. "Not
only am I hallucinating a beautiful woman, but one who speaks
her mind."

She thinks I'm beautiful! Ciara's heart gave a little leap. Then
logic returned. *She's also wasted. Can't put much stock in anything
she says.*

Time to try a different tactic. Something to get Mickey to
open up and distract her from the drinking. Because she was
going a little pale under the bar's lights. Ciara hoped Mickey
wouldn't pass out.

"Look, if I'm a hallucination, then there's no harm in telling
me what's really upset you, right? I mean, your secrets have to
be safe with me."

"If you're a hallucination," Mickey countered, "then I'm
literally talking to myself. And that's a whole different level
of drunk." She raised the glass in her hand and studied it, as
if seeing it for the first time. "I've never had this much before.
Never wanted to." Her face fell. "Jesus, I screwed up tonight."
The words ran together. Ciara had to lean closer to the radio's
speakers to make them out. If she got much drunker, she'd be
unintelligible.

"Talk more, drink less," Ciara advised. She wished she could
reach Mickey through the glass. She'd snatch that shot of gin
away and pour it down the bar's sink. "Tell me why you think
you messed up. I saw it, by the way, your fight with Annie."

Mickey rolled her eyes. "Of course, you did. You're in my
head." She reached for the bottle again, knocked it over, and
cursed under her breath, then flushed with embarrassment.
"Sorry. I was taught better than to use profanity in front of a

lady, even an imaginary one."

While Mickey righted the bottle and sopped up the spill with a bar rag, something pawed at Ciara's leg. She looked down to see EZ wagging his tail and staring up at her, then at the bartender in the mirror. He seated himself beside Ciara's left foot and whined.

Ciara reached down and scooped up EZ in her arms, holding him to the mirror's surface. He barked and licked the glass in front of Mickey's face, leaving slobbery trails that distorted the image until Ciara wiped them away.

Mickey reared back. As if they weren't already wide enough to burst, the bar owner's eyes damn near popped out of her head. Then she set everything down, bent over, temporarily disappearing from view, and came up with . . . her own era's EZ.

"This just gets weirder and weirder," Mickey said while the two canines cocked their heads at each other. She glanced at her office. "Maybe I fell asleep in there, and this is all a very intense dream. Yeah, that's the ticket. I'm dreaming." She turned back and winked at Ciara. "You're a fine dream, doll face."

Ciara blushed, then shook her head hard. This wasn't about her. "Stop trying to change the subject. Tell me what's wrong."

Mickey's face fell, her mood shifting in that abrupt way that only the extremely intoxicated could manage. She took a couple of ragged breaths. Very drunk, Ciara reminded herself. This was so hard to do long-distance.

"I'm sorry about Annie. I know you two were . . . together."

"That . . . isn't it," Mickey managed. She set her version of EZ on the floor where Ciara could no longer see him, and Ciara did the same, letting him curl up on the tile beside her.

When she raised her head again, Mickey's breathing had increased in speed. A tremor ran through Mickey's body, so strong Ciara could see it ripple through her muscles. "Shit," Mickey gasped. "I think I'm—" She wavered where she stood. Both EZs barked in alarm.

"Oh. Fuck," Ciara whispered. "Mickey! Hey, listen to me. Mick! Hold onto the bar and work your way to one of the seats. Come on. You can do it."

Mickey blindly obeyed, hauling herself hand over hand around the bar's edge, then to one of the chairs at the closest table where she fell into it and almost toppled the whole thing including herself. She put her head down, her spine rising and falling much too fast.

Hyperventilating, Ciara realized. At least she hadn't blacked out. She wanted to break the mirror, climb through, and wrap her arms around the stricken woman on the other side.

"Keep your head down," Ciara instructed her. "Easy. Take deep, even breaths. You're okay."

Bit by bit, Mickey's lungs ceased heaving, the raspy breaths slowing over the radio's speakers. Mickey sat up, glanced at the mirror, and closed her eyes. Even with the dim lighting and the new distance between them, Ciara could make out the blush in her cheeks.

"Hey, there's no reason to be embarrassed," she soothed. "It's hard to see a panic attack coming." So much more to this woman than what Ciara had seen in pictures and a hazy presence on Halloween night. So much more to learn about her that "yes" and "no" and "maybe" couldn't answer.

One eye cracked open, squinting at her. "Panic attack? Is that what it's called?"

Ciara nodded, recognizing mental health terminology as more limited in Mickey's time.

Mickey nodded back. "That fits I guess."

"So, what are you panicking about?"

Mickey raised both eyebrows before her face fell once more into despair. Her eyes shone in the dim light, tears held at bay by the force of her will. "I broke the most sacred vow we make," she said, then dashed one escaping tear away with a quick, angry slash of her hand that left a red streak across her cheek from the abrasion. "I threatened to reveal Annie's attraction to women. I can't believe I did that, even after she . . ."

"Hurt you? Promised to out everyone along with the Speak EZ? Mickey," Ciara said, aching to take Mickey's hand and unable to, of course, "what she said she'd do was much, much worse."

Mickey turned to Ciara, fixing her in her guilt-ridden gaze. "You never, ever make that threat. It's the worst possible breach of trust. You never tell without permission, and you never ask. What an incredibly messed-up world. Well, I'm telling you. I like women. Good thing you're a hallucination and I'm drunk. Sober, I would never have said that."

Ciara nodded in acknowledgment. Always good to agree with the intoxicated. "I like women too, very much," she whispered.

"Well, of course you do. You're my imagination."

I like you, Mickey. And I really, really hope I get the chance to tell you that in the flesh someday.

Mickey glanced away. "I don't want to be like Annie."

"Aw, honey, you're nothing like her. For one thing, she was an idiot to dump someone like you. For another, I believe she would have revealed the Speak EZ. But I don't think you would have taken your revenge if she did."

Mickey shook her head rapidly from side to side, then blinked a few times as if she'd made herself dizzy from the motion. "It was an empty threat," she admitted. "I'd never do something like that, not even to her."

"I know you wouldn't."

A few more drunken tears ran down Mickey's face. "Sorry," Mickey said. "I'm not usually a crier. It's been a rough few weeks." Her EZ chose that moment to hop up and lay his head on her lap. She stroked his brown and white coat with an unsteady hand.

"I won't judge. Ever. For anything." Ciara paused. "Not you, anyway. Annie, though, I'll judge her plenty."

Mickey managed a weak laugh, then turned toward Ciara. She blinked as if trying and failing to clear her vision. "I'm going to sleep now," she said laying her head down on her arms crossed on the table. As she drifted into unconsciousness she murmured, "Damn, I wish you were real."

The lights around the shelving on Ciara's side flickered out, and the main ones in the ceiling brightened. The glow in the mirror faded away, and Mickey vanished from her view, leaving her in an empty bar once more. Sighing, she reached out and snapped the radio off.

Chapter 30

????

CIARA HAD TAKEN to doing all her work in the subbasement speakeasy, sitting with her "laptop" and something she called a "hotspot" at one of the bar's tables with EZ curled up on the next seat over. Sometimes her friends would even join her. And all of it to keep Mickey company while they tried to research her on their breaks.

They'd even include Mickey in their conversations. Ciara had told them about the clock trick, and whatever they discussed, they'd toss Mickey a yes or no question or two to make her feel like part of the team. It got frustrating sometimes. She worried that the inclusion was more out of pity than a genuine desire to interact. But it beat standing around mute and invisible and only able to watch.

At the moment, all four were there, seated at the table closest to the clock and drinking beer they'd brought down with them, since they worried over the age of her liquors. And damn it, she still didn't know what year it was or month or day. They always carefully avoided that subject. And she couldn't ask.

The one time she'd managed to scrawl "date?" in the dance floor dust, Ciara had stared at it for a long moment, shaken her head, and wiped the hard-earned question away with the toe of her shoe.

Ciara had told Mickey about being able to communicate with her former self through the radio, but when they tried that with her as a spirit, she couldn't make audible sounds for the speakers to carry. Mickey remembered nothing of that drunken conversation. She recalled the fight with Annie, and drinking herself unconscious, and the horrific hangover that lasted three days, but as Ciara had predicted, she'd been blackout drunk. She had no memory of that first meeting, no idea what they'd said to one another, and she wished she did. Every conversation with Ciara was precious to her.

And if she thought too hard about it . . . was that their *first* face-to-face meeting? Or their most recent one? Time did not work here the way she'd always thought it did.

"Hey, um, guys, I think . . ." Carlos looked up from his laptop thing, a concerned expression marring his features.

Kate frowned. "What is it? Did you find something?"

Jeremy moved to look over the other bartender's shoulder. Mickey liked Carlos. He was funny and seemed competent. She would have loved having him work for her. "Oh," Jeremy said, eyes going wide. "Oh, shit."

Mickey still hadn't adjusted to hearing quite so much profanity spoken out loud, especially in front of the ladies, but she'd come to understand that it had become commonplace when someone was surprised or upset.

Ciara joined Jeremy and studied the device with the screen that seemed able to show them whatever they asked for. Ciara's hand flew to her mouth and her eyes darted to the clock on the wall where she knew Mickey stood.

"We should, um, discuss this in my office," Ciara said.

"Right. Definitely." Carlos pushed his chair back from the table while the others scrambled out of the way.

No. Oh no. The frustration that had been building inside

Mickey threatened to boil over. They were *not* going to discuss aspects of her life and death where they knew she couldn't follow. She might no longer be alive, but somehow, some way, she was still a thinking, *feeling* being. And she was tired of being cut off from the rest of humanity. Tired of not knowing.

And no matter how much she loved it and how much it felt like home, she was goddamn tired of being stuck in this bar.

Extending her spirit self through the casing of the clock, she struck the inner chimes with all the energy she'd amassed.

BONG.

All four visitors startled and turned to face the source of the sound, eyes wide, mouths agape. Then all four expressions fell into a combination of guilt, embarrassment, and shame.

Ciara took a deep breath. She held out both hands in a placating gesture. "Okay, Mickey," she said, voice soft. "Okay." She glanced at her friends, then nodded toward the door. "Why don't you guys head on upstairs. I'll be up after she and I talk."

Talk. Hah. If Mickey had her voice, she'd be shouting. This forced silence threatened to steal what little sanity she had left.

Carlos, Jeremy, and Kate shot her varying sympathetic looks, though none of them faced her quite head-on since they couldn't precisely judge her position in the bar. Then they left, and she and Ciara were alone.

Ciara studied the clock for a long moment, as if she could see Mickey and was gauging her mood. She approached with hesitation, and Mickey realized with a pang of guilt that she'd frightened her.

She never meant to frighten anyone. She never wanted to scare Ciara.

The frustration and anger rose again. She couldn't apologize, couldn't make things right, couldn't do anything.

The lights around the bar flickered.

Ciara gazed up at the overhead bulbs, then back to the clock. "Are you doing that?" she asked.

Was she?

"We've been having a lot of electrical glitches in the lighting system upstairs, too. Is that you? Is that what happens when you're upset?" Ciara reached the table and sat back down, laying both palms to either side of Carlos's abandoned device. "I don't blame you, you know. I can't imagine what it must be like for you, but I'd guess it's pretty horrible. I'm so sorry we hurt you more than you must already be hurting."

Mickey tried to calm herself. She counted to ten. She looked around the home she'd made for herself. But that didn't help. It had become dusty and rundown after however many years had passed—no longer the warm and inviting refuge she'd created. So much love and care poured into this place, all come to nothing.

One of the bulbs Ciara had replaced shattered.

Shit.

Mickey had loved both her jobs in the bar and the theater when she was alive. *And wasn't* that *an insane thought to have?* It pained her to think her out-of-control moments were doing damage to spaces that had meant so much to her in life.

It pained her to think of herself as out of control at all.

She took pride in her stability and calm both at home with her overprotective brother, and in her dual roles as bar owner/operator and set crew member. But this situation . . .

Ciara took a sip from the beer she'd brought down earlier. The bottle trembled in her hand.

Okay. Get it together, Mick. They're trying to help you.

"You asked about Paul and Annie. Carlos found some information. Are you sure you want to hear this?"

Was she sure? Not in the slightest. But she had to know. As gently and softly as she could, Mickey tapped the chimes.

Ding. Ding.

"Okay." Ciara took a deep breath, then another swallow of beer. She was stalling. This must be very, very bad. "I guess I should start with the elephant in the room, today's date." She glanced toward the clock as if she could make eye contact, but of course she couldn't see Mickey there. "Today is November 27th ... 2022."

It was ... when? *Oh, dear god.*

If Mickey still had the ability to pass out, she would have. A hundred years. She'd been stuck in this limbo for a little under a hundred years. How was this even possible? Why had it happened? It meant ...

It meant everyone she'd ever known was dead. Long dead. Decades dead.

Her brother, her friends, Annie, her coworkers. Everyone. Gone.

Except for EZ who still sat on the chair beside Ciara, Mickey had no one left in the entire world.

She'd known. Of course, she'd known. Deep down inside, she knew it had been a very long time. But hearing it spoken out loud dashed every desperate but pointless hope to dust.

Ciara continued to look in her general direction, face sympathetic. She waited for a couple of minutes, giving Mickey time to digest that revelation. But how did someone digest something that huge?

"I'm so sorry," Ciara said. "We should have told you sooner. But I didn't know how to break that to you. And there's more ..."

Right. About Paul and Annie. Breakup or not, she and Annie had shared something special for a time, and Paul had been her only family. Still reeling from the first news, Mickey chimed the clock.

Ding. Ding.

Ciara reread whatever was on the screen of the machine on the table, frowned, and rubbed her hands over her eyes. When she looked up again, her face was stricken. "This really should be done in person," she said, standing and pacing away toward the bar. "I could use a shot right now."

Instead of pouring herself something and taking her chances, she snapped on the now-antique radio. After a moment to warm up, it hummed.

"Are you sure you can't—"

Heartbroken, devastated, Mickey poured all her emotional overload into a roar of anguish only she would hear. It filled the space with its pain, bounced around and echoed and then ... it exploded through the radio's speakers.

Ciara leapt away from the shelf where the radio sat and covered her ears. She reached out and braced herself against the edge of the bar, her knees almost buckling. EZ barked and barked and twirled in frantic circles of panicked energy.

Faint panting followed the shout. It took a minute before Mickey realized it was her own unnecessary breathing. She'd discovered early on that even within her shadow of a body, when she was self-aware, habit made her go through the motions of intaking and expelling air. And the more upset she became, the more rapidly she did it.

As heartbroken as she was, she had to focus on her breakthrough. She'd made the radio work!

She had to focus on Ciara, too, trembling against the bar. Now that she'd learned how to talk as a spirit, after a scare like that, would Ciara still want to hear her?

No. The radio wasn't good enough. If she really concentrated on her emotions, could she rematerialize? She needed to apologize, and she needed ...

Mickey wasn't sure what she needed, but whatever it was, it involved Ciara.

Chapter 31

November 27, 2022

SHE'S DEAD. SHE'S a ghost. And she's angry.

No. Not angry. Not like Mickey was a few minutes ago when Ciara and her friends intended to hide information from her yet again. No. Mickey was upset and hurting and she'd lashed out vocally and scared the bejeezus out of her. Ciara needed to get a grip.

But what if she is *dangerous? What then?*

If a ghost could cause lights to shatter and influence electrical flow, could she do other more serious harm? Could she start that fire Kate worried about? Could she throw things around? So far, she seemed pretty limited, unable to even cross the room without taking several days to do it.

Apparently, frustration was the key to improving her abilities in the afterlife.

"Okay," Ciara said, keeping her voice calm and hating the way it wavered. "Okay. I'm sorry. I'm so very sorry. I can't imagine what this is like for you. It must hurt so much."

No response. Was that good or bad?

She glanced toward the mirror. "I really wish I could see your face. It's like texting . . . erm . . . talking on the phone. It's so hard to gauge how you're responding to what I'm saying."

Something flickered, like an image wavers when heat rises off a steamy surface. And then, quite unexpectedly, Mickey's spirit appeared.

Ciara sucked in a breath and blinked, but no, she was really there, standing in the spot where she'd died, semi-transparent and frozen in place just as she'd been the first time Ciara had encountered her. She'd managed to cross most of the way back across the room and turn to face her, so the ghost was getting much better at manipulating her non-corporeal form. Was it all about emotional energy?

Ciara approached with caution, moving slowly until she stood directly in front of Mickey, but the spirit didn't move, didn't blink, didn't react to Ciara's proximity in any way. She resembled a mannequin more than anything Ciara had read about ghosts. Mickey wasn't breathing, but then, why would she? Except Ciara'd heard the breathing over the radio, which had gone back to producing nothing more than a simple hum through its speakers.

She tried waving a hand in front of Mickey's eyes. Nothing. Not even a blink.

"Well, EZ, what do you think?" Ciara asked the dog standing beside her right ankle.

EZ looked up at her, then at Mickey, shook himself, and trotted away to lie down beside the dance floor.

Okay then. "Okay," Ciara repeated aloud. "Let's try a different approach." She stared into Mickey's unblinking but no less compelling eyes. "How do I wake you up? Give me a clue here."

A clue. Wait a minute. Maybe she'd already received one. Something niggled at her brain.

The radio hummed. Maybe the scene from the past she'd witnessed wasn't the end of its usefulness.

Ciara shifted around Mickey to the wide shelf behind the

bar where the radio sat, still and nearly silent. Fingers hovering over the center dial, Ciara hesitated. Her hand shook. Whether she wanted to admit it or not, Mickey had terrified her with that outburst. Did she really want something more to happen?

I'm in the midst of the most incredible, unbelievable, fantastical experience of my entire life, which has been woefully devoid of incredible, unbelievable, fantastical experiences up until now. I've been led to this place at this moment for a reason, a purpose.

Oh, sure, I could leave, tell the others to bring in a team of ghost hunter experts who might claim to know what they're doing but wouldn't have any more of a guess than I do. But why do I feel like Mickey would vanish like so much smoke?

Other than the look through the mirror into the past, she didn't appear for the others. She appeared for me.

It has to be me.

Doesn't change the fact that this is by far the stupidest thing I've ever done in a growing list of stupid things.

Before she could talk herself out of it any further, Ciara grasped the dial and twisted it to look for a working station.

For a moment, nothing happened. She didn't know whether to be disappointed or relieved, when the soft glow emanating from the depths of the radio's interior pulsed brighter, then dimmer, then brighter again.

Like a heartbeat of warm orange light.

There was a sound, too, coming from the front speaker panels, so faint Ciara couldn't make out what she was hearing. She leaned down to place her ear against the right speaker and strained to understand.

Whispering. The radio was whispering to her.

"Don't freak out," she told herself while EZ put his paws up on her leg, ears pricked. He heard it too. "It's probably just trying to pick up an AM station. This thing's a hundred-plus years old. Maybe this is what it looks and sounds like while it's doing the job it was designed for and not transmitting ghostly screams." Damn if she knew. Yet one more thing to ask Claudia Waters the librarian.

Assuming she survived to get out of the bar.

Ciara glanced over her shoulder, double-checking that Mickey was both still there and hadn't moved. Yep, and nope. Nothing had changed in that department. But the whispering grew louder.

A male voice. The station announcer? Had to be. She couldn't understand what he said. It was a miracle the thing could get a signal at all down there in the subbasement. Did concrete and cinder block conduct radio waves? AM was stronger than FM; Ciara knew that much. She wished she could hear the words. What station was she listening to? She never tuned in to AM radio. It was always talk shows and religious sermons mixed with music for old people.

One of the other two dials had to be the volume control. She didn't want to lose the station, but she needed to hear. Ciara flipped a mental coin and twisted the right-hand dial to the right. *Click click click click.*

Loud crackling erupted from the speakers like the sound old phonograph records made in black-and-white movies. The whispering rose up around her, shushing and hissing and murmuring, a chorus of nonsense coming from a thousand voices all at once, maddening and disorienting, then wailing and crying. They sounded miserable.

They sounded angry.

But they didn't sound like Mickey.

Dear god, were there others?

Ciara pressed her palms over her ears, afraid she might lose her mind when suddenly and without warning, the sounds resolved into a single male and even pleasant voice. Slowly she drew her hands away.

"—hope all our listeners are enjoying this evening's program of music. Next up we have 'If You Close Your Eyes' performed by the All Night Jazz ensemble featuring vocalist Isabelle Jones, with band leader Adam Rothfuss conducting."

The first notes from trumpets and saxophones slid into the bar, soft and smooth and soothing. She'd never been a jazz fan, but she found the slow rhythm relaxing, and the soulful melody made her heart ache.

And her memory . . . twitch, for want of a better word. She knew this song. She'd heard it in her office, through the walls, through the vents. More attempts to reach her that she hadn't recognized.

The performance wasn't perfect. She caught a few botched notes, and she could have sworn someone coughed. A live broadcast? Did anyone do live music broadcasts anymore?

Her brain wanted to follow that question further, but the vocalist's rich alto interrupted her thoughts.

"Knew your face when you walked through that door.

Knew I might be the one you looked for.

Let me tell you, you're in for surprise

If you close your eyes."

EZ barked, interrupting the reverie Ciara had fallen into. The dog turned around, then lay down in a tight ball and tucked his head between his legs.

"What are you doing?" Ciara asked. EZ didn't move from the odd position. She shrugged and went back to listening to the music.

Was the singer's voice getting louder? It was. It definitely was. The instrumentation had faded away into the background, barely audible, but the vocalist . . . It almost felt like the woman was singing in Ciara's ears, both of them, in stereo, and directly to her.

"I'm the one that you want to see most.

Hoping our love won't give up the ghost.

But I still think that it would be wise

If you close your eyes."

211

The lights in the bar flickered, then steadied, then began increasing in brightness. Some sort of surge, maybe, only gradual and continuous?

If she blew all the theater's power, she was going to be in so much trouble.

The lights grew brighter and brighter, and the woman's singing pouring through the radio's speakers became louder and louder. Shielding her eyes with one hand and pressing the other against one ear, Ciara staggered away from the bar area into the shadows around the tables.

Which weren't so shadowed anymore.

Even though only a handful of bulbs were lit, they'd become so brilliant they illuminated the entire bar. And they were growing brighter still—so bright everything around her began to white out.

"Impossible!" Ciara shouted over the blaring vocalist. "This is impossible!" She directed her rant at Mickey's frozen form, as if the ghost could do anything to help her.

The ghost's eyes were closed.

"Oh, I'm an idiot." She'd been searching for a clue, and the powers acting upon this place had practically force-fed three to her. The song. The dog. Mickey.

Ciara closed her eyes.

Even through her eyelids, she saw the intensity of the light, so glaringly white she wondered if it would have blinded her had she not heeded the radio's warning. It brightened and brightened to the point where she feared it would burn right through her lids. Then it gave one last vicious flash—

—and went out.

Click click click. Isabelle's sultry voice faded away to be replaced by the announcer once more, but much, much softer.

Someone had turned down the volume on the radio.

Ciara stood panting in the center of the clusters of tables and chairs, fists clenched at her sides, eyes squeezed shut, but still able to detect the warm glow from the overhead bulbs as they returned to normal.

A warm, firm hand fell on her shoulder. Ciara wanted to open her eyes, but terror wouldn't let her, even though she knew what, and whom, she would see. She took a deep breath. Let it out slowly. It shuddered through her panicked lungs.

"Hey doll, you okay? You look like you could use a drink."

Ciara opened her eyes and stared into Mickey's bright blue ones.

Chapter 32

????

MICKEY SLOWLY RELEASED Ciara's shoulder. She could hardly bear to let go, but she'd scared Ciara enough for one day. Human contact. Physical connection. God, she'd missed the feel of soft skin beneath her fingertips.

"I'm . . . I'm . . ." Ciara stared around Mickey's bar, eyes wide and wild. Her breath came in short gasps. "Where . . . *when* am I?" she stammered.

Mickey grinned and shrugged. "Not sure. Limbo maybe." She turned toward the bar—the pristine, undamaged, dust-free bar. No cobwebs, no bullet holes. It looked freshly polished with the wax she kept in the back office. Maybe it was. "I was in my time over and over for a while, reliving the night I . . . um . . . never mind. Can't be then. The place was packed that night." *Not later. Not when I couldn't find my keys.*

She swallowed hard, forcing down the sick feeling that rose in her stomach, chest, and throat. "Then I was stuck in yours. And there was a long period in between when time passed me and EZ by. Before you found your way in. Before EZ found his way out." She waved a hand around to indicate the welcoming space she'd built from a storage closet, empty of other souls save herself, Ciara, and EZ curled on the floor and now raising his head to woof a greeting. "Now we're here."

EZ stood and trotted over, and Mickey scooped him into her arms to cuddle him to her chest.

"Hi, boy. Such a good boy. Been a while since I got to hold you." The trickle of tears down her cheeks surprised and embarrassed her. Not the image she wanted to display to the first guest she'd entertained here in a hundred years, to *Ciara*. She buried her face in EZ's soft fur and wiped the tears away.

Ciara's hand touched hers on EZ's back and she looked up. "I've seen you cry before," Ciara said, her tone sympathetic. "You don't have to hide it."

"The night Annie came back. So you said." She set EZ on the tile before her shaking hands dropped him.

Ciara nodded.

Mickey shook her head. "I barely remembered my own name when I woke up the next morning." Taking Ciara's hand—a forward move for her, but she couldn't help herself and Ciara didn't object—Mickey led the way to the bar and indicated the open stool at the end of it—of course all the stools were open, but the end one was her favorite seat in the house. Even though Ciara could have used the bar itself for support to climb onto the seat while wearing that short little flared skirt, Mickey extended her arm.

Ciara accepted the offer of assistance and situated herself by wiggling her very attractive rear end into the perfect position. "Such a gentleman," she purred.

Damn if Mickey didn't blush. She turned away to hide it and stepped behind the bar, hesitating a moment at the end of it when an unexpected chill passed through her. She hoped she wasn't coming down with something, then caught herself. Heaven forbid she should be sick *and* dead. Talk about overkill. No, it was the spot where she'd died. It bothered her to stand in it in her current, more solid, form. Weird.

She shook it off and faced her guest. Ciara had her elbows on the bar and her chin in her delicate hands, and all chills fled from the rush of heat that came from looking at her. Her short black skirt rode up high on her shapely thighs.

Realizing she was staring, Mickey averted her gaze and met Ciara's eyes. Ciara smiled at her. Caught. She didn't apologize. "You've got nice gams," Mickey said, reaching behind the counter for the ingredients she needed to fix her guest a drink: gin, an egg from the tiny ice box beneath the bar, lemon juice, simple syrup, club soda, and ice. She grabbed a clean shaker from the rack by the sink and began combining things.

Ciara's brows drew together, wrinkling her forehead in the cutest expression of confusion. "Gams?"

"Yeah, you know. Legs?" She didn't look up. Removing the yolk from the egg white took a bit more concentration than the rest. "You've got nice legs." Actually, Ciara had nice everything, but Mickey didn't say that. She stopped moving, freezing in place while her mind caught up with her mouth. "Does that bother you, me giving you compliments? I really shouldn't have—"

"I'm lesbian," Ciara said with firm confidence. "I told you that same night you were so drunk, but since you don't remember, let me remind you. It's not a problem at all."

"Oh. Whew." Mickey wiped imaginary sweat from her brow. "Then I have permission to continue?"

"Complimenting me?" Ciara laughed, the joyous sound brightening the somber atmosphere that had closed in around them. She waved a hand in a 'keep going' gesture. "Please don't stop."

At some point, Ciara's voice had taken on a breathy quality that sent shivers of pleasure coursing from Mickey's chest to her abdomen where they shifted into waves of warmth. She longed to hear those exact words in a somewhat different context.

Mickey cleared her throat as Ciara raised one eyebrow, then winked. Oh, damn. The woman knew exactly what she was doing to her. "Um, I, um, really liked the flapper number you wore the first time you saw me, too. Got any more like that?"

Ciara laughed again.

"What?" she asked.

"That was my Halloween costume," Ciara said, still giggling.

Mickey stopped, holding the two halves of the egg she'd broken in her hands. "You're serious?" People in the 2020s dressed like people from the 1920s for *Halloween*? Had her entire era's fashion become a joke in the future? She opened her mouth, prepared to defend her decade's choices, even if she didn't tend toward following fashion herself, but Ciara cut her off.

"I've been trying to . . . um . . . wear nicer things for you the last few weeks, rather than my jeans and baggy sweaters." A very endearing faint blush suffused her cheeks.

Oh, really? Mickey noticed. A tighter sweater here, a short skirt there, fine stockings or slinky black tights. She'd figured those were for work—that maybe Ciara's boss had complained about her being too casual.

But she'd been dressing for Mickey. The corners of Mickey's lips curved upward in a slow grin, but she didn't look up again. Instead, she drained the egg white into the shaker and discarded the yolk, then went to cover and shake the whole mixture together when Ciara reached out and caught her wrist.

"Wait!"

Mickey raised her eyebrows at her.

Ciara waved her free hand at the shelves of bottles behind Mickey. "Look, I'm maybe willing to risk drinking hundred-year-old gin. I mean, it's probably not toxic, just terrible. But I'm drawing the line at century eggs. You might be dead, but I'm not."

Ciara kept her voice light, obviously meaning it as a joke, but the reminder still sent a pang of hurt through Mickey's heart. This, all this, was impossible. She could imagine no course that would let them be together. Mickey willed herself to keep the hopelessness off her face and focus on this moment here and now. Whatever powers existed here had given them this time to share, and she was determined not to waste a second of it.

"Right," Mickey said. "Look, the eggs are cold." She placed the shaker on the bar and passed one of the other uncracked eggs to Ciara, setting it gently into her soft palm. Her fingers brushed Ciara's wrist and sent a shock of intensely pleasurable sensation up Mickey's arm and straight to her core. Judging from Ciara's quick inhalation, she'd felt it, too.

Mickey swallowed hard and shifted her feet, trying to regain her composure. For someone who no longer had a living body to arouse, she certainly was reacting to every contact with Ciara.

"There was no bad smell when I broke the first egg open," she managed to continue, her voice oddly low and rougher than normal. "And look around. The place is clean. Everything appears to be new. I don't think normal rules apply here, wherever or whenever here is."

Ciara set the egg on the bar and gave it a gentle twist. She watched it spin around and around, not making eye contact with Mickey, but her cheeks had turned a darker shade of pink. "Okay, but what about salmonella?"

Mickey squinted at her. "Um, there's no fish in this drink, promise. I'm not aware of any fish drinks, and I've been tending bar for years."

Ciara stared at her for a long beat. Then she burst into a louder fit of giggles than before. "Fish drinks!" She laughed so hard tears ran down her cheeks. She swiped them away on the back of her hand and gained control of herself. "No, the sickness salmonella." She frowned. "You'd heard of it in the 1920s, right? You can get it from raw eggs."

"Oh, yeah, sure. From uncooked meat, though, not eggs. Heck, my brother eats raw eggs for breakfast on the regular. Says it makes him strong. Not one of my habits."

Ciara's gaze traveled over Mickey's biceps in the fitted suit jacket she wore. "You are delightfully muscular enough," she said.

That heated Mickey up even more than she already was. Then it occurred to Mickey exactly what she was wearing, and a chill cooled all her fire. Pinstripe suit, black-and-white leather shoes, fedora hat. Shit.

A quick glance at the wall calendar confirmed her fears. Woman in a black evening gown holding a red feather fan. But where were all the other customers? Maybe it only looked like that night.

She finished making the gin fizz and nudged the glass toward Ciara. "Here. Try it. Live a little. I don't think you can get sick here."

But you can get shot.

Ciara lifted the glass and took a tentative sip. Her lips puckered, but she swallowed and forced a smile.

"Too sour? Too strong?" Mickey asked.

"That obvious, huh? Maybe a little of both?" she replied in an apologetic tone. "I'm a wimp when it comes to hard liquor. You have to mask it with something sweet for me to really enjoy it."

"Not a problem. I'll drink yours and make you a Bee's Knees with extra honey." Mickey put the second egg away and retrieved the mostly full glass, taking a swallow herself. Perfect if you liked lemon, but not Ciara's preference, which was fine. She'd memorized recipes to appeal to a wide variety of tastes. Two minutes later she set a new concoction in front of her guest.

Ciara wrapped her long thin fingers around the glass's stem, her nails painted the exact same shade of blue to match the unusual streak in her hair. She lifted the drink, took a sip, and closed her eyes as a blissful expression spread across her features. "Mmm, wonderful," she murmured, tongue darting out to catch the last bit of flavor on her full, red lips.

Oh my god. Mickey didn't know much about a real bee's knees, but she was definitely going weak in her own.

Ciara drank a few more swallows, each as good as the last judging from her cat-that-ate-the-canary smile, then pushed her glass a few inches to the side and folded her arms on the bar. "Now that I've had some liquid courage," she said, letting her expression settle into something much more sobering and serious, "we should talk about your brother and your ex. I said this should be discussed in person. Didn't think I'd actually get to, but who knows how long I'll be allowed to stay here."

Right. Time to dial back her libido. She came around the bar and took the stool next to Ciara, sitting sideways so she could watch Ciara's face. "Tell me," Mickey said, and braced herself for the worst.

Chapter 33

????

THE LAST THING Ciara wanted to do was distract Mickey from making her drinks and sharing small talk and admiring her legs, but she couldn't shake the thought that they were here now, in the un-aged Speak EZ together, face to face, because she'd mentally asked the powers that be for a chance to break her news to Mickey gently.

Some force beyond Mickey had made this happen. And she had no idea how much time—hah—they had.

She shifted on the stool to face Mickey, noting the rigidity with which the bar owner held herself, the tightness of her muscles, the hard line of her jaw.

The raw pain in those unbelievably blue eyes.

Ciara rested her hand over Mickey's on the bar, marveling at its warmth, its *realness*. She was so damn *alive*. She wished she knew how to keep her that way.

"I'm ready," Mickey ground out between clenched teeth.

Right. "Okay." Ciara kept her tone soft. "You know how long it's been, that they would be dead regardless, right?"

Mickey nodded once, an abrupt, angry motion.

"Okay," she said again. "No way to sugarcoat this. Your

brother and Annie died shortly after you did."

"What? How?" Mickey's voice came sharp and shrill, several notes higher than her usual sexy alto.

Turning around on the stool, Ciara searched the table where she and her friends had been sitting for Carlos's laptop, but that hadn't made the "crossing" to wherever she was now. "Damn. The details were on the computer . . . um, the machine Carlos was typing on. But from what I read over his shoulder, the police at the time thought it was some sort of lovers' quarrel. About a month after your death, Paul, um, shot Annie."

She stopped speaking, afraid to say the rest given how deathly pale Mickey had gone. The fingers under hers gripped the edge of the bar.

"And Paul?" It came out as a whisper.

Ciara took a deep breath. "He killed himself later the same night."

"Oh god," Mickey moaned. She tugged herself free of Ciara's hand, seized her glass in her trembling fingers, and downed her drink in one gulp. Then she slid off the stool and stood, presumably to pour herself another, but her knees buckled.

Ciara jumped from her own seat and caught Mickey beneath one arm, propping her back on the barstool. "Stay put. I'll get it." She hurried to the other side of the bar and grabbed the open bottle Mickey had set aside. "I'm no bartender, but I can slosh some whiskey in a glass."

"Slosh a lot," Mickey mumbled, barely intelligible.

Ciara did not, in fact, slosh "a lot," instead pouring only slightly more of the brown liquid than Mickey had started with into the glass she'd abandoned. She'd seen Mickey dead drunk and had worried for her. It was not a vision Ciara wished to revisit.

Mickey gulped down the second drink without commenting on the amount. Ciara doubted she'd even taken notice of it. Mickey set the glass aside with great care as if she were afraid of shattering it. The knuckles of her fingers had gone white from her grip.

"They were seeing each other, right? Annie and Paul?" Ciara asked softly.

Mickey stared at her knees. "Yeah. And Annie and Bobby. Any word on him?"

No concern or remorse in that question. Whoever Bobby was, Mickey had no fondness for him.

"Who?"

She raised her head, her face stricken, and Ciara's heart hurt for her. To lose so much so quickly and definitively. "Bobby," she growled, "the guy supplying booze for this place."

Ah, right. Ciara remembered the name, now, from the scene she'd witnessed in the mirror.

"Well, the go-between negotiating for me with his mob friends," Mickey finished.

"Mob?" Ciara's voice squeaked. "For real? I mean, my friends and I had speculated, but I didn't think you'd really . . ."

Mickey gave her a wry smile. "You want illegal liquor, you gotta go to the disreputable sources. Other than the bathtub gin dabblers, the mob runs the entire alcohol game in this town from the smugglers bringing it in from overseas to the guy who drives the truck and carries it down to your storeroom—in this case, Bobby."

Mickey had mafia contacts. Ciara had known about the bootlegging that must have been going on, the smuggling, but to hear that confirmation . . . It felt like she'd stepped into an Al Pacino movie, and in a way she had. Her mental list of Mickey's possible murder suspects kept getting longer and longer.

"Alcohol is legal again," she said. "Prohibition ended in the early 1930s. I don't know what happened to this Bobby guy. Do you have a last name for him? Carlos can look him up."

"Yeah, Valinkov. Parents came over from Russia, I think." She swept an arm toward the shelves. "Just like most of the liquor served here."

Ciara pulled her phone from the side pocket of her skirt, bought mostly because it *had* pockets in the first place. She clicked the on button, a tad surprised that it functioned in this in-between space. The screen lit up. She opened the notepad app and typed in Bobby's surname.

Mickey leaned forward. "So, it's a flashlight and a . . . typewriter? What else can it do?"

Turning the screen to where Mickey could see it, Ciara smiled. Anything to distract Mickey from the horrible truth of the death of her ex and her only family. "Primarily, it's a phone," she explained, swiping until the calling digits appeared on screen.

"You can *call* people with that? That tiny thing?" Mickey stretched across the width of the bar and snagged the whiskey bottle, then poured a more generous slosh into her glass. At least this time she sipped rather than gulped, but her hand still shook, betraying her calmer façade.

Ciara went along with the obvious attempt at a change of subject. "Yes, though I doubt highly I could do that from wherever here is, and almost no one actually calls anybody anymore. Mostly, we type messages to each other, but they are delivered instantly."

The bar owner ran a hand through her hair and gazed in the direction of her office. "When I had a line installed down here, I thought I was the Queen of Sheba. It was such a luxury, you know?"

Ciara nodded, though it was difficult to imagine a time when phones were considered luxury items.

"We had one at home. Had to with Paul being a cop and all." She choked a little on her brother's name, then hurried on. "But not down here. I put it in so management could warn me if cops showed up upstairs. You know, if they thought I was about to be raided. So we could double-check that the door was locked, or maybe make it up the stairs and out the back of the theater while they stalled them in the lobby. It always amazed me how I could hear another human being's voice even from miles away on the telephone. Such a vast improvement from writing a letter and waiting for a response, or even from the telegram because you could *hear* the other person. You could make that emotional connection." Mickey tilted her head up to focus on Ciara's face, though she looked a little bleary-eyed. "That's why I wanted so desperately to make you hear me. And then I went and frightened you with my shouting. I'm sorry."

"It's okay. You had reason to be upset. Still do."

"May I?" Mickey asked.

Ciara nodded, and Mickey took the phone from her, turning it over in her strong, callused hands. A little shiver passed through Ciara at the thought of how those hands would feel sliding over her skin. She pushed that thought away. This wasn't the time for it.

Mickey shook her head. "Amazing. And you say people choose not to talk on these . . . phones? Why would anyone choose less emotional connection when they could have more?"

"They could have even more than that. I can see people to talk to them with that phone. It uses cameras. You had cameras, right?"

"Sure. And silent films. But we didn't know how to combine the two—picture and sound. I think that's where we were headed, though."

"You were," Ciara assured her. "Maybe we can watch some together sometime." She tilted her head toward the device in Mickey's hands.

"On this?" Mickey held up the phone. "Incredible." She passed it back. "So, what do you think? Any idea who killed me? You think it was Bobby's crew?"

Ciara licked her lips while she thought, then grinned inwardly at the way Mickey's eyes locked onto the movement of her tongue. And it hit her. A hundred years. Before they both arrived in this place, it had been a hundred years since the woman beside her had been touched, held, or . . . anything else.

Still not the time.

"I don't know," Ciara said, answering Mickey's question while the bar owner stood on steadier limbs and wandered over to the radio, switching through a few stations of news before finding another one with soft jazz. She turned and leaned back against the rear shelf, her long, lean figure attempting a calm, collected pose when Ciara knew Mickey barely had a leash on her tension. "A mob hit would make sense if you stopped paying them for the counterfeit bottles."

"Figured that out, huh doll? I thought you had when I watched you and your friends in my office, but I couldn't hear what you were saying. Beauty and brains. My favorite combination."

And damn if Ciara didn't blush. Was Mickey flirting with her? She got so flustered she almost missed Mickey's next words.

"I didn't stop paying them."

Mickey stepped right up close, her face inches above Ciara's. She could smell whatever cologne Mickey wore—a combination of leather and vanilla maybe—as well as the gin and lemon on her breath.

"You didn't?"

"No. I had an obligation to my customers, not to mention a healthy sense of self-preservation." She chuckled without humor. "Lot of good that did me. And as far as I know, neither Paul nor Bobby knew about my prior relationship with Annie. She and I and Jimmy, my best friend, were the only ones who knew she'd been seeing all three of us at some time or another. Maybe even all of us at once, though I never got the sense she was two- or three-timing *me*. I'd like to think I would have noticed, but considering I didn't see my own death coming, who knows?" Mickey closed her eyes and took a deep breath, then let it out slowly. "We may never find out who killed me or why the murder took place."

Ciara hated the defeat in the tone of Mickey's voice and the slump of those broad shoulders, hated that she was the one who had caused it. But she wasn't ready to give up yet. Annie was the connection between all of them. Ciara had to keep digging.

The wheels were turning in her head, but they spun out of control in four directions: Mickey, Annie, Paul, Bobby. "I'll have Carlos look into what happened to Bobby," she said, tilting her head toward the radio where a big band number emanated from the speakers. "Of course, I can't do that until I get back, and I'm not sure how that's going to happen." Whatever or whoever controlled all this hadn't left instructions.

"Well," Mickey said, "maybe we shouldn't worry about things we can't change." She studied Ciara for a long moment, and the smoldering heat creeping into those blue eyes and chasing the anguish away made Ciara tingle from her head to her toes.

Chapter 34

????

TELLING CIARA SHE was a beauty hadn't been idle flattery. With that long, black hair and its striking blue streak and those amazing curves, the woman's photograph would have belonged in any pinup calendar. "So, what's with your hair?" Mickey couldn't help asking as she moved to clean up their used glassware. Whether this was an illusion of her speakeasy or the actual place, Mickey never liked to leave a mess for very long. "I mean, it suits you, but why blue? And how did you get it that color?"

"Oh," Ciara said, reaching up to twirl the dyed strand around one finger. Adorable. "It's, um, the cat's pajamas where I come from."

Mickey laughed and shook her head.

"Did I say that wrong?" she asked, eyes wide with an innocence Mickey couldn't resist.

"No, you got it right. But you aren't comfortable using it. It came off like a line from one of the productions upstairs in early rehearsals." The tune on the lowered-volume radio shifted away from the big band number that had been playing and on to more slow and sultry jazz. Mickey tossed the bar rag she'd been using to wipe down the polished surface into the sink. She extended her hand. "Dance with me?"

Ciara bit her bottom lip, eyes shifting between Mickey and the empty dance floor, clearly debating her decision.

"Please?" Mickey whispered. "I've missed holding someone."

Why the hell did she say *that*? It made her sound weak and vulnerable. Mickey didn't *do* weak or vulnerable if she could help it, and definitely not both at the same time. But with a hundred years of isolation, loneliness and, yeah, celibacy, she had plenty of vulnerability stored up, and not a little weakness, too.

And vulnerable worked. Ciara reached out and took Mickey's hand. The reaction was electric—a spark that went beyond anything mere static might produce but not the least bit painful. More like . . . exhilarating.

They reached the center of the dance floor and stared at one another. "I'm guessing you prefer to lead," Ciara said with a small smile.

Mickey gestured down at herself in her men's suit, then at Ciara in her short skirt and tight-fitting top. "Good guess. That okay?"

Placing her hand on Mickey's shoulder, Ciara nodded. "Absolutely okay."

Mickey's body flushed with heat. She took Ciara's right hand in her left and placed her other hand at Ciara's waist. They moved around the floor a few turns during which it became clear Ciara hadn't done a lot of dancing, not that Mickey minded. For Mickey's part, she'd had to attend all the lessons her brother had been forced to endure, sitting on the sidelines, wishing she were the one twirling those adolescent girls around. Then she'd go home, stand in front of her bedroom mirror, and practice the steps she'd memorized.

"It's a good thing you know what you're doing," Ciara laughed as Mickey shifted her foot out from under getting stomped on for the third time. "I'm so sorry. We don't really dance like this—"

"Anymore?" Mickey finished for her. "Show me how you dance now."

Ciara looked up at her, that mischievous smile Mickey had already come to both appreciate and fear a little spreading across her face. She dropped Mickey's hand, let go of her shoulder, and instead wrapped both arms around Mickey's neck, stepping in so their bodies were pressed together full-length.

"Oh, um . . ."

"Is this okay?" it was Ciara's turn to ask. She held herself still, though the song played on.

Everywhere they touched, Mickey was on fire. Her body wanted a lot more than a dance from this woman, and it was letting her know it. When Ciara shifted so Mickey's thigh pressed slightly between hers, Mickey swallowed hard and took a long, slow breath.

"Don't you dance like this, too? In your time, I mean," Ciara continued when Mickey failed to answer.

"Not usually on a first . . . date," Mickey responded, struggling to complete a coherent sentence, or thought for that matter. Ciara had begun to sway them back and forth, bringing her own thigh to brush against Mickey's center. Mickey might have been leading when the dance began, but there was no doubt Ciara was in control now.

"Women move a little faster in the 2020s," Ciara said, resting her head on Mickey's shoulder, her warm breath tickling the base of her neck. "At least some girls do," she amended. "I'm not usually this forward, either, but with you—"

"With me?"

"It feels right."

Yeah, it does.

"I think I'd like the 2020s," Mickey murmured, breathing in Ciara's unique scent—a mix of bubble gum and vanilla. "I like your perfume," she said.

Ciara laughed. "I'm not wearing any. Must be the hair dye."

Huh. Annie had sometimes gotten her hair dyed, always said it wasn't light enough. It smelled wretched for days afterward.

They continued moving around the floor as one song shifted into another. Mickey didn't want this moment to end, but when her hands wandered a little lower and her thoughts shifted away from the dance and more toward the cot she kept in her back office where she very rarely had taken a one-night stand, she ended their swaying and put some space between them.

She studied her polished shoes, afraid she might have offended her dance partner. "Hey, doll, if we don't stop this now, I'm gonna want to take it farther than we should go for two people who've barely met in person." When she looked up, relief flooded her at Ciara's nod and regretful smile.

"Agreed," Ciara said, fanning her face with one hand. "I'm all hot and bothered, and it's not the lack of air conditioning down here."

Mickey raised one eyebrow. "Air conditioning is only for the very wealthy. Besides, it's chilly."

"Not to me."

Me neither. At the moment.

Ciara watched while Mickey dried the glasses they'd used and replaced a couple of bottles on their correct shelves. Then they took seats at one of the lower round tables and just . . . talked.

Mickey was pleasantly surprised to discover they shared a love of science fiction. She'd read the popular novels by Wells and Verne, and Ciara had studied them in high school. Prior to the shooting, Mickey had finished *The Chessmen of Mars* by Edgar Rice Burroughs, and though Ciara recognized the author, she'd never heard of the book. "You didn't miss much," Mickey assured her. "The female main character was hopelessly helpless for the most part. Burroughs's other work is much better, even if it mostly features male leads."

This drove them into further discussion of the fantastical and a shared laugh over the fact that they were living it rather than reading it. Mickey described what it had been like to watch the bar age over the decades and her comparison to being in Wells's *Time Machine*, and Ciara told her about a film called *Ghost* and a love that transcended death.

"And at the end of that film, did they stay together?" Mickey asked, not meeting Ciara's eyes but rather focusing on the wall calendar set to January 1924.

"No," she whispered. "Her lover moved on."

Swallowing hard, Mickey reached out and covered Ciara's hands on the table with her own. "EZ managed to stay," she said. "I want to stay, too. We just need to figure out how the little bastard did it."

They turned to look at the "little bastard" curled up beside the bar, fast asleep.

"Damn, I wish dogs could talk," Ciara managed. "Though it's probably something simple, and he'd tell us we're very stupid humans."

The clock on the wall gave two *bongs* followed by a *ding*, making them both jump, and Ciara confirmed the time with her tiny portable telephone that apparently also acted as a clock as well as a camera and so much more it made Mickey's head spin.

"2:30 a.m., I'm guessing. But it wasn't nearly that late when I left. Time definitely doesn't work the same way here, but my phone still adjusted for it, without internet. That shouldn't be possible, unless it's another clue."

"Or a warning," Mickey said, sitting up straighter in the chair and listening hard. No sounds of footsteps overhead, but then the radio would drown those out. "Did you notice it chiming one? Or two at the hour, for that matter?"

Ciara shook her head, eyes going wider.

"I don't think it's a clue." Mickey now understood the phrase "blood turned to ice" as the chill in her veins made her breath catch and her heart race. "We still have a little time. It was after two thirty when . . . well, when. But I don't remember exactly how long past the half hour it happened. I was kind of distracted at the time." Somehow, she managed a small chuckle at herself. "Nothing is going to save me right now if history's going to repeat itself yet again. We haven't got that answer yet. But you being here is a wild card. I don't know what will happen to you if the killer shows up and you're here, and I don't want to find out." What if the murderer killed Ciara, too? Was that even possible? Not a chance she was willing to take. Even if Ciara was her only hope of escaping this limbo.

She'd developed feelings for her. And she'd protect her. Somehow.

"How do we get you back?" Mickey almost managed to hide the tremor in her voice. Almost.

"I'm not sure. How did EZ leave? I don't mean how did he come back to life, but when was the last time you saw him trapped with you and what did he do that you didn't?"

Mickey squeezed her eyes shut and thought hard. There was something. Something she couldn't quite remember, as if reality had overlain reality and buried one set of actions under another and another. Then it clicked. She opened her eyes. "The door!" she shouted, leaping from her seat and crossing the bar in four quick strides.

"Seriously?" Ciara stood with her hands on her hips. "He just walked out the door?"

"It wasn't quite that easy, but yeah," Mickey said, calling for EZ, then fumbling in her pocket for the keys that, of course, weren't there. "Dammit."

EZ stood and shook himself, looking back and forth between them.

"That night *is* repeating itself again. I couldn't find my keys then, either. EZ had carried them off somewhere." Mickey felt the panic rising. Even over the radio, the sound of an upstairs floorboard creaking reached them.

"Maybe it isn't locked. That was the point, right? You couldn't lock the door and keep the killer out. You haven't locked it since we've been here, and you have a habit of leaving it open." It was more scolding than statement, but Mickey couldn't argue, considering the outcome. Ciara moved to the door, grasped the knob, and pulled before Mickey could stop her.

"No, wait!"

The door swung wide. They stared into the thick cloud of gray fog beyond.

Except this time, something darker moved within its depths.

Chapter 35

????

CIARA STARED INTO the shifting tendrils, certain she'd spotted something solid moving in there, but her eyes couldn't penetrate it enough to determine what it had been.

"You see this, right?" Mickey said, moving to stand beside her. "It's how EZ got away. He ran into it and . . . left me behind."

Nails clicked across the dance floor as EZ joined them in the doorway. He didn't seem alarmed. Maybe she hadn't seen anything but fog after all. The swirling made it difficult to focus.

"Yes, I see it. I think maybe it's my way home. And EZ's." Ciara stepped forward but Mickey grabbed her arm and held her in place.

"Are you crazy? That's . . . that's not normal. And there's a murderer out there." Though she tried to hide it, clearly she teetered on the edge of terror, her emotional edge betrayed by the clench of her jaw and the rigidity of her shoulders.

Despite the seriousness of the situation, Ciara laughed. "What about this has ever been normal?" She followed Mickey's eyes to the clock, saw the panic, and reached up to turn her face away from it. "There's nothing out there. At least not yet. I have to go."

EZ trotted past her, straight into the fog and reassuring her there was no immediate danger. His head, body, hindquarters, and finally his stubby tail vanished. A moment later he reappeared, stepped fully out of the mist, and shook himself, then sat, watching them both. Reaching out, Ciara attempted to put her hand into the grayness.

And failed.

"What the hell?" Ciara flattened her palm and pressed it up against the swirling barrier. Her arm muscles tightened. She extended one leg back for extra leverage, leaning her whole weight on the one hand. By all the laws of science, she should have tumbled forward head over heels. But she didn't. The mist held her up. Mickey added her own weight to the attempt as side by side they pushed, but neither of them made it half an inch past the threshold.

Impossible. Like everything else.

Out of breath from their exertions, they stared at each other.

With a growl of frustration, Ciara slammed the door shut, closing them in the speakeasy once more. She turned to Mickey. "Guess that wasn't the way out for me after all. It's like the air is heavier out there, so heavy I can't push through it. Did you feel it? It was harder to breathe in the doorway."

Mickey ran both hands through her hair. "Since I've been dead for a hundred years, it feels odd to be breathing for real at all, so I didn't notice, but I believe you." She'd raised her voice to be heard over the blaring radio, the words almost unintelligible with the noise.

Wait.

The lights flickered overhead. She stared at the speakers on the front of the no-longer-antique radio blasting its smooth jazz across the bar. Ciara quickly walked over to it and placed her hand on the dial. "Cover your eyes!" she shouted.

"What? Oh. Oh hell." Mickey's voice was growing hoarse. She covered her eyes. She was clearly still trying to say something, but Ciara could no longer hear the words over the deafening sound.

She looked at EZ who'd curled in a ball at her side, snout between his paws. The bar lights grew brighter, the radio even louder. Before it was too late, Ciara grabbed her phone from her pocket and snapped photos of the bar, Mickey, and EZ. She knew Kate had tried videoing what they'd seen in the mirror, but no one had taken pictures. Maybe she'd bring back some kind of evidence to prove what she was experiencing to the others. She shoved the phone into her skirt. Leaving one hand on the dial, she pressed the other over her eyes and waited for the flash she knew she'd detect regardless. When it came, she twisted the radio off.

Click.

Silence. Blessed silence. And the glare through her eyelids had also faded to some kind of normalcy. Ciara eased her palms away from her eyes, blinking furiously to hurry them to adjust. On the floor beside her, EZ uncurled his body, stood, and shook himself, then looked up and wagged his stubby tail.

The remaining working lightbulbs, plus the couple more she'd added, left the bar in the hazy glow she'd become accustomed to, much dimmer than Mickey had intended for it to be.

And Mickey, of course, was gone.

A wave of longing so great it caused her physical pain had Ciara grabbing for the closest seat. Only after she'd sunk into it did she realize it was the same chair Mickey had occupied only minutes . . . and maybe a hundred years . . . ago, and she shivered. Except that hadn't *really* been the Speak EZ of 1924, but rather some in-between representation of it, a manifestation of Mickey's own memory perhaps.

But then, that meant the Mickey she'd spoken to, touched, danced with, held . . . wasn't the real Mickey, either. Not a ghost. Not then. Warm skin, pleasant scent, sensuous touch. But if not a spirit, then what *was* she? Whatever Mickey had been in those few hours, it hadn't been something of her own doing. So, either there really was another force at work, or . . .

Or Ciara had imagined the entire experience. After all, ghosts were one thing. Transport to an entirely different plane of existence? That was a whole new level of crazy.

Her thoughts raced as she fumbled her phone from her skirt pocket and brought up the saved images.

The Speak EZ appeared on the tiny screen, and Ciara's breath caught. Dim lighting. Cloudy bottles and silvered glass. Worn wood in desperate need of polish.

She double-checked the date and timestamp. Ciara had taken this image minutes before, when she thought herself to be in that in-between version of her surroundings, but the photo showed her exactly what she saw right now—a hundred-year-old bar in need of care and refurbishment.

Hand trembling, she swiped the screen with her thumb to the next image—EZ. And her eyes almost popped out of her head.

The dog glowed.

Literally glowed.

In the picture on her phone, an ethereal light surrounded EZ, radiating from his tiny body outward to a distance of about a foot in all directions. Ciara glanced from the screen to the real live dog standing beside her foot. Noticing the attention, EZ stood on his hind legs and placed his front paws on her knee. He cocked his head to one side as if studying her.

No glow here, but in the picture he looked like a tiny canine angel.

Except EZ wasn't dead.

But he should have been. Was that it? What did the light mean? And just because she couldn't see it now didn't mean it was gone. The glow hadn't been visible to her human eye in the in-between Speak EZ either.

She snapped a new picture of him and checked the result.

No glow now. But why?

Ciara wished she'd taken a selfie, wondering what the lens would have shown her of herself in that other realm between times. Would she have glowed? Or was that reserved for beings that died and managed to come back?

And how would it render a living being who'd died and *hadn't* come back?

Dread gnawing at her insides, Ciara forced herself to open the final photo she'd taken in that limbo . . . and promptly turned her head to the side and vomited on the black tile floor.

"Oh god," she gasped, then took a ragged breath through her still open mouth to avoid the smell of the former contents of her stomach. Fumbling with her hand but not looking, her fingers found and flipped her phone over, screen down, so she wouldn't have to review the image again. Not that it helped. It had ingrained itself in her memory.

Murder mysteries, cold cases, crime scenes—television and film had done a decent job of giving the public an idea of what dead bodies looked like, and yet . . .

And yet.

When the body belonged to someone you were attracted to—no, scratch that—someone you were *falling for*, someone whose body you'd been literally touching minutes prior and hoping to touch a lot more, in a lot more places, that altered the experience in new and much more horrific ways. The best word Ciara could come up with for what she'd witnessed in the phone's display was *grotesque*.

Under normal circumstances, if someone tried to hide the specifics of something unpleasant from Ciara, her vivid imagination would fill in the gaps with the most awful details possible. Roommate running late getting back to the dorms? Ciara's mind decided she must have had an accident or been attacked, and it provided mental images of what that would look like. Runaway pet? It had to have been hit by a car. A complete stranger reported missing on the evening news? Murdered. Definitely.

And in any conversation, the worst four words anyone could say to her were, "We've got a problem," because she'd jump to the worst possible assumption of what that problem could be.

When she and her friends had figured out that Mickey had been shot to death, Ciara expected nightmares about the event, terrors in which her subconscious would reexamine the murder in all its potential gruesomeness, but there'd been no bad dreams.

She bet she'd be having some now.

The picture she'd taken of the oh-so-handsome Mickey McFadden bore little resemblance to a human being at all— blackened bones with ragged bits of equally blackened flesh and strips of clothing still clinging to them, empty eye sockets, but all of it upright and facing the camera with its mouth in a lipless, lopsided, yellow-toothed grin.

Ciara fought to think. What was this trying to tell her? Was it another hint or clue? Had the body been burned after the murder, or was this what a hundred-year-old corpse looked like in general? A question for Carlos to research.

Pulling herself together, Ciara rose on shaky limbs and rinsed out her mouth with a bottle of water she'd brought down on an earlier trip followed by a travel-sized mouthwash from her purse, spitting the liquid into the bar sink. She fetched the cleaning supplies Jeremy had left behind the bar and mopped up the mess she'd made, careful not to look at the spot where Mickey had died, or the clock, or the radio, or her own phone still lying on the table face down.

She'd finished cleaning and was pouring out the now-brown water into the bathroom toilet while the pipes groaned and growled around her. They'd given up on worrying about a pipe break or leak. It was impossible to carry bucket after bucket of clean water from upstairs to the subbasement, so they'd resorted to taking the chance, and so far nothing had burst.

Ciara took the empty bucket in hand to set it on a table to dry when the radio turned itself on.

Click.

Chapter 36

November 27, 2022

MICKEY REMEMBERED. She remembered interacting with Ciara in the past, or the in-between, or limbo, or whatever the hell it had been. Her body remembered holding her, dancing with her, warming from the heat she gave off.

Being snapped back into the future—Ciara's present—was a bucket of ice water poured over her head in the heart of winter. And yet a little bit of Ciara's warmth remained, deep in her chest cavity, a tiny spark that widened and burned when she saw Ciara become ill in the center of her bar.

What had gone wrong? Ciara had been looking at something on that device of hers—the pictures she'd taken at the end of their visit together maybe. At least Mickey assumed she'd been taking photos. Ciara pointing the phone at her and the following flash of light had suggested as much. What had Ciara seen in those captured images?

When Ciara raised her chalk-white face and refused to focus on any of their means of communication, Mickey knew something was seriously wrong. It spurred her to action, and before she realized what she'd done, she'd crossed the length of the bar from the clock to the radio against the farthest wall.

She'd *moved*. She'd moved *fast*.

Ciara had done something to her. And it felt good.

But not so much right now.

She reached out with ghostly energy, focusing it to snap the radio on. It had worked to transmit her voice before, but she'd been angry and upset, unleashing all her strength in an effort to force her anguish through its speakers. Would it work again?

"Hey doll," she said, keeping to what she hoped was a whisper not a shout. "You okay?" The glow from within the radio's depths flared brighter for a moment, pulsing in time with the syllables in her words before returning to its normal dimmer hue. Did that mean it worked?

When she turned toward Ciara, the beautiful brunette's eyes had fixed themselves on the radio.

Yes!

Then, to Mickey's horror, Ciara squeezed her eyes shut and covered her ears with both hands, shaking her head. Too loud? Too creepy? To herself, she sounded normal enough. What did she sound like to Ciara? Why had she reacted that way?

It's a disembodied voice coming from a dead woman, you idiot, she chastised herself.

Mickey worried about trying again, but she couldn't lose Ciara now, not when they'd come so far, not when contact with her seemed to be helping Mickey regain her sense of her corporeal self. She raised her ephemeral voice a tad and leaned closer to the speaker. "I'm sorry. I'm worried about you." She paused, considering her words. "The last thing I want is to scare you."

"Well, that's what you're doing!" Ciara shouted. She stood and made for the door, her knees trembling, and her steps unsteady. Tears ran down her cheeks, making Mickey feel even worse. This was all going so wrong.

Ciara made it to the entrance and twisted the doorknob, throwing the door open so hard it banged against the exterior wall of the bar. Not knowing what all the commotion was about, EZ barked and ran in circles around her feet, almost tripping her.

In a flash, Mickey was beside her, invisible to Ciara's eyes but well within touching distance. What would happen if—

Mickey laid her palm on Ciara's shoulder.

A cold wind howled through the open door and into the bar, so strong it lifted Ciara's long hair, blowing it across her face and into her eyes and knocking Mickey's fedora clean off her head so it skittered across the nearby dance floor. Mickey released Ciara and bent to retrieve her hat, knowing in her heart that when she straightened, Ciara would be gone.

Instead, Ciara's fingers closed around the hat's brim at the same time as her own.

Mickey turned her head to meet Ciara's gaze, inches away from Mickey's face. They straightened together, drawing the hat up with them. Ciara sucked in a sharp breath. The hand not grasping the fedora reached around to rest against Mickey's cheek. All the panic over Ciara's fear rushed out of Mickey at the touch of those soft, delicate fingers on her skin. Mickey's eyes slid closed, and she exhaled, reveling in it. "Please don't run away from me," Mickey breathed. "Please don't go and leave me alone again. I'm not sure my mind can take another hundred years of isolation."

"You're ... solid," Ciara whispered, awestruck. "I can see you, touch you, feel you."

"Can you?" Mickey whispered back, eyes fixed on Ciara's full lips. Acting on pure instinct, she lowered her head and brushed her own lips against Ciara's.

Ciara responded, letting the tip of her tongue tease Mickey's lips apart and briefly dart inside. The fedora dropped from both their hands at the same moment and clattered to the floor.

Chuckling while still engaged in the kiss, Mickey let Ciara's tongue continue to explore. Normally she was the one taking the lead, but very cognizant of Ciara's prior fears, Mickey gave control over to Ciara.

She didn't regret it.

Ciara kissed sensually and slowly, determined to draw the most pleasure from the experience and making Mickey's heart race—something she'd only been imagining for the last century but which now felt very real. She slid her hands around Ciara's waist and tugged her closer, leaving enough looseness in her grip so Ciara could resist if she wanted, and thrilled when, instead, Ciara pressed herself full length against Mickey's contact-starved body.

Heat sped from the top of Mickey's head to the tips of her toes. They came up for air only to dive under again with Ciara threading her arms around Mickey's neck. Like two pieces of a puzzle, they fit together.

Ciara broke the kiss first, leaning her forehead against Mickey's shoulder and breathing heavily.

"That was . . . wonderful," Mickey murmured, stroking her hair. "I've been wanting to do that since I first saw you."

"Same," Ciara admitted.

"Are you okay now? What happened before? I really didn't mean to upset you."

"Oh. Um." She pointed a hand in the direction of the phone on the table.

Okay. Mickey released Ciara and strode over to it. When she went to pick it up, Ciara said, "Wait! You might not want to look. It's . . . you."

One eyebrow was raised; Mickey offered her most rakish grin. "I'm a little rumpled from the smooch, sweetheart, but I think I clean up pretty nice."

"That's not what I—"

But Mickey had already flipped the phone over. The screen lit from within by itself, maybe triggered by the movement. And she got a good long look at what had upset Ciara so much. "Is this . . . me?" Mickey forced out, studying the skeletal remains. One of the bits of ragged fabric clinging to the bones appeared to retain a few pinstripes. She tilted the phone sideways, but the picture turned with the phone. She tried again, this time rotating it a hundred and eighty degrees, but the image righted itself no matter which way she held the device. Frustrated, she thrust her hand still clutching the phone toward Ciara. "Can you make it stop . . . moving? I'd like a better angle."

Only then did she realize Ciara hadn't moved, her feet seemingly riveted to the tile by the dance floor. She had her arms wrapped around her own midsection, and she shook her head from side to side.

Mickey looked from the screen to Ciara and back again. "I'll admit, you didn't capture my best side—"

"H-how can you joke about it? You're dead!"

Releasing a sigh, Mickey set the phone back on the table, face down once more, and tried holding her hand out again. Moving like a skittish puppy, Ciara crept forward until she took Mickey's hand and let Mickey draw her the rest of the way to her side. "Yeah, doll. That's right. I'm dead. And a little beyond caring what this thing thinks I look like. Ya follow?"

Ciara took a deep breath. "Yeah."

"And I look pretty damn good right now, don't I?" Mickey struck a pose, fists on her hips, biceps flexing in the suit jacket, and a toothy grin.

Ciara couldn't help smiling. She sobered and rested a hand on Mickey's shoulder. "Yes, right now. But—"

Mickey dropped the pose. "But what? Look. I understand if you want to back off." She lifted the phone again. "'Dead' isn't usually on people's lists of things they're searching for in a romantic partner. It's hell on our dating options and makes a long-term relationship a significant challenge." She glanced pointedly at EZ. "But not an impossible one. I haven't given up. And I think we're onto something here. I was able to move a lot faster after our visit to that limbo Speak EZ, and I can appear to you now and move and talk all at the same time. Progress without a doubt."

Mickey held up the phone in front of herself. The image had vanished. She fiddled with it a bit and managed to accidentally get it to flash but couldn't get the picture to return. Shrugging, she set it back on the table.

"And I can touch you without passing through you," Ciara reminded her, stroking her hand down Mickey's arm and sending shivers beneath her skin.

"Um . . . yeah . . . you can do that. But—"

"But?" it was Ciara's turn to ask.

"But if you keep touching me that way, I'm going to have to kiss you again. So if you don't want that, speak up now."

In response, Ciara pressed her lips tightly together in the cutest pout Mickey had ever seen.

"Okay then." Mickey leaned in and resumed her exploration of Ciara's lips and tongue.

They kissed. They danced. They talked until Mickey's grasp on solidity began to fade. Eventually, when she went to take Ciara's hand and raise it to her lips, she found herself unable to do so.

A few minutes later, she vanished from Ciara's sight, but not before they'd said their goodbyes for the night.

Still able to see Ciara, Mickey smiled to herself as Ciara tucked her discarded phone back into her skirt pocket, blew a kiss to the empty room, and stepped through the door.

Chapter 37

November 28, 2022

"IT WAS THIS weird in-between place," Ciara repeated to Carlos, Jeremy, and Kate who watched her, wide-eyed, like campers listening to the counselor relate scary stories by the fire. They sat on the couch opposite her, side by side, Jeremy with a bottle of beer balanced on one knee and three empties on the low table between them and Ciara. Kate had both hands wrapped around a short glass of whiskey, knuckles white, while Carlos had his fingers clasped and folded over his abdomen—the calmest of all of them.

"So, not really New Year's Eve then?" Kate said. "Or was it?"

"I don't think it was. I think we were suspended somehow. But I'll know better if we see another flashback into the actual events of the past."

Carlos nodded once. "Good. Because I truly believe when that clock runs out again, it will mean bad things for everyone involved, but especially for Mickey."

Kate reached out and touched Ciara's hand across the table. "You two are getting awfully close," she said.

Well, at least they weren't disbelieving her. "I guess so," she admitted, the blush rising in her cheeks.

"Do you think that's wise, girlfriend?" Carlos put in. "While I still have faith in our sleuthing skills, you should consider the possibility that we might fail to solve this in time."

Ciara's stomach muscles clenched. "That's not an option. We'll figure it out. Anything on that Bobby Valinkov guy? And what's with the American first name? He came over from Russia, right?"

"Yes, he did. Along with three brothers and a sister, all of whom were part of the family 'business,' which, on the surface, appeared to be importing furniture from the motherland— conspicuously legit." Carlos leaned forward and pulled his phone from the back pocket of his black trousers. They all wore their work clothes—Jeremy and Kate in backstage black from head to toe, Carlos in his dress pants and a red satin button-down, and Ciara in a knee-length skirt and a conservative V-neck sweater. The theater had cleared out an hour prior once the evening show ended. They had the entire place to themselves, and the lobby echoed their voices back to them. "The Valinkovs had a store on Grand Avenue, just a block over from here, on what's now called Big Band Way."

"A front, you mean," Kate put in, taking a sip of whiskey.

"Yep, for sure. It got raided and shut down in 1932. They were hiding bottles of vodka and other spirits in hollow table legs, couch frames, and chair cushions, as well as manufacturing their own gin in a back room and printing fake labels to make them look like legitimate brands. They also bought cheap varieties of alcohol from different countries, shipped them here, and replaced their labels with others that badly imitated more expensive distilleries, so they had a reason to charge more."

"Like the ones in Polish that Mickey was studying," Ciara said.

Carlos nodded. "Yep, just like those. The cops arrested the entire family, including 'Bobby' whose real name was Sergei— but immigrants often adopted American-sounding first and

249

sometimes last names as well to better blend in with a foreigner-fearing population. According to the police report I uncovered, they all went to jail for almost ten years for smuggling alcohol and other illegal imports."

Ciara straightened, pressing her spine against the seat cushions. "Huh. So Sergei/Bobby was the only member of the love triangle to survive. Does that mean he's the killer?"

Jeremy shook his head. "Or does it mean he wasn't involved in the murder at all? He's a smuggler and a bully, and he had a gun, I'm pretty damn sure, judging from his behavior the night you witnessed him threatening Mickey, but you said he didn't even draw it. He didn't have the balls."

"And Paul killed Annie and then himself a month after Mickey died. Was that really a lovers' quarrel? Could it have been a fight about Mickey's murder? Or guilt? Or loss? We're still missing pieces." Ciara punched the closest throw pillow, stood, and paced beside the cluster of seating.

"Okay. Let's focus on something else," Carlos said, forever the calming influence. "Maybe there's a clue in the photo of Mickey you told us about. Can you show it to us?"

The blood drained from Ciara's face at the mention of the hideous image. She reached out where she stood and grabbed the armrest of the nearest couch. Carlos was up in a flash, wrapping warm arms around her and hugging her close.

"Never mind. We'll try a different angle," he soothed, pressing his lips to her hair. "Shh. It's all right."

"No. We have to examine everything." She handed her phone over to him. "But you look. It's in my saved images. I took it yesterday, so it shouldn't be buried too deep."

Rather than release her, Carlos passed the phone over to Kate while he rocked Ciara gently. Her taut muscles loosened, and her shivers stopped. With a shaky sigh, she stepped out of the circle of his arms, nodding her thanks.

They knew when Kate found the image. Her sharp intake

of breath gave her away. But when Ciara glanced at her, Kate didn't appear horrified. "Is this the picture you took?" Before Ciara could turn away, Kate reversed the phone and showed her the screen.

"No, don't show—oh." Ciara leaned in and took a closer look, then looked again. "That . . . isn't the one I got. I'm not sure . . ." She studied the picture of a confused but intent Mickey, eyes focused a little lower than the camera lens like she was trying to figure out the screen. Ciara remembered the flash going off when Mickey had followed her into present day and was studying her phone. She must have taken an accidental selfie.

Only this image reflected how Mickey had appeared to her both in their limbo space and afterward—handsome, dashing, and a little cocky with her rakish grin and bright blue eyes.

And she glowed.

Ciara swiped back to the picture of EZ, which had the same effect, an odd outline of white light that now appeared in both images around their subjects.

"What's that light?" Kate asked.

"No idea. But you can't see it in person, and it wasn't there before, though EZ had it earlier. Also, this isn't the picture I was talking about." Ciara scrolled back and forth through her saved images. "It looks like she deleted that one while she was messing with my phone." Hmm. Had that been an accident, too? Or had Mickey figured out how to discard the upsetting photo on her own?

She quickly brought up her recycle bin folder. Not there, either. Smart, Mickey. Very, very smart, if that's what happened. She'd gone to the restroom at one point during their lengthy conversation, realizing she needed to clean up a bit after her bout of nausea, and she'd left her phone on the table. That would have given Mickey the perfect opportunity. Or had those other unseen forces intervened yet again? She doubted she would ever know.

"So where do we go from here? I feel like we've reached a dead—" Kate stopped, catching herself. "Sorry. An impasse. And the clock is still ticking. We've made progress. That glow and Mickey's increased abilities indicate that. But she still can't walk through that fog you told us about. What's next?"

The lobby fell silent as they stared at each other.

Carlos cleared his throat. "I hate to say it, but I think we need professional help after all."

Ciara's first impulse was to object. She didn't want to turn this into a media circus or, worse, have some scam artists take advantage of them, running their time off Mickey's ticking clock. But after a moment, she had to nod. They had run out of trails to follow. They needed to forge new ones.

"Okay, but who? My contacts are a little short on ghost hunters," Jeremy said.

"The Bolini brothers," Kate stated, sitting forward. She turned to Ciara. "You probably have their info on your office computer."

"Um, who?" Ciara asked.

Carlos snapped his fingers. "Right! Before the pandemic. I remember." He turned to Ciara. "They came here a few years back. They were investigating all the old buildings in the area—anyplace that had reported ghost sightings, and you know this theater was always rumored to be haunted, well before Mickey and her bar showed up."

Jeremy took up the narrative. "They brought all kinds of equipment—special cameras, soundwave detection thingies—"

"'Thingies?'" Kate laughed. "Very scientific, babe."

"Look, I wasn't into it, and I wasn't paying that much attention. I remember because the set crew ended up carrying in most of their gear for them, and some of that shit was heavy. But it all looked expensive and was definitely high-tech, and management paid us overtime to humor them, so we did."

"But did they find anything?" Ciara asked.

Kate nodded. "Yeah, they did a write-up on it in their book on urban ghosts. Cold spots, subaudible whispering, light orbs on film, weird electrical surges. Nothing definitive, though. They said we had multiple spirits here, but they couldn't tell us who they were."

"Well, maybe they'll do better now that one of our spirits has a name. How about you give them a call, Ciara?" Jeremy said.

She looked at each of them in turn. "It will mean telling them about the Speak EZ."

Carlos rested a hand on her shoulder. "We'll work something out. A nondisclosure agreement or something. We've hit a wall even my detective skills can't break through. We're out of other options."

Ciara searched her brain for an alternative. She didn't want to share this with anyone except her friends.

She didn't want to share Mickey with anyone else. But if she wanted to save her, she couldn't think of another choice.

"Okay," she said. "I'll dig out their number."

Chapter 38

November 30, 2022

TWO DAYS AND several exhaustive computer searches later, Ciara conceded defeat. There was no finding the contact information for the Bolini brothers on her office computer's hard drive. The internet didn't provide enlightenment either. She found their blog with ease. "Yes, Go into the Light" popped up with a simple search. But the last entry had been uploaded in 2018, not long after they'd investigated the theater and surrounding area.

Their book had been released in 2019 to lukewarm reviews and a lot of accusations of fraud and fakery, including a class action lawsuit brought about by people who'd hired them to investigate their homes and places of business and claimed they'd been promised "results." By the end of that year, all references to the siblings ceased, as if they'd dropped out of existence. The "Contact Us" info on their website yielded a disconnected phone number and a Mailer Daemon response to the email Ciara attempted to send. To her surprise, their snail mail address listed a street in town not far from the theater, but a swing-by took her to a boarded-up brownstone with broken second-floor windows and no signs of life.

Okay. Maybe the library could help. Claudia had an interest in parapsychology. And the Bolini brothers were local. She might have interacted with them at some point.

"Claudia Waters. You know . . ." Ciara moved one hand in an ocean-wave-like motion across the line of sight of the woman operating the help desk. She stared blankly back. "W-A-T-E-R-S." Surely someone working at the library could spell, right?

Nothing. Not a blink of recognition. Then, "She doesn't work here," the woman said, breaking eye contact and pushing a couple of keys on her computer keyboard.

"Yes, she does. She's helped me several times now. She works in the section that has local records and blueprints."

Another two clicks. "Nope."

Someone in line behind Ciara cleared his throat. Ciara ignored him. She'd waited her turn for assistance, and with only one person behind the desk, that had been quite a while. Mickey's afterlife was at stake. She needed to see Ms. Waters.

"Maybe she's a volunteer," Ciara suggested. Claudia had said she "worked" at the library, that people like Ciara helped her keep her "job," but that didn't mean she got paid. "Would volunteers—"

"Volunteers are listed in the computer for security reasons." The woman held up a hand to forestall further questions. "There is no 'Waters' in the sign-in file for the last six months."

Another throat-clearing. This one female. Ciara turned to glare and froze.

Claudia Waters was beckoning to her from inside the nearest elevator, a wide smile on her wrinkled face. She waved her arm a couple more times, then stepped all the way in and let the elevator doors *clonk* shut. A moment later the lit numbers above it indicated a stop on the third floor where the parapsychology section was located.

A shiver passed through Ciara.

Muttering a halfhearted thank-you since the woman hadn't been all that friendly, Ciara hurried to the bank of elevators, pressed the button to call for one, and rode it to the third floor. As before, the section echoed with her footsteps, the emptiness tangible. She passed no other living souls, but the familiar librarian waited for her at the end of an aisle.

"Hello, dear. It's been a while. I was wondering when you'd continue your research into the spirit world." The woman's voice creaked a bit like a rusty hinge but welcomed her warmly with a hint of mischievousness underlying the words of greeting.

Ciara stopped a few feet in front of the librarian and crossed her arms over her chest. "Pandemic concerns, huh? Didn't want me to shake hands or touch you." She paused, then flushed with embarrassment at her inconsiderate words. "Oh! Is Covid what—?"

Claudia gave a little laugh, then turned toward the shelves on her immediate right and ran a finger along the bindings as if searching for a particular one. "No, dear. That's not what killed me. I passed on long before the pandemic began. Old age. Simple as that. But the virus provides an easy excuse to not give myself away. I'm not sure what's going on with your dog friend—yes, I know you petted him. You've got dog hair on your sweater, and it's glowing to my sight. But the living cannot touch me."

A sudden thought occurred to Ciara. "Is that . . . common? I mean, do people see ghosts all the time without realizing it because they don't touch?"

The librarian paused in her search and glanced at Ciara. "Sometimes, yes. Mostly no. Few retain a connection to this world. But I loved this place, and it loved me in return, and when the time came for me to cross over, I found two paths laid out before me. I chose this one, and I've been here ever since."

"Is that what happened to Mickey?" Had she loved the

Speak EZ so much that she'd somehow chosen to stay without realizing it? "Oh, you don't know who Mickey is," Ciara said.

"Oh, I most certainly do. She's the spirit trapped in the bar beneath the theater. The one you're trying to help." Claudia paused, pulling a book from the shelf just above her, and added, "The one you're in love with."

"I—oh! I mean, how ... I mean, I'm not—"

The wizened older woman shook her head, smiling. "Young people. Never want to admit love to themselves or others. Such a gift to be ignored." She passed the book to Ciara who took it in both hands. "I haven't met Mickey personally," Claudia went on, "but she sounds like a lovely young woman. And before you ask, some spirits are more mobile than others. Some get around. They don't make themselves known to everyone, including other ghosts, but I'm something of a touchpoint for the local spiritual community, a repository of information as I was in life. When you left the last time, I asked a few friends to check on your theater and its inhabitants. Had to make sure you weren't going to make trouble for us before I spoke with you again. Your dog is the talk of the afterlife, by the way."

As bizarre as this entire conversation was, Ciara felt no fear. Constant exposure to the supernatural had accustomed her to the onslaught of oddness. "I left him at my place," she said, waving a hand at the empty space by her side. "Only service dogs allowed in the library." She paused. "EZ's alive. I want to figure out how he managed it, and ..." She blushed. "I want to bring Mickey back, too."

The librarian clucked her tongue. "Don't know how he did it. Don't know if it can be done again. But if you figure it out, be sure to let me know, hmm? Now," she continued, nodding to the book in Ciara's grasp, "take that. I'm finished reading it. Check it out properly. And track down its remaining living author. He was on the right track, that one, and he had respect for the dead. If a ghost preferred to remain anonymous, he kept it that way.

257

It's what got him into trouble with the living. But if anybody can offer assistance, he can. Oh!" She fixed Ciara with a hard, authoritative stare she could easily imagine being used on noisy patrons. "And be careful. Not all the local ghosts are as attractive and warm as your Mickey."

Ciara raised an eyebrow, and Claudia chuckled.

"I'm dead, dear. Not blind. And at times I can see things beyond these walls. It was a gift I carried from life into death. So . . ." She sobered again. "Be wary. Some ghosts are downright rude and others dangerous." And with that, the spirit of the librarian walked forward, right through the shelves of books, and disappeared.

Ciara blinked once. Twice. But her heart rate didn't speed up. She didn't hyperventilate or feel faint. She laughed. "Quite the exit," she commented out loud.

And from somewhere deep in the rows and rows of shelves Claudia's joyful heartfelt laughter echoed back to her.

She glanced down at the book in her hands. *Urban Legends—Urban Realities—Urban Ghosts.* This was the book the Bolini brothers had written after investigating the theater and other city structures for paranormal activity. Ciara flipped through the pages until she located the entry on her place of employment.

"Big City Little Theater—Readings indicate multiple haunts here including those of frequent patrons, performers, and employees, though we were unable to obtain definitive identifications for any of them. In particular, one of the light orbs captured on both video and still photography behaved in an oddly animal-like manner rather than that of a human's residual energy. It kept low to the ground, rolled from one of us to the other, stopping at our feet for up to fifteen seconds at a time before returning to the first of us to encounter it. After its appearance (which occurred each of the five times we visited the theater property) small objects would be discovered discarded in the area: paperclips, keys, lens caps and the like. So, perhaps the spirit of a toddler?"

No. EZ. It had to have been EZ. Now Ciara's heart pounded, but in excitement, not fear. EZ had tried to get their attention but hadn't been able to . . . what was it called? Manifest. He hadn't manifested for them the way he finally learned to for her and the others working in the theater.

Ciara skimmed through several more reports until the final one stood out to her. "Our most satisfying discovery with regard to the unearthly inhabitants of the Big City Little Theater came weeks later when we paused our investigations into other buildings in the area due to a heavy snowstorm and power outage and had time to sit and listen to all the audio recordings we'd gathered via devices set up in a number of different locations throughout the theater structure. Imagine our surprise when white noise and background sounds from our team gave way to intelligible whispering from the recorder we'd left in the subbasement. 'What can I get you?' in a husky female voice came through clearly and distinctly, along with what might also have been, 'What'll you have?' and possible sounds of clinking glassware in the background that could not be attributed to our own people or their equipment as virtually nothing in use was made from that material. Interviews with the theater's owners and long-term staff revealed that the building never housed a restaurant of any kind, and the lobby bar had always been situated two floors up from where the recordings were captured.

"While some skeptics postulated that perhaps our devices had somehow intercepted the same frequency being used by microphones in a drive-thru fast food restaurant in the area, my brother and I truly believe that the speaker had passed on and was continuing to carry out their day-to-day job of taking orders in some sort of service industry, maybe even from a business in one of the other buildings nearby, oblivious to her passing into the afterlife."

Ciara continued reading, the final paragraph chilling her to the bone.

"Finally, multiple members of our team reported uneasiness and an anxious urgency while in the theater's expansive subbasement. One swore she felt a hand pushing her toward the exit to the stairs, while another heard someone whisper in her ear, 'Don't forget to lock the damn door,' as she was leaving the lowest level. Was this the same woman we captured on our audio recordings? Was the last voice a woman at all? There's simply no way to know."

Chapter 39

December 1, 2022

ALLESSANDRO AND MATTEO Bolini had been twins. Were still twins, depending on how one defined such things. Matteo had killed himself not long after the lawsuit against them had been filed. The brothers had been broke, their reputation ruined, and were being hounded by dissatisfied customers, the media, and bill collectors. Ciara located their heartbreaking story and Matteo's obituary easily once Ms. Waters had pointed her in that depressing direction. According to the article, the deceased brother's final words before pulling the trigger had been, "I will prove there is life after death. I will prove it myself!"

The writer of the article had added a snide comment at the bottom about how, several days past the brother's demise, no such proof had come to light.

In the aftermath, Allessandro vanished, but by all accounts the siblings had been close. And before going into hiding, he'd had Matteo's body laid to rest in a nearby public cemetery.

Ciara bet that Allessandro wouldn't have strayed too far from his brother's grave.

When she told her friends what she'd learned from Ms. Waters and her plan to visit the graveyard after work, Kate paled, an unusual reaction from Ciara's fearless coworker. "You're telling me I was chatting with a ghost the entire time I was researching blueprints, and I didn't even know it? She stood right next to me!"

Ciara pointed down at the dog sleeping in her lap, then glanced at Kate in the chair across from her. "You're sitting right next to one now."

Kate shook her head and leaned forward to scratch EZ behind his ears. EZ opened his eyes, licked her hand, and returned to his nap. "That's different," Kate said, settling back into the plush lobby chair and running her palms over the velvet-covered arms—a rare nervous gesture for her. "He's alive now."

"We have the weirdest conversations," Jeremy muttered.

Ciara barked a laugh, which made EZ glare up at her with indignation, which made her laugh all the harder, bordering on hysteria. When she regained control, she found Jeremy and Carlos exchanging concerned looks until Carlos raised his hand and said, "I'm going with you, girlfriend. Meeting dead people on our home turf here at the theater is one thing. Going to a graveyard after dark is a whole different level of spooky."

"I'm coming too," Jeremy added. "No harm in having extra backup."

Kate dropped a hand to the hammer hanging off the toolbelt at her side, stroking the heavy head of it like a familiar friend . . . or her favorite weapon. "I'm in," she said. She glanced at the guys. "Somebody needs to keep you two knuckleheads focused." That sounded more like the Kate Ciara recognized.

The time between their lunch hour planning session and the end of the workday crawled by more slowly than a sedated snail. Ciara finished about an hour or so before the set crew, so she headed down to the subbasement to check in with Mickey before the cemetery excursion.

And found the door to the Speak EZ unlocked. Again.

She stepped inside, EZ trotting ahead of her, and flipped

on the original lighting. She knew she hadn't left the door open after her previous visit. Her trip to Mickey's past had scared her, and she took care to remember what the consequences for the bar owner had been, even if the same threats didn't exist in 2022. She'd set a reminder on her phone to lock the door and had angrily stomped down the stairs after climbing all the way back up in order to do so more than once.

And yet.

Mickey's time is running out.

There had to be a connection between the approach of the new year and the consistently unlocked door. The flash to Mickey's past had been a warning. More and more, Ciara felt the urgency to find a way for Mickey's spirit to rest, alive again or crossed over, before ringing in 2023.

Because if she didn't . . . she had no idea what would happen.

"You're looking awfully serious, doll," came a soft alto from the doorway to the backroom office behind the bar. A moment later, Mickey appeared in the entry wearing black trousers and a white button-down, her short hair tousled without being messy—very sexy. She carried EZ on one arm, the other hand stroking him from neck to tail. "I wish you wouldn't worry so much." She stepped around the end of the bar, careful to avoid the "death zone" as they'd nicknamed the place where her body had fallen. Setting EZ down, Mickey crossed to Ciara, searched her eyes for consent which Ciara gave readily, and rested her hands on Ciara's waist. "What's eating you?"

You, I wish.

Ciara flushed at the unbidden thought while Mickey raised an eyebrow and quirked a grin. Without a doubt, the bar owner knew exactly what went through Ciara's mind at that comment, and likely intended to elicit the reaction with her choice of words. In response, Ciara slapped her lightly on the arm and marveled at her ability to do so. "Quit it," she mumbled. "This is serious."

Mickey sobered, tightening her hands at Ciara's hips. "I know it. But worrying won't help. It's a distraction. And there are good distractions and bad ones." She leaned down and kissed her, softly, then deeply, leaving them both breathless when she broke away. She used her thumb to rub the crease of worry that had formed between Ciara's brows. When it didn't fade, Mickey released Ciara and wandered over by the clock that had been their only source of communication for so many days. "You've been gone. Have you learned anything new?" She kept her tone casual, but Ciara could hear the tension beneath it.

Mickey was worried, too, but she didn't want Ciara to know it.

Ciara let Mickey in on what she'd discovered and her plans for the evening, chest tightening as Mickey's frown grew deeper with each step she relayed.

"That . . . doesn't sound like the safest move, sweetheart." She paced to the front of the bar and leaned her elbows on it. "Not all ghosts are friendly like me and EZ." A shadow passed over her face as she likely remembered the experience they'd both had in the speakeasy's "past." Whatever had approached the bar from upstairs hadn't had good intentions for them.

A sudden thought occurred to Ciara. "Have you met others? Ms. Waters said there were more here. So did the Bolini brothers in their book."

"I don't remember—" Mickey took a step toward her and froze, then caught her breath in a sudden gasp. The blood drained from her complexion, a neat trick considering she had neither blood nor complexion, and she went to one knee, her right palm planted against the tile floor to prevent a total collapse.

EZ let loose with a string of worried barks, running around and around Mickey's fallen figure, but to Ciara's surprise, keeping a few feet of distance between them.

"Hey!" Ciara shouted, dropping to her knees beside the tangible spirit. "Hey, what's going on? Look at me." She took

Mickey's chin in her hand and tilted her face up to meet wide panicked blue eyes and lips twisted into a grimace of pain.

Mickey gasped again, then wrapped one arm around her midsection. She jerked her chin from Ciara's grasp and doubled over with a low groan. Ciara scrambled closer on her knees and pulled Mickey to her. The ghost's entire body shook in her arms.

What was happening? Had their time run out? Could a person die twice? Because it certainly looked and felt like whatever energy Mickey had retained after her death was leaving her in a hurry.

Mickey moaned, an agonized sound, then whispered something Ciara couldn't catch. She leaned in closer until Mickey's harsh, uneven breathing blew hot and rapid against her ear.

"Move . . . me . . ." the bar's owner wheezed.

"Move . . . Oh, shit." In her need to impose upon Ciara the riskiness of her upcoming cemetery visit, Mickey had stridden forward . . . right into the spot where she'd died.

On other visits, Mickey had accidentally edged into the innocuous-looking area, identical in appearance to all the rest of the bar's black polished tile. Even a few inches within the perimeter resulted in exposure to what Mickey described as a "freezing, airless, hopeless space," and they'd worked together to identify its boundaries and avoid the area.

Ciara had suggested taping it off. Mickey refused, saying it would ruin the décor.

Now she was smack in the middle of that space.

"Okay, you're okay," Ciara murmured, hoping her tone was soothing despite the adrenaline rushing through her veins, because Mickey clearly wasn't anything close to okay. Ciara shifted her position to get behind the larger woman and circled her arms around Mickey, covering Mickey's own arms around her abdomen.

Then she pulled.

Or tried to.

Mickey's form rippled around Ciara's straining forearms, Ciara's limbs sinking several inches into Mickey before Ciara pulled herself free with a yelp of surprise. "What the hell?"

She tried again to get a grip on the bar owner. Disconcerting didn't begin to describe the feeling of one's body *melding* with another. And she couldn't get a firm grasp without allowing herself to quite literally sink into Mickey's fading form.

EZ gave it his best effort as well, sinking his teeth into the back of Mickey's waistband and tugging with all his might. It clearly hurt the little dog, and he whined and growled and trembled but refused to let her go.

When Ciara's arms had sunk in so far they should have intersected intestines, the sensation ceased. So. Mickey hadn't returned to her ghostly existence. Not completely.

Not yet.

Ignoring the weirdness as best she could, Ciara hauled her backward, dragging and pulling Mickey an interminable inch at a time. Her muscles burned with the strain, and she cried out while Mickey tried to help her by pushing back against her, the heels of her work boots squeaking on the tile.

Ciara had gotten Mickey's form about halfway out of the death zone when she felt the sticky warmth seeping through the sleeves of her fuzzy sky-blue sweater. Dread and horror settled over her like a thick fog.

Don't look. Don't look. Don't look.

Easier thought than done. Besides, she knew what she would see.

A glance forward over Mickey's shoulder showed dark crimson soaking into the soft fabric and spreading outward around her arms and across Mickey's once-immaculate white button-down.

"Oh god, please not again," Mickey murmured before she went limp in Ciara's arms.

Chapter 40

December 1, 2022

EZ'S ROUGH, WET tongue bathed her face while someone else poked her in the stomach. Repeatedly. Annoyingly. Her brother, Paul, no doubt, rousing her for work, not knowing it was her day off. Mickey swatted the offending finger away, surprised by how much effort that took.

Her arm weighed a ton. And it moved as if encased in molasses. What the hell was wrong with her? Had she been drinking again?

That had never been her go-to vice. At least not before Annie broke up with her. Things had slid a little downhill after that, though she'd kept it under control for the most part. No point in making a bad situation worse.

"Hey, wake up," a soft, feminine voice called to her. Kind. Familiar.

Mickey wanted to hear a lot more from that voice. She opened her eyes and looked up into Ciara's concerned expression. Blinking against the glare from the overhead lights, she squeezed her lids shut again. "Why are you poking at me?" she groaned, nudging EZ away with one heavy hand. He dropped into a perfect sit and cocked his head at her as if judging her condition.

Ciara cleared her throat. "Um, I was checking how solid you are."

"How *what?*"

"You were fading."

"I . . . oh." The reality of her situation roared to the forefront of her befuddled ghostly, not-really-existent brain. "Right." Mickey let her head roll to one side, taking in the dance floor she lay on, well beyond the edge of the dead zone. "You got me out."

Ciara nodded. "And you solidified. And we're using tape to mark that off. I don't care what it looks like. I'll bring some down tomorrow." She wagged a finger in front of Mickey's nose. "You need to stay out of that area until then. You weren't just disappearing. You were . . . bleeding."

That spurred Mickey into action. She slid her elbows higher up her sides and raised her upper half enough to look down her torso. No bloodstains. No blood. But she remembered the sticky, warm feel of it as it flowed from the wounds in her abdomen, remembered the oozing, remembered the pain and the smell . . .

Pushing off with her right arm, Mickey rolled herself over to the left and dry-heaved above the parquet wood flooring. Of course, nothing came up. She hadn't eaten solid food in a hundred years, and besides, she didn't really have a stomach, or a throat, or . . .

Defeated, Mickey let her forehead *thunk* against the wood. "This is impossible," she mumbled from the awkward position. But what difference did it make?

Ciara worked a hand under her chin and raised her head to search her eyes. "What is? What hasn't been?"

"Us." Mickey sighed.

Ciara's face fell. "I know it probably is, but I'm not giving up while there's still a chance. Are you?"

Mickey thought about it—too long, judging by the sudden set of Ciara's jaw and the hardening of her stare. But the last thing Mickey wanted was to hurt this woman who'd brought her out of the dark, empty loneliness she'd inhabited for so long. She was dead. Ciara was alive and had a chance to find real happiness with someone else, and regardless of what EZ had accomplished, they seemed no closer to figuring that out than they had been the day they first encountered one another.

"Maybe," she whispered, defeated.

Ciara grabbed her shoulders and shook her, making her head spin. "No. Uh-uh. No way. You are *not*. Not while I'm around. My whole life, every friend I've ever had, every woman I've ever liked . . . or loved," she said, never breaking eye contact, "has left me, or I was forced to leave them. I am *not* letting you quit."

Mickey tried to focus on Ciara's words, Ciara's pain and her past. She'd told Mickey about her childhood and all the times her military family had to move. Must have been brutal. And lonely. But none of that compared to the one single word in the middle of it all: "loved." Ciara loved her.

Mickey had to fight harder. She couldn't be yet another person who left Ciara behind. God, what else could she do?

"When I first got here, you couldn't even appear to me, couldn't cross the room or write in the dust without it taking days. Now I can see and hear you, touch you." Ciara's voice softened on the last two words, and Mickey got the distinct impression she wanted to touch Mickey a lot more than she had been so far.

That feeling was mutual and had been for a while, but wouldn't that make everything worse if they failed?

Scooting around behind her, Ciara slid her arms under Mickey's shoulders and pulled upward. "Come on. Get up. You need to lie down."

"I'm already lying down," Mickey groused, but she dragged her weary not-body upright to a seated position, then somehow got her legs beneath herself and stood. Her knees trembled. Her limbs shook. She leaned heavily on Ciara. "I'm going to drop and take you with me."

"I'm stronger than I look." Ciara half-walked, half-carried her toward the back office.

Yeah, doll. I'm figuring that out. But are you strong enough for both of us?

Ciara eased Mickey down on the lumpy cot. A cloud of dust rose from the pillow when she laid her head on it, but that didn't bother her. It felt so good to be horizontal. She closed her eyes and let her temporary body breathe.

Ciara ran her hand through Mickey's already tousled hair, smoothing a few strands from her forehead.

That felt really good, too.

Without looking, Mickey reached out, found Ciara's waist, and grasped it, tugging her closer until their lips met. The heat of Ciara's mouth melted the icy cold within her chest, and a deeper heat began to build lower. Much lower.

God, it's been so long.

A groan escaped her throat, urgent with need and desire, and Ciara answered the call, teasing with her tongue and untucking Mickey's shirt to slide cool hands against heated skin. In a rush, Mickey's strength returned and in one swift move, she rolled them until she was on top, her weight pressing Ciara into the mattress. The springs squeaked in protest.

"Careful," Ciara panted, "you're going to topple this thing like I did."

Mickey glanced over the edge of the tilting cot, one of its legs indeed looking as if it might buckle at any moment. She sighed. "Not exactly the romantic setting I'd envisioned for this," she admitted.

Ciara blinked up at her. "You envisioned this?"

Ah hell. Mickey hadn't meant for that to slip out. But in the dark, all alone, she'd held, undressed, and made love to Ciara a thousand times in a thousand passionate ways. All of which eluded her at the moment. Mickey was no stranger to seducing a beautiful woman, but Ciara . . . she was different. A little shy but still somehow in control, wearing her tight-fitting dungarees and yet oh so very feminine. Ciara was a *modern* woman, and Mickey had no idea what that meant anymore. Did women want the same things in 2022?

She shifted above Ciara, her groin coming into brief contact with Ciara's hip, and groaned again. So did the cot's frame.

"Yeah, I thought about it," Mickey admitted. "But in my imagination, the bed didn't fall apart beneath us." An idea formed, and she pushed herself up, chuckling at Ciara's pout.

"You aren't giving up, are you?"

"No way, doll. Just give me a minute." She stood and moved to the office door, her strength having returned. Ciara revitalized her. It amazed Mickey how Ciara's touch gave her energy. "And close your eyes."

Ciara's brow furrowed, but she did as Mickey asked, closing her eyes and resting on the dusty pillow. Like a princess waiting for her knight in shining armor. In a room covered in filth. Mickey shook her head and stepped into the bar proper, went to the radio, and switched it on. She clicked through the stations until jazz flowed like honey into the room, then watched and waited, her breath held, and her fingers crossed.

The lights flickered. The music swelled to fill the bar. Mickey closed her own eyes, waited a few beats, and clicked off the radio.

When she blinked her eyes open, she grinned at the polished wood and glass around her, the pristine bottles reflecting the yellow glow of the overhead lights. Mickey strode into the office and shut the door. She studied the clean and dust-free space and nodded once in satisfaction.

"You can open your eyes now."

Ciara opened her eyes, blinked, and stared at her. "How did you know that would work?"

Mickey shook her head. "I didn't. But I hoped it might. Better?"

"Well, it's clean, but the cot is still lumpy. And there's something hard under the pillow." She grinned.

Oh. That. Yeah.

"Um—" Heat crept into her cheeks.

Ciara laughed. "Don't worry about it. We all keep something around for flying solo, right?" She patted the mattress. "Come over here and distract me from the lumps."

Mickey sank down next to her, turning her words over in her head. Finally, she blurted, "Do all 2022 women keep . . . things like that around?" She tilted her head toward the pillow.

Now it was Ciara's turn to blush. "My tastes run to the mechanical, but sure, lots of women do."

Mickey had no idea what she meant by "mechanical," but she got the gist.

"Forget it. Come here." Ciara leaned back, pulling Mickey to her and over her so that Mickey's body stretched out along her length. She paused, running her hands over the long-sleeved shirt Mickey wore. "I like this on you, but I feel a little casual by comparison."

Mickey glanced down at herself. She still wore the pressed white collared shirt and black trousers—her clothing of choice when she had time to change between running theater lights and mixing drinks.

"You look swell," Mickey reassured Ciara with a crooked smile. She did look beautiful, and Mickey stroked the fuzzy fabric of Ciara's sweater up her sides until she'd covered her firm breasts with her palms. Then she paused, a shiver running through her. "Did you—?"

Ciara fixed Mickey with a half glare. "I locked the door. Now get your head in the game." She brought Mickey's chin down for a long, sensual kiss that set Mickey's blood on fire.

Mickey wasn't sure what "get your head in the game" meant, but as she slid down Ciara's length and snapped open those tight-fitting dungarees that showed off every sensual curve, she knew she'd figure it out or give it a whole new meaning of her own.

Chapter 41

????–December 1, 2022

TWO HOURS LATER, Ciara roused herself from a warm, hazy doze. Mickey lay curled tightly beside her. She'd pulled Mickey in close after their lovemaking, both to hold her in this bubble of time, and to prevent the two of them from rolling off the narrow cot.

She raised one arm to stretch it over her head; the other was pinned beneath Mickey's warm body.

Warm. Body.

So real. So solid. So freaking sexy.

Mickey had given her everything she'd ever wanted in a lover. She knew her way well around the female form, bringing her to orgasm twice before she'd allow Ciara to reciprocate. And even then, she'd tried to hold herself back, to ensure Ciara had everything Mickey could give her.

In the end, Mickey's willpower broke, hard, and she came with such force she slammed the cot against the cinderblock walls. Mickey gave her a sheepish grin, reminding Ciara she was "coming off the longest dry spell in history," then fell into a heavy sleep.

Now Ciara had to extricate herself.

As a testament to Mickey's exhaustion, she didn't rouse at all when Ciara tugged her arm free an inch at a time and clambered off the cot. It took only moments for her to scramble into her discarded undergarments, jeans, and sweater. EZ raised his head from where he lay by Mickey's feet and gave Ciara a forlorn look as she headed for the office door.

The little dog looked between them, Mickey and Ciara, clearly torn.

"You can stay here," Ciara offered, though she'd grown to love the terrier mix as her own, "but I'm not sure how easy it will be for you to get back." She wasn't sure how easy it was going to be for *her* to get back.

EZ gave a soft whine, hopped off the bed, and lowered his head to his bent front legs, extending his backside up in a long stretch. When he trotted to Ciara's side, she opened the office door wide enough for them both to slip out and closed it behind them.

The bar lay quiet and still, the yellow bulbs warming the empty space. Her gaze went to the wall calendar where a redheaded pinup girl wore a glittery dress covered in tinsel with a pair of large ornaments over her . . . yeah. Tasteless or not, though, relief spread throughout Ciara's body. December. Not January. Not yet.

The pinup girl's image seemed to follow her every move as Ciara stepped over to the radio. She pulled her cell from her pocket and activated the screen. 6:58 p.m. At least in her time. Maybe. The minutes had flown while she and Mickey made love, and she couldn't be sure of the exact hour. Regardless, she had to get back there. Her friends were waiting to accompany her on their cemetery expedition.

She reached for the knob on the antique radio but froze as her fingers brushed the ridged dial. Her breath caught in her throat. Had she heard a footstep outside the speakeasy door?

Ciara strained her ears, cupping one with her free hand.

Tap. Tap. Like high heels approaching with purpose.

"Oh god," she breathed. She'd locked the door. She remembered locking it. No one could get in. And yet . . .

And yet she found the speakeasy door unlocked on a regular basis, even when she was sure. Why hadn't that occurred to her before she slept with Mickey?

Because you wanted her so much. Nothing would have stopped that train from leaving the station, even the threat of death.

The clock on the wall chimed the three-quarter hour. 2:45 a.m. Hadn't Mickey said her death had occurred sometime shortly after 2:30? But it was the wrong day. It was December, wasn't it?

Or had Ciara's presence interrupted Mickey switching the calendar over to January first?

No. No, no, no. Mickey wasn't wearing her fancy suit. The details were wrong. It wasn't the night she died. It couldn't be.

Beside her, EZ growled deep and low in his throat, the fur on his back stiffening along with his small but powerful muscles. *Oh please don't bark.* Ciara scooped him up in her arms and clutched him to her with one hand while clasping his muzzle closed with the other. "Shh," she whispered.

The doorknob jiggled.

It turned.

"Shit." She had to find somewhere better than behind the bar to hide. She'd never make it to the bathroom before the intruder entered.

Back in the office then. If the door locked from the inside, they might have a chance.

She hadn't taken two steps before both the office and the entry door swung open. Ciara faced the office, her eyes widening and locking with Mickey's—she stood in the doorway, hair tousled, clothing askew, and eyes heavy-lidded with recent sleep. "Oh good," she said, voice hoarse, "I caught you. I was afraid you'd already—"

"Get down!" Ciara screamed, doing so while Mickey dropped into a crouch, her eyes darting to the front door.

The open front door.

But it wasn't a gun-toting madman who strolled through the entrance.

It was Annie.

Annie tossed her long, blond hair over one shoulder where it fell in perfect waves Ciara could never hope to emulate even with the help of a salon and an entire team of stylists. She raised an eyebrow, cocking her head to the side to study first Ciara half-hidden behind a useless wooden chair, then Mickey low behind the bar.

"Mick? Honey? What are you doing?"

"Um—"

"And what's this floozy doing here?" She pointed a finger at Ciara who straightened and planted her hands on her hips.

"Hey! I'm not the one skulking around in the middle of the night. What are *you* doing here?"

Annie blinked at Ciara, her brows drawing together in confusion. Right. Ciara had spoken to her as if she knew Annie, which, in a way, she did. She'd seen the confrontation between them that had ended with Mickey banning Annie from the Speak EZ. But Annie hadn't seen Ciara through the speakeasy's one-way mirror into the past. Annie had no idea who Ciara was, but given the glare Annie was giving her, she had a pretty good idea what Ciara meant to Mickey.

EZ slunk over to Annie to give her a brief sniff, but she shoved him away with the side of her shoe and stalked over to stand in front of Ciara. Before Ciara could move away, Annie seized her by something hanging from the front of her sweater—the washing instructions tag.

Heat rushed to Ciara's cheeks. In her haste and the darkness of the office, she'd put on her sweater backwards and inside out. Could she have been any more obvious?

Annie gave the tag a sharp, quick tug like correcting a misbehaving dog on a leash, then pushed her away so that she banged a hip into the nearest table.

"Woah woah woah," Mickey said, scrambling between them and holding both hands up in a blocking gesture signaling a cease and desist. "That's enough. Ciara's right. You shouldn't be here. It's . . ." She glanced at the clock. "It's almost three in the morning. And I told you not to come back. What do you want?"

The woman's eyes widened. If she could have fired the lasers in her gaze, Ciara and Mickey would be lying dead on the floor.

Oh, bad choice of thoughts. Ciara tried to shove away the mental image of Mickey pierced by bullets and sprawled across the tile, but failed with a shudder.

"You don't waste time, do you?" the woman sneered. "I say I'll take you back and you immediately play house with someone else. And a spic, no less. *Ciahhrrrrahh.*" She stretched the vowels and over-rolled the *r*'s, turning Ciara's name into a mockery. "You couldn't replace me with a nice American girl? Instead, you insult me with this trash? And what's with the blue hair? Dye job gone wrong, honey?"

Mickey slid around to Ciara's side, laying a cautionary hand on her shoulder, holding her in place to prevent a physical altercation. Ciara almost laughed. Mickey needn't have worried. Ciara didn't start fights. It wasn't her nature. She'd defend herself if the woman took a swing at her, but she wouldn't make the first move.

"Tell me something, *doll,*" Annie said, her voice a hissing mockery of a conspiratorial whisper all three of them could hear, "does she call you that? Does she call you 'doll'? When she kisses you, does she run her tongue along the bottoms of your top teeth? And when you make love, does she—"

"That's enough, Annie," Mickey growled, tightening her grip on Ciara. But was that possessive? Or was it panicked? Because, yes, Mickey had done those things, and probably whatever

Annie had been about to suggest next as well.

Jealousy and hurt flared in Ciara's chest but she tamped both down. It wasn't like her own repertoire of romantic moves was all that long. People tended toward certain terms of endearment. "Doll" was common in the 1920s. And you kissed the way you kissed.

Right?

Annie grinned like she knew she'd hit the mark. "I came for my earring," she said, pointing at a single diamond clip-on in her right earlobe, the left one bare. "You remember the set you gave me for my birthday, don't you? Anyway, one fell off the last time I was here. I'm betting you found it while cleaning up. Are you going to return it? Or is that one more thing you're taking away from me?"

Mickey released Ciara and crossed her arms over her chest. It was her turn to grin. "EZ found it and gave it to me."

"Perfect. So, if you'll just—"

"And I pawned it. Paid off the price difference with the increase on the booze your mob lover sells me. Seemed fair all things considered."

Ciara stifled a laugh. Oh, that was priceless. Any remaining concerns about Mickey's previous attachment to Annie vanished in that moment.

"Pawned it? One earring? Who would want one earring?"

Mickey's grin faded and her gaze dropped to the tile floor. "They were real diamonds, Annie. Good ones. I saved for months and dipped into the rest of my inheritance to cover the difference."

She looked up, her expression hard and her jaw set. "You weren't nearly as attached to them when I gave them to you. Barely glanced at them and put them back in their box. You know what I think?" She leaned forward, right into Annie's face the way she'd done when she'd banned Annie from the bar. "I think you dropped the one I found on purpose. I think

279

you wanted an excuse to come back and needle me some more. You had no idea what they were worth. Those earrings held no financial or sentimental value for you. I'm glad I pawned the one I found. I'm glad I got anything back."

Ciara took a step backward as Annie let out something between a hoarse cry and a shriek. She reached up and yanked off the remaining earring, raised her hand as if preparing to throw it at Mickey, then thought better of it and closed her fist. She shoved it hard into the purse she had slung over her shoulder.

Turning on her heel, Annie made for the door. When she reached it, she stopped and faced them one more time. "Go to hell, Mick."

Mickey laughed, but there was no humor in it. "I've been there," she said. She slid her arm around Ciara and pulled her close against her side. Ciara rubbed her back, soothing the tight muscles. Mickey glanced down at her, and the heat of Mickey's gaze almost melted her on the spot.

"If it weren't for this woman," Mickey continued without breaking eye contact with Ciara, "all of me would still be there. She set the important part free. Get out, Annie. And this time, don't come back. I don't care what reason you have. I've moved on." She stopped, laughed again, and shook her head. "In every possible way."

It wasn't until Annie had been gone for several minutes that Ciara thought to ask, "Did that really happen?"

Mickey paused in her fiddling with the radio, tyring to help Ciara go home to her time. "Hmm? Did what really happen?"

"Annie. Coming back like that. Did she really show up demanding her other earring sometime between Christmas and New Year's? I'd always thought when we got together in 'your time,'" she explained, making air quotes she wasn't certain Mickey would understand, "that we existed in some sort of, I don't know, time bubble that manifested as the speakeasy in 1923, but that we weren't *really* in 1923. But now I'm not sure.

That felt awfully real to me. Am I part of your history now? Or are you reliving part of it and we're making a *new* set of events in your past?"

Mickey stared at her for a long moment, then blinked and shook her head. "I don't know," she admitted. "It's hazy, like I've got two memories for that time period, one where she came back and startled us, and one where she came back and found me alone." Mickey fell quiet, studying the floor tiles while she contemplated.

"When she found you alone," Ciara asked in a soft whisper, "did she stay?"

The bar owner's head snapped up, her eyes flashing. "No. She didn't. I didn't let her. If I'm remembering the other time chain clearly enough, she wasn't as angry, but the general series of events was the same. I had pawned the other earring, regardless. And I threw her out again, regardless. You being here just added fuel to her fire."

Something squirmed at the back of Ciara's brain. If the events could be altered, even a little, by her presence in them, could Ciara prevent the murder from ever having taken place?

Or more concerning, could Ciara have somehow *caused* Mickey's death in some sort of weird feedback loop by enraging one of the prime suspects?

Chapter 42

December 2, 2022

BETWEEN THE SEX and Annie's unexpected visit, Ciara and EZ arrived in the lobby thirty minutes later than planned to be greeted by smirks and knowing smiles and a wink from Carlos. For the time being, she kept her time fuckuppery questions to herself. If it made her brain hurt to think about, and she'd actually been there, she couldn't imagine how her friends would take her theories.

"Jeremy wanted to send a search party," Carlos said. "It took both me and Kate to hold him back. You okay?"

"Fine," Ciara said. "More than fine," she admitted, "and no, you're not getting details." She glanced at Kate. "Well, maybe later, between girls."

Carlos pouted. "I'm fabulous enough for girl talk."

She patted him on the shoulder. "You are fabulous. Period. We'll see."

"It's already dark. Sun sets early this time of year. And cold. Grab your coats and let's get going." Jeremy held Kate's coat for her to slip into, and she kissed him on the tip of his nose in thanks.

That. That was what Ciara wanted with Mickey, and not just

within the walls of the Speak EZ. Somehow, someway, she'd get it.

A fifteen-minute walk in the freezing windchill, and the four of them huddled together outside the cemetery gates with EZ bouncing around on the opposite side after slipping between the bars.

"Gentle Hills Cemetery," Kate read on the metal sign hanging from the right-hand gate. "Fitting."

Even in the middle of the city, the local government had carved out this space generations prior and designated it for the deceased. Indeed, the grounds rose and fell with gradual inclines upon which sat a variety of headstones and here and there a small family mausoleum. Ciara had passed this place many times during the day. It was never empty. There was consistently someone leaving flowers on a grave or a groundskeeper tending to the grass or pruning the numerous trees throughout the property. The staff was always friendly, waving and smiling at her as she strolled by.

Now the scene made Ciara shiver, and not only from the icy December wind. The trees stood bare in the winter cold. Any flowers had shriveled to black, brittle husks on the chilled gray markers. Nothing moved except the branches in the gusty wind.

Kate gave the left gate a shove. It swung open on well-oiled hinges. An unsecured lock dangled from a chain by the handle. "Someone forgot to lock up?" she said, stepping through while the others followed. EZ hurried to Ciara's side looking up expectantly.

Carlos shrugged. "I live near here. I've never seen it locked. Lights are always on, too." He waved a hand along the dark gray asphalt path leading straight ahead. Tall black metal lampposts lined it on either side about ten feet apart, the tops aglow with soft yellow light, separated enough to cast eerie shadows while still providing enough illumination to walk by. "There's usually a night caretaker patrolling around. I've seen him through the gates on my way home lots of times."

"Oh, that'll be great on our resumes. Caught wandering around an empty graveyard in the middle of the night." Jeremy crossed his arms over his chest but continued following the others as they made their way along the path, stopping every so often to examine names and dates on the headstones.

Ciara paused, staring into the darkness at the rows upon rows. Markers more than a few feet from the walkway were illegible in the dark. "We're never going to find him this way."

Carlos slipped an arm around her shoulders. "Instead of wandering aimlessly and getting arrested for trespassing, maybe we could find the night watchman. There's got to be some kind of office or something somewhere, right? A caretaker's building? We could ask where this Bolini guy's grave is, say we're friends of the deceased and want to pay quick respects."

"That sounds like an excellent idea," a voice Ciara didn't recognize responded from the darkness to their left.

Everyone jumped. Ciara squeaked in surprise. Jeremy shifted in front of Kate who promptly smacked him on the shoulder and shoved him out of her line of sight.

They stared at the new arrival, a youngish slim man dressed in black jeans and an open knee-length black coat revealing a red sweater beneath. He had a red-and-black checkered scarf covering his neck and the lower half of his face, but his warm brown eyes twinkled with amusement. He brought up a black-gloved hand to tip his black woolen scally cap at them in a gentlemanly fashion.

Carlos cleared his throat and extended his hand for the man to shake. He had his thousand-watt smile going, all the bartender charm coming through. "Hello!" he said. "Would you happen to be the caretaker? We're sorry to bother you at this late hour. We were on our way home from work and thought we'd pay respects to a friend of ours, Matteo—"

"Bolini," the man finished for him. "Yes, I take care of things around here." He gestured broadly across the graveyard with a sweep of his arm. "I'm here every day. Seen you walking by a few times," he said, nodding at Carlos, then Ciara. "But you've never come in before. And I don't know the rest of you. Not very close friends if you've suddenly decided to visit now. He's been gone several years." The voice held a trace of a European accent, adding a softness to the rebuke, and although the amused glint remained, a bit of sadness had joined it. "You more of those ghost hunters? The family is done with that."

Ciara frowned. "Really? After a lifetime of pursuing them? Hard to believe the brothers would quit privately even if they gave it up publicly. It was their whole life."

"And Matteo died," Carlos said, voice full of sympathy. He glanced over his shoulder at her then turned back to the caretaker. "Look, you're right. We didn't know Matteo. We were hoping to locate Allessandro, his brother. We've got an . . . unusual situation at the local theater."

"A ghostly one, I assume," the caretaker said, shaking his head.

"Yes," Ciara admitted, a hint of suspicion forming in her gut. "Look, it's impossible to explain, but she needs help, and Ms. Waters at the library said Allessandro might be her best chance."

The stranger's eyebrows flew up at the mention of the librarian, almost touching the underside of the brim of his cap. He stared at each of them in turn, finally focusing on EZ. His gaze remained fixed on the dog for a long time as if studying him. Then he turned on one heel and headed off into the darkness, beckoning over his shoulder for them to follow.

"This is really stupid, following the creepy graveyard guy into the dark," Jeremy muttered as he stumbled over a tree root.

Ciara grabbed his arm to steady him. "I don't think we're getting the whole picture here. He's more than the caretaker, that's for sure. And he absolutely recognized Ms. Waters' name."

Carlos glanced sideways at them, a broad grin on his

face. "Yes. Exactly. I was wondering if you'd figured it out. The question is, is this Allessandro . . . or Matteo?"

Kate gasped. "Oh. Oh! Of course. But then, it's Allessandro. You shook hands with him, Carlos. And . . . you did that on purpose, didn't you? You suspected all along!"

"Even with the scarf, I recognized the eyes from the photos of the brothers on the internet. They're cute." He kept his voice low, but the excitement bled through. "I did some research of my own while we waited for you, Ciara."

Damn if she didn't blush again.

"And it could be either brother. He's wearing gloves, so I didn't actually touch him, or Matteo could have come back . . . just like EZ did. Maybe that's why the librarian thinks they can help—"

Carlos broke off as the figure leading them abruptly stopped and turned to them, an incredulous expression on his face. He dropped to a crouch, removed his right glove, and held a hand toward the dog who trotted over to sniff, then lick his fingers. "I knew it," the man breathed. He looked up at Ciara. "This dog. He's the light orb we traced at the theater, isn't he?" Without waiting for an answer, he scratched EZ behind his ears. "You like little shiny things, don't you? I'd still like to know what you did with my lens cap."

EZ barked once in response.

"Allessandro, I presume?" Carlos said.

The caretaker straightened, fixing each of them with a stern stare while he slid his glove back on. He opened his mouth to speak, but another male voice beat him to it.

"Actually," the pleasant tenor explained from the darkness between two nearby trees, "no." The new arrival stepped beneath one of the lampposts. He was dressed identically to the first, only this man had his scarf pulled down to reveal his entire handsome face bearing a soft but sad smile. "Good evening. I'm Allessandro Bolini. You've met my deceased sibling, Matteo."

"But how?" Jeremy demanded. He turned to Matteo. "You touched EZ. EZ's alive. You're dead."

"Things aren't always as they seem," Matteo said with a soft smile. Before anyone could ask another question, he turned and headed away from them toward a small, shadowy structure near the edge of the cemetery.

Allessandro shook his head. "Please forgive my brother's rudeness. He never was fond of pleasantries, and death hasn't improved his manners any. Let's go inside and we can talk further."

The six of them, along with EZ, gathered in the warmer interior of the caretaker's cottage office at the far edge of the property. It was a snug fit with Allessandro seated behind the desk, Matteo in a folding chair beside him, and EZ on the ghost's lap. Ciara and Kate took the seats in front of the desk, and Jeremy and Carlos stood behind them.

"Now that we're settled out of the cold, please, tell us your story." Allessandro leaned forward over the desk, his excitement evident in his posture. Matteo tapped one foot against the wood floor in an equally eager gesture.

"We've been trying to figure out a few things," Matteo explained.

"And confirm others," Allessandro added.

"What sorts of things?" Carlos asked.

Matteo and Allessandro exchanged a glance. Then Matteo shook his head. "Your story first. Your ghosts predate my experience. Once we compare notes, they may hold the key to all the answers."

Chapter 43

December 3, 2022

THE CLOCK ON the wall, an old-fashioned miniature grandfather clock complete with quarter-hour chimes, rang the half hour bells. Half past midnight.

Ciara made herself comfortable in the padded leather guest chair, crossing one leg over the other, while Allessandro fiddled with a teapot on a hot plate beside the desk, along with some delicate china cups and saucers. While he made and poured the tea, then doled out sugar, lemon, honey, and real cream, she related her tale of first meeting EZ, saving him, and their discovery of the hidden bar. She mentioned the strange mist and how EZ had seemed to find his way back to the living after a few trials and errors.

This brought her to her first encounters with Mickey's ghost, the glimpses into her life, and the travels with her to the past. The others chimed in with their theories of who the murderer might be and what they guessed could be happening as Ciara grew misty-eyed relating her fears that they would run out of time. They had less than a month before New Year's, and in 1923 it seemed even closer to Mickey's death date.

When she finished her tale, she took a long sip from the tea with honey that Allessandro had passed to her; she had no idea when he'd done so. For a moment, everyone remained silent, lost in their individual thoughts.

Matteo broke the silence first. "It's incredible!" he said on an exhaled sigh, looking at Allessandro. "Similar to what happened with us, but not quite the same."

"In what way?" Kate asked, getting to the heart of the matter.

"Well," Allessandro said, waiting until Matteo nodded at him before he continued, "the way in which your dog there returned from the dead for one thing. We thought we were onto it when we discussed self-sacrifice," he added to Matteo. "I think we're right."

Jeremy waved a hand in the air. "Hey. We're over here. Can you explain this to us rather than confirming whatever it is with each other? It's late and still cold even with the hot drink, and I have work in the morning."

Kate smacked him on the arm, but Allessandro nodded. "Yes, you're quite right. So sorry." He poured himself a bit more tea. Matteo refrained from having any, and Ciara wondered if that had to do with him being a ghost. Mickey seemed capable of drinking gin both in present day and in the trips they'd made to her past. Or had she?

She tried to remember specifics of when Mickey had imbibed. Definitely in the past, but had she actually swallowed anything in the present?

"Anyway," the living Bolini brother went on after blowing across the surface of the steaming liquid, "sacrifice. The key to returning from the dead seems embedded in it. And, especially, it seems to depend upon the person making the sacrifice not knowing the one they're saving is already dead or very close to it."

"That's a guess, not a proven fact," Matteo put in. "It might only be the sacrifice, or the sacrifice plus a strong affection. Or there might be even more to it."

Ciara swallowed hard. She knew Mickey was dead. If that was a vital factor in saving her, then . . .

Kate reached over and laid a hand on hers. "It'll be okay," she whispered, then leaned toward the brothers and said, "We need specifics."

In response, the brothers exchanged another look, and Allessandro nodded once. Matteo locked gazes with Kate, and said, "I'm not the Bolini brother who tried to kill himself."

"What?" Carlos exclaimed. "But the news reported—"

"It was me," Allessandro said, his tone soft and solemn. He stared down at the cup in his hands. "I'm ashamed to admit it, but we were discredited, bankrupt, accused of being fakers and kooks and many other worse things by both the media and our clients. We were trying to be honorable to the spirits we investigated, not giving away the more personal secrets we learned, not sharing that some were passing for the living. You said you met Ms. Waters?"

"Yes," Kate and Ciara said together. "She's a lovely woman," Ciara added. "Oh, and Antoine, the owner of the café next to the theater."

"And me," Matteo put in. "Most spirits pass on to another existence entirely, from what we've been able to gather. But others are tied to this plane by places ..." he paused, glancing at Allessandro, ". . . or people they love. They can come and go as they please and interact with the living to some extent, so long as too much attention isn't drawn to them. Some are never detected by the living at all while others have full contact with one or more. My brother's experience, and now yours, allows you more perception. But can you imagine Ms. Waters trying to assist library visitors in finding a particular volume with a media team trailing behind her? And if word got out that your friend, Antoine, still puttered about his beloved café, it would be overrun with ghost hunters and any number of religious fanatics seeking proof of the afterlife. We learned this from a couple of other spirits we encountered along the way during our investigations. We listened to their stories, their desperate needs not to give up what they cherished most and, after some deliberation, decided to remove ourselves from the parapsychology world altogether."

"You're saying that ghosts are all around us posing as living human beings," Jeremy said, shaking his head. "I'm not buying that. It's too much."

Allessandro shrugged. "Believe what you like, but you can't deny your own experiences here. I will admit, you've encountered more than most people, but that merely reinforces a theory of ours. Think of it this way. One of the biggest arguments against the existence of ghosts is that, given how many human beings have been born and died throughout the centuries, the world should be overrun with them. Even with the vast majority moving on to elsewhere, and no," he said, holding up a hand palm out to forestall any questions along those lines, "Matteo and I know nothing about where they go when they leave this plane of existence."

"Or you've decided not to say," Jeremy grumbled under his breath.

"Regardless, even discounting all of them, there would still be a significant number remaining on Earth. Naysayers argue that living people would be bumping into them constantly. They aren't. So, therefore, ghosts must not exist. Except, ghosts are pretty savvy about those they can allow themselves to 'bump into.' They have an instinct about which individuals they can interact with and which they can actually reveal their secret to." Allessandro took a sip of his tea.

Matteo nodded. "Allessandro and I believe that some people are 'ghost magnets,' tagged as such by some higher force to help those of us who linger, which would explain why your group has had contact with so many knowingly. I don't tell just anyone who strolls through the cemetery who I really am, but something compelled me to open up to all of you without really thinking about it."

Jeremy raised his hand. "But I didn't believe in ghosts before all this started."

"That doesn't matter if you've got this 'ghost magnetism' they're talking about," Carlos said. "Some supernatural force knows you'll be open to it eventually or makes you open to it when you're faced with it." He looked to Matteo for confirmation.

"Exactly," Matteo said. "Or that's our theory, anyway."

"So what's all this about the attempted suicide?" Jeremy said, earning a smack from both Ciara and Kate.

"Rude much?" Kate said, glaring at him.

"It's all right," Allessandro said. "It was what it was." He took a deep breath, opened his mouth to speak, and closed it again.

"Hey," Carlos said, reaching across the desk to touch Allessandro's arm. The living Bolini brother looked at it, then at Carlos's open smile, and smiled back. Something passed between them. Ciara wondered if the attraction was mutual. Carlos continued, "It's nothing to be ashamed of. Sometimes you end up in a place so low you can't see the daylight. It's not always something you see coming."

Ciara studied Carlos out of the corner of her eye. Yes, she could see how he might have gone through some difficult mental health moments when dealing with his sexual orientation. She knew she had. She'd have to let him know she was always willing to listen once all of this was over.

Allessandro shot Carlos a more grateful smile and another look of none-too-little interest before continuing. "As I said, it wasn't Matteo who tried to kill himself. It was me. We kept a gun for protection against some of the overzealous individuals who hounded us after we shut down our ghost-hunting business. You'd be amazed at the lengths some will go to if they think you know more about their deceased loved ones than you're letting on."

"I can imagine," Carlos encouraged.

"Matteo was out at the bank trying to extend one of our loans so we wouldn't lose our townhouse. I was upstairs in that house, alone, the electricity shut off, the water about to follow. I wanted a shower, but the water would be cold. I wanted tea, but there was no way to heat it. I wanted to be undisturbed with my thoughts, but the phone rang and rang with demands from our creditors, and finally I grabbed the gun from its case and . . ." He trailed off.

"And I came in and found him with it pointed at his head," Matteo said. "I couldn't process it. I just reacted. I threw myself at him, knocked him to the floor. The gun fired."

"And the bullet hit you instead of Allessandro," Carlos finished for him.

Matteo nodded. "Yes."

"I don't remember much after that," Allessandro went on. "I held him as he died. I pleaded for forgiveness. I begged whatever forces might be listening to take me in his place. Even well after he was gone, I screamed to the walls that death should accept me and return him. Finally, I reached for the gun and put another bullet in the chamber. But when I went to finish what I'd started and join my brother in death so that I might make amends for eternity, I was stopped."

"By me," Matteo said.

"But how? You were dead." Ciara looked from one brother to the other, then jumped in her seat when Matteo's now ungloved hand closed firmly over hers, his fingers warm and slightly calloused.

"Not as much as I was when the bullet first pierced my heart, no," he said, and grinned.

Chapter 44

December 4, 2022

"AND HE WAS able to walk around? Able to touch you?" Mickey asked for the third time since Ciara had joined her in the Speak EZ for a late lunch a full day after her visit to the cemetery and the Bolini brothers. She hadn't come the first day. She explained one of the owners had come in and asked her to "crunch some numbers" for him, eliciting a pang of guilt from Mickey, but she'd headed down to the subbasement as soon as she could drag herself away from recording receipts and balancing the accounts.

My death is interfering with her life. That needs to stop.

Mickey caught herself and laughed internally at her foolishness.

Right. It will. As soon as the repeat of my final year of life ends and I die again. At least that's what she believes. I can see it in her eyes every time she looks at me. She's sure she's going to lose me, lose what we have begun to create . . . and I think she's right.

Her heart ached, or what passed for her heart, as she sat across the table from Ciara. Mickey raised her glass of gin and tonic and took a long sip, then paused when Ciara stared at her. "What?"

Ciara pointed at the half-empty glass. "I hadn't noticed

before, but . . . you drink? Here? Now?"

Mickey raised both eyebrows. "Um . . . it's a bar. I own and run this bar. Of course, I drink. And of course you've noticed. You've had drinks with me several times." What was this?

"No. I mean yes, but no. I'm talking about here, now, in my present. You're long dead and you're consuming a beverage. And it isn't passing through you and spilling all over the floor. You're solid inside, too." She studied the lunch spread out in front of her—a bologna sandwich, some potato chips, and a half-eaten apple—and nodded with excitement. "Look! There're potato chip crumbs on the table in front of you. Did you steal one?"

A blush flooded Mickey's cheeks. "Yeah, sorry. I should've asked first—"

"You can have all the chips you want. Take them!" She nudged the bag in Mickey's direction, then laughed. "This is progress."

"You've lost me, doll."

Ciara paused, flushing with pleasure at the endearment, and Mickey winked. For a moment, Ciara seemed to lose her train of thought. "Oh. Oh, right. The food. You're ahead of Matteo Bolini. He can't eat or drink anything, even though he's solid to people he trusts."

Huh. Well, that was something, at least. "But he can walk all over the cemetery grounds, and in and out of the caretaker's office. That's a lot more freedom than I have."

Ciara had explained that while Matteo had also managed a semi-return from the dead, he had his own restrictions, very similar to Mickey's. He, however, wasn't traveling back and forth between past and present reliving the moments leading up to his death. The brothers theorized this might have been due to Matteo's death being so close to his return. And there was also really nothing more to be done to stop it. If Matteo hadn't intervened, Allessandro would have died. Of course, if they could go back further, perhaps Matteo could have talked

Allessandro out of the attempt altogether, but they weren't getting that opportunity the way Mickey and Ciara were.

"Everyone's death experience is personal. So is their afterlife. We can look at some similarities, but we can't explain the differences," Allessandro had told Ciara, and she'd passed that information along to Mickey, much to Mickey's frustration.

"Look, I'll admit it's ... something ..." Mickey said, taking another chip and wagging it at her before popping it into her mouth. She savored the salty taste that complemented the gin. Potato chips hadn't existed in her time. Delicious. "But we need more than that."

Ciara proceeded to explain about the Bolini brothers' "sacrifice" theory.

Well, she explained it as best she could because it *was* theory.

"They think it's a combination of having an affinity to ghosts, a personal connection to a particular one or a person about to be one, and a willingness and opportunity to sacrifice their life for that individual. It also takes a spirit that's strong enough to manifest in the first place. That mixture, in any form, be it sacrifice on the part of the party that's still alive, or on the part of a spirit with enough energy to intervene after its death, seems to result in the spirit having the potential to return from death, in part or in whole, with varied restrictions. Some can maintain solidity. Some can move back and forth from ghost form to solid and 'alive' in appearance and action. Some come all the way back to the living but can't leave certain areas or can't eat or drink. Others, a very few the brothers believe, return completely to live an entirely new life."

She paused to think, then resumed.

"Take EZ for example. He had more 'spirit energy' than most. He could appear and disappear to a lot of people with or without an affinity, even before I 'saved' him from an oncoming truck. But after I saved him, he became more and more solid. I put my life at risk to make sure he didn't 'die' because I didn't know he was already dead. I also had a connection to him because I thought he was cute and wanted to adopt him. And apparently I have a natural affinity for ghosts. Jeremy, Carlos, Kate, and I are ghost magnets, and I think me in particular. EZ eats, drinks, can come and go from the theater, and do everything a living dog does, though he can also still move in and out of locked rooms from time to time without thinking about it. He's got the best of all worlds."

Mickey tried to follow everything she was saying, but it made her head spin. She nodded as if she understood.

"You're definitely getting there," Ciara added. "We've got the 'closeness' part, the connection we need." She paused to turn away, attempting to hide the blush that had bloomed in her cheeks. "I think the key factor missing for the two of us . . . is sacrifice. I think . . . I think I have to be there when we hit New Year's Eve again in your past, when you die again . . . and stop it."

Oh. Oh hell no.

Mickey opened her mouth to protest, then closed it again. Ciara's face was so open and eager, her eyes shining, her jaw set with determination. There would be absolutely no way to dissuade her from taking the risk.

And it was a risk. A huge one. Judging from the Bolini brothers' experience, though not quite the same, Ciara could end up dead in Mickey's place. She had no idea what that might mean for Ciara or Ciara's soul or whatever this was that Mickey existed in. Would Ciara be trapped in the past while Mickey walked alive and free into the present? It wasn't *really* the past they'd been visiting, though, was it? Rather, it was some kind of alternative set in motion by Ciara's presence in Mickey's reality. The details of the days didn't match up exactly.

Or *was* it Mickey's real past, and somehow she and Ciara had gone back and Ciara had changed it? A headache began at the base of her skull, working its way over the top and down into the bridge of her nose to pound between her eyes.

Maybe it wouldn't work that way. Maybe they'd both die and be trapped together in their little pocket of reality, which might not be so bad . . .

Mickey jerked her head once from side to side, sharply and painfully, trying to clear that thoughtless, selfish, horrible idea from her mind. How could she even consider imprisoning Ciara with her for her own comfort and companionship needs? The pain ratcheted upward, and she winced. The bar rocked around her. She squeezed her eyes shut.

"Hey! You okay? Mick?"

Chair legs squeaked across the tile floor. Firm hands gripped her shoulders from behind.

"Talk to me. What's wrong?"

Mickey forced her eyes open, then squinted, even the softer lighting of the old yellow bulbs too much for her. "Headache," she ground out between gritted teeth. "Bad one. It'll pass." She took another swig of gin. The torture eased. She let out a long sigh and managed a grin. "Definitely glad I can drink in this time."

That earned her a smile, and Ciara returned to her seat, though she kept a wary eye on Mickey. "Okay, so the plan. I'll visit every night from now forward. We'll use the radio to go . . . wherever it is we go. And if it's New Year's Eve—"

"You'll what?" Mickey asked, the exhaustion with all of it seeping into her tone and expression. She was so very tired. "Can you fend off some guy with a gun? Can you stop a bullet?" Her voice edged on anger. She fought to keep it even.

"Well, we could start by making sure the door is locked."

Yeah, she could do that. She *would* do that. And maybe it would be enough. But either way, she wasn't letting Ciara be anywhere near the man who shot her.

No matter what it cost.

Ciara shut the storeroom door behind her, pausing outside in the exterior space until she heard the lock snick. So weird to think that if anyone had been with her beyond her immediate circle of friends, they might not have heard the bolt slide home, or maybe they would have, and been freaked out by locks locking themselves from the inside of what would be to them a room empty of anyone appearing to be living.

Wait a minute. How was Mickey locking the speakeasy door, especially here in the present? Ciara patted her pocket, feeling the key inside. Yep, still had it. So . . . what? A ghost key? She thought about it. Okay, yeah, maybe. Mickey wasn't naked (though Ciara certainly preferred her that way). Her clothing had traveled with her into the modern day and solidified when Mickey did. Why not the key to the speakeasy as well? So now they each had one.

My life is so weird.

It felt good to have a plan, though. She didn't trudge so heavily up the subbasement stairs, and her head didn't hang low with disappointment. However, her heart beat a little faster at the thought of the risk she would take.

Knowing the murder was approaching for weeks in advance was much different than what had happened that day on the street with EZ. Then, she'd reacted on pure instinct to save the little dog from being run over by the oncoming truck. Now she had time to think about everything, and she wished she didn't.

I'll be fine. I can't die in the past. I'll just be reborn again and be alive in the present.

Unless . . . a little voice whispered in the darker recesses of her mind, *that isn't the past at all, but some other place where you can die for real. This isn't a game. It isn't a play being performed upstairs on the stage. Mickey is dead. You could be too.*

But if she succeeded, she might bring Mickey back. She told the voice to shut up.

Ciara touched her lips with her fingertips as she reached the top of the stairwell and stepped into the lobby. The memory of Mickey's hot parting kiss replayed itself, causing a flush to race into her cheeks and a pool of warm desire to gather in her core. She'd gotten used to those kisses, and she didn't want them to end.

She'd do anything to keep Mickey in her life, even risk losing her own.

Chapter 45

December 5, 2022

MICKEY FLOPPED BACK on the lumpy cot, her muscles turned to limp rags and her lungs heaving. Ciara followed her down, landing on Mickey's chest, her own hot breath panting across Mickey's bare breasts and hardening her nipples. Again.

"Geez babe, stop. I can't go another round like that last one," Mickey wheezed. No dame had ever worn her out like this one did. And judging from the flush throughout Ciara's skin and the lack of focus in her eyes when she weakly raised her head to look in Mickey's face, Mickey had given as good as she'd got.

Ciara blinked, focusing, and grinned down at her. "You sure about that?" She tweaked a taut nipple.

Mickey groaned in response, stunned when her clit twitched in sympathy. With a chuckle, she tugged Ciara's hand away. "Yes, I'm sure. Three's my limit." She shifted out from under the pleasantly soft body above her and swung her legs over the side of the bed. EZ hopped up from his snoozing spot near where they'd left their clothes—on the floor by the foot of the cot, and wagged his stubby tail in a blur of excitement.

"Where are you going?" Ciara asked, rising up on one elbow to openly admire Mickey from head to toe while Mickey pulled on her trousers and black T-shirt.

Didn't seem to matter what she wore, even her casual work clothes, Ciara loved her in it.

Reading her mind, Ciara added, "Those muscles of yours make everything look good."

Mickey fought a blush and lost. Damn, this woman could undo her with nothing more than a once-over. "I need some water. I'll bring you a glass, too." She creaked open the door and stepped into the bar while Ciara lay back on the cot.

As she closed the door behind her, something shifted—a subtle rustling Mickey couldn't quite identify, like fabric brushing against her arms and legs. The sensation passed, and she shrugged it off, moving farther into the familiar space. The radio played softly, filling the main room with sultry jazz. She'd left the string lights around the bar on, but the rest lay shrouded in shadows, quiet and empty, and for a moment, Mickey was besieged by all she'd lost in her past: friends, family, coworkers, her entire world gone. She shook her head once, a sharp, angry movement. Look at all she'd gained. A whole new existence. Granted, a limited one, but *she'd gotten to see the future!*

Ciara had shown her unbelievable things on her portable telephone's screen: new inventions, technology, music, film. And then there was Ciara herself.

Mickey hadn't recognized the empty place inside her until Ciara filled it. Ciara had said the words, even if a little indirectly. Mickey hadn't been quite ready. But she was ready now.

I'm in love with her.

Damn terrible timing.

She shook her head again, poured two glasses of water from the sink, and turned toward the office, then paused. Something niggled at her, the same unsettled, "off" feeling she'd had when she'd entered. She studied the bar intently, peering into corners, scanning the walls . . .

The calendar was missing. Her ghostly heart stopped.

But . . . that didn't make sense. She'd taken it down and put up the new one almost immediately. . . sometime very early in the morning of January 1, 1924. And right before her world had come to an end.

Her heartbeat shifted from zero to a million beats per second. Three steps took her to the garbage can behind the bar where she found the balled-up 1923 calendar in its otherwise empty interior.

Okay. So why wasn't the new one hanging on the wall? And what did this mean?

She stared at her feet in her black-and-white leather shoes beside the trashcan.

She hadn't been wearing shoes when she left the office.

One step to the left took her in front of the mirror behind the bar, revealing her crisp white button-down and pressed black suit pants. Her jacket hung off the edge of the bar.

Had she somehow stepped into the speakeasy in the moment of time exactly *between* throwing the old calendar away and hanging the new one?

With a trembling hand, Mickey reached into the space immediately beneath the bar where her fingers closed around the replacement calendar. She'd stored it after purchase, waiting for January 1.

The clock on the wall chimed the half hour. She didn't need to look to know it was 2:30 a.m., but a quick glance confirmed it.

Oh god.

She had to get Ciara out of there. But first she had to make it look like any day but New Year's or Ciara would never leave.

Mickey gave the new calendar a hard, crumpling shove to the rear of the interior shelf where Ciara wouldn't see it. She snatched up the suit jacket and jammed it into the same space, then kicked off her shoes and tucked them beneath the sink. Maybe Ciara wouldn't notice the change of shirt and

303

trousers. The light was dim, and they were both tired from their lovemaking.

She snatched the old calendar out of the trash, pressing and smoothing out its creases as she crossed to the wall, then slammed it back on the nail from which it had hung throughout the previous year.

The noise brought a sleepy Ciara out of the office, rubbing her eyes and blinking at her. "What are you doing?"

"Oh! Oh, the damn calendar fell off the wall again. I was putting it back up. Sorry I woke you." She gestured at the glasses of water she'd set down on top of the bar. Anything to get Ciara's attention off the condition of the calendar and the state of her own clothes. "There you go."

Ciara took a glass and drank deeply from it, then cocked her head toward the radio. "Wanna dance?" She had that gleam in her eye.

It was the gleam that meant she wanted to dance Mickey back to bed, and she didn't have time for that. "Actually," Mickey said, faking a yawn, "I'm ready to flop over. And you're probably pushing dawn back in your time, too."

Ciara fumbled her telephone out of the pocket of her unzipped dungarees and lit the screen. Her eyes widened. "Oh! Yeah, it's late. I've got work in a few hours." She placed her glass in the sink. "I should go." Regret darkened her tone.

Yes, you should. As fast as possible. Trying not to look like she was hurrying, Mickey joined her behind the bar and placed a kiss on her lips—a distraction from her hand fumbling for the radio dial. She cracked one eye open, checking to make sure Ciara's were closed. Ciara always closed her eyes when they kissed, and given her current cross-eyed view of the bridge of Ciara's nose, Mickey now understood why everyone smooched blind. But it meant their vision would be protected.

She switched the radio off. Ciara jerked a little, catching a strand of hair around one of Mickey's buttons, but Mickey freed her, then held her against her chest as the lights flared then dimmed to normal level. When Ciara opened her eyes, the gray of age had once more settled over Mickey's beloved establishment, the calendar had switched to the 1924 version, and she was back in her work pants and black T-shirt.

"I hate seeing the place like this," she muttered, taking Ciara's arm and guiding her toward the door. She didn't hurry now. No one was coming to murder her in 2022. At the entrance, she wrapped her arms around Ciara's waist and pulled her close, resting her chin on top of Ciara's head and breathing in her scent, a combination of lavender and vanilla Mickey loved.

This was it. Goodbye. The hour was upon her, and the next time she turned on that radio, death would be at her door. She couldn't let Ciara come back before that happened. She wouldn't let Ciara be part of it.

"When we bring you back," Ciara said, "we'll reopen this place. It will be all the rage. Speakeasies are hot right now. Management will love it. We can run it on the nights when we don't have performances, so it doesn't compete with the lobby bar. The revenue might even buy us the new roof we've been needing for the theater."

Mickey swallowed a lump in her throat. "Yeah, doll. That sounds swell." She forced a smile. "You know I've fallen hard for you, right? No matter what happens, I want you to know that."

"Sure, Mick. I know. I love you, too." Ciara frowned up at her. "It's going to be okay. I'll be back tonight. We've got to be close to New Year's. When that happens, I'll remind you to lock the door. We'll block the entry with some tables and chairs. We'll change history, and then . . ." She trailed off, took a deep breath, and squared her shoulders. "Then we'll see what happens."

Except Mickey always knew she had to lock the door, and every time the night had repeated itself before she met Ciara, the fates had conspired to keep the keys away from her. Every New Year's Eve had ended in her death, no matter what she did.

She didn't believe for one moment that Ciara's presence would alter the events of that night.

It would mean two human deaths instead of one, plus EZ of course. Or maybe not EZ. Now that EZ lived again, would he be present in the repeat of her last moments?

As if on cue, EZ trotted out of the office and hopped on his hind legs for Mickey to pick him up. When she did so, the little dog licked her face over and over, then pressed his head up under her chin and shivered against her.

He knew what day it was in her time. Somehow, EZ knew.

Mickey's eyes filled. She buried her face in his fur, wiping away the tears so Ciara wouldn't see them, then thrust the whining dog into her arms. "Hurry now," she said, "or we'll be back in bed before you can get going." Her laugh sounded hollow to her own ears, but Ciara didn't seem to notice.

"Right. I'm off." She took the squirming EZ under one arm, stroking his head with her free hand. "Hey, there's a full dog bowl waiting for you at my place. We'll be back later. Goodnight!" Ciara tossed over her shoulder, and with that she was out the door and closing it behind her.

Mickey waited by the closed door, listening to Ciara's footsteps recede, then pause about halfway across the exterior space leading to the stairwell. With a sigh, she took the key from her pocket and clicked the lock into place. The footsteps started up again, fading into silence when Ciara went upstairs.

Mickey crossed to the radio and clicked it on, flooding the room with big band swing. The lights brightened, then dimmed.

On unsteady limbs, she returned to the door and reinserted the key in the now-gleaming lock, the brass freshly polished when she'd prepared for her customers that fateful night. Her hand trembled as she unsecured the internal bolt and left it unlocked. No more running.

Back at the bar, she felt for the hidden latch built into the underside of the top shelf. A hidden compartment released.

Something heavy and metal tumbled out. She palmed the pistol in her right hand, closing her grip around its pommel. Mickey had never needed to use the weapon, but she knew how. Her brother was, after all, a cop, and running a bar got dicey sometimes. She gave the chamber a quick check—loaded.

Okay then.

She glanced at the clock. 2:33. Still a few minutes. She wasn't clear on exactly when the shooting happened, but she guessed somewhere around 2:45 or so. Her gaze fell on the wall calendar, back in its place, the new one this time. The woman in the black dress with the red fan smiled at her from its glossy pages.

"Happy New Year, doll," Mickey said and poured herself a final shot of the good stuff.

Chapter 46

December 5, 2022

CIARA PAUSED FOR the third time on her walk home to her apartment. She had her arms wrapped around herself, the coat she'd retrieved from her office insufficient against the December chill and a brisk wind. EZ tugged on the leash clutched in her right hand and gave a soft whine. He hadn't wanted to leave the speakeasy. Granted, he never wanted to leave after spending time with Mickey, but tonight . . .

Usually, he gave up about a block from the theater, thoughts of a warm bed and a full bowl distracting him from missing his first owner. Tonight, he jerked and pulled against Ciara's urging him toward home. She'd managed to get him moving again with a quick pat or an encouraging word, but when he plopped his backside beside a fire hydrant and flat-out refused to take another step, her patience snapped.

"Dammit EZ! It's cold out here. I've got to be back at work in a few hours, and you're freezing your furry ass on the sidewalk. Why? We do this all the time. You know Mickey will be there in the morn—"

EZ barked, interrupting her, then shook himself, for all the world indicating that the answer to her statement was a resounding *No.*

Ciara stared at him. She knew he had intelligence surpassing the average canine. And she'd had an uneasy feeling as well ever since Mickey locked the door behind her and she ascended the basement stairs. Rationalizations buried it, but it niggled at her.

She stood on the otherwise empty walkway, staring down at EZ but not really seeing him anymore while her brain turned over every action Mickey had made tonight, every word she'd said. All around Ciara the city slept, never truly silent but close enough for her to think. The blinking traffic lights and streetlamps lit the asphalt and sidewalk in random color patterns, almost hypnotizing her.

When had things begun to get strange at the bar?

When you walked out to Mickey rehanging the old calendar.

Mickey had jumped away from it, spun around to face Ciara with an almost guilty expression on her face. But why would she act that way?

Ciara concentrated, picturing the scene in her mind, the glasses of water on the bar, the crumpled calendar with the woman using a pair of large Christmas ornaments to hide her voluptuous breasts . . . Why had the calendar been so crumpled and crushed?

A shiver passed through her that had nothing to do with the cold.

The calendar had fallen. Sure, okay. That might account for a crease or two. But the image of the pinup girl had hills and valleys bent into it as if it had been rolled into a ball . . . and thrown away, then retrieved and smoothed unsuccessfully.

Because Mickey had run out of time when Ciara emerged from the office.

The calendar *had* been in the trashcan. She'd thrown it in the trash in the early morning of New Year's Day.

Oh god, no. No no no.

She'd been in such a hurry to get Ciara out of there. When

she'd switched off the radio, Ciara had caught her hair on one of Mickey's buttons.

Except Mickey hadn't been wearing a button-down when they'd been in the past tonight. Ciara had made a point of admiring the way Mickey's biceps stretched the sleeves of her black tee.

But she'd been wearing a dress shirt with buttons the night she'd died.

"No!" Ciara cried, out loud this time. She scooped EZ into her arms and raced back the way she'd come, toward the theater. Only minutes from her place of employment, but was it too many?

Swinging EZ under one arm, she used the other hand to fish out her phone, the movement lighting the screen and the clock display on it. 2:38 a.m. Mickey had told her she'd been shot sometime after 2:30.

Still, she'd have to turn on the radio to get back to when it happened, she thought as her shoes pounded on the sidewalk. At least that's how things *had* been working for the two of them lately, but did that rule apply if Mickey was alone? Certainly, Mick had relived her death experience any number of times prior to Ciara's arrival, according to her.

If the time in the past matched the time in the present tonight, Ciara would never make it, but she damn well intended to try. She picked up her pace, slipping and sliding on some patches of ice from an earlier drizzle, then forced herself to take more care. Breaking a leg or twisting an ankle wouldn't help Mickey. And Mickey had locked the speakeasy door. Ciara remembered hearing it click behind her.

But if what was happening was what Ciara thought was happening, why had Mickey wanted Ciara out of there?

Her brain whirled as she ran and skidded and slid. Mickey hadn't liked Ciara's plan of staying with her through the morning of January 1, 1924, when it did arrive.

And it had.

Did Mickey think the murderer would break the door down? It was extra thick and would be hard to get through, but Ciara supposed it could be done, especially by someone with a gun. Mickey was trying to protect her. That much was obvious. But what extremes had Mickey planned in order to do that?

The answer almost knocked Ciara to the icy pavement.

Mickey wanted her out of there because Mickey planned to end this. They'd theorized that if the bar owner died again, it would be permanent. And that would ensure Ciara's safety.

"Damn you, Mickey McFadden," Ciara breathed.

She raced up the theater's steps, slipped on the top one, and came down hard on both knees, barely missing crushing EZ beneath her. The impact tore open the fabric of her jeans and scraped the skin beneath, leaving it raw, burning, and bleeding red into the thin layer of snow covering the marble stairs. She ignored the pain and fumbled in her purse for the keys, fished them out, dropped them, and grabbed them up again.

Pushing to her feet, she forced her hands to stop shaking long enough to jam the key into the lock and shove open the heavy door. With the exception of a few lights in back hallways left on to deter thieves, the lobby was dark and shadowed. Ciara banged her shin on one of the low tables, but she made it to the stairwell.

Her breath came in rasping gasps both from the frigid air outside and her breakneck-speed run. EZ squeezed past her on the stairs, the sound of his toenails scrabbling on stone echoing back to her as he disappeared below. She hurried to catch up with him.

When she reached the subbasement level, EZ barked frantically and hopped up and down on his hind legs at the door.

"Mickey!" Ciara shrieked, crossing the open space between the storage rooms in four strides. She grabbed the doorknob in both hands and twisted it hard.

Locked.

That should have given her relief, but it didn't. It felt wrong. Everything felt wrong.

Ciara slammed her fist against the door, rattling it in its frame again and again before she remembered she had the key. She fished it from her pocket, catching it on the weathered and ancient dog collar she kept on her person at all times. She yanked harder. Both came free and flew across the floor, landing with a plop and a clink of fabric and metal on the concrete.

Before she could stop him, EZ picked up the key in his mouth, then turned toward the speakeasy door. He gave a soft and muffled whine, hindered by his teeth clamped around the key, then looked from the door to Ciara and back again.

Ciara sucked in a sharp breath, lunging at him when he raced headlong at the entry, then passed *through* the solid wood and metal leaving her alone in the subbasement.

"Oh Jesus," Ciara breathed. She'd forgotten, in her interactions with what appeared to be a living, breathing Mickey and EZ, that they'd been, and Mickey still *was*, a ghost, capable of actions that defied disbelief. She pressed both palms flat on the door. "Mickey, open up! Come on, I know you're in there."

A muffled bark answered her call.

"EZ? Stop playing around. Bring back that key!"

She turned her head to the side and pressed her ear to the door. Was that . . . jazz?

The radio was on. And if it was on, that meant Mickey was already back in the past. She had to get in there, but she wasn't doing that without help.

Her eyes scanned the subbasement, but the open space between storerooms was empty except for the dog collar she'd dropped—a splash of dingy red against the white floor. Her brain inventoried the items she and her friends had found in the other storage areas over a month prior, but rubber chickens, scarves, and fake flowers weren't breaking down any barriers between her and the woman she loved. Even the few bits of furniture tucked away were props made of particle board and painted to look fancy. They'd crumble to dust if she swung one at the door.

Okay, she couldn't use an object, but what about a person? Some of the set crew worked well into the night after a performance, and they were all muscular and strong. Could one of them still be around at this hour?

She dragged her cell phone out and dialed Kate, but it went to voicemail as a call to any sane person's phone would in the wee hours of the morning. Next came Jeremy who did answer but mumbled something unintelligible into the phone in a semiconscious state and hung up on her. Carlos often went out with the performers after a show. He might be up.

She tried his number, but it rang and rang and rang until she hit "end call."

Other than those three, she didn't have any other contact information in her phone for anyone local. She hadn't bonded with anybody else, and she had no other numbers memorized except for her parents' cell, and they lived in another state.

Who else could she call? What other numbers did she know?

Okay, sure, 9-1-1. And what would she tell the dispatch operator? "Hey, I need assistance to break into a hidden bar to rescue my ghost girlfriend from a killer who's been dead a hundred years"?

Ciara paced the empty space, back and forth between the speakeasy door and the stairs, her shoe brushing the discarded dog collar out of her path.

She stopped and stared at the bit of red fabric with the round metal tag—the tag with two phone numbers engraved on its surface.

I can guarantee if you try to call either of those numbers, the only ones likely to answer are ghosts.

Ciara swore she caught a whiff of Claudia Waters' rose perfume as the elderly librarian's words echoed through her memory. With a trembling hand, she reached down and picked up the collar, fumbling the metal disc until the sequences of letters and numbers were visible.

"This can't work. It can't possibly work," Ciara mumbled over and over to herself. She balanced her phone in her other hand and punched in the first series of characters with her thumb.

Nothing. Nothing but a faint hissing sound from the speaker now pressed to her ear.

You're wasting time. Every second that passes brings Mickey's killer closer to her. And what would you say if you could connect? "Hey, stupid, I love you. Now open the door"?

Ciara pulled the phone away and checked the screen. Yep, she was on the theater's Wi-Fi. Plenty of signal. If the call could be made, she'd be making it right now.

Except . . . there was no Wi-Fi in the 1920s.

An odd chill sent a shiver through her, followed by a strange calm that settled over Ciara's frayed nerves like a heated blanket. With a steady finger, she swiped open the Motorola's settings and switched the Wi-Fi off.

All the bars of signal vanished. Without the internet, the subbasement was the ultimate dead zone.

A semi-hysterical laugh escaped her at her choice of descriptors. Impossible. Everything about this was completely, utterly, entirely impossible.

And yet . . . she punched in the alphanumeric sequence one more time.

And hit "send."

Still nothing. But a tingle in the air around her, almost like it was electrically charged, suggested she was on the right path. Wait. People didn't make person-to-person calls in the 1920s. They had to use an . . .

Ciara hit "0."

Silence. Then the faintest sound of . . . ringing? No, it couldn't be. It couldn't—

"Operator," came a tinny voice that sent Ciara jerking her head away from her cell in surprise. "Hello? This is the operator. Number please."

She took a steadying breath and drew the phone back to her ear. Hoping she hadn't somehow connected to a modern-day facility, Ciara gave her the ancient calling code. A moment later, it was ringing again, then a *click* as someone answered.

"McFadden residence. Officer McFadden speakin'. Who's callin' at this hour? Annie, if that's you, you better have a damn fine reason to—"

Ciara almost dropped the phone. She'd called Mickey's *house*. The one she'd shared with her brother. The brother who'd died over a hundred years ago. "Paul? Is this Paul McFadden?" Her voice shook. Why *this* should be the event that almost sent her swooning to the floor again, after all she'd experienced over the past few weeks, she had no idea.

"Yeah, that's me." A pause, followed by muffled shouting, as if he'd covered the mouthpiece and was calling to someone in the background. Then, "Who is this? Whaddya want? It's the middle of the damn night."

And he'd been drinking. She could hear the slurring in his words. Mickey had once mentioned Paul had the graveyard shift the night she was killed, but apparently, he'd been doing some illegal whiskey celebrating of the new year while on duty. A door opened on the other end of the phone, followed by him yelling Mickey's name, and then a low curse.

"Um, I work at the theater," Ciara said without thinking, trying to come up with some reason to be calling and hoping to get him off the phone as quickly as possible. Paul wasn't the one she needed to reach.

"Mickey ain't home. She with you? You know where she is? 'Cause she better get her ass back here right now. Workin' all hours, stayin' out all night. No way for a woman to act. You tell her—"

Ciara thought fast. "Um, she's sorting through the prop storage rooms. She said I should call so you wouldn't worry." And go back to bed, she hoped.

Paul barked a laugh into the receiver. "Worry! Worry? I'll show her worry. You tell her I'm on my way over there to bring her home where she belongs. You got that? Enough is enough. New year, new rules. No sister of mine is gonna be out all night, working of all things. Can't cook. Can't clean. I walk my beat eight hours plus overtime and come home to no dinner on the stove, but *I'm* the one payin' most of the bills while she's playing at a job and having her fun off an inheritance because—" his voice dropped to an angry sneer "—because our parents figured women shouldn't be supporting their damn selves and gave her half." Then he hung up on Ciara.

Okay, not what she'd wanted, and not while he was angry, but maybe it would help having a cop on the scene. Surely once he saw Mickey was in danger, he'd stop worrying about her being a proper lady and protect her like the big brother he was. Right?

Mickey was his baby sister after all.

A trickle of worry slithered up Ciara's spine. Paul was a suspect in Mickey's killing. He and Annie had both died not long after Mickey did.

And Paul had been sleeping with Annie, just like Mickey had been.

But if Paul was answering his home phone, then he wasn't in the theater, hadn't been on his way to the theater until Ciara set him on that path. So he couldn't be the killer.

Unless . . . what if—

Oh god.

What if it had been *Ciara*, through some sort of time loop turning back on itself, who had sent *Paul* the actual killer *to* Mickey by calling him on the phone?

What if Ciara was the real murderer, and Paul was merely the instrument of Mickey's death?

The more she thought about Paul's feelings concerning women, the more she realized how angry Paul would be when he discovered the speakeasy . . . and Mickey wearing a pinstripe suit and fedora.

Ciara had to warn her. As fast as she could, Ciara reconnected to the long-dead operator and rattled off the second phone number on EZ's broken collar.

Chapter 47

January 1, 1924

THE PHONE WAS ringing. In the Speak EZ. But . . . how?

Mickey stood over her desk, staring at the miracle invention as it jangled, stopped, then jangled again. Jazz carried through the open door leading into the bar. She was in the past, or some version of it. She supposed someone long gone could be trying to reach her, and nostalgia threatened to knock her to her knees. What she wouldn't give to hear one of her old pals one last time. Even the familiar voice of the theater manager or her booze supplier would have been welcome.

But in her—granted spotty—recollection, no one had called that fateful morning of New Year's Day.

A muffled bark interrupted her consternation, and EZ came tearing into the office from the bar. This dog, with his ability to transcend time and death, had managed to find his way home to her once again. He dropped into a sit at her feet, his whole body vibrating with nervous energy. Something shiny stuck from the corner of his mouth.

EZ lowered his head to the floor, set the key on the tile, then scooped it up again. His tail wagged, stopped, wagged some more, like his conscience warred with his doggy nature.

"You tryin' to make it up to me?" Mickey said with a sad smile while the phone continued ringing behind her on the desk. "Tryin' to set things right?" She gave a bitter laugh. "Can't quite bring yourself to do it though, can you? Don't wanna give up the shiny. It's okay. That ship sailed a hundred years ago. Besides, I want the door unlocked. Locked in the future. Unlocked now. Get it over with once and for all, you know?" Except her heart hurt, for herself, for EZ, and for the pain she'd cause Ciara, because the dame had gone and fallen in love with her, same as Mickey had with her. "Can't live with 'em. Can't live without 'em. Never been as literally true as right now."

A surge of frustrated impatience with it all ran through her. Mickey snatched the handset off the cradle.

"Yeah?" she snapped.

"Mickey? Oh god, Mickey, it's really you."

Mickey reeled herself in, tamping down on the anger. "Ciara? How?" Had Ciara gotten transported back somehow without having to be in the bar? Mickey knew she'd locked the door in 2022. And EZ had the key right here in front of her, so—

"Ghosts," Ciara blurted on an expelled breath. "They've been giving me hints all along. I used the number on EZ's broken collar. But . . . I also dialed your brother by accident. He's on his way to you in your time. He sounded furious. And Mickey—" She broke off from the rapid-fire explanation and took a quick breath. "Mick, I think, maybe, I just sent your killer to you."

"No. Paul would never." She stopped. Had a floorboard creaked overhead?

"He doesn't like your lifestyle, Mick. And he's mad about the inheritance."

Mickey laughed. "He doesn't know the half of it about my lifestyle. Thinks I'm a tomboy, you know? Tries to make me grow my hair and wear a damn dress, but he doesn't know . . ."

"I think maybe he has a clue."

Or someone had tipped him off, like Annie maybe? In a rage

about being thrown over for Ciara and kicked out of the bar? Or maybe one of the other patrons had let something slip around him. Or Bobby. Mickey could see him taunting her brother with the news she was a dyke.

"And what about the money?" Ciara repeated.

Another creak of the ceiling above her. She wondered what time it was, but she didn't have a clock in the office, and the phone wouldn't reach out into the bar. "Yeah, money's an issue, sure. He blew his half on gambling. I told him I had, too, but really I invested it in this place and stashed everything I made so he wouldn't bet that away. You tellin' me he thinks I've still got it?"

"If he didn't think so before, he's going to know as soon as he sees your bar, Mick." Ciara was almost in tears, her voice choking on the other end of the line. "Oh god, this is all my fault."

"No. No it isn't. It couldn't be. It's not possible." Mickey stopped speaking. None of this was possible. Why should one more unbelievable thing surprise her? She shook it off. "If Paul's coming here, he would have come anyway. Woke up in the middle of the night, saw I wasn't home, and came looking for me. That's all there is to it." She wouldn't let Ciara blame herself for this. Mickey's life had been her own to lead, both the things she could help and the things that were her nature. She couldn't have changed how she lived and which sex she loved any more than she could change her own soul.

"Whatever the cause, whatever the reason, you need to turn off the radio and open the damn door. You are *not* in this alone this time. I'm in it too, even more than before. And if you don't come back to this time and let me in there, I swear I'm going to find a way to break that door down."

Mickey closed her eyes. "Then that's what you're gonna have to do. I'm sorry." And she hung up the phone, Ciara's final "Wait!" echoing in her ear.

Almost immediately it rang again, but she picked up the earpiece, clicked the receiver to disconnect the incoming call, and set the handset aside on the desk. If Ciara kept trying, she'd only get a busy signal.

"Yeah, busy," Mickey muttered to herself while feeling for the gun she'd tucked in the rear of her waistband beneath the jacket—still there and easy for her to draw. "Busy dying." She stepped into the main room, then nudged EZ back into the office with her shoe. "Not this time, boy," she told him. "No need for you to go through that pain again." She shut the door and ignored the scrabbling of his nails against its inner surface.

Huh. Had there been scratches on it in the future? She couldn't remember. If Ciara was right, the entire series of events around her death was one big loop, but where did the cycle begin and where did it end?

Well, she wouldn't go down blind and easy this round. The clock on the wall said she had a handful of minutes at most before her unwanted guest arrived. Mickey crouched behind the bar and used the mirror to watch the reflection of the front door.

What she didn't expect was the creak of the *bathroom* door swinging open, or the confused voice that asked, "What the hell are you doing?"

Mickey nearly jumped out of her own skin. She stood slowly until her eyes cleared the top of the bar and met those of a very amused-looking Annie with her hands planted on her hips, staring at her.

"Searching for loose change?" Annie said, laughing.

Mickey's mind raced. What the hell? Her killer had absolutely come in through the front door, from behind her while she faced away toward the office and EZ with her key. That night . . . that night she'd cleaned the bathroom before straightening the rest of the bar. No one had hidden inside. So how had this changed—

"I thought I'd hang around, see if your new girl was about."

321

That's how. Ciara was right. Her actions, and her interactions with Mickey in their trips to the past, had changed the course of events. Mickey hadn't cleaned the bathroom this time around because she'd been making love to Ciara. And Annie was here again also because of Ciara. Could Ciara be right about sending Paul to kill her? Regardless, she didn't have time for this.

"What do you want? And how did you get in? You aren't supposed to be here." She studied Annie. No weaving. No glassy eyes. Her ex was sober and . . . cheerful. That smile on her face looked like the genuine article.

No gun, either, and no handbag to pull one from. Annie wore a glittery dress of silver sequins that hugged her figure but covered her to the knees. She'd never been a flapper, but she filled out that sheath damn fine. Always had.

And she paled in comparison to Ciara.

"Look, Mick. I came to apologize. Lily let me in while you were in the back room, and I hid until everyone else left. I hoped your girl might be here, too, so I could include her in the sorrys." She cocked her head to one side, eyeballing Mickey. "You gonna come out from behind there or what?"

Mickey flushed, slipping the gun onto the shelf behind the bar before Annie saw it but still within easy reach. "Yeah, sure, Annie. So what changed? Why're you so full of apologies all of a sudden?" *And how can I get you out of here before Paul shows up? Because if Annie isn't the killer . . .* Her heart sank.

Or maybe Annie *was* the killer, but Ciara's interference had changed that, too.

"Your girl, Ciara," Annie said, getting the pronunciation correct for the first time. "You got a good thing there. You deserve a good thing, Mick."

"Mighty generous of you," Mickey said, easing toward the front door to lock it now that she had Annie involved, then remembering EZ still held the damn key. She stopped and faced her uninvited guest.

Annie laughed, a girlish sound Mickey had never heard come out of her before. "Yeah, well, I've got a good thing too, and if it's gonna work, we need to come to an agreement."

Ah.

"You're talking about Paul," Mickey said, the pieces clicking into place. She eyed Annie thoughtfully. "You love him?"

Annie shrugged. "Not yet. But I think I could if I get half a chance. And that means what you and I had needs to stay a secret. A huge secret. If he ever found out—"

"He'd kill us both." She'd never thought Paul capable of murder before, but with all the evidence mounting against him, Mickey knew she'd been blind.

"You're being a little overdramatic, I think. But he'd definitely dump me. And I like being with a cop. Gives me some protection, you know?"

"From Bobby? You were sleeping with my booze connection, too."

"That . . . ended badly."

And now Mickey knew why Annie needed a cop's protection. What a mess. She shook her head. "You sure know how to pick 'em."

Annie shot her an almost sad smile. "I picked *you*, remember?" she said, soft as a whisper. "You just had to go and be a woman."

Mickey rolled her eyes. "You knew that going in. Not something I could change." But she could change the course of current events. All she had to do was get to the radio and turn it off. Only now Annie had slid herself between Mickey, halfway to the door, and the bar area where the radio played an upbeat big band number that clashed with the tone of their conversation.

Of course, then Ciara would come storming in like an angry bat out of hell and Mickey would have to set up this whole damn scenario all over again. She was tired. So damn tired. She wanted it to be done, but even after everything, she didn't want to watch Annie die.

"Out of the way," Mickey said, nudging Annie aside and reaching for the radio knob.

At the same moment, EZ scratched harder on the inside of the office door and Annie grasped its handle to let him out.

Chapter 48

December 5, 2022

SOMETHING ... NO SOME*ONE* was clomping down the theater basement stairs. Boots on concrete. *Thud, thud, thud.* Ciara stared at the open doorway leading from the stairwell into the subbasement.

God, let it be one of the set crew working late. Or maybe a cop who saw me come in and wants to check.

An inhuman howl of despair echoed down the stairs, then blew into the open space where Ciara stood, carried on an icy, unnatural wind. It lifted her hair from her shoulders and froze the blood in her veins. There were no doors or windows accessing the stairwell. It was completely internal to the theater. No way that gust had come from outside.

The bootsteps drew closer. Unable to unglue her feet from the floor, Ciara traced the sound as it crossed from the stairs toward her, closer and closer, until whoever or whatever it was stood directly before her, about halfway to the speakeasy door.

Something warm puffed repeatedly against Ciara's ear. It took her a moment to recognize it as breath. Then, "Get out of my way," a low, distinctively male voice growled and was gone. The steps continued behind her. The doorknob to the speakeasy rattled in its socket.

It turned a fraction to the right.

The music drifting from beneath the door stopped.

The knob ceased turning.

The speakeasy had returned to 2022. In this time, the door was locked, and all the participants in Mickey's death were ghosts. The lock to the speakeasy door snicked. Open! Mickey's doing? Or had that unseen force acted upon it again?

Ciara ran to the door to throw it open, but before she could do so, she stepped into the coldest space she'd ever occupied. Her heart raced. Her breath caught in her throat, then exhaled on a sharp burst of cloudy mist.

I'm standing in *Paul's spirit!*

She thought she might throw up, but she swallowed her mouthful of bile, twisted the knob, and stepped into the warm glow of Mickey's ancient bar, leaving the pocket of frigidity behind her. Ciara closed the door and turned to face the room, halting at the unbelievable sight that awaited her.

"Um. Hey," Mickey said, tossing her a weary wave from beside the radio. She wasn't alone. A blurry outline of a woman in a silvery dress stood behind her, her fingers wrapped around the handle of the office door. The woman's transparency reminded Ciara of how Mickey had appeared when she'd first encountered the bar's owner—foggy and faded and moving so slowly it couldn't be seen with the naked eye of the living.

The door to the office was open by about a foot, and EZ squeezed himself out the gap, then walked *through* the second ghost and trotted over to Ciara as if passing through spirits was something he did every day.

Actually, that might be true.

"Who's . . . that?" Ciara waved a hand at the see-through woman.

"Annie," Mickey said.

"Annie," Ciara repeated, frowning. She rested her palms on

her hips. "Quite the dress."

Mickey glanced over her shoulder at Annie as if she hadn't paid much attention to her choice of attire before that moment. "Oh. Yeah, I guess."

"Mickey's a bit of a dog, isn't she?" One more time, Carlos's earlier comment floated through Ciara's recollection. She tried to shake it away and failed. It was New Year's Eve in Mickey's time, or New Year's Day. And here was Annie.

"She isn't trying to kill you," Ciara observed.

"No. She's not the murderer." Mickey squinted at her. "What's bugging you?"

"She's heading into your . . . office."

The clouds in Mickey's expression cleared. "Oh. Oh! No. Jesus, doll." She crossed to Ciara in two long strides and wrapped her arms around her. "She's after Paul. Wants to make a husband out of him. And she wants to swear us to secrecy about her . . . varied preferences."

Ciara leaned to the side to study Mickey's ex-lover. Annie was getting the hang of moving through modern day in ghost form a lot faster than Mickey had. She'd already pivoted about ninety degrees and stood in profile to them now, facing the mirror behind the shelves of liquor bottles. Their eyes met in the reflection, Annie's showing frustration and confusion.

Yeah, Ciara could imagine. One minute you're walking and talking. The next, you're half frozen in time, fighting your way through each motion inch by painstaking inch. God, what Mickey had gone through to communicate with her these past few weeks.

A muffled bark drew her attention away from the slow-motion spirit. EZ pawed at her jeans, then dropped into a sit. A bronze key hung half out of his mouth.

"This is how it happened, isn't it? EZ had the key and you couldn't lock the door."

Mickey nodded. "And it's about to happen again. Look, you

327

need to go. Let me turn the radio back on and finish this." She released Ciara and went to the bar. Reaching around Annie who now faced the radio, Mickey drew out a revolver from the lower shelf. She studied the weapon in her hands. "When Paul gets here, maybe I can use this to convince him to take Annie and leave. I'll get my own place. I've got enough saved up."

"And I'll never see you again."

Mickey's grin was sad but determined. "Not necessarily. I won't kick the bucket then, but I'll still die before you found the speakeasy. Maybe my ghost will end up here regardless. It's my favorite place to be, except for by your side."

"And that," Ciara said, squaring her shoulders, "is why I'm not leaving." Before Mickey knew what was happening, Ciara snatched the gun away from her and took up a position between Mickey and the door. "Paul's already here in my time. I felt him, heard him. He's right outside the door. If I protect you, and what the Bolini brothers said is correct, then you can come back with me, for good."

"We're not doing this," Mickey said, trying to grab the weapon back, but Ciara stepped forward out of her reach. The bar owner gave an exasperated sigh. "We don't know that will work. We do know Paul will definitely shoot a stranger pointing a gun at him."

"Then I'll die. In the past. Before I ever existed. And I'll be born again and grow up and discover the bar and meet you, and you'll be able to walk out that door!" Ciara gestured at the entrance with the muzzle of the revolver . . . just as the radio snapped on, and the lights flashed bright enough to blind them all.

Their eyesight returned to normal in time to watch the doorknob turn back and forth.

Ciara risked a look at Annie's ghost, no longer a ghost at all now but wide-eyed and solid, with her hand wrapped around the radio dial. She'd figured out the connection and switched it back on.

"The door!" Mickey reached a hand toward her beloved pet, but he skittered away, wagging his tail. It was all a game to him.

"Speak, EZ. Speak!" Ciara shouted.

EZ barked twice. The key fell to the tile.

Ciara held the gun down at her side while she scooped the key up and swung toward the door.

Paul stood framed in the entryway, his own weapon pointed right at her heart.

Chapter 49

January 1, 1924

"PUT IT DOWN!" Paul commanded, his weapon never wavering.

Ciara slid the gun onto the bar and pushed it away from her. "We thought someone was breaking in," she tried, but he cut her off with a chop of his free hand. Behind her, EZ growled. Mickey nudged him back with the edge of her shoe and he calmed a little.

Paul stared from Ciara to Mickey to Annie and settled there. "So, it's true then. You're some kind of queer? And with my fucking sister?" His face twisted in disgust.

Mickey's heart twisted in her chest. It had been years since they'd been close, but still she'd clung to some hope that he might, just might, accept her for who she was if he ever found her out. Well, now she knew.

"My own goddamn sister a fucking bulldagger, a dyke." He wouldn't even look at Mickey. "Shoulda seen it. Shoulda known." His gaze shifted to Ciara. "And who are you? You the one who called me, or are you part of this . . . threesome?" He spat the final word.

"I'm . . ." Ciara began, but Mickey interrupted her, the

tendrils of a plan forming in her head.

"*She's* my girl. Annie's a coworker. You know we work together upstairs in the theater. She's not one of my regulars. She lost an earring and came down here to ask if I'd found it backstage."

That seemed to mollify him a tiny bit. He lowered the gun to his side, though he didn't holster it, and the corner of his eye twitched. "Not one of your regulars. In an illegal bar." Paul glanced around the Speak EZ, settling on the clock on the wall. "Our parents' clock. Thought you pawned that piece of shit." He shook his head. "You own this joint, don't you?"

Mickey nodded once, slowly, none of them making any sudden moves.

"You really don't give a damn, do you, Michelle? I'm a *cop*! You know what'll happen to me if this gets out? Do you? I'll be kicked off the force, a laughingstock. And you! You'll go to jail if you survive long enough to get there. I won't be able to protect you!"

"I'm not asking you to, Paul."

"Then what *do* you want from me? I *raised* you. I went and got a respectable job. I made sure you were taken care of. What else do you want?"

Mickey sighed. "I want you to walk away. I want you to take Annie, marry her, be happy, raise that family you used to talk about, the one me being around kept you from having. I'll move down here. You don't owe me anything. I make good money. I'll be fine."

"Oh no. No, no, no. You don't *get* it." Paul began pacing back and forth across the empty dance floor, his footsteps in time with the jazz number playing on the radio, though Ciara didn't think he was aware of that detail. "You're the one who's going to walk away. Far away. Go to New York, or Philly. Go to hell for all I care and take her with you." He jerked a hand in Ciara's direction. "Find another theater and another bunch of queers to work with." His voice dropped to a low growl. "But I never, *ever* want to hear from you again. You get me?"

"Yeah, Paul, I get you," Mickey whispered. "If that's what it takes, I'll go."

Annie seized the moment to scramble to Paul's side and wrap her arms around his bicep. "Come on, baby. She said she'll leave. Let's get outta here before someone else finds us in this dump." She tucked a strand of blond hair behind her ear. "We can go back to my place, celebrate the New Year."

All the fire seemed to drain out of him with those words. Paul's shoulders dropped, and he tucked the gun into the holster strapped to his side under his jacket. "Yeah. Okay. Sure. We can do that." They turned toward the door. As they stepped out, into the gathering gray mist, Annie tossed a wink and a smile back over her shoulder.

And they were gone.

"What . . . was that it?" Ciara stammered when Mickey closed the door. "Did we stop it?"

Her energy sapped, Mickey sank into the nearest wooden chair and looked up at her. "Maybe?" She shook her head. "I can't believe Paul would have killed me."

Ciara took the seat opposite her and covered Mickey's hands with her own. "I'm sorry. I know he's your brother." They sat in silence for several long minutes, EZ curled up beside them on the tile. "So, what happens now?" Ciara finally asked. "I mean, we changed history, right? This wasn't the way it originally went down. You didn't die. Or did we only change things *here* in this pocket of time?"

Mickey shook her head. "I have no idea, but yeah, you definitely shifted the chain of events. Annie wouldn't have been here if you two hadn't quarreled. She wanted to make good with both of us so we wouldn't tell anyone, especially Paul, about me and her and ruin her opportunity to play house."

Ciara nodded, but she was frowning.

"What?"

"It's just . . . well, Paul wouldn't have been here, either, if I hadn't called him thinking he could protect you. Stupid, I know, but I wasn't thinking clearly. I didn't really consider him to be the killer."

Mickey's shoulders slumped. "Neither did I."

Above them, one of the floorboards creaked. They both turned to stare at the ceiling, then at each other. "Mick . . ." Ciara glanced at the clock. It was well past three in the morning, but . . . "What if—?"

"What if all this just delayed the real killer?" Mickey said, rising from her seat.

Footsteps sounded from outside the speakeasy door.

Shit.

Three strides took her to the bar. She was reaching across it from the end, stretching her fingers for the gun Ciara had left there, when the door opened. Mickey caught a glimpse of something metal in the mirrors. Ciara screamed and moved, a blur in her peripheral vision. Then two loud pops.

Mickey dropped her gaze to her abdomen, fully expecting to see the holes, the bloodstains spreading across the white, but there was nothing.

Behind her, something hit the dance floor with a thud.

EZ barked and whined, then skittered back through the cracked-open office door.

She whirled to see Ciara, sprawled across the wood between her and Jimmy framed in the doorway. His pistol dropped from his fingers to clatter on the tile. He went to his knees beside Ciara.

"Aw, no. No, this ain't right. Why the hell'd you go and move between us like that? Where did you even come from?" Jimmy was babbling, wringing his hands in his lap, while Ciara lay there, facedown, unmoving.

Mickey hit the floor hard on her knees, stopping him when he reached a tentative hand toward Ciara. "Don't!" she snapped. "Don't you fucking touch her!" Her fingers found Ciara's shoulders more by feel than sight since hers was blurred by the tears streaming down her face. "Hey. Come on, don't do this to me. Ciara?" She rolled the body over, releasing a groan of anguish at the sight of Ciara's eyes wide and staring up at nothing, two dark stains soaking through the fabric of her soft sweater.

The radio blared on, some kind of jaunty number sung by a tenor about dancing under the moon.

Mickey's hands clenched into fists. "Why?" Her voice broke. "Why? Why! Why would you do this? Why on earth would you want to kill me? We were friends, Jim. What reason could you possibly have had?"

Jimmy's gaze went from Mickey to Ciara and back again. His whole body shook, but his eyes were hard when he spat out, "Annie. You couldn't just let her go, could you? You and Paul. I thought you'd figured it out on Thanksgiving, throwing her out on her ear. I told you you'd done the right thing. But no. She's been sneaking back down here, over and over, to see you! Like tonight! I saw her come in. I saw her stick around. I thought maybe, maybe I'd give you one more chance to leave her behind, so I offered to walk you home tonight before she snuck out of her hiding place, but no, you just couldn't leave her be, leave her to me. None of you could. Well, except the bootlegger. Crazy, right? The smartest one of all of you is that Bobby guy who can't even spell vodka right on the invoices he leaves you."

"I don't get it. I don't understand." Something warm and wet seeped through the fabric of her pant leg. Ciara's blood.

Ciara's. Blood.

EZ's barking continued from the back office. The song on the radio shifted to something heavy on drums and horns, completely incongruous to the scene playing itself out before Mickey.

What was going to happen? To Ciara? To *herself*? Right now, she cared nothing about continuing her life. The only life Mickey wanted was with Ciara.

Jimmy pushed to his feet and Mickey didn't even try to stop him. He threw his hands in the air. "You. Paul. What, are you sharing her now? I saw them leave together. Can't go after a cop, so I'll have to wait for Annie to come to her senses and realize he's the wrong guy for her, but I could get rid of you." He pointed a shaky finger at her, then shifted it toward Ciara's body. "Except then she shows up. Out of nowhere. I never saw her head down the stairs from the main basement."

Where he'd been waiting for his chance to kill her because … because …

"You were seeing Annie, too." Mickey spoke without inflection, her voice unrecognizable even to herself.

"No," Jimmy said. "I wanted to. The rest of you kept getting in my damn way."

Mickey had heard enough. She grabbed up the gun Jimmy had dropped, aimed it at the blasting radio, and fired a single shot. It tore through the wooden housing, bursting the glass tube components in a shower of sparks and shards. The music stopped.

Everything stopped.

Chapter 50

????

"THAT ISN'T HOW it happened, you know."

Mickey tried to focus on the familiar voice, tried to turn toward the sound, but of course she was once again frozen and alone, standing behind the bar in the darkness, the fixtures and furnishings outlined in glowing bluish-white light.

"What isn't, Jimmy?" she said, identifying her unwanted guest. Tired. So damn tired. Too exhausted even for the anger she knew would come if she let it.

"I'm sorry, Mick," Jimmy said from right beside her left ear, but now he was whispering, and she knew where else she'd heard that voice.

He was the entity who had come to her early on. The one who'd apologized and sworn to make things right. And had he? The tiniest glimmer of hope burned in her chest, but she hardly dared to kindle it. *What* did *happen?* She couldn't talk, but she thought the words at him.

"I killed you. Shot you in the back. EZ, too. I was out of my head. You gotta believe me. Seeing her with everyone else, including you, hearing you talk about her, how you were when you were together, I didn't know what I was doing."

If she could have, Mickey would have grimaced. Yeah,

guy talk. She wasn't one to kiss and tell, but with Jimmy, she'd confided in him. About everything—the ups, the downs, the intimate details. She'd trusted him to keep her confidence.

Well, as far as she knew, he had done that much.

"I didn't even know you liked both women and men," Mickey said. So much she hadn't known about a man she'd considered her closest friend.

Jimmy chuckled. "Something Annie and me had in common," he said.

Yeah, she guessed they did have that.

"I took your body to the old crematorium. You know, the one on Eighth and Oak? They'd been shut down for years. Nothing worked right. Flames never got hot enough to turn you to ash, but I buried the rest. Nice spot in a field. I think it's a parking lot now."

Well, that explained the photograph Ciara had taken.

God, Ciara. Where was she? What had happened to her?

"Then Paul and Annie had that fight and killed each other and I . . . well, I offed myself a week after that."

Jesus. Carlos hadn't looked into what happened to Jimmy. It hadn't seemed like a good lead to follow.

"But I promised you. I promised I'd make this right. I used my energy. Got you this second chance."

"Second chance? What second chance?" She was still a ghost, still alone.

A creak sounded, the office door slowly opening as if on its own. Mickey expected to hear toenails scrabbling on tile. EZ could push that door open if she left it ajar. But instead of her dog emerging from within, a bright, white light poured through the new opening, bathing the entire bar in its blinding glare.

"Heh, guess that's my cue," Jimmy said. He slid past her behind the bar, pausing a moment to gaze across the empty tables and chairs. "Despite Annie, despite everything, this is always where I was happiest. Thanks for making this place,

Mickey. You did good here."

From the corner of her eye, she watched him step through the glowing doorway, becoming nothing more than a dark shadow in the brightness before vanishing into its depths. The door swung shut with a soft click.

Awareness left her.

December 8, 2022

The speakeasy door swung open.

Ciara walked in, *alive*, breathtakingly beautiful if Mickey were breathing, tentative at first, pausing barely past the threshold before her searching eyes landed on Mickey behind the bar.

Mickey felt the energy within her shiver with recognition, longing, anticipation, and love.

Something between a cry and a shout tore from Ciara's throat, and a moment later she was standing beside Mickey, staring up at her, one hand hovering above her shoulder before she brought it down and made—

Contact.

An explosion of sensation suffused Mickey's being, Mickey's *soul*, all five of her senses on overdrive registering everything from the faint exhalation of Ciara's breath to the ticking of the clock on the far wall, from the pungent residue of the cleaning solutions they'd used, to the overwhelming pleasantness of Ciara's vanilla and lavender perfume, from the scratchiness of the long-sleeved button-down Mickey was wearing, to the infinite gentleness of Ciara's hand on her shoulder.

Mickey's heart pounded in her chest. She filled her lungs with air and brought her mouth down on Ciara's in a searing kiss that went on and on.

When they broke apart, Ciara wrapped her arms around Mickey as if she'd never let go. "Three days," she gasped. "It's been three days. I thought you weren't coming back."

"I thought *you* were dead," Mickey managed, holding her just as tightly.

Ciara shook her head. "I don't remember anything after getting shot. One second, I felt the bullets hit me. The next, I was here, behind the bar, in the dark, and alone. Except for EZ." On cue, the little dog trotted through the still-open main entry, paused for a moment, then lay down on the dance floor, sprawling on his belly with a sigh. "I've been down here every day, waiting, hoping."

"I'm here," Mickey soothed, rubbing Ciara's back. She glanced toward the entry and sucked in a sharp breath.

No fog.

There was no gray mist beyond the doorway, just the empty space between the prop storage rooms, almost unchanged from when she'd begun working for the theater.

"What is it?" Ciara asked.

Taking Ciara's hand, Mickey strode toward the doorway. "I think . . ." She stuck a toe through the opening. Her foot met with no resistance. "I think . . . I'm really, *really*, here." She dropped Ciara's hand, closed her eyes, and walked forward and out of the bar for the first time in almost a hundred years.

Epilogue

December 31, 2022

MICKEY SIGHED WITH contentment and joy. The Speak EZ had never been so packed with people. Every chair and barstool had an occupant. The dance floor was full of couples. Carlos stood with her behind the bar, mixing a martini for Kate who'd commandeered one of the stools when someone went to dance.

Mickey should have been pouring liquor herself, but she couldn't stop simply taking it all in. In just over three weeks, they'd sold off some of the sealed antique bottles she'd owned, paid off someone for some fake identification papers, and brought in a professional cleaning team to return the Speak EZ to its original glory in time for New Year's Eve.

The mostly undamaged housing for the radio had been retained and repaired. Its innards had been replaced with modern components set to something called Pandora, and the "channel" they were currently listening to was "Hits of the Roaring Twenties." The current owners of the theater, Jack and Samuel, swayed to a steamy jazz number on the dance floor. They'd been informed about the finding of the hidden bar and loved the idea of opening it to the public at night as an additional destination if one didn't wish to attend a performance, or as an after-spot for those who wanted to linger longer when a show ended and the lobby bar shut down.

The Speak EZ would also be included in a daily "historical ghost tour" of the building, led by Mickey herself, telling tales of what life had been like in the area during her lifetime, while leaving out the part about having actually *lived* through it.

In addition to tending the bar, which she bought out with the rest of her remaining inheritance (ancient bills stuffed into her "lumpy" mattress worth a lot more than face value due to their age), that tour guide was to be her job in the new year. It irked her to pay for the bar at all, but Mickey couldn't exactly claim ownership under the circumstances.

For now, all the guests were employees of the theater along with their spouses or partners—a private celebration for them.

Carlos nudged her with his elbow, cocking his head toward the door since his hands were full of glassware. She followed his gaze, her eyes widening and her breath catching in her throat.

Ciara stood, framed in the open doorway, her hands on her hips—hips clad in a full-length, form-fitting black velvet evening gown. The plunging V-neck tantalized Mickey with a view of her cleavage. From a strap around Ciara's right wrist, a red feathered fan dangled. Ciara's lips turned up in a mischievous grin. She knew exactly what she was doing to Mickey, and from her expression was loving every second of it.

She was the spitting image of the woman from the pinup calendar.

Carlos waved a hand in front of Mickey's face. "You *are* a bit of a dog, aren't you?" he teased.

"Nah. I'll leave that to EZ."

A bark answered her comment from the back room where EZ was keeping himself out of the way of too many high-heeled shoes.

Lowering her fedora rakishly over one eye, Mickey went to take Ciara for a turn on the dance floor.

Acknowledgments

I could not do this without my biggest supporter and fan, my spouse. They are also an author, so they "get it," and that makes it so much easier when things become difficult. Also, thanks to my two daughters who are constantly asking when they get to read the next book.

Thank you to my in-person and online friends and fans who offer encouragement and enthusiasm for my work. There are too many to name, but I love each and every one of you. Special thanks here go to "SnowBunny" on Twitter/X for winning my contest and getting a character named after her real name. I hope she enjoys her as much as I loved writing her.

Thank you to my writing support/promotion group, the Feisty Foes, who are always ready with great advice and ideas as well as a sympathetic ear when things go awry: MB Austin, Virginia Black, Meredith Doench, Riley Scott, and our newest member, Cathy Pegau.

So much appreciation goes to my amazing agent, Naomi Davis, who stuck it out with me when I needed to change publishers. *Again.* You have so much more confidence in me than I have in myself. You are the best cheerleader!

And to Bywater Books and everyone there who gave me my new publishing home——Salem West, Ann McMan, and

Christel Cogneau, you really know how to make a writer feel welcome and valued. Anna Burke, your editorial feedback was spot on. I love your work and was honored to have you as my editor. I can only hope I lived up to your expectations. Thank you also to Elizabeth Andersen and Nancy Squires. And Ann McMan (again) for the cover. I hope I'm not missing anyone.

As with anything, despite all the editing in the world, mistakes do still happen. Any that remain in this novel are entirely my own.

About the Author

Weapons training? Check. Ziplining down a mountain? Got it. Paying someone to mock-kidnap her? Oh yes. How about cave swimming with bats overhead? Absolutely! When Goldie Award-winning author Elle E. Ire isn't seeking out wild and crazy experiences to do firsthand research for her characters, she writes speculative romance featuring kickass women who fall in love with each other.

Elle is the author of ten books including *Vicious Circle*, the *Storm Fronts* series, the *Nearly Departed* series, *Reel to Real Love*, *Harsh Reality*, and her first novel with Bywater Books, *Speak EZ*.

She is represented by Naomi Davis of BookEnds Literary Agency.

Twitter | @ElleEIre
Instagram | @ellee.ire
BlueSky | @elleeire.bsky.social
Facebook | facebook.com//ElleE.IreAuthor/
Website | https://www.elleire.com//

Bywater Books believes that all people have the right to read or not read what they want—and that we are all entitled to make those choices ourselves. But to ensure these freedoms, books and information must remain accessible. Any effort to eliminate or restrict these rights stands in opposition to freedom of choice.

Please join us by opposing book bans and censorship of the LGBTQ+ and BIPOC communities.

At Bywater Books, we are all stories.

For more information about Bywater Books, our authors, and our titles, please visit our website.

https://bywaterbooks.com